Other Books by MaryLu Tyndall

The Blue Enchantress

Charles Towne Belles
Book 2

MaryLu Tyndall

The Blue Enchantress
Charles Towne Belles, 2
by MaryLu Tyndall

All Scripture quotations are taken from the King James Version of the Bible.

Library of Congress Cataloging-in-Publication Data is on file at the Library of Congress, Washington, DC.

ISBN-13: 978-0-9908723-7-5
E-Version ISBN: 978-0-9908723-6-8

Cover Design by Ravven

Ransom Press
San Jose, CA

Dedicated to anyone who has ever felt worthless and unloved and who has sought to obtain value through the lies of this world.

"He also that received seed among the thorns is he that heareth the word; and the care of this world, and the deceitfulness of riches, choke the word, and he becometh unfruitful"

Matthew 13:22

Chapter 1

St. Kitts, September, 1718

"Gentlemen, what will ye offer for this rare treasure of a lady?" The words crashed over Hope like bilge water. "She'll make a fine wife, cook, housemaid"—the man gave a lascivious chuckle—"whate'er ye *desire*."

"How 'bout someone to warm me bed at night," one man bellowed, and a cacophony of chortles gurgled through the air.

Hope slammed her eyes shut against the mob of men shoving one another to get a better peek at her as she stood on the tall wooden platform displayed like a piece of ripe fruit at market. Something crawled on her foot, and she pried her eyes open in time to see a black spider skittering away. Red scrapes and bruises marred her bare feet. When had she lost her satin shoes—the gold braided ones she'd worn to impress Lord Falkland? She couldn't recall.

"What d'ye say? How much for this fine young lady?" The man grabbed a fistful of her hair and yanked her head back. Pain, like a dozen claws, pierced her skull. "She's a handsome one, to be sure. And these golden locks." He tried to slide his fingers through her matted strands, but they caught in a tangled knot, and he jerked his hand free, wrenching out a clump of her hair. More pain etched across her head.

"Have ye seen the likes of them?" He flicked her hair into the wind, and Hope watched it blow away like all her dreams.

Ribald whistles spewed over her.

"Two shillings," one man yelled.

Hope dared a glance at the throng undulating before the auction block. A wild sea of lustful eyes sprayed her. Men dressed in stained garments bunched toward the front, yelling out bids. Behind them, other men in velvet waistcoats leaned their heads together, discussing her value as if she were a breeding mare. Slaves knelt in the dirt along the outskirts of the mob, waiting for their masters. Beyond them a row of wooden buildings stretched in either direction. Brazen women emerged from a tavern and draped themselves over the railings, watching Hope's predicament with interest. On the street, ladies in modish gowns averted their eyes as they tugged the men on their arms from the sordid scene.

Hope lowered her head. *This can't be happening. I'm dreaming. I am still on the ship. Just a nightmare. Only a nightmare.* Humiliation swept over her, along with an ever-rising dread as the reality of her situation began to take root.

She swallowed and tried to drown out the grunts and salacious insults tossed her way. Perhaps if she couldn't hear them, if she couldn't see them, they would disappear and she would wake up back home in Charles Towne, safe in her bedchamber, safe with her sisters, just like she was before she'd put her trust in a lying snake.

"Egad, man. Two shillings, is it? For this beauty?" The auctioneer spit off to the side. The yellowish glob landed on Hope's skirt. Her heart felt as though it had liquefied into an equally offensive blob and oozed down beside it.

How did I get here? In her terror, she couldn't remember. The auctioneer's cold eyes—hard like marbles—

met hers, and a sinister grin twisted his lips.

"She looks too feeble for any real work," another man yelled.

The sounds of the crowd grew warbled and muted. Fists forged into the air in slow motion as if pushing through mud. Garbled laughter dribbled from yellow-toothed mouths like molasses.

Hope wished for death.

The gentle lap of waves caressed her ears, their peaceful cadence drawing her gaze from the nightmarish spectacle, past the muscled henchmen who'd escorted her here, out onto the bay. Two docks jutted into sparkling turquoise water where several ships rocked back and forth as if shaking their heads at her in pity. Salt and papaya and sun combined in a pleasant aroma that lured her mind from her present horror.

A flicker brought her gaze to the glimmering red and gold figurine of Ares at the bow of Lord Falkland's ship. When she'd boarded it nigh a week past—or was it two weeks—all her hopes and dreams had boarded with her. Somewhere along the way, they had been cast into the sea. She only wished she had joined them.

The roar of the crowd wrenched her mind back to the present and she faced forward.

"Five shillings."

"'Tis robbery and ye know it!" the auctioneer barked. "Where are any of ye clods goin' t' find a real lady like this, a beauty to warm yer bed at night?"

A stream of perspiration raced down Hope's back as if seeking escape. But there *was* no escape. She was about to be sold as a slave, a harlot to one of these cruel and prurient taskmasters. A fate worse than death. A fate her sister had fought hard to keep her from. A fate Hope had brought upon herself. Numbness crept over her, even as her eyes filled with tears. *Oh God, this can't be happening.*

She gazed at the blue sky dusted with clouds, hoping for some deliverance, some sign that God had not abandoned her.

The men continued to haggle, their voices booming louder and louder, grating over her like demon howls from the pit of hell.

Her head felt like it had detached from her body and was floating up to join the clouds. Palm trees danced in the light, salty breeze coming off the bay, their tall trunks and fronds forming an oscillating blur of green and brown. The buildings, the mob, the whole heinous scene joined the growing mass and began twirling around Hope. Her legs turned to jelly, and she toppled to the platform.

"Get up!" A sharp crack stung her cheek. Rough hands clamped her arms and dragged her to her feet. Pain lanced through her right foot where a splinter had found a home. Holding a hand to her stinging face, Hope began to sob.

The henchman released her with a grunt.

"I told ye she won't last a week," one burly man shouted.

"She ain't good for nothing but to look at."

"She can lie on her back, can't she?" another man brayed, sending the crowd into a fit of ribald laughter.

Planting a strained grin upon his lips, the auctioneer swatted her rear end. "Aye, but she's much more stout than she appears, gentlemen."

Horrified and no longer caring about repercussions, Hope slapped the man's face. Shock followed by fury twisted his features before he raised a fist to strike her.

"One pound, then!" a tall man sporting a white wig called out, stopping the auctioneer. "If her looks aren't marred by your abuse, that is. I could use me a pretty wench." Withdrawing a handkerchief, he dabbed the perspiration on his forehead.

Wench. Slave. Hope faced the auctioneer, appealing one last time for his mercy. "As I have told you, sir, there's been a terrible mistake. I am no slave!"

He snorted his disbelief.

Hope searched the horde for a sympathetic face—just one sympathetic, chivalrous man to hear her appeal. "My name is Miss Hope Westcott," she shouted. "My father is Admiral Henry Westcott. I live in Charles Towne with my two sisters."

"And I'm King George," a farmer howled, slapping his knee.

"My father will pay handsomely for my safe return." Hope scanned the leering faces. Not one. Not one look of sympathy or belief or kindness. Fear crawled up her throat. "You must believe me," she sobbed. "I don't belong here."

Ignoring the laughter, Hope spotted a purple plume fluttering in the breeze atop a tricorn in the distance. "Arthur!" She darted for the stairs but two hands grabbed her and held her in place. "Don't leave me! Lord Falkland!" She struggled in her captor's grasp, ignoring the ache across her back.

Swerving about, Lord Falkland tapped his cane into the dirt and tipped the brim of his hat up, but the distance forbade Hope a vision of his expression.

"Tell them who I am, Arthur. Please save me!"

He leaned toward the woman beside him, said something, then coughed into his hand. *What is he doing?* The man who once professed an undying love for Hope, the man who promised to marry her, to love her forever, the man who bore the responsibility for her being here in the first place! How could he stand there and do nothing while she met such a hideous fate?

The elegant lady beside him turned her nose up at Hope. Then threading her arm through Lord Falkland's, she pulled him down the road.

With each step of his boots away from Hope, her heart, her very soul, sank deeper into the wood beneath her feet.

Had the world gone completely mad?

"Two pounds!" a corpulent man in the back roared.

A memory flashed through Hope's mind as she gazed

across the band of men—of African slaves, women and children, being auctioned off in Charles Towne. How many times had she passed by, ignoring them, uncaring, unconcerned by the proceedings?

Was this God's way of repaying her for her selfishness, her lack of charity?

"Five pounds."

Disappointed curses rumbled among the men at the front, who had obviously reached their limit of coin.

The auctioneer's mouth spread wide, greed dripping from its corners. "Five pounds, gentlemen. Do I hear six for this lovely lady?"

A blast of hot air rolled over Hope, stealing her breath with the odor of sweat, fish, and horse manure. The unforgiving sun flung sparks atop her head until she felt she would ignite into a burning torch. She prayed she would. Better to be reduced to a pile of ashes than endure what the future held for her.

"Six pounds," a short man with a round belly and stiff brown wig yelled from the back of the mob in a tone that indicated he knew what he was doing and had no intention of losing his prize. Decked in the a fine damask waistcoat, silk breeches, and a gold-chained pocket watch, which he kept snapping open and shut, he exuded naught but wealth and power.

Hope's stomach turned in on itself.

The auctioneer gaped at her, obviously shocked she could command such a price. Rumblings overtook the crowd as the short man pushed his way through to claim his prize. The closer he came, the faster Hope's chest heaved and the lighter her head became. Blood pounded in her ears, drowning out the groans of the mob. *No, God. No!*

"Do I hear seven?" the auctioneer bellowed. "She's young and will bear you some fine sons."

"Just what I'll be needing." The man halted at the platform, glanced over the crowd for any possible competitors, then took the stairs to Hope's right. He halted beside her too close for propriety's sake and assailed her with the stench of lard and tobacco. A long purple scar crossed his bloated face as his eyes grazed over her like a glutton at a feast. Hope shuddered. Sweat broke out on her palms.

The auctioneer gazed over the crowd.

The man squeezed her arms, and Hope jerked from his grasp and took a step back, horrified by his audacity. He chuckled. "Not much muscle on her, but she's got pluck."

He placed his watch back into the fob pocket of his waistcoat and removed a leather pouch from his belt. "Six pounds it is."

The silver tip of a sword hung at his side. If Hope were quick about it, perhaps she could grab it and fight her way to freedom. She clenched her teeth at the ludicrous thought, for she had no idea how to wield a blade. If only her pirate sister were here. Surely Faith would know exactly what to do.

As the man counted out the coins into the auctioneer's greedy hands, Hope reached for the sword.

Chapter 2

"Seven pounds!" Nathaniel Mason charged toward the platform, shoving his way through the unruly throng. "Seven pounds." Even as he bellowed the amount, he wondered if he had lost his mind. That was over half the coin in his pouch, and he needed all of it to purchase his supplies for the return trip to Charles Towne.

The stout man purchasing Miss Hope swung about and glared at Nathaniel as if he were naught but an annoying bug. His hand froze in midair, a gold coin clenched between his stubby fingers. "What is the meaning of this?"

Eyes glinting, the auctioneer doffed his tricorn and swept it through the air with a bow of deference. "Seven pounds from the gentlemen in the blue waistcoat. Do I hear eight?" He raised a questioning brow toward the first man.

"I wouldn't pay eight pounds fer me own mother!" a man in front of the crowd cackled, eliciting squawks of laughter from those around him.

"Eight." The red-faced man continued to count out his coins into the auctioneer's open pouch as if he would tolerate no opposition.

Shoving through the horde of sweaty, cursing men, Nathaniel leapt on the platform. "Nine pounds!" he shouted above the clamor and allowed his gaze to brush over Miss Hope.

When he'd first seen her from across the street—where he'd been arranging with a merchant to load the man's goods aboard ship—his heart had plunged like a stone into his boots. Though the woman resembled Miss Hope in hair and fairness of skin, he could not believe it was the lady he knew from Charles Towne—not so far from the safety of her home, not in such slovenly condition, and certainly not being sold as an indentured servant! Yet as he approached the throng and saw those glistening eyes the color of the Caribbean Sea that had mesmerized him back home...

His heart had rammed into his ribs.

How had she come to such dire straits? *Kidnapped.* The word blasted through his thoughts. 'Twas the only explanation. White women brought a handsome price in the islands, where they were in short supply. And Miss Hope's particular beauty would lure many a slave trader to steal her from her home, take her far away where no one would know her, and sell her to some lonely, desperate plantation owner. In these savage lands, most people looked the other way at such injustices. But how could it be? The last time he'd seen Miss Hope, she'd been strolling down the streets of Charles Towne, her arm entwined with a navy marine's.

And, if he recalled, tossing her snooty nose in the air at him as well.

Like she always had. Belittled him. Ignored him. Treated him as though he were dung on the street.

You owe her nothing.

But now those crystal-blue eyes locked upon his as if he were her only lifeline in a vicious storm. Dirt smudged her face and neck. Dark circles tugged the skin beneath her eyes. Her hair hung in tangled nests onto a stained and tattered gown. "Mr. Mason." She managed to whisper his name, and that one whisper held all the desperation and pleading he needed to continue.

"The lady is mine, sir." The rotund merchantmen gave Nathaniel a cursory glance. "I have already made a bargain with this man, and as you can see I am sealing it with my payment."

"Aye, let 'im have her," a lanky man from the crowd barked at Nathaniel. "Garrison ain't had no lady in years."

Laughter roared across the mob like a sudden thunder storm, and the merchantman's face blossomed in a mad dash of crimson. He shot the man a vicious glare before continuing to count his money.

"Me vote goes t' the young sailor," another shorter man bellowed. "He looks like he's been out at sea far too long." He surveyed the chortling mob. "Who'll care to place a wager on him?"

An onslaught of bets saturated the air like a tropical downpour.

Nathaniel shoved his way between Mr. Garrison and Hope, guiding her behind him, and faced the auctioneer. "Is the auction closed, sir?"

"Nay." The man grinned. "Not as long as the bidding continues." He wiped spittle from his chin. "Truth be told, I may get to my drink early today."

"Then I believe the last offer was nine pounds." Nathaniel reached for his money pouch.

"Ten." Mr. Garrison waved Nathaniel off and snapped open his pocket watch. "Best that or leave."

Nathaniel glanced over his shoulder at Hope. Moist eyes sparked with fear met his. Beyond her, his ship rested idly in the bay. He'd come to St. Kitts to fill her hold with tobacco, sugar, cotton, rum, herbs and salt—a shipload of cargo to take back to Charles Towne. He'd lined up willing merchants and farmers, and if all went well, stood to pocket a huge profit for his trouble. Enough to purchase another ship for his burgeoning fleet.

His gaze settled back on Hope. Tears now spilled from her eyes, winding slick trails through the dirt on her cheeks. "Please help me, Mr. Mason."

Facing forward, Nathaniel swallowed a lump of emotion he could not describe and managed to squeak out, "Eleven." It was all he had.

"Twelve." The man uttered the word without hesitation and scratched beneath a wig as stiff as his resolve. "I intend to have her, sir. I suggest you stand down." He snapped his watch shut and returned it to his pocket.

Nathaniel rubbed his eyes. *What should I do, Lord?* He couldn't leave this lady in these lecherous hands, but he had nothing else to offer. Nothing, except his ... Nathaniel snapped his gaze back to his ship—the ship he had built with his own hands, the ship he had spent four years working as a carpenter to pay for and another year to build.

He clutched his side where an old wound began to burn. *What is the value of a ship compared to a human life?*

The auctioneer tapped his boot on the wooden platform. "Can you best the offer or not, sir?"

Blood rushed to Nathaniel's head. His lungs collapsed under the weight of what he knew he must do. He faced the auctioneer, avoiding Miss Hope's desperate eyes. "I offer ... I offer my merchant brig." He spit it out before he changed his mind.

The auctioneer's eyes widened, and he studied Nathaniel as if to searching for mockery, but Nathaniel knew not an ounce of humor would be found on his expression.

"Which one is it?" The auctioneer gazed over the water.

"'Tis the two-masted brig, there in the center, by the East Indiamen." Nathaniel pointed toward the pride of his fleet even as his heart crumbled within him. "The one with the blue cross painted on her stern. I built her myself."

"Ah yes, I see. She's a beauty." The auctioneer slapped Nathaniel on the back. "I'll take her." He poured Mr. Garrison's coins back into the man's hand then glanced at

Miss Hope. "Though, seems I'm gettin' the best of our bargain." He chuckled.

A collective gasp shot from the horde of men, followed by renewed profanity and further feverish wagers.

Mr. Garrison squeezed his hands over the clanking coins and thrust them toward the auctioneer. "I protest, sir! He cannot offer his ship. This is unheard of." His cheeks budded in purple as his dark eyes darted among the three of them like grapeshot searching for a victim.

But Nathaniel could not care less. He couldn't move. He couldn't breathe. An odd buzzing filled his head. Had he just sold the *Blue Triumph*, his best merchant ship?

And for a woman who did naught but spurn him at every turn.

She wasn't spurning him now. The taut lines in her face had softened, and she smiled up at him with thankfulness and admiration.

He tore his eyes from her. He must think. He could still change his mind. Save his ship and walk away. He clenched his fists until his nails bit into his skin. Maybe the pain would return his senses to him. He released a long sigh, hoping it would stifle the sinking feeling that dragged upon his heart.

Of course there was no other choice. *Oh God, give me a way out.*

The auctioneer faced Mr. Garrison. "Counter the offer, sir, or I suggest you take your money and leave."

"I am not authorized … I mean to say, I cannot," he blubbered and removed a handkerchief to dab the sweat on his neck. After firing one last angry glance their way, he turned and waddled down the stairs, cursing his way through the laughing rabble.

Groans emanated from the men who had lost their wagers as the clank of coins rang through the humid air.

Miss Hope clutched Nathaniel's arm with a grip that said she would not easily release him. A month ago such attentions would have pleased him. Under present circumstances, nausea bubbled in his gut.

The auctioneer swatted at the crowd to dismiss them. "Be gone with ye. I'm done for the day."

Cursing, the men dispersed while Nathaniel begrudgingly made arrangements with the auctioneer to transfer the ship to his care.

Chapter 3

Hope couldn't stop trembling. 'Twas as if she were in the midst of an icy winter on the shores of Portsmouth. Yet it was anything but cold in the stagnant, sweltering tiny room Mr. Mason had thrust her into over two hours ago. Where had he gone?

Hugging herself, she lay back on the lumpy bed and stared at the wooden beams across the ceiling. Once they must have been smooth and beautiful, but now they were marred and stained. Just like her. The sounds of bells ringing, horses clomping, and people chattering reached her through an open window that allowed not a hint of a breeze entrance. Beneath her in the tavern below, men quarreled and laughed as they took to their drink, while some sotted fool hammered out a morbid tune on a harpsichord.

She longed to cry, to let out all the horror of the past few weeks, but she found she could no more force her tears to come than she could will herself to stop shaking.

Nor could she cast away the vision of a hundred filthy grimy hands reaching for her, shouting, cursing, making lewd suggestions. Squeezing her eyes shut, she tried to erase the scene, but instead the flabby face of the merchantman who had nearly purchased her swirled in her mind until her stomach soured.

But she had been delivered.

She could scarce believe it! Nor could she believe the person who had delivered her. Not Lord Falkland, a gentlemen, and the man who claimed to love her, but Mr. Mason, an uneducated commoner—a man she'd done her best to avoid in Charles Towne.

The door to the chamber slammed open, and Hope sprang from the bed. Mr. Mason marched in, tossed a brown bag into the corner, and slammed the wooden slab behind him. Without glancing her way, he stormed to the window and gazed out as if he wished he were anywhere but here with her.

"What is that?" She pointed toward the large bag and leaned on the bed before her wobbling legs gave way beneath her.

"All I have left of my ship." The fury in his voice jarred her.

Though she had thanked him over and over after they'd left the auction block, he had barely spoken two words to her. She couldn't blame him. He had paid a high price for her redemption.

"I am sorry for your loss, Mr. Mason."

He grunted.

"I owe you my life."

Again, a grunt.

"Are you to be angry with me forever?" She used her sweetest voice, the one that melted most men's hearts.

He spun to face her, arms clenched so tight, his muscles bulged beneath his shirt. He had removed his waistcoat— something a gentleman would never do in the presence of a lady—and only a linen shirt covered the wide expanse of his chest. A muscle twitched in his strong, stubbled jaw beneath eyes that reminded her of a panther about to spring.

Spreading the folds of her torn skirt around her, she lowered her gaze, unsettled by another wave of familiar fear rising within her. "You were much kinder back in Charles Towne."

"Back in Charles Towne, I hadn't lost five years of hard work." He rubbed the back of his neck, plopped down in a chair by the window, and closed his eyes.

A gust of wind sent the tan curtains into a feathery dance and brought a moment's relief from the heat. Hope lifted her mass of tangled hair, allowing a whiff of air to cool her heated skin and hopefully ease her taut nerves. Once again she found herself at the mercy of a man's good graces. Since the last time had not turned out so well—and now, this man obviously hated her—she found no reason to feel secure.

When he opened his eyes, the harshness had softened. Placing his elbows on his knees, he leaned forward. "You have no doubt suffered greatly, and my thoughts have been for my own loss. Pray tell, Miss Hope. What happened to you? What brought you here to St. Kitts, and worse yet, to that auction block?"

"Is that where I am?" Hope shrugged. "I've been locked in a cabin aboard Lord Falkland's"—she paused and swallowed against the pain rising in her throat—"ship for two weeks."

He scratched his jaw. "Lord Falkland. Your beau? You and he were the talk of Charles Towne."

Tears burned behind her eyes, yet still they would not fall. "Nay. Apparently, I was mistaken."

"How did you come to be on his ship? I don't recall your sisters mentioning travel plans."

Grabbing a tangled lock of hair, Hope flattened it between her thumb and forefinger. "I wanted to … wanted to …." How could she tell him the truth? It would stain her already begrimed reputation.

But from the look on his face, he was beginning to understand anyway. "Where is your escort?" His tone reminded her of her father. "Or rather *who* is your escort and why did he leave you unprotected?"

Hope stared into her lap, wishing she could sink into the foul-smelling mattress.

"You didn't have an escort, did you?"

Her eyes glassed over. "I didn't need one." She ran a hand beneath her nose. "I wanted to surprise—"

"You intended to run away with him!" His incredulous shout boomed off the walls of the tiny chamber.

Hope shrank. "We were betrothed—not officially, that is—but he promised to marry me when he returned." Sobs crowded in her throat, causing her words to jumble. "I thought we could get married on the ship."

Mr. Mason stood and paced like a caged animal, hands fisted at his sides.

A tear finally spilled down her cheek. "But his wife put a stop to that."

"His wife? Fire and thunder!" he bellowed again, raking a hand through his hair.

"How was I to know he was married and that he would hand me over to the captain to do with me as he wished?" Outrage burned anew in her chest at Lord Falkland's betrayal. Outrage and agony. Biting her lip, she dared a glance at Mr. Mason, who had taken up his pacing again, and she feared she'd lost her only friend in this godforsaken outpost.

His tanned complexion exploded in crimson. "Do you realize the price I have paid for your licentious affair?"

Hope's stomach folded in on itself. Yes, she did, at least as much as she *could* understand. Though it was not the first time her association with Lord Falkland had been referred to in such a lewd manner, it did naught to lessen the pain. "We loved each another."

"Ah, yes. Of course. Every man sells the woman he loves as a slave."

"How can you be so cruel?" She sobbed, seeking a

handkerchief but finding none. "I wish I were dead."

He snorted. "If you intend to kill yourself, I wish you had done it before today, so I wouldn't have been forced to forfeit my ship to save you."

Surely he was taunting her, yet not a trace of amusement rang in his voice. "Am I not worth more than a boat?"

"A brig, if you please, and one that did not come easy to me, as most things have come for you."

She snapped her gaze to his, her jaw tightening. "You think what I have endured has been easy?"

Halting, Mr. Mason narrowed his eyes. "Nay, I think you are a foolish girl with foolish dreams who hasn't a care for the effect her choices have on others."

Hope shot to her feet, ignoring the pain spiking up her calves. She didn't know whether to be angry at his affront or fall to the floor in a heap of despair. She'd never met a man with so little sympathy for a lady in distress. "I thought you were a Christian."

"'Tis the Christian in me that saved you from that vulgar merchantman. So I'd be thanking God if I were you. But the *man* in me will not toss vain flatteries where they aren't deserved." He ran a hand through his wavy hair and turned to gaze out the window as if she weren't worth his time.

Her heart crumbled. How much rejection could one lady endure? "Since you find my company so objectionable, I will relieve you of any further obligation." She took careful steps across the wooden floor so as not to catch another splinter in her already bloody feet. "Truly, I do thank you for all you've done, Mr. Mason." Silence resounded behind her as if he actually intended to let her go. Surely a gentleman like Mr. Mason wouldn't leave a lady alone on a strange island with no means to return home? Even if she deserved it. Yet with each step, her heart beat a little faster and her knees began to quiver.

She reached for the door handle. Her head grew light. Blinking to clear her vision, she stumbled. Boot steps pounded over the floor, and a warm hand grabbed hers. "Blast it all! You don't have to pretend to swoon for me—" Mr. Mason's gaze dropped to her bloodied feet. Cursing, he hoisted her in his arms and carried her to the bed.

He eased beside her, and an overwhelming urge to seek comfort and safety in the arms of a man forced her to fall against him. The scent of wood and tar and man cradled her, and tears began to flow again, turning to sobs when his strong arms encircled her.

"All is well now, Miss Hope." He patted her arm as someone would a pet dog—a dog that might bite him. Was he that repulsed by her? "Never fear. You are safe now."

Safe. Was she truly safe? She had feared for her life for so long, she doubted she would recognize the feeling. But here, sheltered within this man's strong arms, a hint of comfort rose within her.

Gently pushing her away, he peered down at her injured feet. "I didn't realize you had been injured."

She swiped the tears from her cheeks, encouraged by his kindness. "What is to become of me, Mr. Mason?"

"I will take you home to Charles Towne. I've arranged for us to travel on a ship, the *Lady Devon*, tomorrow at sunrise. She heads for Kingston, where I expect my other ship to arrive in a few weeks."

Hope drew in a deep breath. "You are too kind, Mr. Mason, but I thought you had no money left?"

"I don't. I signed on as navigator to pay for our passage."

"I see." Hope bit her lip, realizing the depths to which this man had fallen because of her. "But you have another ship?" At least she had not completely ruined him.

"Aye, and we shall sail her from Kingston to Charles Towne and have you home within a fortnight." He stood, allowing his gaze to wander over her before shifting it away.

But not before Hope saw a speck of desire in his eyes. A speck. And quite fleeting. But enough to give her hope that,

if all else failed, she could use this man's attraction to her to
ensure safe passage home.

Chapter 4

Nathaniel grabbed Hope as she tried to jump from the oscillating bosun's swing and set her down as gently as he could on the rolling deck of the ship.

The scent of honey and sunshine swirled around him as she raised her sapphire gaze to his and smiled. Despite the morning chill—despite all his efforts otherwise—his body heated. Clearing his throat, Nathaniel picked up the brown bag he had dropped in order to help her. Even as angry as he was, even knowing her lack of virtue, her close proximity still affected him like it had back in Charles Towne. What was it about her that made him so weak?

"Thank you, Mr. Mason, but I don't see why I must be brought aboard ship as if I were a crate." She brushed dirt from her green muslin gown that, though stiffened and splayed by the various undergarments ladies were required to wear, did naught to hide her curves.

"'Twould be improper and dangerous for you to climb the ropes above the sailors, miss."

With a huff and not an ounce of embarrassment at his comment, she shielded her eyes from the sun and gazed toward the docks of St. Kitts jutting from the small town like tongues ready to receive their daily bread. Beyond the ramshackle buildings and waving palms, the island swooped up to a tall mountain blanketed in mossy green.

But it was the darkening sky in the distance that gave Nathaniel pause.

"Barbaric place," Hope said with disdain.

But how could he blame her after her horrifying experience? Though exhaustion tugged on her features, morning sunlight shimmered over her pearly skin and glittered in the bouquet of golden curls pinned atop her head. No one would recognize her as the filthy, rag-clad woman being auctioned off yesterday in the town square. And although she held her pert little nose in the air, a hint of shame seemed to weigh down her shoulders. Good. As it should.

She observed the bustling deck with interest, seemingly unaware of the appreciative glances thrown her way from every man aboard. Or was she? Something in her expression, the slight quirk of her lips, the lofty slant of her brow, told him otherwise.

When Nathaniel had tapped on her door that morning, she opened it with such force, he thought she would barrel right into him. The mixture of shock and delight beaming on her face took him by surprise. Had she thought he would abandon her? Like Lord Falkland. Like her father. Like how many other men in her life?

Nay, he'd arranged with the tavern keeper for a bath, a fresh gown, and a meal to be brought up to her, but—as was only proper—Nathaniel sought his night's rest elsewhere. Perhaps he should have informed her he would return, but in truth, he'd been too angry.

Heightened voices drew his attention to the quarterdeck where a group of sailors crowded around the man Nathaniel assumed to be the captain. One crewman's tone was quite emphatic as he kept pointing toward the eastern sky, while others shouted their agreement. The captain's retort came in the form of a loud, booming voice that bore a curse and several colorful names for his crew that quickly scattered the men.

A muscle twitched in Nathaniel's jaw. Captain Conway's reputation among the seamen at port was one of a cruel, overbearing man, and few but the most desperate signed on to his crew.

Desperate like Nathaniel.

But what choice did he have? He would obey all orders and stay away from the man as much as possible.

A net full of barrels hauled by ropes rose over the side of the ship and hovered in midair, and Nathaniel quickly guided Hope out of the way toward the railing. "What type of ship is this, Mr. Mason?"

"A merchant brig."

"Like your ship," she said in a voice thick with guilt.

His ship. A palpable pain struck his heart as he scanned the choppy bay and found her resting idly among the turquoise waves. His brig, the *Blue Triumph*—the ship he'd poured not only his money into, but his blood and sweat. He'd chosen every plank and timber, bolt and nail, canvas and line. He'd designed it, managed the builders, and spent many an hour himself hammering and measuring and sealing with tar and oakum. Yet it was his brig no longer. An ache raged in his gut. He should be pleased Hope felt *some* remorse, but Nathaniel could summon no joy at the thought. It would take him years to recover from the loss, and that meant more years before he could realize his dream of owning his own merchant fleet.

"I am truly sorry, Mr. Mason." Her eyes shone with sincerity. "I made an awful mess of things and have cost you a great deal. You have been nothing but kind and done more than most gentlemen would." She laid a hand on his arm. "When we return home, I'm sure my father will offer some recompense for your loss."

Tugging his arm from beneath her hand, Nathaniel

doubted it. Admiral Westcott's reputation spoke of a gruff, commanding man who was as tight with his fortune as he was in running his ships.

She reached out for him again, and he took a step back. She was a sly one, this one—a charmer. Like a coquettish fox, luring men into her den, well-skilled in the art of female attraction. Perhaps that was what had drawn him to her in Charles Towne, that and his belief that she was a virtuous woman. But a proper lady would not sneak aboard a man's ship with the intention of running away with him, regardless of whether she thought they were betrothed and he was unmarried. Nay, a woman like that was certainly no longer chaste.

A woman like that was too much like his mother.

However sincere her apology, Nathaniel had no intention of allowing his anger to dissolve. Yes, he could forgive her— as was his Christian duty. But forget? Forgetting such a horrendous offense was far beyond his ability and bordered on the divine. And one thing he had learned in his five and twenty years, he was not God.

A gust of wind crashed over them with the smell of fish, salt, and sweat, and Hope raised a hand to her nose and lifted her gaze to a family upon the quarterdeck: A man dressed in silk stockings, black velvet breeches, and an elaborately embroidered waistcoat stood beside a woman who was fretting over her young daughter. Behind them stood Captain Conway, arms locked across his chest, surveying the loading of the ship. A young, light-haired gentleman leaned to whisper in his ear all the while keeping his gaze on Nathaniel and Hope. The gleam in his eyes sent a ripple of unease down Nathaniel's back.

Commanding shouts drew his attention back to the main deck where, amidst the sailors scrambling to follow orders, a small group of passengers popped up from below—satchels, and valises in hand—and scurried across the deck. Several crewmen joined them as they slid over the railing and climbed down to a waiting boat.

The captain marched to the railing and thrust a fist in their direction. "Begone with you, you mush-brained cowards! We have no need of your kind."

Nathaniel reached out and grabbled one of the departing crewman, a young boy with shaggy brown hair.

"Why are you leaving?"

"A hurricane, sir." He gestured toward the angry sky in the east. "Headin' this way."

"Most likely just a summer storm, lad. Nothing to fear," Nathaniel returned.

"Mebbe, but I ain't takin' me chances. Not for the likes o' Cap'n Conway." Fear sparked in the young boy's eyes as he hurried after his companions.

Nathaniel eyed the thick clouds piling atop the horizon. By sailing this time of year, they risked facing one of the monstrous storms that occasionally struck these waters, but many a year passed in which none occurred. He glanced at Hope, whose attentions had shifted to the handsome light-haired man now marching across the deck issuing orders and sending looks of interest her way. Nathaniel huffed. He needed to get her settled in her quarters below—away from the eyes of unsavory men. He needed to escort her safely home. And the sooner the better. His inquiries at port had told him there would not be another ship bound for Kingston for two weeks. And that was far too long to wait on the whim of a possible storm.

A loud crack pierced the air followed by the snap of twine and groan of heavy crates. "Look out below!"

Nathaniel shot a quick glance above him, dropped his bag, grabbed Hope's arm, and yanked her out of the way.

Slam! The crunch and crack of wood shot across the deck as a jarring impact shook the brig. Trembling, Hope leaned against him. "Oh my."

A heap of shattered crates littered the deck where they had just stood. Clothing, jewelry, spices, and coffee spilled from the splintered cavities as ale chugged from a cracked barrel. Nathaniel collected his breath. He and Hope would have been crushed. What *was* crushed was the brown sack containing all his belongings.

"It appears you have saved my life once again, Mr. Mason." Hope raised a hand to her forehead and laid her head on his shoulder. "I feel faint."

Nathaniel desperately needed to move away from the feel of her soft curves pressed against him, but he worried if he did, she'd topple to the deck and he'd be forced to take her in his arms.

The young man Hope had been watching shouted obscenities at the sailors manning the ropes as he marched across the deck, shifting a harried gaze over the splintered chaos and spilled goods, before halting in front of them.

"My apologies, sir, miss. Are you both unharmed?"

"Yes. I believe so." Nathaniel stepped back from Hope. "However my dunnage was not so fortunate."

The young man clicked his tongue and stared at what remained of Nathaniel's bag. "I hope it contained nothing of value."

Just everything I had left of my ship. Nathaniel grimaced. Since he'd come across Hope yesterday, he'd lost his brig, nearly his life, and now everything else he had on his person: clothing, his prized spyglass, his mother's locket, his ship's logbook, among other valued mementos—all in his efforts to save her. If he believed in such things, he might think she was bad luck.

"Mr. Gavin Keese." The young man extended his hand to Nathaniel. "I'm the second mate." He glanced at Hope, admiration glinting in his eyes.

"A pleasure, Mr. Keese. I am Nathaniel Mason, the navigator." Nathaniel grabbed his hand and gave it a strong but friendly shake.

"Aye, good. Then we shall be working together. As you can see many of the crew abandoned the ship in fear of a little storm." His features wrinkled in disgust. "Which has left the remainder a bit overwrought, I'm afraid. No doubt the cause of this mishap." He shifted his admiring gaze back to Hope. "And this is?"

"Forgive me. Miss Hope Westcott, may I introduce Mr. Keese, the second mate, as you heard." Nathaniel forced a smile.

With a gentlemanly bow, Mr. Keese placed a kiss upon her ungloved fingers. Hope gave him a coy smile that would have melted even the most pious priest.

Several seconds—which seemed like minutes—dragged by in which Mr. Keese and Hope's eyes and hands remained locked in a lingering, playful dalliance.

The biscuit Nathaniel ate for breakfast began to rebel in his stomach. He had assumed the burden of escorting Hope safely home, but he had neither the time nor inclination to deal with any more of her troublesome liaisons. Grimacing, he fought the urge to step between them. Instead, he cleared his throat. "I must check in with the captain."

"Good. I shall keep Miss Hope company until you return." Mr. Keese's blue eyes never left hers. "If that's acceptable with her, of course."

She smiled her approval, both of them ignoring Nathaniel.

Growling, he stormed off to report to the captain. Within minutes, he returned with orders to show Miss Hope to her stateroom and get to work. He proffered his elbow to her once again. "Shall we?"

"Nay, I'm quite comfortable here." She waved him off, laughing at something Mr. Keese had said.

"I thought you were feeling faint."

"It has passed," she said in a lighthearted tone but did not meet his eyes.

Mr. Keese scratched the whiskers lining his jaw. "Alas, I fear I must be about my work as well, Miss Hope." He kissed her hand again. "I shall look forward to our next meeting."

Hope watched the young man saunter away before she took Nathaniel's arm with a sigh.

Disgust simmered in his belly as he assisted her down the companionway ladder. "Perhaps you should avoid playing the coquette until you return to Charles Towne?" He intended to keep the sarcasm from his voice but it rang clear in the narrow hallway.

"Coquette? Why, I was doing no such thing." She released his arm. The ship rolled and she bumped into the bulkhead. Rubbing her elbow, she continued beside him. "I was simply being kind."

Kind indeed. Nathaniel led her through the dim hallway to the forecabin, where he was told the women were staying. "Most men will not consider your attentions mere kindness, Miss Hope." He halted at the door. "Ah, here we are."

"And, pray tell, what will they consider them?"

Nathaniel wiped the sweat from the back of his neck and leaned toward her ear. "Perchance it was this *being kind*, as you call it, that caused the mess you find yourself in."

Light from a lantern hanging on the deckhead flickered over her fiery eyes. "If you are implying I am some trollop who throws herself at any man who comes along, you are mistaken! Lord Falkland and I loved each other, or at least I thought." She lowered her gaze. "I would have married him … if … well, never mind. I don't have to explain myself to you, nor bear your insults."

"I'm afraid you do, at least until I bring you home."

Hope opened her mouth to reply, but slammed it shut and looked away.

Opening the door to the cabin, Nathaniel ushered her inside and closed the door before she thought of a sassy retort. Then turning, he stomped down the hallway and back up on deck where most of the sailors' eyes were on the dark boiling sky in the east. Dark and boiling like his insides. Infuriating woman! Already back to her flirtatious ways.

Then why was he so drawn to her?

When she was everything he didn't want in a woman—without a belief in God, without morals, and unwilling to take a good look at herself and see her need for change. The sordid reputation of his mother he'd fought so hard to overcome, the honorable reputation he'd worked so hard to obtain would only suffer should he entangle himself with such a woman. Nathaniel rubbed his aching side and stiffened as a gust of wind struck him, bringing his gaze back to the dark clouds. What if they *did* encounter a hurricane? He prayed he'd made the right decision. Yet risking a storm at sea seemed preferable to spending any more time with Hope than necessary. Women like her caused nothing but problems, heartache, broken lives ....

And orphaned children.

Chapter 5

Removing her shoes from her bandaged feet, Hope plopped onto one of the beds built into the bulwarks. "Ouch." Lifting the thin feather mattress revealed naught but solid wood beneath. Even imprisoned aboard Falkland's ship, she'd been given a real bed.

Falkland ... Arthur.

Her heart felt like a stone, a rather large stone. Leaning over, she rubbed her burning eyes, trying to barricade any further tears from falling. The smell of rotting wood and some foul odor she could not identify wafted around her, permeating her skin and making her feel filthier, more unworthy than she already did. Would the pain ever go away?

Flirting with Mr. Keese had softened it, at least for a moment. It helped to know other men appreciated her beauty and charm, even if Lord Falkland did not. Even with puffy, red circles beneath her eyes from crying half the night, she still could turn a gentleman's head.

All save Nathaniel. What a perplexing man. Whenever she thought he had succumbed to her charms, he would turn away and seemingly erect an impenetrable shield against her coquettish darts.

She huffed. Why on earth did she care? Though he had proven himself to be an honorable man, he was naught but a commoner, a tradesman. Why would she want him?

Why would he want me? Used goods, soiled …worthless.

No doubt that's what he thought of her, for whenever he looked her way—which he made every effort to avoid doing—disapproval burned in his gaze.

Rising, Hope stepped to the tiny window and gazed out at St. Kitts where workers, merchants, and sailors buzzed about the small town like ants. A chill swept over her at the thought that she could right now be at the mercy of that hideous merchantman.

If not for Nathaniel Mason.

All she'd ever wanted was to find a man who would truly love her, marry her, and give her a brood of children … sweet, innocent children, untainted by the cruel world. Though she would never divulge this to her father, she'd dreamt of someday opening an orphanage in Charles Towne—a place where unwanted children would be loved and protected, a place where they could enjoy the sweet childhood she never had. Lord Falkland had wanted children—at least he had told her as much, but now she wondered if anything he said had been true.

She swiped a tear from her cheek. What was she thinking? Women like her didn't run orphanages. Only decent, virtuous women like her sister Grace were entrusted with the care of innocent children.

Tracing the salt-encrusted stains on the window with her finger, Hope closed one eye and peered at the twisted, distorted shape of the island—warped like some maniacal nightmare. Just like her life. How had she ended up in this place? Where had things gone so drastically wrong? She had thrown herself into the arms of a man, given herself away in the hope he would love her and marry her. But her wanton, foolish behavior had nearly cost her everything. Now, she had a second chance. She would strive to improve herself—to become a virtuous lady, strong and brave like her sister Faith, and honest and pure like her sister Grace. Yes, that was it! She would capture the heart of a true gentleman. Then, maybe then, this agonizing emptiness within her would be filled.

The door swung open, and in walked a tall girl in a plain cotton gown, valise in hand. When she saw Hope, her face lit with a huge smile. "Oh, forgive me for intruding." She glanced around the room. "I believe I am staying in this cabin, too. I am Abigail Sheldon." She placed her things on the middle cot and untied the ribbon beneath her chin before removing her bonnet.

"Hope Westcott." Hope returned her smile.

Hair the color of chestnuts spilled from her pins. "'Tis windy aboard ship." She attempted to tuck the loose strands back in place. Sparkling hazel eyes reached out to Hope with more sincerity and virtue than she'd seen in a long while. A cheerful peace cascaded around the young girl like a refreshing waterfall, and Hope liked her immediately.

"I suppose we are the only two unattached females aboard," Miss Sheldon said as the ship swayed, forcing her to hold onto a beam for support.

"Indeed? I hadn't realized." Hope found it surprising she wasn't the only lone woman. Most ladies wouldn't dare travel unescorted, unless they were the type who entertained men for profit.

The snap of canvas and the pounding of sailors' feet above deck filled the room. They would soon set sail, and Hope would once again be at sea. Only this time, she sailed home to the safety of her sisters' arms. This time she sailed farther away from Lord Falkland—Arthur—instead of traveling to a wedding she realized now would be played out only in her dreams.

He sold me as a slave. She could not deny the truth

finally settling in her mind. But she forbade it to penetrate the wall around her heart. Not yet. For she feared it would pierce her so deeply, she'd never recover.

"Miss Westcott ... Miss Westcott."

Hope gazed at the young girl smiling down at her. "Forgive me. My thoughts were elsewhere."

"I was saying that I believe the only other woman aboard is a Mrs. Hendr—"

Instantly the door opened and the modishly dressed lady Hope had seen earlier on deck entered the room, a small girl, no more than six years old, in tow.

"Ah, there she is. I was just telling Miss Westcott we are the only three women aboard. Well, four, if you count your daughter." Miss Sheldon knelt and smiled at the girl clinging to her mother's dress. Red curls spiraled from beneath a straw bonnet as a freckled face with skittish blue eyes dove into the folds of her mother's skirt.

The poor thing looked petrified, and Hope longed to scoop her in her arms and reassure her all would be well.

The woman waved her silk fan about her face and sighed. "I wanted to stay with my husband, but the captain doesn't permit couples together on the ship, though I cannot imagine why. Now, Miss Elise and I must lodge with two perfect strangers." Her blue eyes widened as her gaze flicked between Hope and Miss Sheldon. "Oh, do forgive me. I am quite distraught. I'm not good at traveling, and Elise has not been away from home, and I fear she's caught one of those hideous tropical fevers. Can you feel her skin? Does she feel warm to you?" She pushed the hesitant girl closer to Miss Sheldon and closed the door behind her.

Hope's head spun with the woman's constant chattering, but aside from her unbridled tongue, she was quite lovely. Close to Hope's age, if not a few years older, she carried herself with a lofty urbanity expected of her station. Her flawless skin was crowned with a fashionable coiffeur the color of mahogany. A crimson overgown sat graciously upon her exquisitely laced bodice, which ended in a trim of flowered embroidery. The young girl, dressed no less stylishly, allowed Miss Sheldon to touch her face.

"Nay, Mrs. Hendrick. She feels quite healthy to me."

"My goodness, thank you, but I am sure she is not well. Come, Elise, you must rest." The mother assisted her daughter in taking off her shoes and helped her climb onto a cot. "You can never be too careful." Then, plopping beside the child, she waved her fan about her as if she could swat away the heat and odor saturating the cabin.

"I am Mrs. Hendrick, and this is Miss Elise Hendrick." She eased a lock of her daughter's hair from her brow, and the girl smiled up at her mother then uttered a hushed "Pleased to meet you" in their direction.

"Abigail Sheldon." Miss Sheldon gave a quick curtsy.

Hope nodded at Mrs. Hendrick. "Hope Westcott."

"Well, I suppose 'tis good to have female companionship aboard this vessel, especially with so many unseemly men on board. I mean"—Mrs. Hendrick leaned toward them as if she had a grand secret to share—"you would not believe the way I was ogled when I first arrived. Upon my word, it was most frightening, but at least I have a husband to watch over me." She huffed and eyed the door. "Where is that man with our things? Faith, but 'tis hot in here, and so small. How shall we manage? I cannot believe William has allowed me to suffer so."

"I'm sure we will all get along splendidly," Miss Sheldon said.

Hope felt none of the same assurance. Mrs. Hendrick had naught to complain about. At least she had a husband, a child, and obviously plenty of wealth. Hope had nothing but the dress on her back and the torn chemise and stained corset beneath it. She had lost everything: her dignity, her reputation—and her heart.

All by your own doing. The gentle voice eased over Hope's conscience as her throat burned with sorrow.

A loud *crack* sounded from above, and the ship lurched. At last they were departing this uncivilized island.

Mrs. Hendrick regarded both Miss Sheldon and Hope with a curious eye. "How did you ladies come to be traveling alone?"

Miss Sheldon looked away and swallowed. "My parents were killed recently."

"Oh, my dear, I'm so sorry," Mrs. Hendrick said.

Hope thought of her own mother—of happier times, of feeling protected, loved, and cherished—feelings long since buried beneath the soil of Portsmouth, along with her mother. "I, too, lost my mother."

Miss Sheldon whisked a tear from her cheek. "Then you understand."

Plucking a handkerchief from her pocket, Mrs. Hendrick handed it to Miss Sheldon. "If I may be so bold, what happened to them?"

"They were killed in a slave uprising in Antigua last month."

"Oh my. How horrible." Mrs. Hendrick shook her head. "What was your family doing on such a savage island?"

Miss Sheldon dabbed her eyes. "My parents were missionaries with the Society for the Propagation of the Gospel in Foreign Parts."

Mrs. Hendrick's mouth twisted oddly. "Have you no other relations. Are you all alone?"

"Nay, 'tis only me left. Me and God, that is." A tiny smile broke through her sorrow.

Mrs. Hendrick patted her stylish coiffeur and gazed at her daughter, who had finally closed her eyes.

The brig groaned and creaked over the rising swells as it made its way out to the open sea. Placing her hand over her stomach, Mrs. Hendrick directed her curiosity upon Hope. "And you, Miss Westcott?"

Hope grabbed a lock of her hair. Her story was as far removed from Miss Sheldon's as a bishop's from a trollop's, and she knew the telling of it would bring her neither credit nor sympathy from these two women. "I shall not bore you with the tale, Mrs. Hendrick. Suffice it to say, I am on my way home to Charles Towne where my family awaits me."

"But a young lady traveling alone? Are you not afraid?"

"There is a gentleman who travels with me. He is a member of the crew."

"A relation?"

Though tempted to lie, Hope knew Mr. Mason would not confirm her deceit. But she so dearly wanted these ladies to like her, to approve of her, befriend her. She could use a friend right now, someone who would understand the pain of a broken heart. "Merely an acquaintance who rescued me in a time of great need." She braced herself for the sanctimonious looks of disapproval.

"How romantic." Miss Sheldon smiled.

"I assure you it is not." Hope gazed out the tiny window.

"'Tis most unseemly." Mrs. Hendrick gave a ladylike snort and stared at Hope as if she were naught but an annoying rodent—the same look Hope had received a thousand times from the proper ladies of Charles Towne, a look that made her feel like manure on the street, fit only to be trampled upon.

Averting her gaze before they saw the moisture fill her eyes, Hope knew it would do no good to try to defend herself to Mrs. Hendrick. Lord knew she had tried with her type and never gotten anywhere. Lying down on her bed with a huff, she gave up her dream of making new friends. She never seemed to measure up in other women's eyes. Either they were jealous of her or they thought her too crude, wanton, or too far beneath them. The scorching looks they shot her way never missed their mark, as they might suppose. She felt every one of them like a sharp blade in her heart.

Men were a different sort of animal. Hope rarely had problems befriending men. They adored her, they lavished gifts upon her, they made her feel special. And besides, they were far more interesting than most women she knew, save for her sister Faith.

Hope squeezed her eyes shut, wishing she could shut out the world around her as easily, or at least the two women in her cabin. Or did she? Perhaps stowed away in quarters no bigger than a necessary room with two constant reminders of her inadequacies was a fitting punishment. One she could make the best of. She could learn from these women. Learn how a proper lady behaved. Start afresh and prove to everyone on this ship that she was as virtuous as any true lady.

Excitement jolted through her. No one knew her past here. She could change—she *would* change. And when she returned to Charles Towne, she would prove her new character to everyone—first to her sisters and then to those who had shunned her. Then, maybe then, she could catch the heart of a gentleman, open up an orphanage, and fulfill her life's dream.

Chapter 6

"Miss Westcott, you are looking quite lovely this evening." Captain Conway's gaze took in Hope as if she were a sweetmeat. With a flip of his coattails, he took his seat at the head of the table laden with more food than Hope had seen since she'd began her foolish escapade aboard Falkland's ship nigh two weeks ago. A steaming platter of roast pork perched in the center between two flickering candles. Bowls of plantains, mangos, rice, corn, and biscuits spread across the linen-clad table, their sweet and spicy scents rising to form an enticing aroma. Hope's stomach lurched in anticipation.

"Why, thank you, Captain." She smiled but quickly looked away, not wanting to encourage his attentions. Circling the table, Nathaniel sat across from her, a scowl on his face.

When he'd come to escort her and Miss Sheldon to the captain's quarters for dinner, she was elated—mainly to be freed from the stifling cabin, but also because her stomach had been growling like a wild beast all afternoon. But it was the pleasant way her heart had leapt when she opened the door to see Nathaniel's handsome face that gave her pause.

Pushing aside the uncomfortable reaction, she'd happily taken his arm. Then after Miss Sheldon clutched the other, he'd escorted them both to dinner as if they were going to a ball.

"Thank you for the invitation, Captain." She felt Mr. Keese's eyes upon her from his seat to her right, but placing her hands in her lap, she ignored him. "Surely you do not feast like this every night?"

Captain Conway fingered his pointed gray beard. "Nay, miss, especially when we've been long out to sea." Pockmarks marred his sun-blistered skin that looked as thick as a cowhide, and although the gray streaking his hair told a tale of a hard life at sea, his lively eyes revealed a much younger man within.

Over his shoulder, through the stern window, the sun sank wearily behind the horizon, waving glorious ribbons of crimson, gold, and copper onto the choppy sea in its evening farewell.

A pudgy well-dressed man burst into the room, grumbling his apologies, and took a seat to the right of the captain.

"Ah, now that we are all here," the captain announced, "may I introduce Mr. Herbert Russell." He gestured toward the man, who nodded with a grunt. "And beside him, Major Harold Paine."

The stiff man, dressed in a military red coat crossed with a white baldric, slid a finger over his thin mustache and narrowed his eyes over the guests.

"Then, Mr. Mason, my new navigator." Nathaniel gave a cursory glance around the table, his gaze skittering over Hope as if she didn't exist.

The captain continued. "Miss Abigail Sheldon, I believe?"

"Yes, Captain." Miss Sheldon smiled.

Turning in his chair, Captain Conway nodded to the dashing man at his left. "Mr. William Hendrick." Hope leaned forward to study Mrs. Hendrick's husband, the man she'd seen on deck earlier. Still attired in his stylish garb, he barely acknowledged the introduction, nor anyone else in the room for that matter, as he poured wine into his glass from a pewter decanter.

"Beside him, Mr. Gavin Keese," the captain continued. "My second mate." Mr. Keese nodded toward everyone before he winked at Hope.

"And finally, the lovely Miss Hope Westcott."

Hope smiled as sweetly as she could at all the guests, searching for some kindness, some approval in their eyes. Back in Charles Towne, her inappropriate deeds—along with those of her sister Faith—had put a stain on their family's reputation. But here among these strangers, Hope could start anew. And what better way than with a military officer, a captain, and two wealthy businessmen—obvious gentlemen all. She longed to be treated like a lady, not like a stained handkerchief to be used and tossed aside.

Like Falkland had treated her.

"A fine spread, Captain." Mr. Russell rubbed his hands together, his eyes gleaming as he examined the banquet.

"For our first night at sea, and with such important guests, I could think of no better way to start our journey." Captain Conway poured wine into his glass. "Besides, 'twould be a crime indeed to have two such lovely ladies on board and not enjoy their beauty."

A red hue crept up Miss Sheldon's face as the captain shifted his eyes her way.

"Indeed." Mr. Keese agreed.

"Speaking of beauty, where is your wife, Mr. Hendrick?" the captain asked the modish man on his left.

"She is not well." He sipped his drink. "You know how women cannot handle the sea."

"I'm sorry to hear of it."

Hope bit her lip. *Cannot handle the sea, indeed.* She wanted to correct him—to inform him that if he tore his eyes from his drink, he might see two healthy women seated at the table, but she thought better of it. No sense in stirring up trouble, especially for poor Mrs. Hendrick. Hope had left her casting her accounts into her chamber pot, and although Miss Sheldon had wanted to stay and care for her, Mrs. Hendrick would have none of it. Nor would she allow Hope to bring Miss Elise to dinner.

The ship bucked over a wave. Plates shifted on the table. Hope gasped, and Mr. Keese placed his hand on hers beneath the table and smiled. The warmth of his skin and his playful dalliance lifted Hope's spirits, and she longed to encourage his affections—if only to ease the agony wrenching at her heart. Instead, she snatched her hand back and looked away.

"Shall we begin?" The captain reached for a plate of steaming rice.

"Should we not bless the food, Captain?" Miss Sheldon asked.

Nathaniel's stiff lips finally cracked in a smile as he nodded approvingly at Miss Sheldon. They exchanged a glance that sent unease prickling through Hope, befuddling her mind as to the cause. She took a sip of wine.

"Of course. Of course." The captain blew out a snort and stared at his plate. "God in heaven, bless this meal and keep us safe on our journey. Amen." He said the prayer with such rapidity, it seemed he feared the food would vanish before he finished.

"Amen," Miss Sheldon and Nathaniel said in unison.

Bowls and platters were passed, and everyone piled food onto their plates. Hope spooned portions of tasty pork, corn, and rice into her mouth as fast as ladylike decorum would allow. She had not had a meal like this since she left Charles Towne, and her stomach sang in thanksgiving with each bite. Succulent, moist, and spicy, the pork reminded Hope of Molly's cooking back home. *Home.* Part of her missed it terribly—the security, the love of her sisters—but part of her dreaded going back, dreaded the memories of Lord Falkland on every corner, dreaded the accusing whispers behind her back, the ruined reputation she dragged behind her like a cannonball on a chain.

But for now, she was far from home, enjoying the attentions and admiration of reputable men. Helping herself to more wine, she forced a smile. Her sister Grace would never allow her to indulge so at home.

Nathaniel stabbed a chunk of pork. "Captain, I hear you are new to the Caribbean. If I may ask, where did you sail before you arrived in these waters?"

"I sailed a run between Boston and Liverpool for many years." He pushed his food around with his fork.

"What brings you south?" Nathaniel leaned back in his chair.

"I grew tired of the cold seas and North Atlantic storms," he mumbled. A momentary glimpse of sorrow burned in his eyes before their gleam returned. "And word is, there is a fortune to be made here in the West Indies. Mr. Russell here knows all about that." The captain slapped the back of the man sitting to his right. "Don't you, Herbert? He's found his pot of gold trading on these seas."

Mr. Russell smacked his moist lips together, sending his pendulous jowls swinging. "Quite so. Quite so. Currently, I am on my way to purchase land in the Carolinas."

"Indeed?" Hope said. "I am sailing to Charles Towne, Mr. Russell. My family resides there."

"Then we shall see much of each other, my dear. I hear the land is plentiful and well suited for rice and indigo."

"You are correct, sir. There are plantations and farms springing up everywhere, and the town itself is growing so rapidly, they are being forced to knock down the city walls for lack of room."

"So I have heard. A perfect time to purchase land in these burgeoning colonies." Mr. Russell plopped a chunk of pork into his mouth, chewed it to satisfaction, and then faced the man beside him. "Major Paine, pray tell, inform us of the happenings on the Leeward Islands."

The major straightened his already rigid posture and set down his fork. "As you know, the lieutenant governor is sick with malaria. Hence, I am traveling to England to convince Whitehall to instate me as the new governor should he die." He glanced around the room as if expecting looks of esteem.

Mr. Keese chuckled. "Sink me. The poor man's shoes will still be warm when you snatch them from his body."

Miss Sheldon brushed hair from her forehead. "Heaven forefend, Major. We should pray for the lieutenant governor's recovery instead of plan his demise."

"Well said, Miss Sheldon." Nathaniel dropped a slice of mango into his mouth and gave the young missionary a look of approval.

Another sting of discomfort struck Hope. Without thinking, she leaned close to Mr. Keese—so close she could smell the sea in his hair—and asked him to pass the corn. Their shoulders brushed, and his eyes glinted with interest, but when she glanced back at Nathaniel, he covered a yawn with his hand and looked away.

Fisting her hands beneath the table, Hope chided herself for her behavior. A proper lady did not draw so close to a man—for any reason. This task of transforming into a genteel lady was not going to be easy. She rubbed her brow, trying to still the dizzying effects of the wine and make sense out of her unusual reactions to Nathaniel. Honorable, god-fearing Mr. Mason. He reminded her of Captain Waite, her sister's beau, back home. Stodgy and dull.

Major Paine's jaw stiffened. "Of course I pray night and day for the man's recovery, but in the best interest of England and due to the distance, the transfer of power must be done promptly or chaos will rule on these islands."

"Aye, and we wouldn't want chaos to rule." Mr. Keese's eyebrows arched mischievously.

"Indeed, sir, we would not." Major Paine huffed and adjusted his black cravat. "I hope, Mr. Keese, that despite your insolence, your loyalties lie with England."

"I am loyal to none but myself." Mr. Keese shrugged and scooped a spoon of rice into this mouth.

"I have heard pirates say as much."

"Indeed? Perhaps I am one."

The major slowly rose to his feet. "You should know, sir, that it is my duty to capture and hang as many of the vile blackguards as I find."

Mr. Keese also stood, a challenging grin on his mouth.

Hope's breath quickened. Was there to be a duel right here in the captain's cabin? She had heard seamen were rash, cruel fellows, but this ... over such a small inference.

Nathaniel pushed back his chair and glanced between the men. "Ignore the boy, Major. He is clearly jesting with you and means no harm. Do you, Mr. Keese?"

Before he could answer, the captain bellowed. "Aye, Mr. Mason is correct," he said, a crumb flying from his mouth as he waved a biscuit toward the major. "I know the boy's father. A good Dutch merchant. His mother is from Southampton. Mr. Keese is an excellent seaman and is loyal to whomever he sails with. But the man is no pirate."

The major sat down with a growl. "A man should know how to control his tongue."

Mr. Keese took his seat. A daring gleam shone from his eyes.

"More wine, Miss Westcott?" He held the decanter and began filling Hope's cup before she could answer. Charming, brave, and adventurous, Mr. Keese was every woman's dream. If he possessed wealth and land, he could have his pick of ladies. But for now, his attentions had the glorious effect of soothing her broken heart. The difficulty was, she had no idea how to respond to them without being unseemly. He continued pouring wine, caught up in her gaze, and splashed some of the red liquid onto the table.

"Oh, forgive me." He chuckled.

"Truly understandable with such a charming lady at your

side," the captain chortled as he grabbed another biscuit from the tray.

"And what about you, Mr. Keese?" Hope asked, taking a sip of her wine. The warm liquid slid down her throat, setting her belly aflame and her head into a daze. "How did you come to be second mate on this ship?"

"My father was in the Dutch West India Company, miss. He brought my mother and me to Curacao ten years ago. Sooner than I could walk, I learned to sail." He chuckled. "And when I was of age, I left home to seek fortune and fame. I am on this ship because the opportunity presented itself to me and I took it."

Mr. Hendrick leaned forward to glare at Mr. Keese as if he were a commodity unworthy of his purchase. "To procure either, you must have a plan and the forbearance to carry it out. I sense neither in a man so brash."

"Begging your pardon, sir, but I have acquired *some* fortune. Not enough fame as of yet, but I carry a shipload of adventures in my pocket"—he patted his black doublet—"enough to stir a man's soul for quite some time."

Major Paine snorted. "A man without discipline is a man without honor."

The ship lunged in a creaking protest, sloshing water from the top of a pitcher, and spraying rice kernels over the table like sand. The brass lantern in front of Nathaniel teetered, and he grabbed it, steadying it before it fell. Light shimmered across his brown eyes—eyes that seemed to pierce right through Hope—offering a challenge. A flood of warmth swept over her beneath his gaze. Or perhaps it was simply the wine.

"Well, I, for one, find that type of life exciting," Hope declared, knowing full well she was not suited to such a reckless existence. It was her sister Faith who relished in the unknown, who lived for each daring escapade.

"I am sure you will discover fortune and fame are overrated, Mr. Keese." Miss Sheldon's soft tone held neither pretention nor reprimand, but was said as simply a matter of understanding.

Mr. Russell belched while Mr. Hendrick turned to face the young girl, a smug look on his handsome face. "Easily said coming from someone who clearly has neither."

"What a cruel thing to say." Hope's voice blared louder than she intended. Still, she couldn't let the pompous man insult such a sweet lady.

Nathaniel directed a hard gaze toward Mr. Hendrick. "Apologize to the lady at once, sir."

"'Tis no matter." Miss Sheldon suffered the insult with a grace that seemed to sweeten her face—if that were possible. She swept a reassuring gaze over Hope and Nathaniel before turning to Mr. Hendrick, whose face had purpled at Nathaniel's command. "I assure you, Mr. Hendrick, I know of what I speak. My parents possessed great wealth back in England, in addition to land. They gave up their worldly possessions to become missionaries."

"Perhaps so, Miss Sheldon." Mr. Hendrick stifled his anger beneath another swig of wine. "But a lot of good it has done them. I heard they were murdered by the very people they were hoping to convert."

Miss Sheldon lowered her gaze.

"Enough!" Nathaniel barked. "Can you not see the lady is still distraught over the loss of her parents?"

Envy burned within Hope. She could not recall any man coming to her defense so vehemently, not even her father—and certainly not an honorable man like Nathaniel.

The captain slammed down his glass. "Calm yourself, Mr. Mason. Mr. Hendrick is my guest. But"—he pointed a finger at the man—"I insist you treat all my guests with respect while you are on board my ship, sir."

Mr. Hendrick waved a hand through the air. "Egad. Cool your humors. I meant nothing by it."

Captain Conway turned toward Miss Sheldon. "I do hope you'll forgive the outburst, Miss Sheldon. I fear the company is not what you are accustomed to. Please tell us what brings you aboard my fine ship."

Miss Sheldon's smile had returned. "I am traveling to Kingston. A family friend, Reverend Hickman, has offered me a place to stay and a chance to continue my parent's missionary work there among the natives and slaves."

"Quite admirable." Nathaniel's eyes reflected admiration, but he quickly narrowed them and looked at Hope as if comparing her to the pristine, selfless angel beside him.

But of course, there was no comparison.

Instead of enduring his disappointment, Hope watched the last traces of light fade from the horizon as darkness hovered over the sea like a bird of prey.

The food soured in her stomach, and she took another sip of wine.

"Not sure you can save these savage Indians. They are far too ignorant to understand the complexities of Christianity," Mr. Russell commented, in between shoving forkfuls of food into his mouth.

"The Christian message is not complex sir," Nathaniel said, "but easy enough for a child to understand and embrace."

"Are you a religious man, Mr. Mason?" The captain shoved his plate aside and settled back in his chair.

"I was raised by a reverend, but I would consider myself more god-fearing than religious."

Hope flinched. She knew Nathaniel had been reared by Reverend Halloway, but god-fearing? Truly, he and Miss Sheldon *were* a perfect match.

Mr. Hendrick huffed. "There is no money in God's work. And a man is nothing without wealth and land. When I began my own business at age eighteen, I had not a shilling to my name. Now I own a fleet of merchant ships and a plantation on St. Kitts. Respect, power, and freedom." He raised a condescending brow. "That's what money can buy you, sir."

"It cannot buy you freedom, Mr. Hendrick," Mr. Keese remarked, and Hope wondered why he dared to cross the man again. "Freedom you must take at your own risk. Money and land, they hold you captive, while I am free to go and do whatever I want."

"'Tis my wife who holds me captive, sir," he countered with a chuckle as he poured himself more wine.

Hope's skin crawled at the man's disparaging remark about his wife, and she hoped the alcohol, and not his true sentiments, spoke for him.

"But pray tell, Mr. Mason, what is your business?" he asked.

"I am a merchant as well. I own two ships or, rather, one now." He huffed but did not look at Hope. "I built them myself."

"Built, you say? Odd's fish." Captain Conway wiped his mouth with his sleeve. "Incredible feat. But how did you lose your ship? Storm? Pirates?" He seemed to be holding back a chuckle.

Nathaniel hesitated as his somber gaze flickered over Hope, renewing her guilt. "An unfortunate circumstance."

"Humph. Any captain who loses his ship deserves his fate. Makes me wonder if you are fit to navigate."

"I assure you, I am quite capable." Nathaniel's jaw tightened. "I have captained my own ships for years and intend to find another to replace the one I lost as soon as possible."

The captain's brow grew dark. "And how, pray tell, do you intend to replace it?"

"I will either purchase one or build another." Nathaniel shrugged.

Captain Conway shifted in his seat. "I run a tight ship, Mr. Mason, and my crew is loyal to me." His eyes simmered, making Hope wonder if his statement were true.

"I have no doubt, Captain." Nathaniel regarded him

curiously.

"As you know, sir, we are undermanned on this voyage." The captain pointed his spoon at Nathaniel. "And I will expect you to do more than a navigator's duties."

"I assure you, you will find my work to your satisfaction, Captain." Nathaniel's calm, methodical tone belied the stiffness of his jaw.

"Very well." The captain downed the rest of his wine and glanced at Hope, a grin creeping over his lips. "I believe you are escorting Miss Westcott home, Mr. Mason, are you not?"

"Aye, Captain."

"And how did you come to be in need of escort so far from home, Miss Hope?"

Cringing, Hope stared at her lap, searching her wine-clouded mind for an explanation that would not mar her standing with these people. "'Tis a long, arduous tale, Captain. Suffice it to say, I took the wrong ship, ended up at St. Kitts abandoned, and Mr. Mason graciously offered to escort me home."

"I take it you are familiar with Mr. Mason?"

"Yes, we are acquainted from Charles Towne."

"I am a friend of the family," Nathaniel offered, finishing the last bite of pork from his plate.

Major Paine clicked his tongue, while Mr. Hendrick snorted. "I'll wager."

Hope's heart melted at their accusing looks.

Mr. Mason narrowed his eyes. "I assure you our relationship is quite respectable."

"Respectable enough to have sold your brig to purchase the young lady from a slave auction?" The captain snickered and exchanged a knowing glance with Mr. Keese. Gasps burst through the cabin, followed by chuckles.

Hope felt as if she'd crashed into a brick wall.

"Sold a ship to buy a woman?" Mr. Hendrick held his glass of wine in midair as if he were too shocked to know what to do with it.

"Ah, that explains it, then." Major Paine's eyes lit up.

"And what would that be, Major?" Hope asked sharply, wondering what other sordid details were to be disclosed about her.

"Yes, quite curious. I wondered what the man was doing," Major Paine announced to the whole table with a chuckle.

"Whatever do you mean?" Hope asked.

"Outside your door last night."

Hope wondered if the man had consumed too much wine.

As she had. She tried to fixate on his face, but the red and white of his uniform blurred into a bloated pink cloud, hiding it.

"You didn't know? My word." Major Paine pointed to Nathaniel. "He slept outside your door. I thought perhaps you two had a lover's spat." Chuckles rumbled over the table—chuckles directed at her virtue. "Now I realize he was protecting his investment."

Hope stared at her plate of food, stunned. All through the night, she'd wrung her sheets into knots, fearing Nathaniel would either come in and collect his due or abandon her altogether. Instead, he had sacrificed a decent night's sleep by guarding her door like a true gentleman.

"I'd say she'd had enough for one night and tossed him out." Mr. Hendrick scoffed.

"I beg your pardon!" Hope sprang to her feet then wobbled and clung to the table. Tears swam across her already fuzzy vision. "How dare you?" For once she didn't deserve these people's scorn. For once she had done nothing wrong. At least nothing they knew about. But perhaps they could smell her shame like a festering wound. Perhaps she would never be healed of it.

She glanced over the muted shapes at the table, searching for an ally, a champion, but she couldn't focus on anyone. She thought she saw Nathaniel rise from his seat, she thought she heard his deep voice bellow in her defense, but all she heard in the end were her shoes clomping over the wooden deck as she dashed from the room.

Chapter 7

Hot wind, tainted with the scent of salt and wet canvas, buffeted Nathaniel as he stormed up the companionway ladder. Fear rippled down his back. He had already knocked on the forecabin door looking for Hope, but Mrs. Hendrick's feeble voice squeaked from the other side, insisting she was alone. He knew Hope had partaken of too much wine. He knew she was distraught. What he didn't know was what she might do in that condition. He hoped nothing foolish. Yet he had a sense, in the brief time he'd known her, that Hope gave rule to her emotions over her reason far too often.

Silly, selfish girl. Like a wave tossed to and fro upon the sea, she was at the mercy of whatever winds happened to cross her path. How could anyone control such an erratic creature? Why should he care? He sighed. Perhaps God meant for him to help her. But he feared if he did, he'd lose himself so deeply in her charms, he would never find his way out.

Scanning the deck, he examined every dark shadow, finding only barrels, ropes, and a few sailors well into their cups. He nodded to the night watchman and leapt upon the quarterdeck where the helmsman pressed a steady hand upon the wheel. The man gestured ahead to the foredeck where Nathaniel made out a dark figure standing at the bow of the ship. The shadow of another figure hovered nearby, causing his heart to jump. Was someone harassing Hope?

He barreled down to the main deck then jumped up the foredeck ladder and marched toward the bow. But as he approached, the second figure dissipated like a shadow blown by the wind, leaving Hope standing alone. Nathaniel halted and rubbed his eyes, aching from lack of sleep. No doubt the reason for the strange apparition.

He eased beside her.

She flinched and swiped what looked like tears from her eyes. "What are you doing here?"

"You left so suddenly I … I wanted to make sure you were all right."

"I am quite well, Mr. Mason. Go back to your party."

"Who was here with you?"

"No one. I am alone, as you can see." Leaning over, she gazed over the railing. "The water looks so enticing, does it not? I had the strangest urge to throw myself into it a minute ago. I don't know why."

A chill slithered down Nathaniel. He said a quiet prayer of thanks he had arrived when he did.

The fetid odor from the head pricked his nose. "Miss Hope, the stench here is not fitting for a lady. Allow me to escort you back to your cabin."

Her red-rimmed eyes teetered over him as if looking for a place to land. "'Tis exactly where I belong, then."

The ship rose over a swell, sending a warm, salty spray over them. But instead of cringing like most ladies, Hope spread her arms out as if she wished to take flight. She stumbled, and Nathaniel readied his hands to catch her, but she caught her balance and stood like a wild bird with wings outstretched.

"Miss Hope, you shouldn't be—"

"There's something beautiful about the sea, isn't there? Something almost magical." She staggered. Nathaniel tossed his arm out behind her, but then she clutched the railing again and smiled. And in that smile, beyond the fear, beyond the facade, beyond the pain ... beamed an innocent little girl.

A protective yearning cluttered Nathaniel's throat, and he gazed over the dark waters. "Aye, the sea can be soothing at times." The wind eased into a light breeze, yet the ship rocked above massive swells that had grown higher throughout the day. "But I've spent enough time upon it to know it carries many hidden dangers as well."

Her frown returned. "I suppose you are correct. Nothing is as good as it seems."

"They were wrong to impugn your character, Miss Hope. Many men, even good men, can be quite crude in their assumptions." Yet even as he said the words, he wondered if something beyond the men's lewd opinions had caused her distress.

"Their crude assumptions were not incorrect, Mr. Mason. As you well know." Squeezing the remaining tears from her eyes, she drew a shuddering breath and then stared down at the bow slicing through ebony waters.

"The past is in the past." Nathaniel uttered the only thing he could think to say, but deep down, he wondered if it were true. His mother's past—and hence, his past—haunted him day and night.

"You are wrong, Mr. Mason. The past follows us like a dark cloud." She tugged upon a loose strand of hair at her neck and scanned the black line of the horizon, though her eyes seemed to stare far beyond it.

"Then start right now to ensure a better past follows you." Precisely what he intended to do—to remove the stains his mother had left on him, on his life, to pull out from under the shame, the poverty, until the past was so far behind him, he could no longer see it, could no longer smell it.

She snickered. "I wish it were that easy. Perhaps it is, for someone like you."

"You know nothing of me."

"I know enough." She tightened her lips. "You are the type of man who rescues foolish girls by selling half of all you own in the world. You're the type of man who sits outside a lady's door at night, forfeiting your sleep to protect her, even after she's ruined your life."

A tear slid down her cheek, and though he tried, Nathaniel couldn't resist wiping it away. Then, easing his fingers down, he caressed her delicate jaw, astonished at the softness of her skin. Desire shot through his belly. It sickened him. Was he so much like his mother, he couldn't resist a simple temptation? He dropped his hand and took a step back. "Any honorable man would have done the same."

"I am not so sure, Mr. Mason." Stumbling, she gripped the railing again as a blast of wind struck them—oddly, from the west—freeing more of her curls to flutter like ribbons of gold behind her. "I had thought … I had wanted … I wanted to know what it felt like to be treated like a respectable lady." She sniffed. "At least for a time."

Nathaniel swallowed against the burning in his throat. He didn't want to feel sorry for her, didn't want to care. She had brought all her trouble—including the way people treated her—upon herself. *So much like his mother.* Still, her tears seeped into his heart, penetrating the hard crust of his childhood and softening a part of him that longed to take her in his arms—longed to comfort her. "Of what import are their opinions?"

"Of great import." She took in a deep breath.

Nathaniel flinched, realizing the hypocrisy of his question when he himself had sought for years to cast off the shroud of dishonor from his past and emerge into respectful society. "You need no one's approval save God's," he said as much to himself as to Hope.

Her sad, hollow chuckle was snatched away on the wind. "I fear I lost *His* approval a long time ago."

"Perhaps you lost His approval of your behavior, but never His approval of you." A spark of purpose flickered within Nathaniel. Maybe he'd been sent to help this woman, after all.

She snorted. "Spare me your religious exhortations. I've heard them all from my sister Grace."

Grunting, Nathaniel crossed arms over his chest. How could he help someone who refused to be helped? But for now, he must calm her down and get her below before she lost her balance and fell into the sea, or some sailor came across her alone. Anger knotted in his gut at the position she once again had thrust upon him.

"Speaking of your sisters," he said. "They must be quite worried about you by now. Wasn't your sister Faith locked in the Watch Tower Dungeon?"

The ship plunged over a rising crest, showering a salty mist over them once again. Droplets sparkled over her face, neck, and the rising swell of her bosom, drawing his eyes to a place he had avoided glancing at all night. Coughing, he jerked his gaze back to the sea and rubbed the back of his neck. The wind died down again. Yet the waves increased. Not a good sign.

"Yes. Faith was awaiting trial," she finally said.

"And you left without discovering her fate?" Nathaniel hadn't intended his voice to sound so accusing, but he knew the Westcott sisters were close, and he couldn't imagine one of them leaving another one in danger.

She waved a hand through the air. "She assured me she would receive a pardon. Besides, Lord Falkland was to set sail, and I had no choice."

Could the woman be so selfish as to leave with her sister's fate unknown? Or perhaps she had been so besotted with that buffoon, Falkland, that she had gone temporarily mad. Most likely a bit of both.

Her features hardened. "Don't look at me like that. I love my sisters, and I know they love me. I knew Faith would be all right. She always is." The ship thrust into the next roller, and Hope wobbled and gripped the railing. "Besides, I never fit in with my sisters. Grace is so good, I don't believe she's ever had a vile thought in her life, and Faith is so strong, so brave, so much like our father. There's naught she cannot do, if she puts her mind to it." She sighed. "Then, there's me."

Nathaniel grimaced, growing tired of the woman's self-pity. "I am sure God has gifted you with your own special talents." Though he suspected she'd been too preoccupied with carnal pursuits to find them.

"So I've been told." Releasing the railing, she tilted her head to the side and waved her hands over her voluptuous form, a coy smile upon her lips. "This, apparently, is the only gift I have to offer."

The ship jolted, sending Hope stumbling sideways. Nathaniel flung himself in her path, and she fell against him, her warm body molding to his. She lifted her face to his and giggled. The sweet aroma of wine swirled around him. Her sapphire eyes glowed in the moonlight with an innocent pleading that seemed at odds with her libertine behavior.

His heart ran a race in his chest. He glanced at her inviting, parted lips and searched frantically for the anger of only a moment ago. Gathering his resolve, he gripped her arms, nudged her back a step. "It is not all you have to offer, Miss Hope." Though he attempted a stern tone, his voice emerged guttural with passion.

She dropped her head on his shoulder and nestled closer, obviously as unconvinced by his statement as he was. Her golden hair, blowing in the breeze tickled his nose and smelled of honey.

Lord?

Easing her hands up his arms, she gripped his muscles as if she absorbed strength from them, then she tipped her head up. Her warm breath caressed his chin as she brushed her fingers over the stubble on his jaw. A hot wave crashed over him, and he struggled for a breath of control.

Her lips pressed on his.

His limbs went numb as he gave in to the sensations roiling through him. She tasted of wine and mango, and he grew hungrier for more of her.

Moaning, she melted into him, her soft curves molding perfectly against his body like wind in a sail. How many times back in Charles Towne had his eyes drifted down to her full lips, dreaming of how they would feel against his … of how they would taste? Now, as they caressed his cheeks, his chin, and explored his mouth, his head grew light and his senses reeled. And he knew in that one moment, he could either lose himself completely or save himself forever.

Would it be so bad, to take the path his mother had trodden?

God help me.

No! He could not, would never. Pushing Hope back, he tried to catch his breath.

"What is it?" Shock heightened her voice.

"I cannot do this." Shame assaulted him at his behavior, his lack of restraint. Throughout the years, he'd resisted many women's flirtations, desiring to keep himself pure for his wife, wanting to do things right. But this woman, this luscious woman who was all curvy and soft and who smelled and tasted like honey and sweet wine had penetrated his shell of his control. Yet the way she flung about her charms with ease and gave herself away so freely, reminded him of exactly where he'd come from. A place to which he had vowed never to return.

She backed away from him, the simmer of passion fading from her eyes, replaced with sorrow. "You asked what my talents were."

"I didn't ask for a demonstration." Nathaniel flexed his jaw, his lips still burning from their kiss.

"I heard no complaints."

"Why do you throw yourself at every man you meet?" Her expression crumpled. "I don't want to. I'm trying not to." She gave him an angry pout and shook her head. "I don't know." Her shoulders sank. "I made a vow today to change."

"Try not drinking so much wine."

She shot him a fiery gaze.

"And flirting with Mr. Keese. You barely know him."

"I'm trying."

"Try harder."

She bunched her fists. Her mouth tightened. "Well, perhaps you should try not to accost a lady while she is all alone in the dark when you know she had too much wine. 'Tis most improper. What did you expect me to do?"

"I did not accost you. I *grabbed* you because you were about to fall." Nathaniel raised a brow. "Next time I'll allow you to tumble to the deck."

She wobbled again, but when he reached out to steady her, she snapped her arm away. "Don't touch me, or I'll scream and bring the crew swarming to my rescue."

Nathaniel laughed. "Rescue you from what?"

"From you taking advantage of my wine-befuddled senses."

"Despite the wine, I believe you knew exactly what you were doing." He narrowed his eyes. "An art you have perfected over the years, no doubt. But I do not intend to be your next victim."

"Victim! Pah. Go back to your lady, Miss Sheldon. You two are perfect for one another."

Miss Sheldon? He smiled. Her jealousy delighted him far more than it should have.

The ship lunged, sending white foam over the bow and onto Hope's shoes. She flung her arms out to her sides to keep her balance.

"The seas roughen. I'll escort you back to your cabin." Nathaniel held out a hand.

"I don't need your help. Leave me be." Swinging around, she stomped back to the rail.

"In your condition, you'll most likely fall overboard, and I don't feel like a swim tonight."

"Then leave me be and let me drown." She waved a hand behind her.

"Spoiled brat."

"Pretentious brute."

The ship bucked again. Hope lost her balance and tumbled backward. Nathaniel reached for her, but then jerked his hands back. She thumped to the deck. Her skirts billowed around her as she began to sob.

With a huff, Nathaniel hoisted her in his arms, ignoring her protests and her attempts to free herself as he carefully navigated the foredeck ladder and then the companionway ladder below. Finally, giving up, she slumped against his shoulder and released a quiet sigh.

Lord, why have You put this lady in my life?

The exact sort of woman he'd vowed to steer clear of. Yet he'd done the one thing she needed least of all—he'd given into her advance out of purely physical desire. Like every other man in her life. How could he have done such a thing when he'd strived so hard to maintain godly self-control his entire life, strived to eradicate any licentious tendencies inbred within him?

Hope needed help, she needed healing—she needed God. And he was the last person to give her any of those things.

Lord, take away my anger and my desire for this woman and send her someone who can lead her to You.

In the meantime, Nathaniel must keep his distance from the tantalizing Hope and return her back home as soon as possible. And that's just what he intended to do.

"Here we are." He set her down at the door to her cabin. "Promise me you'll stay here." He peered down at her.

"Forgive me. Mr. Mason." She hiccupped. "It would seem I am a source of constant trouble for you." She rubbed her forehead. "I don't feel well."

"Then I suggest you go to bed."

"I really am not well." She wobbled and her face blanched.

Clutching her arms, Nathaniel steadied her.

Hope's eyes widened. She flung a hand to her mouth then bent over and lost the contents of her stomach all over his boots.

Chapter 8

H ope drew in a deep breath of salty air, rubbed her throbbing temples, and closed her eyes against the mad rush of frothy water dashing against the hull. The gurgle and slap of the sea agitated the churning in her stomach, and she pressed a hand over the complaining organ. Above the crisp horizon, dark, wispy clouds hung like vultures ready to devour what was left of a clear morning. A multitude of sounds crashed over her: the snap of the sails, the sharp twang of rope, the creaks and groans of the brig, and the commands of the officers ordering the seamen to their tasks.

Oh, how she wished everything and everyone would simply *stop. . .making. . .noise!*

Adding to her affliction was the shame of the prior evening: the insults and looks of derision from the other passengers at dinner, her overindulgence of wine, and her encounter with Nathaniel—most of which she could not remember.

Unfortunately, she remembered enough.

Had she really lost her dinner on his boots? She cringed and stared down at the choppy water. Perhaps it wasn't too late to toss herself into the sea. It would be better than facing

Nathaniel after her drunken theatrics. *And their kiss.* She brushed her fingers over her lips, still tingling with the memory. Some lady she was. Throwing herself at the man like a common hussy. When she'd vowed to change. To be different—better.

But truthfully, she had no idea how to change. She needed the attentions she received from men as much as she needed food for her body. They fed an insatiable hunger for value, for self-worth. But like any good meal, the satisfaction they brought never lasted long.

Turning, Hope averted her eyes from the rolling sea and spotted Miss Sheldon on the other side of the brig. The lovely lady waved and smiled as she wove through the working crew toward Hope. Some of the sailors stopped to wipe sweat from their brows and gazed after the young lady. Hope didn't blame them. Though taller than most women, Miss Sheldon glowed with an innocent beauty that reminded Hope of a fresh spring morning. She carried herself with confidence and a propriety that matched her character. Perhaps Hope could elicit her help to teach her how to be a real lady.

"Good morning, Miss Hope." She grinned and tugged her bonnet further down atop a bounty of chestnut curls. "Where is your hat? This sun is merciless."

Hope tugged on a loose curl dancing about her neck, ashamed she could never keep her hair properly secured. Always a rebellious strand or two would break free and flutter about with each shift of the breeze. "I seem to have forgotten it below."

"Shall I retrieve it for you?" Miss Sheldon's caring tone gave Hope a start, but she politely declined. She deserved a far worse beating than the fiery rays lashing down upon her.

Miss Sheldon's brow wrinkled. "Are you ill? You appear a bit pale."

Hope wanted to tell her that her mouth was as dry as a desert, her stomach a brewing caldron, and her head engaged in a battle, but it had all been her doing, and she deserved no sympathy. "Nay, I'm all right."

"I am so sorry the men distressed you last night. It was incorrigible of them to make such accusations." A smatter of freckles on her forehead crinkled into a tiny blotch.

Hope urged a smile to her lips. *If you only knew the truth, you'd not be standing here beside me.* Or would she? Miss Sheldon's eyes carried not a hint of judgment or condemnation.

The captain emerged from below, tipped his hat at Hope and Miss Sheldon, then planted his boots on the deck and his fists on his hips as he surveyed his kingdom. Hope swallowed a lump of disdain. 'Twas the pompous captain who had broached the topic of Hope and Nathaniel's relationship last night. What sort of gentleman discusses such private matters in public? In fact, as he glanced her way now, he seemed to be gloating in his victory.

Hope shifted her attention to Mr. Keese, standing tall upon the quarterdeck. He had nodded at her earlier when she'd come on deck, but he'd made no effort at conversation. The smirk on his face said quite enough. Beyond him, lazing upon a barrel beneath the shade of a sailcloth strung over his head, Mr. Hendrick sipped a drink, unconcerned with his sick wife below.

Movement caught her eye as Nathaniel popped on deck with cross-staff, divider, and chart in hand. Laying his instruments across a table beside the helm, he glanced over the brig. Hope looked away before their gazes met, unable to bear the disapproval she knew would be upon his face.

Captain Conway swerved about. "You there! Mr. Mason. Attend the weather topsail braces."

Nathaniel glanced up at the sails fluttering under a light wind then back down at his captain. Jaw stiff, he stomped down the quarterdeck ladder and headed toward the foremast to do the captain's bidding.

Never once glancing her way.

"Mr. Mason seems quite the gentleman." Miss Sheldon's

gaze followed him.

Hope frowned at the girl's appraisal. Still, as she watched Nathaniel march across the deck, unavoidably admiring the way his tan breeches clung to his narrow waist and muscular thighs, how could she fault Miss Sheldon for her attraction to him? He truly was a gentleman: kind, quick witted, and chivalrous. And he deserved someone like Miss Sheldon—a sweet, godly woman. But somewhere deep within Hope sparked a longing to prove to him she could indeed change, that she could become a proper lady, despite her abhorrent behavior last night.

Miss Sheldon hazel eyes sparkled. "He seems quite taken with you."

"You are mistaken, Miss Sheldon."

"Call me Abigail, please."

"Abigail, I assure you his kindness toward me stems from his godly principles alone. We are naught but mere acquaintances."

Still, she couldn't keep her eyes off him as he tore off his waistcoat and flung himself into the shrouds, white shirt flapping in the breeze and muscles bulging in his arms as he climbed the ratlines up the foremast.

Miss Sheldon giggled. "Hmm, I see."

A burst of heat stormed up Hope's neck, and she shifted her attention back to the captain, who glared up at his new navigator as if he were a Spanish infiltrator.

The brig crashed over a turquoise wave, and Hope glanced aloft again to ensure Nathaniel had not lost his footing. But the man continued his climb with the ease of a hardened sailor until he was no more than a dark shadow at the top of the mast.

"Why is the captain sending Mr. Mason aloft? Is he not the navigator?" Hope asked.

Abigail shrugged. "I suppose because the ship is undermanned."

Undermanned or not, most of those men were casting

glances at her and Abigail from all around. Did Abigail notice the attention she drew? No. A sweet, trusting innocence beamed from her face—an innocence Hope knew she could never reclaim.

"Abigail, have you ever had a suitor?"

"Oh heavens, no." She blushed. "There was neither the opportunity nor any available gentlemen on Antigua, I'm afraid."

"Surely you see the way men admire you."

"I try not to, Miss Hope." She leaned toward her. "They admire only what they see on the outside, a beauty that fades and has nothing to do with who I am." She turned to face the sea. "What a glorious day!"

Hope wiped the perspiration from the back of her neck, pondering what Abigail had said. Hope had not considered the admiring looks she received were something to be shrugged off, meaningless and flighty. Yet she found Abigail's words sparking through her mind, igniting her reason as if a lantern had been lit in a dark room.

She smiled at her new friend. So much like her sister Grace, and yet so different in many ways—more approachable, less judgmental. Yes, Hope could learn much from this pious, strong woman.

A sail snapped, and Abigail tipped her hat up, her hazel eyes sparkling with admiration. Nathaniel stood precariously on the fore top yard. "My word, but he's brave. I would die of fright up there."

A hint of coquetry tinged her voice, and Hope's exuberance of a moment ago shrank like the topgallant Nathaniel furled above. Even if she could learn to be a lady, even if she could put her past behind her, how could she ever compare with someone like Miss Sheldon?

The crown of a flowered straw hat appeared at the top of the companionway, and Mrs. Hendrick clambered onto the deck from below. Her daughter, Elise, gripped her mother's hand and with wide eyes, surveyed the brig. Hope thought she saw a shudder pass through the small child as she enfolded herself in her mother's skirts, and Hope longed to assure her all was well despite the clamoring activity across the deck. But the scowl Mrs. Hendrick directed toward Hope stopped her. Gripping her stomach, the poor woman made her way to the railing, her face as white as the canvas that sped the brig on its course.

"Mrs. Hendrick. How do you fare this morning?" Abigail reached out to assist the woman. "And you, Miss Elise?"

The little girl smiled as Mrs. Hendrick gripped the railing like a lifeline and moaned.

"Can I get you something to eat?" Abigail placed a hand on the woman's back.

Another moan. She leaned over the railing and closed her eyes. "Thank you, but I fear I won't be eating for quite some time."

"I'm glad you came above deck as I suggested. The fresh air will do you good." Abigail took in a deep breath and held down her hat beneath another rush of wind.

Hope smiled at Elise, and the girl giggled in return, hiding in her mother's skirts. But even amidst her nausea, Mrs. Hendrick managed to cast a warning glare at Hope and step away from her as if she were afflicted with some dread disease.

Blinking back the burning behind her eyes, Hope looked up to see Mr. Hendrick glance their way but quickly resume his conversation with Major Paine, who stood beside him, arms across his chest.

As she pondered the man's lack of care for his wife, Nathaniel dropped to the deck with a thump and started for the quarterdeck ladder.

"Mr. Mason, stow those barrels below," the captain hollered, pointing to a cluster of four casks beneath the foredeck.

For a moment, it seemed that Nathaniel would disobey

the order as he stood there, eyes narrowing and fists clenching. But finally, he turned on his heels, headed toward the barrels, and hefted one onto his shoulder with a grimace.

Hope bit her lip. It was her fault Nathaniel wasn't the one giving the orders. It was her fault he was forced to work so hard and be humiliated by a man with half his brains. For the first time in her life, Hope realized how her witless actions affected others. Had they affected her sisters, as well? Her father?

Abigail's gentle touch on Hope's arm startled her. "I must go below. I promised to bring some food and water to a sick sailor. Can you look after Mrs. Hendrick?" She nodded toward the groaning woman leaning over the railing.

Hope started to tell Abigail the woman would surely protest when Mrs. Hendrick, in a severe tone, saved her the effort. "There is no need. I shall be fine."

"I will try," Hope whispered to Abigail, "but only for you."

Abigail smiled and turned to leave, and as Hope watched her disappear below on her errand of mercy, she wondered how someone became so caring and selfless. Perhaps there was something missing from Hope, some part of her heart God had forgotten to insert, for she could barely garner an ounce of sympathy for the suffering woman at her side—especially in light of the woman's contempt for her.

The brig bucked, sending Mrs. Hendrick toppling, and Hope reached out, caught her by the waist, and steadied her against the railing. Elise clung to her mother and began to whimper.

"You're with child." Hope could not hide the surprise in her tone.

Mrs. Hendrick looked down at her belly in horror then back up at Hope and whispered. "How did you know?"

"I felt the tender mound when I touched you just now."

"Well, I'll thank you to keep your hands to yourself," she hissed and glanced at her daughter. "Elise, stop your fussing. Mother is sick. Be a good girl."

"I can care for Elise if you'd like." Despite knowing Mrs. Hendrick would never allow such a thing, Hope couldn't help but offer. She would gladly risk another cruel rejection for the chance to comfort the small, frightened girl.

Mrs. Hendrick gave a ladylike snort.

Which Hope understood as a no. "How many months?"

"Seven."

"Seven? I would have never guessed. You're so tiny."

A smile, the first one Mrs. Hendrick had graced upon Hope, quickly faded from her lips. "Mr. Hendrick detests plump women, so I must try to keep my weight down."

"Surely he understands you carry his child?"

"He is a man and does not bother himself with the details of childbearing."

Hope's jaw tensed. "It is not good for you. The baby needs nourishment."

"What do you know of it?" Mrs. Hendrick snapped. "How many children have you carried?" She paused and allowed her gaze to scour over Hope. "Or perhaps you *do* know."

"How could I? I have never been married." Hope swallowed a lump of shame.

"Humph." Mrs. Hendrick glanced at her husband and adjusted the hat ribbon tied beneath her chin. Though she lifted her graceful nose and cultured eyebrows haughtily, sorrow seemed to weigh heavy on her as she studied the man. Then facing the sea again, she held her stomach.

Hope gazed across the endless ocean, its waves suddenly calm as if some invisible hand pressed down upon them. An eerie silence enveloped the brig. The wind ceased, and Hope rubbed the perspiration from her neck as wisps of black clouds spread their talons across the horizon.

"Eleanor!" A loud growl rumbled across the deck. "Come hither, Eleanor!" If possible, Mrs. Hendrick's face grew even paler.

"I must speak to my husband." Mrs. Hendrick grabbed Elise by the hand. "If you will excuse me."

"Mother. May I stay here?" Elise tugged on her mother's skirts.

"No. Elise, come with me."

"But Father is always so angry. Please let me stay."

"I will watch her for you, Mrs. Hendrick." Hope braced herself for the woman's rebuff while at the same time offering her an encouraging smile.

Mrs. Hendrick shifted her gaze between Elise and Hope, her face in a pinch as if Hope had asked if she could throw her daughter to the sharks.

"What harm could possibly come to the girl?" Hope raised her brows.

"Very well. But I shall keep my eye on you." Mrs. Hendrick wagged a finger in Hope's face before lifting her satin skirts and trudging up the quarterdeck ladder.

Finding a small crate in the shade of the foredeck, Hope sat and hoisted Elise into her lap, grateful to be able to take weight off her sore feet. Nestling her face into the girl's red curls, Hope breathed in the deep scent of innocence. Children always smelled fresh and pure—as if the cruel stench of the world found no place to stick to them. "Are you afraid of the ship?"

Elise nodded, her wide blue eyes meeting Hope's. "A little bit, but Father says never to be afraid of anything."

A gust of wind sent Elise's curls into Hope's face, and she brushed them aside, thankful for the sudden reprieve from the stifling heat. "I think it's all right to be afraid sometimes."

"You do?"

"Yes. But not of this brig. I know there are many men running about and lots of loud yelling, but each is doing his job." Hope straightened the lace on Elise's sleeves. "Do you know what that job is?"

The girl shook her head.

"To get you safely to Kingston."

"It is?" She glanced up at Hope with excitement.

Another blast of hot wind swept over them, fluttering Elise's skirts.

"So, you see there is nothing to fear," Hope announced, settling the fabric. "Except that this wind will whip our skirts off." They both giggled.

A loud shout from the quarterdeck drew their attention. "Blast it all, woman!" Mr. Hendrick's booming voice echoed over the brig.

A shiver ran through Elise, and she began to finger the fringed tips of the lavender sash around her waist. "Are you afraid of your father, Miss Hope?"

Hope glanced at the red-faced man who had retaken his seat and was waving his wife away as if she were an annoying gnat. A deep sigh escaped Hope's lips if only to curb the anger rising within her and the memories it resurrected. Growing up, Hope had often been frightened of her father, and that fear did naught to foster the secure haven in which every child should be raised and nurtured.

"Men can be scary sometimes. They're big and they have deep voices like bears." She dug her fingers like claws into Elise to tickle her, hoping to get her mind off her parents.

Elise's giggle halted in a shriek as her mother grabbed her arm, tugged her from Hope's lap, and stormed below without a word, dragging the poor girl behind. Hope's last glimpse of the child was a flurry of red curls and wide pleading eyes.

She rubbed her arms against a sudden chill, despite the heat of the day, and stood, moving toward the railing. Children—and women—forever doomed to be at the mercy of those in power over them. Thoughts of her own childhood shoved their way into her mind. Her innocence stolen at so young an age. Her trust forever crushed.

Distant thunder growled, and the wind ceased again as if

someone opened and shut a door. Mountainous swells rose like hump-backed monsters beneath a sheet of turquoise. The ship tilted. A black shroud consumed the horizon and sent out spindly fingers toward her as if intent on dragging her back into the swirling void. She trembled. A sense of evil and foreboding gripped her—a feeling that something or *someone* wanted to possess her, a feeling she'd had before, most recently at the Pink House Tavern in Charles Towne. At that time, she'd been rescued by Mr. Waite and her sister Faith.

But who would save her now?

Swerving around, Hope glanced over the deck. Two sailors tying knots in ropes grinned at her. Upon the quarterdeck, Major Paine's eyebrows lifted in invitation. The captain gave her a saucy smirk. Hope turned back around. Better to face the storm than the lecherous gazes of these men. She knew they took such liberties because they thought her wanton. She'd received the same looks back in Charles Towne once gossiping lips had spread the news of her relationship with Lord Falkland throughout town.

"Good day, Miss Hope." Mr. Keese appeared beside her, tipping his bicorn.

"Good day, Mr. Keese."

"You are looking lovely today, I must say."

"Please, sir, I wish you would not say." She stared at the swirling water below.

His head jerked backward as if she'd punched him. "How's this? A woman who doesn't wish a compliment?"

Hope faced him. Strands of loose sandy hair flapped in the wind, and a wild, inviting look beamed from his dark blue eyes. "Forgive me, Mr. Keese. I meant no offense. And I do thank you for your kindness." After the vulgar way the crew eyed her, not to mention Major Paine's bawdy glances, the perpetual smirk on the captain's mouth, and Mrs. Hendrick's insulting manner, Mr. Keese's kindness soothed Hope's wounded heart like salve.

"If you'll permit me yet another compliment, Miss

Hope, this voyage would be pure drudgery without you."
One side of his mouth curved in a handsome smile.

"I am sure you would manage, Mr. Keese." Though Hope tried to squelch it, a grin lifted her lips as well.

"But life is more than managing, is it not?" He took her hand in his, enveloping it with his strength and warmth. But no. She hardly knew him. She snagged it back and stared at the deck.

A jagged streak of lightning crossed the dark sky, followed by a rumble of thunder. The brig rolled over a churning mound, and Mr. Keese put a hand on her back. When her eyes met his, no passion simmered within them. Just a playful gleam as if he were toying with her.

"Regardless of what you and the others may think, Mr. Keese. I am not a woman of loose morals."

He scratched his thick sideburns and shrugged. "I rarely give much credence to the opinions of others."

If that were true, she envied him. "'Tis an admirable quality, Mr. Keese." The brig pitched over another wave, and Hope gripped the railing. "I believe you and Miss Sheldon are my only friends on this voyage."

"Not Mr. Mason?" He cocked a brow.

"Least of all him." The sting of rain filled her nostrils. She brushed hair from her face and glanced over the oddly calm sea lurking between the swells rippling in from the southeast. "I find most of the crew stare at me as if … as if …." Thunder rumbled, and she raised her voice over the din. "As if I extend an open invitation for companionship."

"Indeed?" Nathaniel's guttural voice stormed between them. "How fortunate for you, Mr. Keese." He nodded toward Mr. Keese with a smile that belied the simmering in his eyes.

Hope swallowed the burning lump in her throat. "You misunder—" she started to explain, but Nathaniel's face was as stiff as a sail at full wind, and the words faltered on her lips.

"May I speak to you a moment?" he said without emotion.

Hope lifted her brows toward Mr. Keese, encouraging him to come to her aid.

Instead, he took her hand and planted a kiss upon it. "I shall remember your invitation, Miss Hope." A playful grin twisted his lips before he marched away.

Why hadn't he explained the context of her statement to Nathaniel? Hope growled inwardly.

Nathaniel ran a hand through his moist hair. "I believe your meaning was clear, Miss Hope. The only thing I misunderstood was your desire to change."

Defeat settled in like an old familiar friend, and she pressed a hand over her still-bubbling stomach.

"You're not going to be sick again?" He gave her a lopsided smile. "I don't have my boots on to protect me this time."

Hope glanced down at his large tanned feet. "I hope you can forgive me, Mr. Mason. Regarding my behavior last night, I … I am quite overcome with shame."

He studied her with dark inquisitive eyes the color of coffee. Flecks of gold sparkled within them like flickers of hope until the sun disappeared beneath a cloud and stole them away.

Hope's gaze dropped to his lips. A warm sensation fluttered in her belly and she quickly looked away. What was wrong with her? It wasn't like she hadn't kissed a man before. Just not one who hadn't invited it. Nor a man as decent and honorable as Nathaniel.

"I came to warn you to go below, Miss Hope." He crossed his arms over his damp shirt and stiffened his jaw. "That is, when you are finished with your playful dalliances above."

"I wasn't engaged in dal—oh, what's the use?" Hope waved a hand through the air.

Ignoring her, he nodded toward the horizon. "There's a

fierce storm brewing, and I fear the deck will become most unsafe in a short time."

"Thank you for the warning, Mr. Mason."

"Mr. Mason!" Captain Conway bellowed. "Quite dawdling and get back to work, or I'll send you below to pump out the bilge."

Pressing a hand over his left side, Nathaniel frowned, dipped his head in her direction, and stomped away.

Hope spun to face the sea again. A vicious tempest was brewing, indeed. Both here on the seas and within her soul. Her every attempt to behave like a lady had failed miserably. Not by any fault of her own, but by the presumptions of others. Nathaniel in particular. How could she change if all those around her had already made up their minds as to her character?

Chapter 9

The brig heaved, and Nathaniel braced on the bulkhead to keep from tumbling down the hallway. The muscles in his arms and back throbbed. He hadn't worked so hard in years, not since he'd been a carpenter aboard old Captain Harley's ship. Known for running his merchantman stricter than a ship of the line, Captain Harley had difficulty manning his voyages. But Nathaniel had been young, in desperate need of work, and eager to learn how to sail. In regards to the latter, he owed old Harley a huge debt, for the man took him under his tutelage and taught him everything he knew.

Captain Conway was a different animal. His harsh and unyielding command served no discernable purpose other than to exasperate and demean the crew. And for some reason, he harbored an extra measure of ill will toward Nathaniel. Perhaps he resented Nathaniel's experience as a captain and feared he would attempt a mutiny. *Ludicrous.*

The brig canted, groaning like an old woman, and Nathaniel slammed into the bulkhead, careful not to drop his lantern. Thrusting it before him, he followed the shifting circle of light through darkness as thick as molasses. He must make his way down to the hold, where he had heard Miss Sheldon was tending a patient.

Gripping the rough wood of the railing, he crept down the ladder as another wave jolted the brig and nearly sent him flying.

Outside the thick hull, the storm pummeled the merchantman with waves as high as a building and gusts of wind strong enough to blow a man overboard. The warning signs had been evident ever since they'd set sail from St. Kitts three days ago: the huge swells rolling in from the southeast, the calm winds interspersed with wild gusts from all directions.

The signs of a hurricane—the most feared storm on the Caribbean.

He had tried to warn the captain to seek shelter as soon as possible, but to no avail. The stubborn man insisted it was naught but a summer squall, announcing that he'd encountered many a storm in the North Atlantic, and that he'd be dead in his grave before he'd cower before wind and waves. As he spoke, his eyes had taken on a wild glow as if some wicked force possessed him, and he kept shouting something about his wife and thrusting his fist in the air, cursing the black clouds.

The man was clearly unsettled, which explained his brutal treatment of the crew, but that did naught to ease Nathaniel's fears of what would happen should they enter the hurricane's path.

At least Nathaniel had convinced him to sail south before the worst of it hit. In addition—per Nathaniel's request—he had brought down the topgallant yards and masts, strapped them to the deck, and secured storm lashings on the guns.

With these measures taken, they may well be out of danger by morning. But the ride through the long night would be tumultuous at best. Which was why Nathaniel must escort Miss Sheldon back to her quarters. Down in the hold, she could be crushed by cargo loosened by the storm. The sick crewman shouldn't be down there either, but Captain Conway had insisted he remain as far from the rest of the crew as possible so as not to spread whatever disease ailed him.

Thunder growled like a ravenous monster, shaking the brig from truck to keelson, and Nathaniel hurried downward. As he took the last step, the ship lurched, and he tripped. Tiny paws skittered over his bare feet, and he kicked the beasts aside. The stench of moldy grain and human waste assaulted him. Bracing his feet over the wobbling deck, he followed the flicker of a light in the distance.

"Miss Sheldon!" he bellowed. "Miss Sheldon!"

"In here." A female voice screeched through the roar of the storm.

Pushing the door aside, he entered a tiny room crammed full with crates, barrels, and sailcloth. Amidst the clutter, a cot sat in one corner. Upon it lay a gaunt man shriveled into a ball, his bony face a sunken frame of death. Miss Sheldon sat on a crate beside him, lantern in one hand and wet cloth in the other. She turned and gave Nathaniel a weak smile, her eyes moist with tears. The man moaned and she dabbed the cloth on his forehead.

Dousing his lantern, Nathaniel approached, feeling blood drain from his face. He recognized the stench of death, one he'd witnessed many times before—an ugly, cruel force that knew no mercy. An icy chill stabbed him, shoving away the suffocating heat. "Is there no one but you with medical knowledge aboard the ship?"

"Nay, the captain's wife used to administer medicaments, but word is, she remained behind in St. Kitts with some relations." Miss Sheldon's voice strained with sorrow.

"I don't blame her. The captain probably ordered her to haul barrels all day as well."

She glanced his way, a glimmer of approval in her eyes. "You handle his harsh treatment well, Mr. Mason. With a humble spirit."

He chuckled. "I don't feel very humble."

The sailor moaned and smacked his lips together, and Miss Sheldon soaked her cloth in a bucket of water and squeezed droplets into his mouth.

The brig jerked to larboard. Miss Sheldon held on to the cot, and Nathaniel, still holding his lantern, threw his back against a stack of teetering crates to keep them from falling. "I've come to escort you back to your cabin, miss. 'Tis not safe here in the storm." He steadied the boxes and nodded toward the sailor. "And regardless of what the captain says, we should take him along as well."

The angry sea pounded against the hull with the roar of a broadside.

She shook her head. "The captain will not permit it, and I will not leave him." Facing the sailor, she dabbed the cloth on his neck. "There, there. It will be fine."

Nathaniel rubbed his eyes, stinging from salt, and squatted beside the bed. Admiration welled within him at the woman's selflessness.

Strands of brown hair had loosened from her pins and waved across the back of her neck with every movement of the ship. And though her figure was hidden beneath a loose-fitting cotton gown buttoned all the way to her neck, her modest attire did not distract from her beauty.

How different she was from Hope. He had enjoyed seeing the two of them conversing so easily two days ago. Complete opposites standing together on the deck, laughing and chatting as if they'd been friends forever. But then who wouldn't want to bask in the joy, peace, and acceptance flowing around Miss Sheldon like a morning breeze? Like her parents, she would no doubt make a great missionary. He sighed. But not him. Instead of drawing people to God's love, Nathaniel seemed to push them away.

"I understand your concern for him, Miss Sheldon, but this is more than a summer storm, and we aren't even in the thick of it yet. You risk your life by staying here."

Where most people would have expressed alarm at his statement, Miss Sheldon remained as composed as if he'd just told her there was no sugar for her tea. "You are most kind to come down here for me, but I'm not leaving."

Nathaniel grunted. If he so desired, he could hoist her over one shoulder and the sick man over the other and haul them wherever he wished.

The sea continued its tirade against the hull, threatening to break through to grab them at any moment. The brig pitched and then plunged, knocking Nathaniel to his knees and Miss Sheldon from her crate. Steadying the lantern that teetered precariously in her hand, he assisted her to her feet. "We should not have these lanterns lit. I insist you come with me at once or I'll—"

A loud moan broke through the roar of the storm. The sailor's eyelids flew open and his gaze shot around the cabin—surprisingly clear for one so ill—and finally locked upon Nathaniel. Terror screamed from his face. His pale lips quivered. "They are coming for me."

Nathaniel knelt beside the man. "Who is coming for you?"

"The dark shadows. The dark shadows. Don't let them take me." His gaze flickered about the cabin again as if he could see monsters in the corners.

An icy chill etched across Nathaniel's back. Light from the lantern cast eerie, shifting shadows over the bulkheads. No doubt in his delirium, the poor sailor thought they were real. Then why did the hair on the back of Nathaniel's neck stiffen? And why did it suddenly feel so cold?

Miss Sheldon's wide eyes met Nathaniel's as she lowered herself back to her crate. She patted the sailor's forehead with the cloth. "Shhh, Mr. Boden. You are merely feverish."

Nathaniel grabbed the man's trembling hand, hoping to offer him some comfort. Boney, frigid flesh gripped his. "He has no fever."

The brig lurched and Nathaniel clung onto the cot.

"He did a moment ago." Miss Sheldon touched the man's neck and frowned. "I don't understand."

Before Nathaniel could remove his hand, Mr. Boden squeezed it with more strength than Nathaniel would have thought possible in his condition. "Are you the preacher?" he asked, his voice cracking with desperation.

"No." Nathaniel frowned. How could the son of a harlot be a preacher?

Mr. Boden writhed on the straw cot, clenching Nathaniel's hand in a viselike grip. "Don't let them take me."

"Shhh, Mr. Boden. No one is going to take you anywhere." Miss Sheldon pressed down on his shoulders, trying to calm him, but he bolted and bucked so violently, she stumbled backward.

An impossible blast of frosty wind whirled through the enclosed space, freezing Nathaniel's damp shirt until it was stiff. His heart thudded in achingly slow beats as if the ghostly breeze had the power to freeze a man solid. Evil was in this room—the same evil he had often felt as a child in his mother's chamber.

And he suddenly knew what he had to do.

Bowing his head, he prayed for God's direction and protection, then gripped Mr. Boden's shoulders. "They won't take you," he said. "Look at me!"

The man's desperate gaze fixed on Nathaniel. Labored breaths whistled in his throat as he settled back onto the cot. "Help me. Please."

Nathaniel laid a steady hand on the man's chest. "You must put your trust in the Son of God. Call upon the name of Jesus."

Mr. Boden began coughing, choking, gasping for breath. He thrashed on the cot. The brig vaulted, toppling Nathaniel and Miss Sheldon. A deep wail roared through the ship as if the sea was furious that it could not breech the hull.

Mr. Boden calmed, his gaze focused on the deckhead above him.

Nathaniel placed two fingers on his neck. "His pulse is weak."

"Jesus," the sailor whispered through wet trembling lips. Terror fled his gaze, replaced by a soothing peace as he released a long heavy sigh and closed his eyes.

Nathaniel held his breath, half expecting the unnatural cold to take them all in its grip. But the icy chill was suddenly swept away by a warm sweet scent that swirled past Nathaniel's nose. "Thank you, God," he muttered.

Tears pooled in Miss Sheldon's eyes. "You did it."

"I did nothing."

Thunder boomed. The brig pitched forward. Nathaniel grabbed her arm to steady her and held the lantern with his other.

She glanced at Mr. Boden, whose face wore a peaceful look. Wiping his forehead, she placed a kiss upon it. "I've been speaking to him most of the day about heaven and hell and turning himself over to God, but he wouldn't listen. Then you stomp in here and reach him in less than a minute."

"'Twas God, not me." Nathaniel still couldn't believe ushering the man into heaven had been that simple.

Miss Sheldon swiped away a tear. "Perhaps I don't have my parent's gift of spreading the gospel, after all. I wonder if I will be any use in Kingston."

If we make it to Kingston. Nathaniel stood, balancing on the galloping deck, and wondered why the waves seemed to be growing in size and intensity instead of lessening. "I'm sure you'll be a wonderful missionary." Truthfully, he hadn't the time to discuss it at the moment. He must get above and determine their course. He held out his hand. "Will you come with me now?"

She gazed at Mr. Boden. "Should we leave him?"

"He is no longer here."

"Of course." She smiled.

Holding her lantern with one hand, she clung to Nathaniel's arm with the other as he led the way out into the hold. Spotting a pile of ropes, he grabbed them from atop a crate and carried them up the ladder.

His heart squeezed in his chest as he approached the door to the ladies' cabin. He'd managed to avoid Hope for two days, the storm having kept her below. But he couldn't face her. Not yet. His anger still simmered at her wanton familiarity with Mr. Keese when she had just met the man.

"Here we are, Miss Sheldon." He halted in front of her door. "Tell the other women to tie themselves to their beds." He plucked a knife from his belt and held it out to her, along with the ropes.

Nodding, she took them and disappeared within, not an ounce of fear on her face.

Nathaniel dashed up the companionway ladder. Why didn't his heart jump when Miss Sheldon was near? Why did it leap only for Hope—a woman who reminded him too much of his mother. Yes, she had vowed to change, but his mother had made similar promises—none of which she had kept. And he doubted Hope would either.

But at the moment he had more important things to worry about. From the way the ship lurched and vaulted beneath the growing waves, it appeared Captain Conway had changed his mind about heading south. And if so, it would be too late to change course now. Nathaniel must convince him to seek shelter before the full force of the hurricane struck. The merchantman would sail close to Puerto Rico, and with luck they could find a safe harbor among the bays on the south side of the island.

If they did not, and Captain Conway insisted on running before the wind, then Nathaniel feared they were all going to die.

Chapter 10

The brig heaved to and fro like a seesaw, and Hope
clung to her bed post, refusing to allow her fear to
become panic. The door burst open, and Abigail rushed into
the cabin, bundles of rope in one hand and a knife in the
other. She forced the door shut with her back against the
buffeting wind then squinted into the shadows.

"Oh, finally, there you are." Mrs. Hendrick cackled from
her bed, where she and Elise hugged the wooden frame for
dear life. "Where on earth have you been? Wandering around
a ship full of men in the middle of the night is no place for a
lady, especially during a storm." She squeezed Elise tighter
to her chest. "And leaving us here with no word as to what is
happening above. Where is my husband? He shouldn't leave
Elise and me here alone. I hope he hasn't fallen overboard.
We are beside ourselves with fright. I can't imagine what
he's doing. No doubt he has taken to his brandy again, as he
always does."

Hope rubbed her ears, buzzing from hours of Mrs.
Hendrick's incessant complaining. She'd even considered
going to find Mr. Hendrick and dragging the negligent
husband to his family, or better yet, staying with him in
whatever quiet haven he had found for himself.

The brig quivered beneath the growl of a massive wave, and Abigail leapt to grip her cot as the cabin pitched. She tossed a bundle of ropes to Mrs. Hendrick. "I am sure your husband is fine, Mrs. Hendrick," she shouted over the storm. "No doubt he's strapped himself in somewhere. Which is what we need to do as well."

Abigail handed one end of a long twine to Hope. "Mr. Mason instructed us to tie ourselves to our beds!"

"Mr. Mason?" Hope's stomach soured. So that explained where Abigail had been all this time, as well as the shimmer of fading lantern light Hope had spotted in the hallway before Abigail had closed the door. Of course Nathaniel had not stopped long enough to inquire after Hope's welfare.

"This is madness," Mrs. Hendrick whined from across the cabin.

Hope peered toward the woman, who held the rope out before her as if it were a snake. "How am I supposed to tie myself and Elise up with this?"

"I will help you, Mrs. Hendrick," Abigail said, then turned toward Hope. "I was caring for a sick patient in the hold, and Mr. Mason came to escort me back to the cabin."

Hope grimaced, trying to determine if the young girl's expression matched her gleeful tone, but the darkness mottled her features. "How can you sound so peaceful and happy during such a violent storm?"

But Abigail didn't respond. She continued tying one end of her rope to her bed frame as casually if she were latching a horse to a hitching post. "The most marvelous thing happened below." Her loud voice rose musically.

Something marvelous? Below? With Mr. Mason? Hope clutched the wooden frame as the ship vaulted over a wave and then tumbled downward, sending her heart tumbling along with it. Thunder exploded as angry waves rammed into the hull, reverberating through the ship like a massive gong.

Abigail clambered over to where Mrs. Hendrick slumped in a puddle of despair, fumbling with her rope. "Mr. Mason said the storm worsens and it isn't safe to be unfettered."

"Oh my, I knew it. I knew I shouldn't have ventured on this trip with William," Mrs. Hendrick wailed. "This is all too much. Too much. I cannot bear it. We are all going to die."

Gripping the bulkhead, Hope hoisted herself up and peered out the window. The maelstrom outside the tiny glass oval writhed in an undulating vision of raging, black clouds one second and a hissing caldron of white-capped water the next. Fear clawed her throat like none she had ever known. What if she were to die in this storm? She would never see her sisters again. She would never see her father again. But most of all, she would never have the chance to put her past behind her and become a true lady.

A wall of water rose from the sea and loomed over the brig, curling into a fist. Two flashes of lightning shot from the churning water, sparks from demon eyes. Flinging a hand to her mouth, Hope stumbled back from the window. An explosion of thunder shook the tiny merchantman. Talons of ebony water reached for her. She screamed. The watery claws slammed against the window. The glass rolled as if it had melted, and a ripple sped through the cabin walls. Hope collapsed to the deck, heart thrashing in her chest.

"What is it?" Abigail yelled from Mrs. Hendrick's berth.

The brig bolted and slammed Hope against her cot. She curled into a ball, hiding from the evil presence—the same evil that had sought her on deck earlier. The same evil that had nearly consumed her back in Charles Towne and before that, in Portsmouth—a dark, maniacal power that had followed her from England to the colonies.

And it followed her still.

But she would not give in to it. Rising, she drew a shuddering breath and crawled over to assist Abigail. Better to be doing something than cowering like a fool.

When Elise saw Hope, her eyes widened, and she dashed into Hope's arms. Embracing her, Hope rubbed her back, trying to still the girl's trembling. "Shhh. Don't be afraid."

"Please stay still, Mrs. Hendrick. We shall be safe." Abigail fought with the tangle of rope.

"How can I stay still? The ship jumps like a grasshopper. Why must I be tied up? What if the ship sinks? How shall we escape then? Oh, where is my husband? He is never around when I need him. Will you go find him?" She lifted her pleading, moist eyes to Abigail.

"It isn't safe." Abigail swung the rope around Mrs. Hendrick a second time. "I assure you, it is better if we all stay here. Besides, I have knife should we need to free ourselves in a hurry."

Mrs. Hendrick's sharp gaze landed on Hope. "Get away from her, Elise. Come here!" She motioned for the little girl, then pressed a hand over her stomach. "Oh, my poor baby."

"You must be strong for your mother. She needs you," Hope said as she pried the little girl from her arms and nudged her toward her mother.

Once Elise returned, Abigail looped another rope around her then tied her and her mother to the bed frame.

The growl of the storm grew louder, deeper, angrier, as if they were surrounded by a thousand warriors bellowing their battle cries.

Hope laid a hand on Abigail's arm. "How bad is the storm, really?"

Abigail shifted her gaze above. "By the look on Mr. Mason's face when he left, I suggest you pray, Miss Hope. Pray as hard as you can."

Nathaniel clung to his lifeline and thrust headlong into the raging wind as a giant swell toppled over the stern and swept him off his feet. The bow of the vessel dove, and he gripped the rope with all his strength. A cascade of water pummeled him as the ship darted headfirst down a mountainous wave. He scrambled over the near vertical deck, seeking a hold, when the brig suddenly leveled again. Struggling to rise, he started for the quarterdeck, intending to convince Captain Conway to take shelter in one of the nearby islands.

His hands burned. His eyes stung. And the wind struck him with the force of a hundred fists. Shivering, he shook off water running from his waistcoat like ale from a spigot, then squinted up at the helm, almost hoping—God forgive him—that Captain Conway had been swept over with the last wave. But he made out a blurred, bulky shape clutching the wheel and thrusting a fist into the air. Wild, haughty laughter ricocheted over the ship like some villain in a playact.

Above Nathaniel, the oscillating dark shapes of two sailors clung to the foremast, their arms and legs circling the wooden pole in frozen terror as they tried to obey their captain's command to raise the storm canvas. But as the mast swung like a pendulum over one side of the brig and then the other, all they could do was hang on for dear life. Several other men huddled across the deck, gripping the capstan, the railings, the ladders, or anything solid they could latch onto as they waited for the next surge to strike.

And strike it did. Like a raging monster, the water lifted the ship up by the stern, rolling beneath it until the bow pointed toward the swirling clouds. Diving to the deck, Nathaniel grabbed the hatch combing, grateful he had convinced the captain to lash relieving tackle onto the tiller, for he feared the wheel wouldn't last much longer under this stress. Even so, if the rudder smashed, they'd be without steering ability. And steering was the one thing they needed right now.

Nathaniel struggled to his feet. Lightning flung white arrows toward the foundering merchantman, casting a ghostly pall over the vicious sea. Thick mounds of water rose from the ebony caldron, their mouths salivating in search of victims. Fear squeezed his chest. A sense of pure evil pricked the hair on his arms—the same evil he'd felt below. A relentless, hellish force. Only this time it seemed all encompassing and more determined than ever. A living, breathing entity that focused all its maniacal intent upon swallowing the tiny brig.

Nathaniel closed his eyes and tried to voice a prayer of protection, but the only word he uttered was a name—the name of the only One who could help them. "Jesus." He made his way to the quarterdeck ladder, shoving his arms against the wind. His legs ached from trying to keep his balance aboard the teetering deck. Salt stung his eyes as an explosion of thunder deafened him. They were in the thick of the storm now. He must convince the captain to keep the thrust of wind on the starboard quarter or the brig would broach and offer her vulnerable side to the oncoming swells.

If that happened, all would be lost.

Nathaniel lugged himself up on the quarterdeck and turned his face from the wind to catch his breath. The captain gave him a cursory glance, his face tight as he strained to pull the wheel to larboard. Mr. Keese clung to the binnacle by the railing. Upon spotting Nathaniel, he forged toward him, reaching him as a wall of water cascaded over them. They both gripped the railing. When it passed, Mr. Keese rubbed his eyes and glanced at Nathaniel, frustration and rage on his face.

"We must convince Conway to steer to starboard!" Nathaniel yelled into his ear.

Mr. Keese nodded and leaned toward him. "I have already tried. He refuses to listen."

Jerking his lifeline over the quarterdeck railing, Nathaniel stumbled toward the captain and turned his face from the wind so he could speak. "Captain, you must steer her to starboard. Keep the wind on her starboard quarter!"

"I do not take orders from you, Mr. Mason!" The captain shouted without so much as a glance his way.

"This is a hurricane, sir. I've been in one before. It is the only way to break free of it."

"Coward! 'Tis but a squall. I know what I am doing."
Captain Conway bellowed into Nathaniel's face, rum heavy
on his breath. "A storm like this took my first wife from me.
But I'll not let it get the best of me again!" His sinister,
depraved laugh was quickly stolen by the wind.

Nathaniel's heart stopped. The captain had gone mad.

"Go tie the additional shrouds to the mainmast like I
ordered you, or I'll have you locked up below with the
women!" He waved Nathaniel off and resumed his clamp on
the wheel. "No storm gets the best of Captain Conway!"

Fury sent blood rushing to Nathaniel's fists, and he
longed to smash one into the foolish man's jaw. If he did not,
the captain's stupidity would kill them all. *God, what do I
do?* But he already knew. Lives were at stake: the sailors, the
women below—Hope.

He glanced at Mr. Keese, who gave him a nod of
agreement from the railing. Nathaniel drew the extra knife he
kept strapped to his side while Mr. Keese crept toward them.

The wind howled as if protesting his decision. Lightning
flashed. The sharp smell of electricity filled the air. The brig
jerked violently, sending Nathaniel and Mr. Keese toppling
to the deck. Gripping his lifeline, Nathaniel pulled himself
toward the railing and wrapped his arms around it.

An eerie silence consumed the merchantman as if the
storm were pausing before the final crushing blow. Nathaniel
clambered to his feet, coughing and spitting water. A
towering swirl of black death rose over the starboard side.
The ship had broached and now faced the storm with its
broadside bared to the wind.

Captain Conway stood aghast, staring at it as if he just
noticed the true ferocity of the storm.

Mr. Keese shook his head at Nathaniel and flattened
himself on the deck.

"Hold on!" Nathaniel bellowed and grabbed the railing.

*Lord, please save us. Please save Hope and everyone on
the ship.*

He squeezed his eyes shut as the mountain of water crashed over him, enveloping him, clawing at him, and sucking the life from him. Something solid rammed into his chest. He swallowed water. Choking … coughing … gasping for breath. His lifeline tugged and flung him like a doll through the swirling mass. Darkness pulled on him, drawing him into its black void. His rope went taut, then slack, then taut again. He flailed, seeking any foothold. Salt burned his eyes, his nose, his throat like acid. Terror consumed him. Not only the terror of dying, but the terror of dying so young— before he had a chance to prove himself, before he had a chance to serve God.

Chapter 11

Nathaniel's hand struck something solid. He clung to it as the sea receded. Heaving, he spewed water from his lungs and clutched the capstan, struggling to rise.

The sharp crack of wood split the air—a loud snap followed by eerie creaks and groans. The mainmast tilted, wavered, then finally toppled over as if some giant executioner had taken an ax to it. Sailors scrambled to escape the falling timber as it pounded the deck with an ominous *boom,* crushing the bulwarks and leaving a web of rope and splintered wood over the brig. What men had survived hunched together in groups, some cursing, some murmuring prayers. The top of the mast, along with its yards and spars, hung off the starboard side of the brig, suspended by a tangle of ropes that used to be the shrouds, halyards, sheets, and braces.

Another wave rose off their starboard beam. Lightning flashed. Captain Conway clung to the quarterdeck railing, his face a deathly shade of gray.

The surge struck, crashing over Nathaniel. Watery claws tried to drag him overboard. He gripped his lifeline, ignoring the pain in his hands. The heavy mainmast dragged in the water and tugged the brig on its side, threatening to pull it to the depths.

The wave passed and Nathaniel scrambled to his feet. "Men, get your axes! Cut the mast adrift before we are done for!"

Thunder roared. The brig lurched to larboard then tumbled downward. Grabbing his knife, Nathaniel joined the half dozen men chopping away at the ropes and halyards. If they didn't cut the mast free in time, they would surely sink.

Hope clutched the ropes Abigail had tied around her chest. The brig pitched. The cabin tilted sideways. Though she braced her feet on the deck, the force swept her off the hard wood and tossed her in the air. Her shoes fell off. Her throat went dry. And her heart felt like it would crash through her chest. Surely they would capsize and all drown beneath the convulsing waters. The rough twine bit into her fingers and pinched the skin on her arms and chest. Pain shot through her. She slammed her eyes shut and prayed for deliverance—prayed for the first time in years. She didn't want her legacy to be one of debauchery and wantonness.

Give me a chance, God. Give me a chance to change.

The brig leveled again then began to teeter back and forth as if riding upon a mammoth's back. Thunder pounded on the hull in a deafening roar.

Mrs. Hendrick screamed—yet again—and Hope opened her eyes. Abigail's thin form lay sprawled across her cot, and in the distance, the dark shapes of Mrs. Hendrick and Elise huddled on their bed.

Hope wondered how Nathaniel fared. And Mr. Keese. Were they still on deck manning the brig or had they gone below to ride out the storm? She couldn't even think of the alternative—wouldn't allow herself to think of it.

Releasing the rope, she rubbed her eyes, aching from stress and lack of sleep. A loud crack echoed through the cabin. The crunch and snap of wood sent an icy quiver through Hope. Screams blared from above. Something massive struck the brig with a jarring crunch. The vessel lurched to starboard then canted back and tumbled in the other direction. The ropes scraped over her skin. Hope knew enough about ships to realize they had just lost a mast—a death sentence for a ship in a storm. She glanced at Abigail, whose wide eyes met hers with a knowing look. Whenever the roaring of the storm had subsided, Hope had heard Abigail praying, pleading for God's mercy and the eternal salvation of all on board.

"Never fear, Miss Hope. We will survive."

Was that a smile on Abigail's face? Hope shook her head at the woman's misplaced confidence as another wave struck the brig. She clutched her ropes. The cabin jolted forward and back, sending her teeth clamping into her lower lip.

"God told me!" Abigail shouted with the confidence of an admiral of the line. She turned to Mrs. Hendrick. "We shall live through this, Mrs. Hendrick. Calm yourself."

Mrs. Hendrick let out a fearful wail.

Yet the roar of the storm began to lessen as if in obedience to Abigail's declaration. The bellowing thunder grew more distant, and waves ceased slamming into the hull.

Tearing apart the knots on her ropes, Hope shoved them aside and stood to peer out the window, ignoring Abigail's warning. Through the streaks of water on the glass, she could see naught but darkness, save for an occasional foamy crest atop a distant swell.

The cabin door crashed open. Hope swerved to see Nathaniel's dark form, water streaming from his clothes. Relief eased through her taut nerves. She could not see his face or his expression, but she could feel his eyes upon her. "Untie yourselves and come on deck immediately," he commanded in a voice cracking from strain. He dashed to Abigail to help her. "See to Mrs. Hendrick," he shouted to

Hope, giving her no time to ponder the jealousy surging within her.

"What's happening? What are you doing?" Mrs. Hendrick cried. "Where is my husband? "Don't touch me." She slapped Hope's hand as she fought to loosen the knots of her rope.

Though Hope would love nothing more than to untie Elise and leave her mother bound—and gagged—she continued to untangle the web of twine around them both.

"Make haste. There isn't much time." Nathaniel's commanding voice stung with a sense of urgency, hurrying her fingers. He assisted Abigail from the cot then guided her toward the door. As soon as Hope had freed Mrs. Hendrick and Elise, he ushered them out as well. Then grabbing Hope's arm, he led her down the hall behind the others.

Hope emerged from the companionway to a blast of warm salty water that stung her eyes. She rubbed them and glanced across the deck. Above her, the clouds parted, forming a burgeoning circle of clear sky and allowing the light of a half-moon to blanket the vessel in an eerie glow. Severed timbers marked the spot where the wheel had stood. The mainmast was gone, its stump a cluster of bristling spikes. Where once the brig had been an ordered assembly of scrubbed and polished oak and brass, now it was naught but a dripping mass of splintered wood and tangle of rope. Captain Conway sat on the quarterdeck, clinging to the railing, his face a mask of horror.

Hope's heart clamped. Without the mainmast, without steering, they were helpless against the next major swell.

Over the starboard side, Mr. Keese and two sailors hoisted the only remaining cockboat into the agitated waters. The ship vaulted and Nathaniel clutched Hope's arm. She glanced up at him. His dark hair matted to his head and dripped onto his sopping waistcoat. Water beaded in his lashes, but the look of concern he gave her sent her head whirling.

"Are you harmed?" he asked.

"Nay." She shook her head. "What is happening? Was it a hurricane?"

"It *is* a hurricane. We are still in it. In the center." The lines of his face tightened, and he swallowed hard as if he now carried the responsibility for every life on board. And from the looks of Captain Conway, that was the case.

Mrs. Hendrick's hysterical sobbing drew their attention to the railing, where Abigail tried to console her.

"We must get everyone into the boat," Nathaniel said, leading her to the railing.

The boat? She glanced across the endless expanse of swirling dark waters. "But where will we go?"

"An island, there in the distance." He gestured to a gray mound rising from the sea. Land? It appeared to be naught but another menacing cloud bank sitting on the horizon.

Hope trembled. "Leave the safety of the brig?"

"It is not safe anymore." He gripped her chin and brought her gaze to his. "Will you trust me? I need you to be strong and help the others get into the boat."

Warmth radiated through her, temporarily smothering her fears. *He wants my help?* How many times in the face of danger had she behaved hysterically like Mrs. Hendrick was doing now? Surrounded by strong sisters, Hope had found it too easy to be the weak one, the needy one.

But her sisters weren't here now.

Squaring her shoulders, she drew a deep breath. For the first time in her life, someone needed her—and not just anyone, but an honorable gentleman—and she determined to not disappoint him.

She nodded.

Boots thudded over the slick wood, and Mr. Hendrick emerged from the hatch. "Is the storm over?"

Behind him, Mr. Russell lumbered onto the deck and slipped when his high-heeled leather shoes skidded across a puddle. Major Paine, who followed behind him, grabbed his arm before he fell.

"Oh, William." Mrs. Hendrick dashed to her husband, dragging Elise behind her. The brig pitched over a roller, and she tumbled into him.

"Confound it, Eleanor, what is all the fuss?" He grabbed her shoulders and held her at arm's length then released her and brushed his velvet coat.

"What do you mean, 'all the fuss'?" Her voice cracked. "You left us alone during the storm without a word. Poor Elise was frightened half to death, and we didn't know whether you were dead or alive. Is that any way to treat. . ."

As Mrs. Hendrick poured her complaints onto her husband, Nathaniel sped toward the bulwarks and glanced down. "Steady now, men, steady." He turned toward Mr. Keese. "Go below and gather some lanterns, steel and flint, and weapons, if you please." With a nod, Mr. Keese disappeared down a hatch.

Beyond Nathaniel, clouds as thick and black as giant bears rose on the horizon. White lightning spiked through them. Thunder growled like a beast eyeing its prey. Hope drew a shaky breath and clasped her hands together to keep from trembling. The hurricane would soon return as Nathaniel had predicted. Bracing her bare feet on the moist deck, Hope made her way to where the Hendricks were still engaged in a quarrel. Nathaniel's booming voice echoed behind her.

"We can make it to the island, but we must leave immediately!"

Wind blasted around Hope, stinging her nose with the sharp smell of rain and salt. A light mist began to fall.

"Mr. Mason!" Captain Conway bellowed from the quarterdeck, where he seemed to have regained his senses and clambered to his feet. "What in the blazes are you doing? I ordered you to raise storm sails on the foremast."

Nathaniel glared up at the captain. "We must leave the ship at once, Captain. The rudder is disabled, the wheel is crushed, and the mainmast gone by the board."

"Are you mad? I will not leave my ship! The storm is over, as you can plainly see." Conway waved his hand toward the sky.

Halting, Hope glanced up to see the patch of clear sky of only a moment ago was narrowing under the advancing circle of dark clouds. A gust of wind swirled her skirts around her legs as tiny drops of rain began to fall.

Nathaniel shook wet hair from his face. "The storm is far from over. This is merely the center of it. We must leave at once before the winds pick up again."

"What do you take me for? A dull-witted landlubber?" The captain leaned over the railing and pointed his finger at Nathaniel. "Is this some ploy to take over my ship? I knew you were a mutineer when I first laid eyes on you. Kreggs, Hanson!" Captain Conway yelled at two sailors standing by the capstan. "Arrest this man at once and take him below."

Hope shuddered. Surely they wouldn't lock up the only man who was doing anything to save them.

The two men braced their bare feet over the rocking ship, looking like drowned lynx, but much to her relief, made no move to obey their captain.

"Captain, I have no desire to command your brig," Nathaniel shouted. "In fact, I am trying to leave it, and I advise you to do the same. When the storm recommences, it will be far worse than what we've thus encountered." He glanced across the remaining crew. "We must all abandon ship."

"You will do no such thing!" the captain roared, his face a bloated gray in the dwindling moonlight. "No one leaves my brig."

The two sailors the captain had ordered to arrest Nathaniel came and stood by his side. "We're wit' ye, Mr. Mason."

Nathaniel nodded. "Mr. Kreggs, go below, if you please, and gather anyone who wants to join us." The sailor darted off as Mr. Keese leapt onto the deck from a hatch, a large bundle in his hand.

Mrs. Hendrick's sobbing brought Hope's attention back to the task at hand. The woman clutched her husband's arm as Elise stood shivering by her mother's side. Hope longed to offer the little girl the comfort her mother neglected to give.

"We should go with them, William," Mrs. Hendrick whined. "Better to be on solid land than out here at sea."

Mr. Hendrick snorted. "Surely the captain knows far better than these"—he waved a hand in their direction—"common sailors."

"But for Elise, for the baby." Mrs. Hendrick placed a trembling hand on her belly.

"Mr. Hendrick, please come with us," Hope pleaded.

"And why should I listen to the likes of you?" His mouth slanted sideways toward a strong jaw that would have made him handsome if he weren't such a swaggering peacock.

"Because Mr. Mason is telling the truth."

Thunder rumbled, and Hope glanced at the mushrooming black clouds swirling toward them. She gulped and tried to steady her rapid breathing and the pinpricks of fear traveling down her spine. Why was she helping these people who clearly hated her, when all she wanted to do was make a mad dash toward the cockboat and reach the safety of land?

A wall of rain-laden wind slapped her with such force it turned her head to the side and stung her cheeks. Gulping for air, she braced her bare feet over the sodden wood as another wave lifted the brig.

Hope reached down and lifted Elise in her arms. "Come with us, now, Mrs. Hendrick. For Elise's sake. For your baby's sake." She held out her hand toward the blubbering woman.

"Oh, very well." Mr. Hendrick grabbed Elise from Hope's arms and ushered his wife toward the railing. "Infernal woman. Now you shall cause me to lose valuable time and precious cargo."

Hope shook her head, wondering if the man harbored any affection for his family at all.

Barreling down the quarterdeck ladder, the captain halted before Nathaniel and reached for his sword, but thankfully, the storm had stolen it from him, leaving an empty scabbard in its place. "I will not stand for this! Pure villainy, I say, pure villainy!" His hard, cruel eyes scoured over the remainder of his crew. "The tiller can be repaired and we have the foremast. You will not leave this ship!"

Nathaniel rubbed his left side and cast a quick glance at the agitated black sky then over the remaining crew. "We must depart now!" His deep growl rolled over the ship, competing with the distant thunder. He faced the captain. "Or we will all die."

"Perhaps you didn't hear me, Mr. Mason." Captain Conway seethed. "No one leaves this ship without my permission."

"We are not your prisoners, Captain. The foremast is weakened. It will not last long when the storm returns. I beg you, sir. Leave the brig while you can."

Captain Conway's pock-marked face seemed to collapse. He glared over the lifeless deck, his fiery eyes seeking an ally. His gaze landed on a skinny man with a pointed beard sitting on the foredeck ladder. "Nichols, I command you to arrest Mr. Mason at once!"

Mr. Keese drew his pistol and pointed it at Conway. Nichols didn't move.

The captain laughed. "The powder's wet."

"I reloaded and primed it." Mr. Keese grinned.

"Enough of this." Nathaniel laid a hand on Mr. Keese's arm and eased the gun down. "We are leaving, Captain, with or without your permission." He spun on his heels. "And we will take anyone who wants to go with us."

A group of ten sailors huddled beneath the foredeck. Three more leaned over the railing, watching the proceedings with interest. Was that all that remained of the crew? Hope cringed at the realization that most of them had been swept out to sea.

The captain spit to the side. "Then begone with you all. You'll not last long on that tiny speck of land." Turning, he leapt up the quarterdeck ladder and took his spot where the wheel once stood.

The brig rose and plunged over a wave, and Hope wobbled as she made her way to Mr. Russell, who had remained glued to the capstan ever since he'd emerged from below. Terror sparked in his wide eyes. "Come, Mr. Russell. Time to leave." She placed her hand on his arm and guided him toward the bulwarks.

Kreggs bounded up from the hatch. Another sailor followed him.

Peering over the railing, Mr. Russell glanced at the tiny cockboat rocking in the fuming water as another swell slapped against the hull and lifted the brig. Jowls quivering, his face turned white. "I cannot leave the ship. All my cargo is aboard. It is worth a fortune. I cannot leave the ship." His narrow eyes flitted about the deck like a nervous sparrow.

Hope laid her hand on his arm. "Is your life not worth more than gold, Mr. Russell?"

"If you stay here, you will lose both," Nathaniel said as a crack of thunder split the air. "Now let's be gone." He cast a wary glance at the black swirling clouds. A blast of wind slammed into them, stealing Hope's breath. She rubbed the sleeves of her wet gown.

"Don't listen to them, Mr. Russell. I will get you safely to Kingston." The captain bellowed from the quarterdeck. "Where I intend to charge you, Mr. Mason, with the theft of my cockboat."

"You may come back and retrieve it any time you wish, Captain. I am only borrowing it." "Now, everyone who's going, let's away!" Nathaniel bellowed, leveling his gaze over the remaining crew.

One of the sailors dispatched from the crowd and stood beside him.

"Are you going, Major?" Nathaniel's gaze landed on Major Paine, who, wringing his wig in his hands, had up to now stood silently by the foredeck.

The major's gaze shifted from the brewing tempest on the horizon to the captain and then fixated on Hope. "Since I am in authority here, I cannot in good conscience leave these single ladies in the hands of such unscrupulous men." Approaching the railing, the major swung his legs over the bulwarks and lumbered down the ropes.

Mr. Keese approached Hope and proffered his hand. "May I assist you?"

"Thank you, Mr. Keese, but I'll wait until everyone else is aboard."

She tugged on Mr. Russell's arm. "I beg you, sir."

Nathaniel cast an approving glance her way that sent a wave of warmth through her, despite the cold wind.

A large swell rolled beneath the ship, tossing the cockboat against the hull with a thud as two more sailors climbed down to take their seats.

"We must hurry!" Nathaniel yelled.

"Mr. Russell?" She shouted over the rising wind and gave him her most pleading look.

Shaking his head, he backed away. "I cannot leave my cargo."

Hope's stomach clenched as a scripture her sister Grace often quoted floated through her mind: *For what is a man advantaged, if he gain the whole world, and lose himself?*

Nathaniel held out his hand. "Your turn, Miss Hope."

Taking his hand, she lifted her soaked skirts and eased over the bulwarks. Gripping the rope ladder, she clumsily made her way down as it flapped against the brig, scratching her fingers and crushing her knuckles against the hull. Numb with fear and pain, she wondered if she could descend another inch, when strong arms grabbed her waist and lifted her into the boat. Thanking Mr. Keese, she took a seat beside Abigail, noting the playful gleam normally present in Mr. Keese's eyes had dulled. That sight alone frightened her more than anything.

"Last chance, Captain. Mr. Russell." Nathaniel's booming voice came from above. The tiny boat rolled over a massive wave and slammed into the hull yet again. Mrs. Hendrick screamed.

"You'll pay for this, Mr. Mason!" Captain Conway shouted in reply.

Lightning blazed across the sky as Nathaniel slid down the rope ladder and plopped into the boat, taking a seat beside Hope.

"Shove off, men!" He shouted. "And row. Row as hard as you can."

Using the oars to push the boat from the brig, the crew plunged them into the water and grunted as they fought against the force of the powerful waves.

Hope gripped the edge of the boat. The tiny vessel leapt and vaulted over the sea, lifting her from the thwarts and slamming her down onto the hard wood. Pain shot up her back. Nothing but black ink surrounded them, slick deadly liquid that surged in hungry mounds.

Water crashed over the sides of the boat, drenching them. The wind tore Hope's hair from its ribbons and pins. The saturated strands whipped through the air and stung her face. Perhaps it hadn't been a wise choice to leave the brig, after all. She could no longer see the ship. Would they make it in this tiny boat? She could feel Nathaniel's body heat beside her, the thrust of his muscular thigh against hers as he shoved his oar into the water over and over again. He glanced her way. "We shall make land, Miss Hope." The confidence of his words gave her a measure of solace.

Black, monstrous clouds engulfed the moon and stars, stealing his face from her view, and the warmth from her heart. The rain began. Drops the size of grapes pelted them, stinging Hope's skin.

Abigail slid her hand into Hope's and squeezed it, and Hope leaned on her shoulder, drawing strength from the peace that draped around the young girl like a warm cloak.

Wave after wave pummeled them. Hope's wet gown clung to her. She shivered beneath the constant assault of the wind. Thunder opened its mouth and roared above the tiny craft.

Foamy fingers reached for her from atop the giant swells. Hope squeezed her eyes shut. An icy malevolence gripped her.

The boat lurched, then pitched, then wrenched up on its side. And tipped over. Muffled screams blared over the roar of the waves as Hope plunged into the sea. She gasped for air. Swirling water enveloped her, muting the growl of the storm above. She kicked her feet, her arms flailing.

Her gown tangled around her legs, and she began to sink.

Chapter 12

Water filled Nathaniel's mouth, his ears, his nose. The sound of the raging storm grew faint. His lungs burned. He broke through the surface and heaved for a breath. A wave crashed over him. Squeezing the water from his eyes, he scanned the liquid darkness. Cries for help blared at him from all directions. To his right, part of what remained of their boat floated on the crest of a wave. The Hendricks, their daughter, and two sailors clung to it for dear life. Wheezing, Major Paine gripped a barrel as it rose atop a massive wave. In the distance, Abigail and two more sailors hugged another section of the boat. Mr. Keese swam up to him.

"Where is Miss Hope?" Nathaniel shouted.

Gavin shook his head as another swell took him out of Nathaniel's view.

Nathaniel dove back into the sea and thrust his arms through the churning waters, peering through the shifting shadows for any sign of her.

God, help me find her. Don't let her die!

Terror at the thought of losing her propelled him deeper. His chest burned. His eyes stung. *He must find her!* His hand struck something solid. She floated listlessly, deeper and deeper, as if she had willingly sacrificed her life to the ravenous storm.

He grabbed her waist and sped toward the surface. When they broke through, her head bobbed lifelessly against his shoulder. "No!" *Lord, please.* Pressing her against his chest, he paddled backward through the violent swells toward the sound of waves crashing on shore.

His feet struck sand. With his last ounce of strength, he hoisted her in his arms and carried her through the foamy swells battering him from behind. Finally out of their reach, he gently laid her in the sand. She didn't move. He turned her on her side, gripped her by the waist, and lifted her from the ground. "Come on! Come on! Don't die on me. Spit it out!"

Her body flopped like a dead fish. Sorrow choked his throat and burned his eyes. Releasing her, he sat back, panting. Then she began to cough. Her body convulsed. Elated, he held her as she spewed lungfuls of water onto the sand, until finally, gasping and sobbing, she fell into his arms.

The next morning, Nathaniel dug his toes into the cool sand that was still saturated from the night's storm. *Hurricane, not a storm.* One of the most vicious he'd encountered. He rubbed the blisters on his hands and gazed across the troubled sea. Angry waves pummeled the shore. Lightning sparked from black clouds retreating on the horizon. Behind him, water drip-dropped from the leaves of palms and ficus trees—tears shed for those who had fallen prey to the deadly squall.

Bowing his head, Nathaniel thanked God for delivering them, for although the hurricane had tried to drag them all to the depths of the sea, by God's grace, it had not entirely succeeded. He also thanked God the cockboat had overturned so close to the island. Only Nathaniel, Mr. Keese, and one of the sailors knew how to swim, but the three of them were able to find and tow the passengers to shore.

As Nathaniel shivered in his damp clothes, an arc of brilliant gold peered over the horizon as if the sun was determining whether it was safe to rise and shed its light on another day. It must have liked what it saw, for it rose a little higher, chasing away the clouds with its bright rays and eliciting a cacophony of chirps and twitters from the tropical forest behind him.

"Did you not get any rest, Mr. Mason?" Abigail's cheerful voice startled him. The folds of her salt-encrusted skirt made a grating sound as she lowered to sit in the sand beside him.

He smiled at her apparent ease with her natural surroundings. But then again, being the daughter of missionaries, she was accustomed to rustic conditions.

"Not much, no." He'd woken to find Hope fast asleep in his arms. A wave of desire had swept through him before he could force it away. Ashamed at his reaction, he had slipped from beside her and left her to sleep.

Abigail stretched her arms above her. "As soon as the wind died down, I must have dozed off. How advantageous that you found that cliff to shelter us. However did you see it in the dark?"

Nathaniel picked up a shell and squinted at the sun. After ensuring everyone was safely ashore, he'd known he must protect them from the torrential rain and thrashing wind. But where to go? If they stayed on the beach, a surge of seawater could snatch them back into the ocean. If they hid in the forest, the trees could topple and crush them beneath their weight. But as the ferocity of the waves increased, he chose the former and led them into the dense thicket.

He shrugged. "I felt the wind lessen as we neared and knew that whatever it was, it had to be large and sturdy."

"You're very wise, Mr. Mason. I doubt any of us would be alive without your quick thinking."

Throughout the long night, they had huddled in groups, bracing against the cliff wall to avoid being blown away. Hope, still trembling from her ordeal, had clung to Nathaniel, refusing to let go. So he'd simply engulfed her in his arms and protected her as best he could from the onslaught. Without a word of protest, she'd curled up against his chest all night, not a scream, whimper, or word coming from her mouth.

She'd been so strong aboard the brig, helping Mrs. Hendrick and her daughter into the cockboat and then pleading with Mr. Russell. Although terror had burned in her eyes, she'd waited until the last minute to leave the brig, and not once had she given in to her fears and blubbered like Mrs. Hendrick.

Nathaniel tossed the shell into an incoming wave. Hope's strength had surprised him. When he'd asked for her help, his intention had been to keep her calm and thus avoid the problem of two hysterical women. But she had accomplished much more than that.

He glanced at Abigail as she stared at the ribbons of sunlight winding their way across the blue waters. The warm golden fingers seemed to have a soothing effect upon the waves, stroking away the tension caused by the storm. Nathaniel released a sigh and soaked in their warmth, his own muscles easing from the stressful night.

"There was something ... something different about that storm." Abigail shivered and gripped her arms

Nathaniel rubbed his eyes, still stinging from salt. Indeed. A storm like none he had encountered.

"Something evil, a wicked presence. Did you not feel it?" She stared at him.

He nodded, relieved he hadn't gone completely mad. "Aye, I did. It seemed to have a purpose, a deep hatred aimed directly at us."

Drawing her knees to her chest, Abigail wrapped her arms around her legs. "Perhaps we angered the forces of darkness when you saved the ill sailor in the hold."

"God saved him, you mean."

"Yes." She smiled.

"Or perhaps something or someone wants to stop you from going to Kingston," Nathaniel offered.

"I assure you, I am no threat to the enemy."

"No threat, you say?" He chuckled. "Aren't you going there to be a missionary like your parents?"

She began fingering the sand. "May I speak freely, Mr. Mason?"

"Of course."

"My parents spent their lives spreading the gospel to the descendants of the Arawaks and Caribs on Antigua. And what did they get for it? Murdered." She looked away. "Not just murdered, sliced to pieces in their own bed." Her voice cracked as moments passed. "I cannot shake the sounds of their screams from my ears or the vision of their mutilated bodies from my mind. Why did God allow that to happen? I know He loved them. They gave up everything for Him. And they were butchered for it." She gazed out to sea and bunched sand in her fists.

Nathaniel's gut wrenched. He wanted to tell her God must have had a reason. He wanted to tell her things would work out for good. But the words seemed so trite in light of what she had suffered. "I don't have the answers, Miss Sheldon, but please don't give up on God."

She gave him a half smile. "I'm not giving up on Him. I know He loves me. But I don't know if I can make the same sacrifice my parents did. It frightens me, Mr. Mason, frightens me more than anything."

A band of waves pounded the shore, sending a misty spray over them. "Yet you were so calm through the most violent storm I've seen."

Abigail squinted toward a massive plank of wood floating atop an incoming wave. "The wind and rain don't scare me. Drowning at sea doesn't frighten me"—one side of her mouth tilted in a smile—"Being hacked to pieces does. Besides, God told me we would survive the hurricane."

"Indeed?" Nathaniel eyed the streaks of honeyed gold cast by the sun on her brown hair, amazed at her courage, saddened by her fear, and suddenly envious of her open communication with God. How long had it been since he had heard a word from the Almighty? All the more reason why this pious lady should continue her work for Him. "Then surely God will give you the same assurance in your missionary work."

The freckles on her forehead scrunched. "My parents had assurance. They believed God would protect and bless them for their sacrifice."

Above them a clear patch of blue pushed the dark clouds aside. "Do you think they feel blessed and protected where they are now?"

She gave him a sideways glance, but said nothing.

The birds continued their cheerful chorus behind them as the full sun rose above the cloudy horizon. The petulant waves of earlier that morning becalmed to tumbling rollers depositing debris above arcs of bubbling foam.

"What does it matter?" She chuckled. "We are stuck on this island, and from all appearances, will not be going anywhere soon."

Nathaniel raked a hand through his hair—sticky with salt. If he didn't meet up with his other ship in Kingston soon, Captain Grainer might set sail without him. A spindly crab skittered across the sand by his feet then plunged into a tiny hole. "Never fear. The island has fresh water and a good anchorage. I'm sure a ship will come along soon."

"What do we do in the meantime?"

"We survive. I will build shelters and gather food, and we will pray for God to deliver us in His good time." Nathaniel had been formulating a plan since he'd arisen hours before. In the predawn glow he had seen bamboo, plantain, and palm trees aplenty on the island—great for making a sturdy shelter. Once he crafted a suitable hut for the ladies, he could set about finding food to eat.

Abigail laid her hand on his arm. Dark lashes framed her glimmering hazel eyes. She smiled. "You are a godsend, Mr. Mason."

What decent man wouldn't be attracted to a woman like Abigail? Innocent, pure, godly, devoting her life to others. Yet, as becoming as she was, he could conjure nothing more than thoughts of friendship. It was Hope who made his blood heat, his thoughts jumble, his stomach flip. Why was he drawn to such an unprincipled, wanton woman?

Nathaniel released a heavy sigh, wondering whether he would ever free himself from his past.

Chapter 13

A dull ache throbbed behind Hope's eyes. She rubbed her temples and tried to form a rational thought. The hurricane. The brig damaged. The cockboat. Water—an ocean of water surrounding her, filling her, weighing her down. Sinking. Peaceful and dark. Then strong hands grabbed her. Pulled her toward the surface. Waves crashing all around her. Her feet dragging over sand, solid land. A bad dream.

A nightmare.

She opened her eyes and sat up, chest heaving and beads of perspiration sliding down her neck. A muted blur of green and brown coalesced into trees and branches and clustered foliage. Pressing her hands against the sandy soil, she struggled to rise. Her legs wobbled, her feet hurt, and the throb in her head turned into hammering. Stumbling, she reached behind her. Her hand scraped over something sharp and cold—a rock wall that rose and disappeared beyond the treetops.

Where was she? How had she gotten here?

The sound of snoring drew her attention to people scattered about the filthy ground, sound asleep. Mr. and Mrs.

Hendrick lay to her left—he with his back to his wife, while she cradled little Elise in her arms. Hope smiled, relieved to see the young girl alive and well. Mr. Keese, Major Paine, and several sailors lay off in the distance. But no Nathaniel. No Abigail.

Her throat constricted. Had they drowned?

Despite the thumping in her head, she brushed aside the foliage and forged through a tangle of green. Drops of water sprayed her from the ruffled leaves. The musky smell of moist earth enveloped her. Insects began to swarm around her head like the thousand terrifying thoughts buzzing through her mind. If Nathaniel had drowned in the hurricane, who would escort her to Charles Towne? Who would protect her? And Abigail, her friend—her first real friend—gone before they had a chance to form a lasting bond. Following the sound of the crashing surf, she swatted aside a maze of vines and burst onto the beach.

There on the sand, watching the sun rise, sat Nathaniel and Abigail. Abigail's hand lay on his arm in a familiar touch. She smiled and they chuckled together like old friends.

Or lovers.

Hope's heart plummeted. She swallowed and tried to control her breathing, all the while ashamed at her reaction. She should be thrilled to find her friends alive, not burning with jealousy! Besides, all she sought was Nathaniel's approval, his admiration. Certainly not his love.

Disgust welled in her belly. Was she so desperate for the attention of every man, she would deny these two godly people a happiness they both deserved? She bit her lip. What would a proper lady do in this situation? She would squelch the churning in her stomach and be the perfect picture of grace. Hope had set out to prove she could change, and change she would. Besides, what madness had befuddled her brain? Nathaniel would never want a woman like her, for in so doing, he would deny the very essence of what made him a true gentleman.

Real gentlemen did not consort with women like her.

Chiding herself, she came up beside them.

"Miss Hope." Nathaniel jumped to his feet, brushing sand from his breeches. A breeze wafted over them, tossing his wavy hair across his forehead and flapping his soiled linen shirt, giving her a peek at his strong chest.

Her breath quickened. Suddenly self-conscious, she adjusted her tattered gown and pressed strands of matted hair behind her ear. What a wretched sight she must be.

Abigail rose and took Hope's hands. "I told you we would survive."

Hope greeted her friend with a smile. "Yet, if I remember, you said God would save us, not Mr. Mason." She glanced his way. "Unless of course they are one and the same?" Which would explain Abigail's attraction to him, but certainly not Hope's.

He shifted his bare feet in the sand and cocked his head. "Nowhere close, I assure you, Miss Hope. But God can use the most unlikely people to accomplish His tasks."

"You are far too humble, sir, as I am sure Miss Sheldon would agree. No doubt she has been expressing her deepest gratitude to you this morning for saving her." Hope gave him a sharp smile.

He narrowed his eyes.

Abigail released Hope's hands and brushed a fringe of hair from her forehead. "Indeed. I do find Mr. Mason's humility refreshing."

"Hmm." Hope laid a finger on her bottom lip. "A worthy quality to be sure. And one that you possess as well, Miss Sheldon. 'God resisteth the proud, and giveth grace to the humble.' Is that not correct?" Dash it all, what was wrong with her? She had reduced herself to quoting Scripture.

Nathaniel folded arms across his chest. "I am pleased you know your Bible."

"I know enough of it. But I am sure Miss Sheldon knows

far more than I, don't you, Miss Sheldon?" Hope raised an inquisitive brow toward Abigail, whose expression had crumpled in confusion.

Oh fodders. Hope knew she was behaving like a jealous schoolgirl, but the conflicting emotions swirling within her forbade her to stop. Perhaps she should leave before she made a complete nincompoop of herself.

"Forgive the interruption. I'm sure you two have much to discuss about God ... redemption ... sacrifice ... or whatever pious matters you find interesting." Hope swerved about, but Nathaniel clutched her arm. Instead of the anger she expected, a slow smile spread over his lips. She bunched her fists.

He knows I'm jealous.

Releasing her, he took a step back. Dark stubble peppered his jaw, making him look dangerous. But it was the yearning in his eyes that truly frightened her. "Please don't leave, Miss Hope. We have much to discuss."

Her head started to pound again. She had set out to behave like a lady and had failed miserably—once again. "Forgive me. I must be tired."

"We have all suffered a frightful experience." Abigail's soft voice brimmed with kindness. So unlike Hope's sister Grace. Where Grace would have chided Hope for her inappropriate behavior, Abigail showed her naught but mercy.

Drying salt began to chafe the skin beneath her sleeve, and Hope scratched her arm. She deserved the irritation and far more for her ill-mannered conduct. Visions of the roiling dark waters pulling her down to the ocean depths made her suddenly tremble. But strong hands had clutched her from a watery grave just in time. She raised her gaze to Nathaniel. "It was you who pulled me from the water."

His half-cocked smile set Hope's stomach aflutter.

Further memories of the night surfaced: the dash into the shelter of the forest, Mrs. Hendrick's screams, the pelting rain. "And you who. . ." *held me all night against the raging wind and rain.* His eyes locked upon hers, and something burned within their depths—desire? No. She was quite familiar with that look. This was something far deeper. Heat stormed up her neck and face, shocking her. She hadn't blushed in years—had thought she was far beyond blushing like an innocent schoolgirl. She turned aside and met Abigail's cat-like grin as the young girl shifted her gaze between her and Nathaniel.

"Who what?" Abigail asked.

"Never mind." Backing up, Hope lowered herself onto a boulder and dabbed the perspiration from her brow. Though the sun sat merely a handbreadth above the horizon, its searing rays had already begun to cook the tiny island. "Where are we?"

"From my last calculation," Nathaniel said. "One of the many small islands near Puerto Rico."

Leaves thrashed, and Major Paine and Mr. Hendrick emerged from the web of green.

"Here, here, Mr. Mason." Mr. Hendrick's red hair gleamed like fire in the sunlight. "We have survived your hurricane, it would seem."

"Not my hurricane, but yes, God was merciful."

Major Paine straightened his wrinkled red waistcoat, but there was naught to be done about the mud on his white breeches or that his boots squished as he walked. The periwig that normally sat atop his head was nowhere to be seen. In its stead, stringy brown hair flayed in a chaotic display about his shoulders. A sword hung at his side. He scanned the horizon. "Humph. Now look at the mess you've gotten us into."

"Would you prefer to have remained on the brig, Major?" Nathaniel's playful tone carried a hint of challenge.

"Aye, I would have." He ran his fingers through his hair, attempting to form some style out of the wayward strands. "No doubt she's made anchor at Kingston by now."

Nathaniel frowned as he scanned the shoreline that

stretched to the north and ended in a jumble of rocks.

Shielding her eyes from the sun, Hope followed his gaze to the debris scattered across the beach: buckets, wooden planks, sailcloth, barrels—the same barrels, from the looks of them, that had stood on the deck of the merchantman.

Nathaniel released a heavy sigh. "I fear you are mistaken, Major."

Mr. Keese burst onto the beach and marched their way, rubbing his eyes and spraying sand into the air with his bare feet. Stains and rips marred his tan breeches, and his wrinkled shirt hung loosely about his hips. Seemingly undismayed by his tousled appearance, he winked at Hope and took a stance beside Nathaniel.

Ignoring him, Mr. Hendrick turned toward Nathaniel. "What do you mean, sir?"

"I mean 'tis plain the brig sank." Nathaniel spoke calmly over the distant crash of waves.

"Egad, I do not believe it." Mr. Hendrick and the major stared at him aghast.

Nathaniel waved a hand over the beach. "The sea has spit up the evidence, as you can see."

Mr. Hendrick fingered his beard while Major Paine picked up a chunk of wood and examined it. "This could be any ship."

"Those barrels"—Nathaniel pointed to a group of casks shifting atop the incoming waves—"Are the same ones I tied together on the brig before we left."

Mr. Hendrick snorted. "They could have been swept overboard."

"Aye, I suppose, but the sailcloth, the planking, the shattered remains of crates tell another tale." Nathaniel gestured to the debris. "They all came from a ship sailing close to this island during the storm."

"Poor Mr. Russell." Hope's chest tightened as the realization of Nathaniel's words sank in. "And the captain and all those men."

Abigail sat down beside her and squeezed her hand.

"Not like we didn't warn them." Mr. Keese gazed out to sea.

"If that is true, there will be no ship returning for us." Mr. Hendrick directed accusing eyes toward Nathaniel as if their predicament was entirely his fault.

"Not anytime soon." Nathaniel shook his head.

Hope eyed the belligerent men. They should be grateful to Nathaniel for his quick thinking, for saving their lives.

Major Paine's face reddened. "What shall we do? We can't stay here." He glanced across the beach in disgust then strolled over to where Hope and Abigail sat. "The ladies will not survive in this wilderness." He swatted at some invisible insect hovering around his face.

Hope doubted the major would fare too well, either.

"I know a bit about living under these conditions," Nathaniel said. "We will make the women comfortable, seek food and water, and wait until a ship sails past."

"Balderdash! That could take months." Major Paine placed a hand on Hope's shoulder as if staking his claim. "We must remove the women from this savage place as soon as possible."

Hope squirmed from beneath his touch and shifted closer to Abigail. Didn't the man realize he would be at the bottom of the sea if not for Nathaniel?

Abigail squeezed her hand as if sensing Hope's unease. How could she sit there and allow these men to behave so ungraciously toward Nathaniel, especially in light of her obvious affection for him? But perchance that's how ladies were supposed to behave—quiet, demure, submissive. Hope sighed. Would she ever be able to comport herself in such a manner?

Nathaniel turned toward the major. "And how do you propose to get us off this island?"

"We shall build a raft." He wagged a hand as if he could conjure one from thin air.

Mrs. Hendrick stumbled onto the beach, Elise by her side. Two sailors followed in her wake as she held a hand to her forehead and moaned. Her elegant coiffure had collapsed into a tangled jumble like the vines she emerged from. Her gown was torn and her lips were as white as her face.

Abigail dashed toward her, took her arm, and led her to the boulder beside Hope, but the woman scooted as far away from Hope as the rock would allow. Elise, however, climbed into Hope's lap. Planting a kiss on the girl's cheek, Hope snuggled against her, enjoying her warm, soft feel before Mrs. Hendrick would inevitably pull her away.

Giving his wife a cursory glance, Mr. Hendrick pulled a pocket watch from his waistcoat and snapped it open. "I daresay, a raft is the way to go, Major. It cannot be too far to Puerto Rico."

"You will never make it," Nathaniel said. "In case you haven't noticed, 'tis the season for storms. And this island lacks the materials to build a craft sturdy enough to withstand another squall."

"But you *claim* to be a shipbuilder, sir. Do you not?" Mr. Hendrick dropped the watch back into his pocket. "Surely you can construct a suitable raft? And besides, we may not encounter another storm for months."

"Are you willing to risk your life and the lives of these women on pure conjecture, sir?" Nathaniel swatted an insect and released a grunt of frustration as if he wished he could do the same with Mr. Hendrick. "Nay, our best chance is to make ourselves comfortable until a ship arrives seeking fresh water and fruit. I know this island. It is one of the few blessed with an abundance of both and well known among local sailors."

Hope eyed Mr. Hendrick and the major. Both bore stiff, unyielding expressions. "Even if you build a raft," she said, "and even if you make it to Puerto Rico, isn't that island in the hands of the Spanish?"

Seagulls squawked overhead as if laughing at the

ridiculous altercation below.

Nathaniel's brows rose, and Mr. Keese crossed arms over his chest and grinned.

"My dear lady." Mr. Hendrick shifted his mulish jaw and laid a finger on his chin, reminding Hope of a common gesture of Lord Falkland's. Why had she not noticed how demeaning it was? "I have sailed these seas for a decade. Not to impugn Mr. Mason's knowledge, but I am quite capable of getting us safely off this island." He chuckled. "And since when do we cower before a few inept Spaniards, eh, Major?"

"Quite right." The major thrust out his narrow chin. "Enough of this nonsense. I am the highest authority here, and I say we build a raft."

Nathaniel pressed a hand on his side as if a sudden ache had arisen. "You may be the second in command of the Leeward Islands, Major, but you hold no power here. By all means, build your raft, but my first priority is our survival and the protection of these ladies."

The major's face purpled. His mouth opened and shut as if he were unable to respond.

Mr. Hendrick came to his aid. "Surely the ladies would be better cared for under the authority of a man who is used to commanding and making wise decisions."

"And where would we find such a man?" Mr. Keese grinned and scratched his sideburns.

"Enough of your impudence, sir." The major found his voice and gripped the hilt of his sword. "I issue the orders here, and I'll have you and your friend gagged and tied to a tree if you do not comply. Mr. Hendrick is correct. The ladies should be under our protection, not that of common sailors. It is our duty as gentlemen." He placed his hand once again on Hope's shoulder, slid it down to her elbow, and attempted to tug her from her seat.

Handing Elise to her mother, Hope jerked from the major's grasp. "Mr. Mason saved all of our lives last night!" A swarm of shocked gazes landed on her. "And I, for one, intend to place my trust in him."

Nathaniel's eyes widened.

The major sauntered over to stand beside Mr. Hendrick. "Ah yes, I forgot about your arrangement with Mr. Mason. Not worked off the full price he paid for you yet? Is that it?" He snickered.

Nathaniel's jaw turned to steel. "And you, sir, have insulted Miss Hope yet again. Something I told you at dinner I would not tolerate."

He had? Hope blinked. She had run from the captain's cabin too fast to hear such a chivalrous defense.

The major rubbed his thumb over the silver hilt of his sword. Nathaniel and Mr. Keese were unarmed.

The two sailors stood a few yards away, watching the altercation with amusement.

Hope's throat went dry.

Nathaniel took a bold step toward the major. "Apologize to Miss Hope at once."

The major shifted his glance from side to side as if he would retreat, but then he threw back his shoulders, drew his sword, and leveled the tip beneath Nathaniel's chin.

Chapter 14

Unflinching, Nathaniel eyed the pompous man. The tip of the major's sword pierced the skin beneath Nathaniel's chin, sending a trickle of blood down his neck. But Nathaniel had dealt with his type before—a man bent on gaining power no matter the cost.

Behind him, Hope gasped, while at his side, Mr. Keese made a move toward them, but Nathaniel lifted a hand to ward him off. There was no sense in anyone else getting hurt.

"I will give you one chance to lower your blade and apologize to Miss Hope, Major." Nathaniel spoke slowly so as not to disturb the sharp point digging into his chin, ensuring, however, that his tone carried the threat he intended. Though he assumed the major had been trained in swordsmanship, Nathaniel doubted the man would make the same assumption of a poor merchant.

A flicker of uncertainty, perhaps fear, sped across the major's eyes. His sword trembled, its tip scraping Nathaniel's skin, confirming his suspicions—the man was a coward.

Major Paine thrust out his pointed chin. "And I will give you one more chance to submit to my authority." A burst of wind sent the gold fringe of his epaulet flapping against his shoulder, mocking the severity of his challenge.

Mr. Hendrick moved to stand behind the major, a supercilious grin on his face.

"As you wish." Nathaniel snapped his gaze to the sea, feigning a look of shock, drawing the major's gaze and momentarily distracting him. In a lightning-quick move, he struck the major's blade with his forearm and shoved it aside. Major Paine stumbled backward. Then grabbing a fistful of sand, Nathaniel flung it into his eyes.

The major roared a foul curse, slammed his eyes shut, and began waving his sword out before him. Dodging the riotous thrusts, Nathaniel darted to the major's side and snatched the weapon from his hand with ease.

Grinding his fists against his eyelids, the major growled like a wounded bear, then bent over, hands on his knees, and spit a string of obscenities onto the sand. "My eyes. My eyes. You've ruined my eyes."

Nathaniel flicked hair from his face and caught his breath, happy he had dissolved the situation without injury. "'Tis just a bit of sand, Major. You will recover."

"Scads, Major." Mr. Hendrick rushed to his friend and helped him up. "Quit blabbering like a fool."

Shaking off his grasp, Major Paine narrowed his streaming eyes upon Nathaniel. "You shall pay for this affront."

Nathaniel chuckled and wiped the sweat from his forehead. Though he would like nothing more than to challenge the man to a rematch, he had more important matters to deal with than feeding his pride and belittling the major. Turning, he tossed the sword, hilt first to Mr. Keese, who caught it with a wink then pressed the tip into the sand and leaned on the silver handle.

Hope's blue eyes latched upon Nathaniel's, beaming with admiration. A rush of warmth flooded him as he returned his focus to Major Paine.

"Now, apologize, if you please."

"I meant no insult to you, miss," Major Paine whispered to the sand beside his feet.

"Very well. You may have your sword back, sir, when you promise to behave." Nathaniel grunted. "We are all stuck on this island for the unforeseen future, and we can best survive if we cooperate."

The major shifted his shoulders as if trying to regain his dignity. "You may do as you wish, Mr. Mason, but I intend to build a raft and leave this savage place as soon as possible. With or without you. He puffed out his chest and glanced first at the ladies then behind him at the sailors. Who is with me?" Tears poured from his reddened eyes.

Mr. Hendrick clapped a hand on the major's shoulder. "You can count on me." He peered around Nathaniel toward Mrs. Hendrick. "I have no intention of living under these barbaric conditions until a ship happens along. Absurd! Come along, dear." He crooked a finger toward his wife.

With a groan, she labored to her feet, took Elise by the hand, and joined her husband.

The major raised a brow toward Hope and Miss Sheldon, pasting on what he perhaps assumed was an alluring smile, but instead it made him look like a court jester.

Nathaniel stepped aside to give the ladies a pathway toward the major should they desire to go with him, but neither made a move.

The two sailors ambled over to stand behind Nathaniel.

The major's crimson face broke out in a sweat. Swerving on his heels, he marched away, kicking up sand as he went. Mr. Hendrick gave them all a haughty look, grabbed his wife and child, and followed after him.

Nathaniel plunged into the forest, hacking his way through vines and branches with his sword in one hand and swatting them aside with a bucket in the other. If Mr. Keese hadn't gathered a bundle of weapons from the ship and tossed them into the cockboat, they'd be defenseless. Regardless, Nathaniel had no weapon on his person earlier in the day when Major Paine decided to make himself king of the island. But then a swordfight was the last thing Nathaniel had expected.

He wouldn't make that mistake again.

He slashed through a moss-covered branch. Tie him to a tree, indeed! If Major Paine had succeeded with his plan, they would all be lost. For he doubted the man knew how to survive in the tropics, let alone how to make a raft seaworthy enough to sail to Puerto Rico. Drawing a deep breath of the moist, loamy air, Nathaniel pushed aside a thicket of ferns. He knew he was supposed to love his fellow man, but how did one love such a self-important oaf?

Mr. Hendrick was no better. For some reason, Nathaniel had expected more of him. Surely a man of his position and accomplishments should possess some measure of wisdom and benevolence. Yet he conducted himself with no more civility than that dunderhead, Paine. A vision of the blundering look on Major Paine's face when Nathaniel had dispatched him so quickly filled his mind. He grinned.

But a gentle nudge within put a halt to his thoughts. *Lord, forgive my pride.*

Still, both men had made their position clear. And that position was in direct opposition to Nathaniel. He grunted. Not only must he protect and provide for the survivors of the storm, but now he must battle an enemy camp.

The buzz and whine of insects filled his ears as he stopped to catch his breath. He waved them off, forming the only hint of a breeze in the stifling forest. Sweat streamed down his back, dampening his shirt, which had just begun to dry after last night's storm. He forged ahead, trying to scatter thoughts of Major Paine, but the man's peevish face kept filling Nathaniel's vision. All his life, men of position and power had looked down their noses at him—the son of a trollop, a pauper, a poor merchantman—assuming he had no

more brains than money. All his life, he'd fought against
their disfavor, trying to prove his value, ability, and
intelligence. And wasn't he well on his way? He had built
two ships of his own. And if he hadn't been forced to sell one
…

His thoughts drifted to Hope, and he tried to conjure up
further anger to fuel his expedition through the tangled forest,
but the vision of her tossing her pert little nose in the air as
she stomped away from him and Miss Sheldon cooled his
humor.

Jealous. Why did the thought delight him so? Birds
chirped overhead, and he gazed up at a collage of brightly-
colored feathers flitting against the green canvas. Beautiful
creatures who, just like Hope, drew all admiring eyes their
way—creatures who basked in the attentions they received.
No, couldn't be. Hope wasn't jealous of Miss Sheldon. No
doubt she was simply envious of any attentions not tossed
her way.

The gushing sound he'd been listening for reached his
ears, and he slashed his way toward it, finally bursting into a
small clearing. A cascade of silvery water spilled from a cliff
nigh ten yards high into a large pond of emerald liquid. A
pristine image of the myriad trees and colorful flowers
reflected off the pond as if proud to display God's creation
back to heaven. Amazed at the beauty of the Creator's
handiwork, Nathaniel dropped to his knees and scooped
handfuls of the liquid to his mouth and then splashed it over
his head and neck and eased it over the blisters on his hands.
At least they'd have plenty of fresh water to drink.

He sat for several minutes, breathing in the musky
smells and relishing his time alone, when the rustle of leaves
reached his ears.

"Mr. Mason!"

He jerked around at the sound of his name on feminine
lips. An "ouch" chirped from a cluster of giant fig leaves
before Hope broke through and stumbled into the clearing.

She glanced over the scenery and let out a sigh of delight. "'Tis like paradise." Eyes as blue as the sea gripped him, and Nathaniel sensed that, just like the sea, they covered a depth no one suspected. Her golden hair the color of the sun fell to her waist in mass of tangled curls. She shifted her bare feet over the sandy soil and fingered the torn lace dangling from her neckline, in a futile attempt to put it back into place.

For a moment—a brief moment—she seemed like a fallen angel who against all odds had fought her way into heaven. Shaking the image, he tried to quell the sudden beating of his heart and perched on a boulder under the pretense of stretching his legs "What are you doing here?" he said a bit too harshly. "It isn't safe for you to be wandering about." Fire and thunder, the last thing he needed was to be alone in the forest with this enchantress.

"Why did *you* come here?"

"To find water." He grabbed the bucket and dipped it in the pond. "You could have gotten lost."

Her soft footsteps approached.

"Oh, pah. I followed your trail. Besides, I knew you were hurt." She pointed to the streak of red on his shirt where he'd shoved aside Major Paine's blade. "And I ..." She looked down. "I thought I'd tend to your wound."

He stared at her creamy skin tinted pink from the morning's sun. "Why?" He could think of no rational reason she would struggle through the bugs and vines to dress a scratch on his arm—no reason save the one that frightened him the most.

A flicker of pain accused him from her eyes. "You were injured defending my honor. It's the least I can do."

"You don't owe me anything." He set the full bucket between them, water sloshing over the sides.

"I owe you everything, Mr. Mason." She toyed with a fold of her skirt, glanced his way, then swerved around. "I owe you a ship for one thing, my life for another." He heard the tearing of fabric. "And now I owe you for standing up to that bully, Major Paine. I do not trust him." She angled around the bucket and knelt beside him, two strips of cloth in hand. "Nor Mr. Hendrick. Their behavior toward you was inexcusable."

She dipped one cloth into the bucket and wrung it out. "Now let me see your arm."

"No need." Nathaniel inched away from her, not at all pleased with the way his body suddenly heated. He should be furious at her. She'd caused him nothing but grief since the day he'd seen her on St. Kitts. He wouldn't even be on this island if not for her. And now he'd be forced to do the one thing he sought to avoid the most—spend more time with her.

Birds fluttered and squawked overhead as though warning him.

Her eyes sparked with playfulness. "I promise I don't bite."

Her lips angled slightly in a pert little smile, and he licked his own, remembering the kiss they'd shared on board the merchantman. Her lingering look suggested she had remembered it, too.

"I'm not so sure." He grinned.

She glanced away as her cheeks reddened. "If you're referring to our kiss, I assure you it will not happen again. I am determined to change, Mr. Mason. Now, are you going to let me tend to your wound, or have I forged through this jungle for no reason?"

Nathaniel gazed at the determined look on her face and decided the sooner he complied, the quicker they could part company. He pulled his shirt over his head and tossed it to the ground.

Hope's gaze latched onto his chest, and she fumbled with the cloth.

"Have I offended you?" he asked playfully.

"Of course not. It's not like I haven't seen a man's bare

chest be—" She slammed her mouth shut and dabbed the cloth on his wound. "Well, you know what I mean."

Yes, he did. And the reminder poured a bucket of cold water onto his simmering passions. She was a woman who toyed with men like playthings, a woman familiar with the intimate affections of men.

A woman not to be trusted.

She dipped the cloth into the bucket again then squeezed it and finished cleaning his cut, her face pinched in concentration. Then grabbing the dry cloth, she wound it around his arm. "You were brave today. I've not seen anything like it. Not many men would have handled things so well with a sword pointed at their necks."

"It was nothing." Then why did his chest surge at her praise?

"Nevertheless, I find great comfort knowing you'll be looking out for us until a ship arrives."

Nathaniel's breath took a sudden leap into his throat. Was she flirting with him? After she'd announced her determination to change? He stared at her. But she focused on his arm, wrapping his wound with care, seemingly unaware of the effect her words had on him, not to mention how his skin heated each time her fingertips brushed across it. Purely a physical reaction to a beautiful woman. That was all. Nothing more.

"Why have you really come out here?" he asked, hoping to dissolve the mist of allure that hovered around her.

She gave a ladylike snort, crossed two ends of the cloth together, and tightened his bandage into a knot.

"Ouch." Pain shot up his arm.

"That should take care of it." She struggled to her feet, hiding her face from him. "Good-day, Mr. Mason."

Nathaniel grabbed her hand before she could turn away. Her eyes swam with moisture. Perhaps she *had* come to help him out of the kindness of her heart. He was a cad. He should apologize but instead, changed the subject. "You stood up to them as well."

"Who?" She jerked from his grasp and turned her back to him.

"Major Paine and Mr. Hendrick." Nathaniel stood. His arm burned, and he rubbed his wound, noting that it hadn't pained him before Hope had tended it.

"Not very ladylike, I suppose." She huffed.

"Ladylike or not, I appreciated it." Hope might not be a saint, but she had spunk. Nathaniel's mother had been unable to stand up to anyone—had allowed men and women alike to take advantage of her. But not Hope.

"Truly?" She swerved about, and her hand slammed against his wounded arm.

He winced and let out a ragged breath.

"I am so clumsy. Please forgive me, Mr. Mason." She reached out to touch him, but he backed away, his arm still stinging.

When the pain subsided, he drew in a deep breath. True concern burned within her blue eyes, and an overwhelming urge to protect her rose within him. She exuded a charm, an appeal that transcended her beauty. Coupled with her poor reputation, it made her easy prey. He saw the way Major Paine looked at her, not to mention Mr. Keese's playful flirtations. He must protect her and provide for her …

… if she didn't kill him first. He grinned.

A weight settled on his shoulders like none he'd known before. Many years had passed since he'd been responsible for the welfare of another. Not since caring for his mother as a young boy.

And that hadn't turned out well at all.

"Shall I see to your chin?" She reached up to touch him, but he jerked away. "Nay, it's fine." He doubted his body could handle any more of her ministrations.

"I don't have the plague, Mr. Mason." She blinked and dropped her hand to her side. "You treat me in the same manner as Mrs. Hendrick does."

"That is not my intention. It's simply that …well …" Nathaniel rubbed the back of his neck. "I've suffered more misfortune these past five days than I've suffered in several years."

Her brow puckered. "And you're saying it's my fault?"

"The loss of my ship?"

"I suppose you're still angry about that." She kicked the sandy soil.

"I'm trying not to be."

"Try harder." She mimicked the same words he'd said to her back on the merchantman when she'd announced her efforts to behave. "Besides, I told you my father would give you another."

"Hmm." He wasn't going to count on that. "Then I was nearly crushed by a bundle of crates on board the brig."

"You can hardly blame me for that."

"And I lost all of my belongings."

She pursed her lips and looked away, her face reddening. "Then the hurricane."

"Now storms are also my fault? Next you'll be blaming me for droughts and famines and wars."

"You haven't been to Spain lately, have you?" He grinned, picturing the havoc she might have wreaked amidst Spain's recent attempt to conquer Italy.

"How dare … of course not!"

"And let us not forget that Major Paine nearly sliced me in two." He raised a brow.

She hugged herself and thrust out her chin. "I didn't ask you to defend me."

Moments passed as Nathaniel studied her. The laughter of splashing water and warble of happy birds did naught to ease the tension between them. She stared at the pond, her eyes misting, and Nathaniel swallowed his rising guilt. He'd wanted her to know what he'd suffered at her expense, but found the sorrow lining her face brought him no pleasure. He opened his mouth to apologize when she clutched her skirts and spun about. "Since you find my company so dangerous, I shall relieve you of it."

"Wait. You shouldn't go alone," Nathaniel yelled after her but the wall of green swallowed her whole.

"I am not your concern." Her sharp voice answered from the thicket.

Grabbing the bucket and his shirt, Nathaniel trudged after her, wishing with all his heart that were true.

Chapter 15

Hope reached beneath the hem of her skirt and
scratched the red marks prickling over her legs—
courtesy of unseen fleas that lived in the sand and feasted on
human flesh. Just another amenity of this tropical paradise.
Flipping down the filthy fabric, she drew her knees to her
chest. Before her, the Caribbean Sea shimmered like a giant
sapphire in the noonday sun, while wavelets painted intricate
foamy designs along the smooth shore. Yet despite her
efforts to admire the scenery, her gaze kept wandering to the
tall, bare-chested, sun-bronzed man with tawny hair, who
stood knee-deep in the surf with spear in hand. The muscles
of his arms bulged as he tensed for the kill, reminding her of
their time in the jungle nigh four day ago when he'd doffed
his shirt so suddenly. She hadn't expected to find such a
firmly muscled chest and finely chiseled arms beneath his
soiled clothes. Nor had she expected the sudden heat that
claimed her at the sight. And of course he'd noticed her
reaction, only adding to her mortification.

But from here beneath the shade of a tall palm, she could
admire Nathaniel discreetly. Certainly there was no harm in
that.

"He presents quite a handsome figure, does he not?" Abigail's teasing tone jarred Hope from her daze and brought her eyes to the girl sitting beside her, weaving leaves into some sort of basket. Was there nothing Abigail couldn't do? She'd been so quiet, her presence had slipped from Hope's mind.

Face heating, Hope started to deny she'd been gazing at Nathaniel, but why bother? Apparently Abigail had been doing the same.

"Yes, I suppose he does," Hope finally admitted.

"And resourceful, too."

Hope shot a glance over her shoulder at the shelter Nathaniel had built for them that first day. It had taken him three hours to latch together a wooden frame with vines and cover it with fig leaves and palm fronds, and another hour to make a raised floor laden with soft leaves and moss for them to sleep upon. Watertight and warm, it afforded her and Abigail the privacy they needed among so many men. Several yards away, he and Mr. Keese had slapped together another bigger shelter for themselves and Kreggs and Hanson, the two crewmen who had joined them. The other three sailors had opted to join Major Paine's party, although Hope could not understand why.

"Would ye like some mango, Miss Hope, Miss Sheldon?"

Kreggs grinned down at her, his arms bursting with red and yellow fruit, his gray hair springing in all directions around a leathery face.

"No thank you, Mr. Kreggs, but save one for me, will you?"

"Sure thing, miss."

"I'll take one. Thank you, Mr. Kreggs." Abigail held out her hands, and he tossed her a mango before he lumbered over to the fire and dropped the remainder into a barrel. Plucking a knife from his belt, he sat on a log and whittled away at a piece of wood.

"Are you ill?" Abigail touched Hope's arm, her brow furrowed. "You're pale and you haven't eaten all day."

"Just tired." Truth be told, her stomach had been flopping like a fish all morning.

"It was quite a fierce storm last night."

"But the shelter Mr. Mason built for us held up well." Hope shuddered, remembering the rain pounding on the thick ceiling of leaves and the thunder shaking the frame of their tiny hut. Yet only a few drops of rain trickled down to where Hope and Abigail crouched together waiting for the storm to end.

Abigail bit into the fruit, dabbing at the juice dribbling down her chin with her handkerchief, and gazed back out at Nathaniel. He thrust his spear into the water then yanked it back with a fish on its tip. Adding it to a pouch slung over his shoulder, he sloshed through the water a few paces and regained his stance. Honorable, hard-working, strong, resourceful Hope let out a ragged breath. She had a long road to travel before she could be respectable enough to catch the eye of a man like Nathaniel. And she was beginning to fear that particular road would be all uphill.

A loud curse drew her attention to the motley band under the leadership of Major Paine. Three sailors, all bare-chested and drenched in sweat, hacked away at logs while Major Paine and Mr. Hendrick sat on a rock in the shade, periodically shouting orders to them. Off in the distance, Mrs. Hendrick and Elise sat beneath a huge calabash tree. Elise played with something in her lap while poor Mrs. Hendrick leaned back against the trunk, fanning herself with an oversized leaf. Hope longed to go visit them and see how they fared, especially Elise, but Nathaniel had forbidden her and Abigail to go near Major Paine without an escort.

Shivering, Hope drew her knees to her chest, wondering why the weather had suddenly turned cold. Yet had it? The sun still beat down on them from above, the morning breeze had dissipated, and ripples of heat sizzled up from the sand.

Belying the chill on her skin, beads of perspiration rose on her forehead, and she dabbed them with her sleeve. What she wouldn't give for a bath and a change of clothes. But she was complaining again, and as she gazed at Abigail, humming a tune as she took the last bite of mango, Hope realized she had a far way to go before she could claim such a sweet spirit.

Leaves rustled, footsteps thudded, and the charming Mr. Keese appeared, hoisting two buckets splashing with water. Setting them down, he placed his hands at his hips and gave her a saucy wink. "May I offer you a drink, Miss Hope?"

Hope couldn't help but smile at the tall, robust man who, although but a few years younger than her, seemed boyish in many ways. Straight, sandy hair grazed his shoulders, contrasting with dark eyebrows that were poised in a perpetual sarcastic arch. That coupled with his mischievous grin made him look both dangerous ... and inviting.

"That would be nice, Mr. Keese, thank you."

"Freshly drawn just for you." He plunged a large shell into the liquid and knelt beside her, tipping it to her mouth.

The sweet water cooled her tongue, instantly reviving her. "Thank you."

Turning, Mr. Keese handed the remainder to Abigail, accidentally rubbing thighs with Hope. Or was it accidental? The grin on his face spoke otherwise. Shifting her gaze away, Hope scooted back. She couldn't deny his attentions eased the ache in her heart, especially in light of Nathaniel's blatant disregard, but she must resist the urge to keep returning to her old ways.

After Abigail drank her fill and returned the shell, Mr. Keese dunked it in the bucket again and poured water over his head, then shook his hair, sprinkling them all.

"That be one way to stay cool, says I." Kreggs chuckled.

Giggling, Hope fought off a shiver while admiring Mr. Keese's strong jaw and playful mannerisms, and wondered why her heart wasn't drawn to him. They were kindred spirits, after all—carefree, wild, unbeholden to anyone or any

God—and he certainly had not kept his interest in her a secret. But then again, Hope had never had any difficulty attracting men of his ilk.

When the laughter died down, everyone but Hope resumed their tasks. "I feel so useless. Mr. Keese, you collect water and wood. Kreggs and Hanson pick fruit. Abigail weaves baskets"—she smiled at her friend—"next she'll be making clothes for us all, no doubt. And Mr. Mason catches fish. I can't even crack open a coconut." She grabbed a handful of sand and let it sift through her fingers.

Mr. Keese plopped beside her, took her hand and placed a kiss upon it. "Why distress yourself, miss? Why not enjoy the fortune of having so many to care for you. Like a princess among her admirers."

"A condition Miss Hope should be quite familiar with." Nathaniel's brown eyes locked upon her as disapproval tightened the lines of his face. With a spear in one hand, a sack of fish in the other, he towered over them like Poseidon emerging from the depths to punish his subjects.

"On the contrary, I wish to help." Hope struggled to rise, but the world began to spin. Tiny sparks flitted across her vision as Mr. Keese assisted her to her feet. She forced her eyes to focus on Nathaniel. "I know I can't do much, but I'm not beyond attempting any task you give me, Mr. Mason."

Nathaniel snorted and tossed the sack of fish to Hanson, who had just sauntered into the clearing. "Skin those, if you please, Hanson."

"Aye, sir." The lanky sailor sank down by the fire and went to work.

"How did you learn to fish like that?" Mr. Keese asked. "And to build these shelters? Lud, such skill. It's incredible."

Nathaniel shrugged as he rubbed a long purple scar etched down his side, and Hope wondered where he'd received such a wound. "I spent time on the shores of Barbados fending for myself."

"We owe you a great debt, Mr. Mason." Abigail laid

down her basket and rose to her feet.

"Indeed." Mr. Keese clapped him on the back. "We have all benefited from such an adventurous childhood."

"Adventurous?" Nathaniel frowned. "I wouldn't call it such."

Still, Hope couldn't help but wonder how Lord Falkland would handle himself in such a savage environment. Always adorned in the latest London fashions without spot or wrinkle, Arthur was not a man to be found half-naked thrusting a spear into the crashing surf. She giggled at the vision.

The smell of fish curled her nose as Nathaniel's gaze found hers again and seemed to bore right through her, pricking her guilt once again. She raised her chin. "I may not be able to contribute very much, but I believe I shall take some food over to Mrs. Hendrick and her daughter. They don't look well, and I doubt they're being fed as much as we are." She skirted around Mr. Keese, grabbed some mangos and plantains from the barrel, and dropped them into an empty bucket.

"Why not leave a platter out for them tonight?" Mr. Keese's tone stung with sarcasm. "They've been stealing our food after we retire anyway."

"They have?" Abigail's voice lifted.

Grabbing the bucket, Hope turned to leave, then wished she hadn't moved so fast. Trees and sky spun around her, and she drew a deep breath and waited for the dizziness to fade.

"Aye." Hanson's knife halted over the fish he was skinning. "I've heard 'em more than once. Thought they was rats at first. Then when I peeked out o' the hut, I realized they were!" He chuckled. "Big rats, that is."

Hope had heard rustling at night as well, but the thought that it might be some dangerous animal had kept her frozen in place. "There's plenty of fruit on the island. Why can't they eat that?" She wiped the perspiration dotting her neck.

"Naw, miss," Kreggs pointed his knife toward the trees.

"We've scavenged most o' the food near the shore. Ye have to go deep in the forest, an' it be slim pickins even there."

Nathaniel ran a hand through his damp hair. "I'm well aware of the situation."

"And it doesn't prick your ire?" Mr. Keese snorted.

"I says we post a guard." Kreggs dug his knife into the chunk of wood in his hand.

"They are welcome to whatever fish we have to spare." Nathaniel squatted by the fire and poked a stick into the simmering embers. "We can't very well let them starve."

Abigail moved to stand beside Nathaniel. "Of course not. What's ours is theirs."

Setting down the bucket, Hope glanced toward the incoming rollers, anywhere but at Nathaniel and Abigail united in cause, united in temperament, united in beliefs, united in …

She sighed. The crystalline waters beckoned her.

"But they ain't worked for it." Hanson swatted at a fly hovering over his fish.

"And don't forget the major drew a sword on you," Mr. Keese added.

Nathaniel rubbed beneath his chin. "I can hardly forget that."

"Then why the devil should we supply them with food when they threatened to tie us to trees?" Mr. Keese plucked a papaya from Hope's bucket.

"Because they are fellow human beings, and we are called to forgive," Nathaniel replied.

Abigail and Nathaniel exchanged a smile that pricked at Hope's heart. Regardless, she could not help but admire a man who would share food with his enemies. And Abigail as well. Both of them were saints.

Hope rubbed her forehead against another wave of dizziness. "Mrs. Hendrick is in a family way, and Miss Elise is but a child. Neither have a choice in the matter." She started toward the other camp when a wave of nausea stole her breath. The bucket slipped from her grasp. Fruit tumbled onto the sand. Could she not even do this one thing right? She raised a hand to her head. The trees, the hut, the people, the sea spun around her—a landscape of hazy browns, blues, and greens.

"Miss Hope ... Miss Hope?" Nathaniel's voice sounded hollow and distant. Strong hands clutched her arm. "Blast it all!"

She tried to walk, but her feet turned to jelly and she collapsed—much to her relief—into the safety of welcoming arms.

A cool hand touched her forehead. Abigail's sweet voice eased over her.

"Heaven help us, she's burning up with fever."

Chapter 16

Red flames leapt all around Hope. Crackling …
sizzling … blazing. She bolted to her feet. Fiery
talons snapped at her, nipped at her gown, fingered her hair.
Sweat slid into her eyes. She blinked and ran the sleeve of
her gown across her forehead and swerved, seeking a way
out. The flames spun all around her in a blurred circle of red
and orange.

The hut was on fire.

Her tongue felt like sand. Her heart crashed against her
ribs. Where was Abigail?

"Abigail!" Hope screamed. "Abigail, Mr. Mason!"
Searing pain spiraled through her, starting at her feet then
cinching around her stomach and raging into her head.

Beyond the fire, the gray silhouette of a man shifted in
the darkness. "Mr. Mason?"

The shape took form—eyes, nose, lips, hair, and clothing
appearing on the figure as he approached, stepped through
the flames, and halted before her.

"Arthur." Hope's breath caught at the sight of the man
she'd once thought she loved with all her heart.

The fire disappeared and the bulkhead of a ship's cabin

formed around them.

"I tell you, Captain, I don't know the woman." Lord Falkland's handsome lips flattened, and he turned to face another man who materialized from the darkness.

Captain Brenham doffed his plumed tricorn and tossed it onto his desk. "Then perhaps ye can explain t' me why she insists ye are her betrothed?"

"Preposterous!" A woman suddenly appeared beside Lord Falkland. "My Arthur cannot be engaged when he already has a wife." She waved a silk fan over her elegant coiffure, sending curls dancing about her neck. "Why, look at her. She is no doubt a fortune-hunting strumpet." She eyed Hope with disdain.

"How dare you!" Hope charged toward her, but Lord Falkland held up his cane, barring her passage. Fear and desperation coalesced into a burning lump in her throat. "Arthur, why are you doing this? Tell them who I am. Who is this woman?" Placing her hand on his arm, she searched his eyes for a hint of affection, a hint of the love she'd grown to expect—the love she'd risked everything to possess.

But he would not meet her gaze. He thudded his cane onto the deck and yanked his arm from beneath her touch.

"As I have told you, Captain. I've never seen this woman before." He patted the other woman's hand and placed a kiss upon it just as he used to do with Hope's.

Blinking, Hope reeled backward. Memories danced through her mind like jesters, taunting her—memories of the tender love she and Arthur had shared, of sweet promises whispered in the middle of the night, memories of being loved, cherished, cared for.

"What d'ye intend I do wit' her?" The captain cocked his head and studied Hope as if she were a chest of gold.

Lord Falkland shrugged. "Why should I care?"

"Because you love me! You promised to marry me!" Throwing all propriety aside, Hope clung to him with both hands. The lavender scent he doused himself with snaked around her, making her dizzy. "What are you doing?" Her heart thumped wildly. Her knees shook. Tears poured down her cheeks.

"Madam, control yourself." Arthur tugged from her grasp.

"Release my husband at once!" The woman pried Hope from Arthur's arm, then shoved her back. "Captain, I protest. Must we continue to endure this humiliation? The woman is clearly deranged."

Hope tumbled to the deck. Heat surged through her, and the floor began to spin.

Captain Brenham clamped his thick fingers around Hope's arm and jerked her to her feet. Pain fired through her shoulder. "Me apologies, mam. By all means, take yer leave. I'll be more 'n happy to deal wit' her."

"Very well, then." Casting one last repugnant look toward Hope, Mrs. Falkland turned and pulled Arthur along behind her.

Lord Falkland glanced at Hope over his shoulder. Through her tear-blurred vision, she thought she saw a flicker of remorse cross his features. And then he was gone.

Along with all of Hope's dreams.

Greed glinted in the captain's eyes. "Aye, I know jest what t' do wit' ye."

Flames shot up around her again, suffocating her and consuming all her remaining strength.

Something touched her forehead. Soft and cool. "She's dreaming," a muffled voice said.

"Seems more like a nightmare." A deep male tone responded. *Nathaniel's voice.*

Had he come to save her? Hope tried to pry her eyes open, but someone seemed to have sewn them shut. She lifted a hand to her face, groping for the cause, and found naught but moist, simmering skin. Thrusting out her arms, she probed for the source of those wonderful voices.

A large, calloused hand gripped hers and held it tight.

"'Tis us, Miss Hope. We are here." She clung to it with what little strength she could muster, drawing comfort from the caring touch of another human being.

"He left me. He lied to me."

"Shhh … Hope, you have a fever." Abigail's soft voice caressed her like the cool cloth brushing over her forehead. A spark of joy assuaged her grief. Her friends had not perished in the flames.

"The hut is on fire." The words squeaked from Hope's dry throat.

"No, you are safe. Nothing is on fire," Nathaniel said. Was he caressing her hand? And what was that infernal pounding in her head?

She rubbed her eyes and managed to pry them open, but only blurry mirages met her gaze. "Where am I?"

"You are in our hut." Abigail's hazy figure leaned over her and dabbed a cloth on her neck.

Hope shifted her gaze to Nathaniel. The slight wave of his brown hair came into focus, then those dark eyes that reminded Hope of the coffee her sister Faith liked to drink. He shifted his jaw, dusted with black stubble. But it was the look in his eyes that drew her attention. Concern, fear, and something else. Such a different look from the one she had just seen in Arthur's eyes.

"Lord Falkland was here." She shook her head, trying to jar loose the tangled web in her mind.

"It was only a dream."

"Only a dream," she repeated. An unrelenting heaviness pressed upon her eyes, and no longer able to fight it, she closed them and faded into darkness.

Nathaniel released Hope's hand with a sigh and rubbed his aching eyes. The first hint of dawn glowed through the leaves of the hut as the crickets hushed to silence. After Hope had collapsed in his arms, he and Abigail had diligently cared for her during the rest of the day and then all through the night. But despite their continuous ministrations, she had remained unconscious, save for the brief moment when she'd just woken. Regardless, her fever still soared, and Nathaniel feared the worst. "At least she awakened."

Abigail smiled as she dabbed the wet cloth over Hope's face, pink with fever. "'Tis a good sign." But her unsteady voice stole conviction from her statement. "Who is Lord Falkland?"

"The man who abandoned her in St. Kitts." Nathaniel flexed his jaw. From the few intelligible words Hope had uttered, he gleaned her memory of Lord Falkland's betrayal had been quite traumatic—and quite painful.

"Ah, no wonder she has nightmares about him." Abigail sank back, folding her legs beneath her, and dropped the cloth into the bucket. "Her fever is far too high."

Nathaniel grimaced and sat on a barrel on the other side of Hope. "Do you know the cause?"

Abigail swallowed, her hazel eyes stricken. "I fear it is marsh fever. I saw much of it on Antigua when I worked with my parents."

Marsh fever. Nathaniel's stomach coiled in a knot. "But isn't that ..." He didn't want to say the word *fatal* aloud, couldn't bear to think it, let alone hear it.

"It can be." Abigail's eyes swam, and she stood, wiping sand and leaves from her skirt. "I'm going in search of Indian Fever Bark. I believe I saw some in the jungle." She headed for the flap of sailcloth that served as a door. "I can make some tea from it. It's all I know to do."

"Ask Kreggs to accompany you. I heard him up and moving around earlier."

She nodded, pushed aside the cloth, and left the hut.

Several hours later, Nathaniel shielded his eyes from the sun as he emerged from the tiny shack. Stretching his cramped legs, he stared at the breakers glistening in white, foamy bands across the blue sea. Yet their beauty held no allure for him today. Gavin stood knee deep among the incoming waves, spear in hand, battling to keep his balance, but as soon as he spotted Nathaniel, he ploughed through the water onto shore.

Hanson entered the camp, his arms full of firewood, as Gavin rushed toward Nathaniel.

"What news?"

Nathaniel shook his head. "Abigail … Miss Sheldon and I gave her some tea, but I don't know how much she swallowed. She's resting now."

Hanson dropped the load of wood onto the sand and scratched his chest, eyeing the hut nervously.

Panic sparked across Gavin's boyish face. "And the fever?"

"It hasn't broken." Only worsened. Nathaniel's gut hardened into a ball of lead.

"I must see her." Gavin tossed down the spear and started for the hut.

Nathaniel held up a hand. "I'm told it is contagious. Miss Sheldon and I have already been exposed. No sense in putting yourself in danger."

"I'll jest go find some fruit." Hanson darted from the clearing.

"But if there's something I can do," Gavin said. "Some comfort I can give her."

So Gavin *did* harbor some affection for Hope.

Shrugging off the uncomfortable feeling, Nathaniel released a heavy sigh. "She's not conscious. We can do nothing now but pray."

"A desperate measure for weak men." Gavin snickered.

"Or a powerful measure for courageous men," Nathaniel responded with authority, even as he wondered where the words had come from. For he felt naught but weak and desperate as Gavin had said. He needed to pray—and pray hard.

Nathaniel pointed to a flounder lying on a bed of leaves

near Gavin's spear. "I see you've caught a fish."

"Only one in two hours." Gavin's boyish smile returned. "And a tiny one as you can see. I fear I don't possess your skill with the spear." He raised his brows in invitation. "We could use some fish for supper."

"I need some rest first." Nathaniel hated spending even a few hours away from his vigil over Hope, but if he didn't, he wouldn't be much use for anything.

He headed toward his hut, but a red and white figure storming toward him caught his eye. Major Paine. Nathaniel groaned.

Drawing up to his full height, the major gripped the hilt of his sword. "What has happened to Miss Hope?"

"She is ill with fever." Nathaniel rubbed his eyes, willing the man to disappear.

"Fever? Egad, I knew you couldn't take care of her." He brushed past Nathaniel, leaving the stench of sweat and moldy clothes in his wake. "I'll take her back to our camp where she can be tended to properly."

Nathaniel turned "Be my guest, Major. Perhaps you have discovered a cure for Marsh Fever?"

The major stopped in mid stride. "Marsh Fever you say?" He faced Nathaniel, his ruddy face fading to white. "Miss Sheldon attends to her?"

Nathaniel nodded.

"Then 'tis best not to disturb her." He stretched his neck. "But be advised, Mr. Mason, I shall return to check on her soon."

"I wait for the honor." Nathaniel bowed, an unavoidable grin on his lips.

With a snort, the major sauntered off to where the sailors still hammered away on a raft that was beginning to take shape.

But Nathaniel had neither the time nor the inclination to worry about that now. The totality of his thoughts and his heart focused on the lady burning up with fever not five yards away. As he plodded toward his hut, memories twisted through his mind, setting off a blaze of panic. His mother had been deathly ill, eaten alive by some unnamed disease. Her vocation and poverty kept all physicians at bay. Even the priests would not set foot in her house. Nathaniel had been only eleven years old, but he had done the only thing he could think to do. He prayed. But his prayers had fallen lifeless before God's throne, leaving him an orphan.

Staggering into his hut, he fell to his knees. "God, if you answer just one of my prayers, please let it be this one."

Chapter 17

Two days passed and exhaustion crushed Nathaniel like an anchor. Sitting beside Hope in the stifling hut, he dabbed her burning face and neck with a wet cloth and eased moist hair from her forehead. A shroud of darkness as black as ebony had fallen outside the hut, and although he and Abigail continued to do what they could to keep Hope cool, her fever remained high. Now, with her breathing shallow and labored, he feared the end was near.

Dark lashes fluttered over her inflamed cheeks as she moaned and writhed on the leafy bed. Oh, how he longed to see those clear sapphire eyes staring back at him again—even when they shot sparks of biting sarcasm his way—instead of the dull hazy blue which had fixated on him of late.

He bowed his head. "Oh, Lord, don't take her. Please let her live."

For the life of him, he couldn't understand the dread that consumed him at the thought of losing her. He'd seen many people die—friends, shipmates, even his own mother. But as grievous as their passings were, he could not shake the feeling that if Hope died, he would lose a part of himself forever.

Rubbing his eyes, he wondered at his sanity—this strange obsession he'd had with this lady ever since he'd first laid eyes on her. The woman had brought him nothing but trouble. Even back in Charles Towne, she'd made a habit of either ignoring him or belittling him whenever their paths crossed.

A burning rose in his side, and he rubbed his old wound and released a sigh of frustration. His fascination with her was surely due to a flaw in his character—something passed down from his mother, and perhaps her parents before her.

Hope gasped and tossed her head back and forth. Sweat beaded on her neck and chest and molded her chemise to her body. He eased the sail cloth they used as a blanket a bit higher, forbidding his gaze to wander into danger. Then drawing his knees to his chest, he dropped his head onto his arms and allowed his tired eyes to close, if only for a moment.

"Nathaniel?"

The sound seemed to come from far away. "Nathaniel?"

Rubbing his eyes, he lifted his head and smiled when he saw Hope staring up at him. She reached a trembling hand toward him, and he took it between his. Heat scorched his skin and radiated up his arm, but he didn't allow the stab of fear to weaken his smile. "You spoke my Christian name."

"Surely," her faint voice cracked, "formalities can be excused when one is dying."

"Dying … Nonsense, you're not dying."

"You're too honorable a man to be a good liar. You forget I've had much experience with liars."

Nathaniel swallowed. "The tea Miss Sheldon has been giving you may yet perform its magic."

"I fear I shall need more than simple magic." She struggled for a breath and glanced around the hut. "What of Mrs. Hendrick and Elise? Did you take them food?"

"You concern yourself with them when you are … in such a state?" By the board, this lady constantly surprised him. Her eyes remained locked on his, one determined brow arched, awaiting an answer.

"Yes, never fear, I took them enough food to last several days."

"Thank you." She squeezed his hand, the miniscule effort visible in the lines on her face.

"Nathaniel." She coughed. "I must tell you something."

"You need your rest." Nathaniel patted her face with the cool cloth. The normal pearly glow of her skin had faded to a gray sheen, broken by red blotches where the fever consumed her. She struggled to breathe.

"Nay. I must. I know I've told you this before, but it weighs heavy on my heart." She paused. "I am so sorry about your ship."

"Fire and thunder." He dropped the cloth into the bucket and raked a hand through his hair. "You think that matters to me now?"

"Why wouldn't it?" Her forehead wrinkled. "It was worth a fortune." She drew a ragged breath. "I've caused you so much trouble."

A chill scraped down his back, stiffening every nerve, followed by the eerie sense *something* was in the hut with them. Running a sleeve over his sweaty forehead, he scanned the palm fronds that formed the walls and roof where dark shadows cast by the lantern light hovered like beasts about to pounce.

"See. You cannot deny it." Hope choked out a laugh.

Shaking away the prick of unease, he faced her. "I will not deny misfortune has followed me lately, but as to the cause, I cannot say."

"Cannot, or will not?" She brushed her fingers over his hand in a familiar way that shocked and delighted him. "You are too kind, Nathaniel, but then, that is your nature, is it not?" She closed her eyes as if they were too heavy to keep open.

Releasing her other hand, Nathaniel wrung out the cloth

and brushed it over her cheeks and forehead.

Hope blinked and drew a deep breath. "Please tell my sisters how sorry I am to worry them so. I've not been a good sister." A smile faltered on her lips. "And tell my father he owes you a ship."

"Shhh, now. You can tell him yourself."

"Nay." She chuckled then broke into a cough. "He won't listen to me. He has never had much use for me, I'm afraid."

Sorrow constricted Nathaniel's throat. He'd always assumed Hope had grown up in a good home, sharing her life with an adoring father and loving sisters.

"Now, now, your father loves you."

"He's oft gone, and when he's home, he makes no effort to hide his disapproval."

"I doubt that. Some fathers can be gruff is all."

"Now I know I'm dying." Her lips curved. "You're being far too kind."

Nathaniel eased a finger over her cheek. He'd not seen such bravery in the face of death, even from hardened sailors. *No!* He would not relinquish her to the grave. He would not give up!

"Death need not be the end, Hope. God has offered a way to eternal life." Nathaniel detested the fear muffling his voice. He hated talking about death. Just saying the word gave the devouring spirit more power. But he had to ensure Hope's eternal destiny—just in case.

She groaned. "For some, I suppose. For people like you. But not for me."

He dropped the cloth and took both her hands in his. "For all. You have only to accept His gift."

"I fear in my case, your God has withdrawn His offer."

Nathaniel opened his mouth to respond, but she squeezed his hands and shook her head.

The stench of decay and hopelessness crept around him, prickling his skin despite the heat. Crickets harped their shrill cries into the night, vying with the thunderous crash of the surf.

"Please don't laugh when I tell you this," Hope whispered, her eyes closing again. "I always dreamed I would open an orphanage—take in every unwanted child I could find and raise them with more love than they would ever need."

Nathaniel stared at her agape. Children? *Hope?* Somehow he'd always pictured her marrying a wealthy landowner, surrounding herself with opulence, and being waited on by a bevy of servants. Yet he could not deny the ease with which she had befriended Miss Elise and the way the child adored her.

But *children?* Nathaniel had abandoned his desire for children long ago, for he did not trust himself to be a good father. No doubt he'd corrupt them with whatever depravity slithered through his veins.

Hope moaned and began wheezing. Easing his arm behind her shoulders, he winced at the heat radiating from her frail body, then lifted her and brought a shell-full of water to her mouth. "Drink."

She parted her lips and took a few sips but then folded into his arms with a wretched sigh and faded again into unconsciousness.

Nathaniel laid her down, forcing back tears.

"How is she?" Abigail's soft voice jarred him from sinking deeper into grief.

He shook his head as she lowered to sit on the other side of Hope and rubbed her arms. Outside, wind whistled against the leafy walls of the hut.

"Sounds like a storm is coming," he said.

"Yes, but I …" Abigail's voice trailed off as she scanned the hut, still rubbing her arms.

"What is it?"

She nodded toward Hope. "How fares her soul?"

Guilt churned in Nathaniel's gut. "If you mean, did I speak to her of her eternal destination, I tried, but her heart remains locked."

She took Hope's other hand. "Something dark pulls her. I feel it."

Nathaniel studied Abigail, remembering their time in the hold of the ship with the dying sailor. "You have a sense of these things, a spiritual sense."

Truth be told, he believed he did as well. How many times had he sensed the same malevolent force in his mother's chamber when he'd been a boy?

"Perhaps." She shrugged. "My parents told me I saw things as a child that were not there. Beautiful beings, angels and butterflies and bright lights." She huffed. "But as I've grown, the things I perceive are not so beautiful." She took the cloth and wiped Hope's neck. "Perhaps this is no sickness at all, but a spiritual battle."

A battle? Of course. The enemy wanted Hope, wanted to kill her and drag her down to hell. What did Paul say in Ephesians? "For we wrestle not against flesh and blood, but against principalities, against powers, against the rulers of the darkness of this world, against spiritual wickedness in high places," he quoted and Abigail gave him a nod of agreement.

Righteous anger welled up inside him. "What can we do?"

"We must pray."

"I *have* been." He struggled to rise and fisted his hands.

"Pray like they did in the Bible." Abigail rose and gripped his arm. "James, the brother of our Lord, said that if anyone was sick among us, we should have the elders pray over him and anoint him with oil in the name of the Lord."

The wind began to howl outside, flapping the loose leaves of the hut.

"I have no oil, and I am certainly no elder."

"You have water, which I'm sure God would bless, and I'm not so convinced about the other." Abigail released him and brushed the hair from her forehead.

Nathaniel snorted.

"What harm could it do?" Her voice held a challenge.

Nathaniel glanced at Hope. Her lips had turned a bluish gray, her chest pitched as she struggled for each breath. Sweat glistened on her skin. His palms grew sweaty and a metallic taste spilled into his mouth. He was afraid. Afraid to pray for the healing of another woman. Afraid he would fail—again.

A burning sensation ignited in his hand. A warm tingling. He shook it, trying to stir his blood, but it only grew.

Abigail stared at him expectantly ... waiting.

Nathaniel closed his eyes. *Lord, is this Your will?*

No answer, save a soft whisper floating on the breeze. *"Believe."*

Dropping to his knees, Nathaniel dipped his finger into the bucket and traced a cross on Hope's forehead. "In the name of Jesus, I command you, sickness, to leave this woman."

His shout echoed against the green walls, pounding through the moist air like the sound of a judge's gavel.

Hope didn't move. The wind ceased howling outside, and silence shrouded the hut as if they'd been plunged to the bottom of the sea. The lantern flickered. Nathaniel stared at Abigail. Instantly, the heavy presence fled. The bristling over his skin eased. His muscles relaxed, and the stink of death dissipated, leaving the smell of moist earth and leaves in its wake. The insects resumed their chorus outside as the wind danced once again through the leaves.

Wide-eyed, Abigail scanned the enclosure then smiled. "Thank God!" She clapped her hands.

Nathaniel laid the back of his hand on Hope's forehead. Still searing hot. He nudged her but she did not awaken. "She's still sick."

"Did you not sense it? Something powerful happened here." Abigail's voice rang with excitement.

Truth be told, Nathaniel *had* felt something, not in the

physical sense, but somewhere deep inside of him. Yet perhaps it had just been wishful thinking.

"Call me if she wakes up." He rose, pushed the flap aside, and stormed from the hut.

His prayers had failed once again. And once again, a woman he cared for would die.

Chapter 18

C lank cling chime clank! The jarring sounds jolted Hope from a deep, peaceful place. She peeled open her eyes. Glittering patches of sunlight twirled across a dome of green like dancers flitting across a stage. A light breeze, laden with salt and the sweet nectar of flowers, feathered over her. She breathed deeply, allowing the air to fill her lungs. The breath of life. She was alive!

Pressing her hands onto the leaves on either side of her, she struggled to rise, but leaned back on her shaky arms as a wave of dizziness threatened to plunge her back into oblivion.

Clank clink clank. Male laughter blared above the pounding waves.

To her right, a damp cloth sitting beside a bucket of water invoked memories of angels holding vigil throughout the long hours of the night. A plate of half-eaten mango near the leafy wall brought a vision of Abigail tenderly coercing the sweet fruit into Hope's mouth.

Raising a hand to her chest, Hope dropped her eyes to her ragged petticoat, whose worn fabric did not leave much to the imagination, and then to her gown draped over a branch strung across the ceiling of the hut. Heat blossomed up her neck. How much of her state of undress had Nathaniel seen?

Cling. Clank.

After several attempts, Hope rose onto wobbly legs and managed to slip into what remained of the once-attractive green muslin dress she'd borrowed in St. Kitts.

St. Kitts. Just thinking of that infamous port sent a shiver through her. Yet, for some reason, the harrowing day she'd spent there seemed an eon ago.

Clank clink clank. If not for the accompanying laughter, she would think they were under attack. Pushing aside the door flap, Hope leaned on the bamboo pole forming the front brace of the hut. The trill of myriad birds announced her entrance even as sunlight caressed her face with warmth. The glint of flashing steel drew her gaze to Nathaniel and Mr. Keese hard at swordplay upon the shore. Sweat glistened on their bronzed chests in the morning sun. Beyond them, the glittering turquoise sea billowed toward the island as if it hadn't a care in the world.

Nathaniel twirled the tip of his sword over Gavin's midsection and offered some taunt Hope could not make out. Chuckling, Gavin dove to the left, spun around, and met Nathaniel's blade with a *clank*! Back and forth they parried, their feet spitting up sand as they shuffled across the beach. Nathaniel moved with the confidence and ease of a man who had been weaned on the sword, but how could that be? Hope's head grew light watching them, and she raised a hand to her brow.

"Hope!" Abigail entered the camp carrying a bucket of water and smiled as if Hope were the queen of England. "You should have called me to assist you." She set down the bucket and clutched Hope's arm, bearing her weight, assisting her to sit on a fallen log at the center of camp.

Returning her smile, Hope struggled to catch her breath. "You've done far too much for me already."

"How are you feeling?" Abigail placed a hand on her cheek. "The fever is gone. Thank God."

"A bit feeble." Hope dug her toes into the sand. "How long have I been sick?"

"A week."

A week? The past few days jumbled together in a blur that seemed at times only minutes and at others as long as months..

"Let me get you something to eat." Abigail started to rise, but Hope placed a hand on her arm. "How can I ever thank you, Abigail? I don't remember much, but I do remember you—your soothing voice, your gentle touch. You seemed always to be at my side."

Abigail's eyes moistened, and she patted Hope's hand. "'Twas my pleasure. But I wasn't the only one who tended you."

Laughter and another *clank* drew Hope's attention back out to the beach, where Nathaniel sprang to the left just as Gavin thrust his sword toward him.

Abigail followed her gaze and smiled. "I've not seen Mr. Mason so distraught. He barely slept during your illness and refused to leave your side for more than a few minutes at a time."

Shock sped through Hope as fleeting memories flickered across her mind—Nathaniel's firm grip on her hands, his scent of wood and tar drawing her from her sleep, his whispers of encouragement tantalizing her ears. Were the memories real, or had she conjured them from her feverish dreams? "I should think he'd be pleased to be rid of me." She let out a tiny chuckle that belied the jab in her heart.

Abigail's eyes sparkled with playfulness. "Rid of you? Why, he was struck with grief at the thought of losing you." She leaned toward Hope. "I do believe the man fancies you."

Hope flinched, trying to ignore the sudden thrill surging through her. Yet Abigail's tone carried none of the jealous sting Hope would expect from a woman who had set her affections upon the same man. In truth, the more she became acquainted with Abigail, the more Hope realized what a high standard she set.

And how unattainable that standard was becoming for Hope.

"Preposterous." Hope chuckled. "The man is a saint. He cares for everyone." *And he deserves someone like you. Someone who won't tarnish his reputation and break his heart.*

"Hmm." Abigail grinned as if she withheld a secret.

Kreggs scampered into the clearing and scratched his mop of gray hair. "Well, I'll be a two-legged swine. Look at ye. Up and well after we all thought ye were knockin' on the gates of Hades."

Hanson followed on his heels and tossed an armload of coconuts onto a growing pile. His wary gaze wandered over her, and he turned to Abigail. "There be no more fever?"

"Nay. God healed her."

God? Impossible. Fresh water, salty air, bark tea, the love and care of others, perhaps. But God, save *her*? Why would He waste His time?

The clanking stopped. Nathaniel held the tip of his sword at Gavin's neck, a victorious grin lighting up his face. Lowering his blade, Mr. Keese shrugged his surrender, and the two men started for camp.

Hope's heart lurched in her chest. She hurriedly attempted to brush aside the tangled curls from her face and straighten the torn lace at the bodice of her gown, but it was hopeless. She must present such a horrid sight. Then why, when she lifted her gaze, did Nathaniel stare at her as if she were a lone spring of water in the middle of a desert.

Gavin plopped down beside her. "Miss Hope, 'tis wonderful to see you up and looking so well."

She couldn't help but smile at the playful gleam in his blue eyes. "Thank you, Mr. Keese."

"Gavin, if you please. Surely being stranded together on

an island calls for dispensing with formalities, don't you think, Nathaniel?"

Nathaniel shoved a wayward strand of hair behind his ear. "Indeed." Yet his eyes still pierced her with an intensity that made her lower hers. Unfortunately, they landed on his thickly corded chest, still flexing from exertion. Fingering the lacy cuff of her sleeve, she shifted on the log and focused her attention on the incoming waves.

"I owe you my heartfelt thanks, Mr. Mason," she said without looking at him. "I understand from Abigail that you spent many hours caring for me."

"It pleases me to see you well again." At the sound of his voice, scattered memories flashed through her mind, bits and pieces of intimacies she shared during her feverish trance—intimacies about her sisters, her father, her dreams. Horrified, she scanned the shoreline, wondering what other things the fever had loosened from her tongue. A flush sped through her as if she'd been doused in hot water. The sensation intensified when she caught sight of Major Paine striding in their direction.

"Perhaps something to eat?" Gavin hopped from his seat and plucked a guava from a pile of fruit, then tore off a piece of dried fish hanging over the fire.

Hanson broke a stick on his knee and tossed it into the flames. "What baffles me is how she sits here to tell the tale. I ne'er seen anyone with Marsh Fever rise from their bed again."

Marsh Fever. Fear bristled the back of Hope's neck.

"God is more powerful than Marsh Fever, Mr. Hanson." Abigail straightened her skirts. "Nathaniel simply did what God's Word instructs. He anointed Hope and prayed the prayer of faith over her." Her dauntless tone attempted to cast all doubt away, yet a frown marred Gavin's brow, echoing the niggling questions burrowed deep in Hope's heart.

For if what Abigail said were true, if God was real, and if He loved Hope enough to heal her … well, it would change everything.

"Two hours later, the fever left her." Abigail sent an admiring glance toward Nathaniel as if he were Moses parting the Red Sea, and a nod of intimate understanding passed between them.

Gavin snorted as he sat beside Hope and offered her the guava. "Perchance this smacks of some divine touch, perhaps not. I care only for the outcome, and that is to see this beautiful lady restored to full health." He winked at her, his flirtatious ways temporarily soothing her pangs of jealousy. Accepting the fruit, Hope took a bite. The sweet pulp burst in her mouth and slid down her throat like a soothing balm. "Thank you, Gavin." She admired the sharp cut of his jaw and handsome features, but against her will, her attention drifted back to Nathaniel.

Kreggs's forehead puckered. "Ye healed her? Ye aren't some kind o' witch, are ye?" He took a step back.

Nathaniel raised a palm. "Nay. Wrong source of power, my friend. And I didn't heal her. God did. I was merely His instrument. In truth, I'm ashamed to admit that I wasn't sure He would."

"Well, I can't deny me own eyes." Hanson rubbed them and squinted toward Hope once more.

"There are those who recover from Marsh Fever." Gavin bit a piece of fruit and dragged his bare arm over his mouth, wiping away a trickle of juice.

"None this quick." Kreggs rubbed his chin. "'Tis a rare thing."

Abigail smiled at the aged sailor as Hope took another bite of the guava.

Hanson sank onto a boulder and stretched his lanky frame. "It do make me wonder about God. Whether what I heard about Him is true."

Nathaniel glanced over his shoulder at Major Paine heading toward them, and his expression tightened. "If you've heard He is good, loving, and almighty, then you've heard correctly."

Suddenly losing her appetite, Hope set aside the remainder of the fruit and tugged on a lock of her hair, remembering the terror she'd felt as she approached death's door. Hopeless, endless terror, as if some hungry, malevolent force greedily waited for her to pass beyond this world.

"I daresay, Miss Hope, so good to see you well again." Major Paine's nasally tone snapped Hope from her dismal musings. He stood at the outskirts of their camp, one hand at his waist and an insincere leer upon his lips. "Mr. and Mrs. Hendrick and I were most concerned."

Gavin snorted.

"Why, thank you, Major, How kind of you." Hope nodded but did not return his smile. A breeze tossed the coils of his hair over the shoulder of his tattered red coat, where a gold epaulet once sat. The missing ornament seemed to set the major off balance as he leaned slightly toward his other side.

"Very good. Very good, then." He perused Nathaniel with disdain. "I perceive you and your friend here"—he wagged a cursory finger toward Gavin—"were partaking in a bit of swordplay."

"Indeed." Nathaniel smirked. "'Tis best to keep one's skills sharp. A man never knows when a sword might be drawn on him."

Hanson chuckled.

Tossing his fruit into the bushes, Gavin rose to his feet. "What do you want, Major? More food?"

The major stretched his neck and gripped his baldric. "I have come to inform you that we plan to set off the day after tomorrow. Our raft is complete, and we are confident we shall be able to sail safely to Puerto Rico." He shot Nathaniel a haughty glance.

"I bid you bon voyage, then." Gavin waved him off, eliciting chuckles from Kreggs and Hanson.

Nathaniel grunted and rubbed the back of his neck. "Did

you use bamboo instead of pine as I suggested?"

"By the time we received your *wise opinion*, it was too late, I'm afraid." Major Paine swatted a bug hovering about his head. "Never fear, we have tested her, and she floats quite well."

"In these shallow waters. But out at sea is a different matter." Nathaniel pointed toward the ocean and huffed. "Even if you make it to Puerto Rico, how do you hope to procure passage to Jamaica from those loyal to Spain? I beg you one last time, Major, to wait for a ship to arrive."

Hope blinked at Nathaniel's kindness. Even after all the major's cruel affronts, he still cared for the man's fate.

The major snorted. "I have every faith we shall be delivered from the sea by one of the many merchant ships sailing to Jamaica. But if we do land on Puerto Rico, I am not without my resources, I assure you." He grinned. "I'm a man of action, Mr. Mason. That is what separates you and me. You choose to wait. I choose to act."

"Let him go, Nathaniel," Gavin spat. "We'll be better off without him."

"What of Elise and Mrs. Hendrick?" Hope asked, her gaze finding them down shore nestled in the shade of a tree. "Surely you aren't planning on taking them along on such an arduous journey?"

"Mr. Hendrick will not part with his family." The major shrugged. "Besides, we have every confidence in the sturdiness of our craft."

She bit her lip. Poor Elise. She'd been frightened on the merchant brig. How much more terrified would she be on a tiny raft? And Mrs. Hendrick, with her *mal-de-mer,* would certainly fare no better, feeling the full brunt of every wave.

But it was the look of concern on Nathaniel's face that sent a wave of dread washing through Hope.

No doubt sensing Hope's dismay, Abigail took her hand in hers. "Major, I implore you. There is no sense in risking your lives. I am confident we shall be rescued soon."

"Dear lady, I have not achieved the rank of second in command under the Captain General of the Leeward Islands by following the instructions of a common sailor." He raised a haughty brow and brushed a leaf from his coat as easily as he brushed off Abigail's concern. "But I do wish that you, Miss Hope, would consider joining us."

Hope cringed, too weak to disguise her disgust. "I thank you for the offer, Major, but I prefer to stay here."

"With these"—he wrinkled his nose—"men?"

"Indeed." She gave him a labored grin then turned to Abigail and whispered, "I would prefer the company of savages to him."

Abigail giggled, but Major Paine huffed. "Very well."

"I will pray for you, Major, for all of you." Frustration edged Nathaniel's tone.

"Pray if you will." Major Paine waved a hand through the air. "But when we sail into Kingston Harbor, you will regret your stubbornness." He fingered his mustache, paused to study Hope, then spun around and strutted away.

Hope stared across the beach toward Mrs. Hendrick and Elise, fear clawing at her unsettled stomach.

"The fool," Nathaniel said, staring after him. "He's leading them all to their death."

Chapter 19

"Ah, the water is so refreshing." Abigail dove beneath the surface of the pond, sending ripples across the clear aquamarine water. Hope chuckled. No sooner had they arrived at the pool than Abigail had stripped down to her chemise and leapt into the water, seemingly unconcerned with the utter lack of privacy.

When she broke the surface, it was with a smile and a burst of laughter. "Come in, Hope. It will do you good and improve your humor, which I daresay still wallows in the mud after Major Paine's visit." Water dripped off her chin and cheeks and glittered in pools in her lashes, making her look all the more like the angel Hope suspected she truly was.

Hope dug her bare feet into the silt lining the shore and allowed the cool mud to steal away the last remnants of both her fever and her frustration. "He is an odious bore."

"You mustn't say such things, you know," Abigail said. "We never know what causes a man to behave a certain way."

In the major's case, Hope believed it was an overblown sense of his own importance coupled with a mind as shallow as a basin, but she doubted she would find agreement with the saint splashing in the water.

Loosening her final bindings, Hope stood. "Is there no one who meets your disapproval?"

Abigail dipped below the surface again and swooped back up, then drew her long chestnut hair in a bunch over her shoulder and squeezed out the water. "Some. But I try not to voice those opinions. They serve no purpose other than to invoke pain."

Expounding on the faults of others had always made Hope feel better about herself, but perhaps Abigail was right. To malign someone's character, no matter how true the observations were, was not the mark of a proper lady. As difficult as it would be to practice such restraint with someone like the major, Hope must try to follow the same rule.

Putting all thoughts of the offending man aside, she glanced at the abundance and variety of plants surrounding the pond, reflecting its beauty in the tranquil waters. Colorful birds flitted from branch to branch, their sweet melody—joined with the soothing rush of the waterfall—helped loosen the tightness in her back and chest. When she had been here last, it had been with Nathaniel to wash his wound. Their playful banter brought a smile to her lips, but she brushed the memory away. That meeting had not ended well.

The clear water of the pond beckoned, reminding Hope she hadn't had a proper bath in weeks. She shot a wary gaze at the surrounding trees, not altogether sure they were alone. Yet they had only told Nathaniel of their intended destination, and Hope knew he would not intrude upon their privacy. Major Paine, Mr. Keese, and the sailors were another sort of animal altogether. But the major had stormed off in a huff. Gavin and Nathaniel had gone fishing upon the reefs, and when Hope and Abigail had left the camp, Hanson and Kreggs were fast asleep in the sand.

Abigail dunked beneath the water again, then rose and

with arms spread, twirled around and around, creating a
pinwheel of foamy waves. "Come in, dear Hope."

Eyeing the surrounding brush, Hope slipped from her
gown and plunged in the pond after her friend. Careful not to
go beyond where she could feel the soil beneath her toes, she
took a breath and sank into the water, allowing it to envelop
her and leech away all her tension. "Oh, sweet mercy, I
forgot how good it feels to bathe!" she said when she rose for
a breath. A spray of water showered her and she turned to see
Abigail, a mischievous twinkle in her eyes.

"Of all the. . ." Hope giggled and splashed her friend in
return, and soon they were frolicking like schoolgirls on a
summer day without a care in the world.

Except Hope *did* have a care in the world. She had many
cares. Not the least of which was getting back to Charles
Towne safely.

Abigail flung water into the air then closed her eyes as
the droplets sprayed over her. There was such joy and peace
on her face, Hope could only stare at her, envious, yet also
happy to have such a friend whose very presence made her
smile. A flower petal floated by, and Abigail picked it up, her
face and eyes aglow with delight as she examined it. The
lady lived her life as if every moment was a precious gift—
even when she had neither love, family, nor fortune.

Hope could make no sense of it. Diving beneath the
water, she scrubbed her chemise, her skin, and her hair,
washing away all the filth, the sickness, and the despair of
the past months. The next hour passed by quickly as they
swam, splashed, and played like little girls, enjoying the
scenery and the refreshing water. Afterward, Hope perched
on a boulder in the sun, trying to dry her undergarments,
while Abigail stretched out in the sand beside her.

Shaking the water from her hair, Abigail leaned back on
her elbows and gazed over the pond. Her sodden chemise
clung to her tall, thin body—a body which did not lack
feminine curves in the appropriate places. Long chestnut hair,

glinting with gold and red in the sunlight, tumbled down her back in the light breeze. With those striking hazel eyes and noble cheekbones, the lady could make a fine match back in the colonies, where title or fortune did not matter as much as in England. Yet she chose to deny herself the basic comforts of life and follow a God who had allowed her parents to be butchered.

Lifting her face to the sun, Hope drew a deep breath of the fresh air, perfumed with musky earth and tropical flowers.

"How are you feeling?" Abigail asked.

"Much better. The fish and guava Gavin gave me seem to have given me a burst of energy, though I'm still a bit lightheaded."

"'Tis to be expected. You will soon regain your strength in full. I've no doubt." Abigail cocked her head and smiled. "You are the perfect example of one of God's miracles, you know."

Hope snorted. "Most who know me would not agree."

"It matters not what most would say, does it? It was God who valued you enough to save your life. His opinion is all that matters." Abigail inched her feet into the edge of the pond.

Hope swallowed. She was not fully convinced God had healed her. Nor did she want to be convinced, for that would present the confusing question as to why He would do such a thing? "You wouldn't think so highly of me if you knew me … if you knew what I'd done."

Abigail reached over and took Hope's hand in hers. "You could have killed a hundred men and been the town harlot, for all I care. God values everyone."

Hope chuckled. "I haven't been *that* bad." How different this lady was from her sister Grace and from all the haughty, self-righteous women in Charles Towne.

"Well, there you have it." Abigail grinned and released her hand.

A light breeze rustled the leaves of a nearby fern and brushed a lock of Hope's hair from her face as if God Himself had reached down to caress her. Warmth that came not from the sun blossomed within her.

"Do you believe someone who has been …compromised"—Hope gauged her friend's reaction, but Abigail stared out over the water unmoving—"who has been sullied, can be restored?"

Abigail drew her knees to her chest. "God is a God of fresh beginnings. He makes all things new." Though she said the words with assurance, a hint of sorrow rang in her tone.

"But surely He cannot restore one's purity?" Could Hope dare to believe she could start over?

"He cannot erase things that happened in our pasts, but He can erase the stain of them."

Hope sighed. "But isn't that the same thing?"

"Not at all. If you allow your past to dictate who you are now, then it still holds you in chains, does it not?" Joy suddenly fled the woman's expression as a wounded look filled her eyes.

Scooting off the boulder, Hope took a seat beside her. "Did something happen to you?"

Abigail lowered her gaze and twirled a finger through the sand, even as a shudder passed through her.

"What is it?" Hope asked.

Abigail shook her head.

Hope took her hand. "You can trust me."

Abigail raised her gaze to Hope's, searching her eyes as if deciding whether she should proceed. Finally she took a deep breath. "On Antigua, two years ago, I wasn't feeling well, and my parents left me home while they delivered food to a nearby village. A wealthy landowner who had just purchased a nearby sugar plantation sent his son to call on my father. Apparently, there was some disagreement between his father and mine regarding his treatment of slaves. When he found me alone in the house …" Abigail squeezed her eyes shut, and Hope grabbed her hand and swallowed the burning in her throat. She didn't want to hear the rest, didn't want to know what her heart was already telling her, but she waited in silence for her friend to continue.

A tear slid down Abigail's cheek, and she wiped it away. "He assaulted me."

Heart sinking, Hope drew Abigail close. How could anyone hurt this precious lady? "What did your father do?"

"I never told him."

Hope nudged her back. "Why not?"

"It would have killed him. Besides, the damage was done, and the young man sailed back to England within a fortnight."

Hope wondered if she should share her own harrowing story, but her mind refused to budge beyond the shock of what she had just heard. "I don't understand."

"What?" Abigail drew her shoulders back and a gentle smile returned to her face as if the telling of the tale had released some burden.

"One would never know such a travesty happened to you. You are so kind and sweet, so humble and willing to serve others. And this God of yours. This God who did naught to protect you." Anger raged through Hope, anger at the spoiled landowner's son, anger at her own attacker, but mostly anger at God. He had not protected Abigail …

And He had not protected Hope.

"Why should I blame God for the actions of men?" Abigail picked up a stick and twirled it in the sand. "If I did that, I'd be perpetually angry at Him."

"But He could have prevented it."

"Of course. Why He didn't, I may never know." She shrugged. "Perhaps for the very purpose of sharing it with you."

Horrified, Hope shrank back. "I could not bear it if that were so."

Abigail patted her hand. "Let us let God be God, shall

we?"

Hope could only stare at her. While Hope's heart had grown bitter and angry, while she'd allowed her dreadful incident to define who she was—who she'd become—Abigail had risen above it and had allowed it to make her a better person, a stronger person.

Abigail rose to her feet and stretched her arms above her. "Let's not talk of such things. 'Tis too find a day to be in ill humor. We have food and safety, your good health is restored, and I'm sure we shall soon be rescued."

Hope laughed at her friend's exuberance. "No one even knows where we are."

"God knows." Abigail grinned.

"I wish I could be more like you. I wish I could erase my past and start over."

"But you can." Abigail knelt and took Hope's hands in hers. "If you allow God to help you."

A flash of red over Abigail's shoulder caught Hope's eye.

"What is it?"

"I thought I saw something in the bush."

"We should be going anyway." Abigail grabbed her dress from a nearby bush. "It grows late, and I'm sure Nathaniel will begin to worry."

After donning her gown, Hope tried to shake off the foreboding that threatened to sour one of the most glorious days she'd had in a long time. She continued to try to shake it off as she followed Abigail down the narrow path back to camp, but the lady was walking too fast and Hope had difficulty keeping up with her. Leaves and fronds starting spinning around her, and she clutched her forehead. Her foot hit something hard. Sharp pain spiked up her leg, and her toes refused to budge.

"Oh my!" Abigail dashed to her side. "Let me help you up. I'm so sorry. I should have realized you still required my assistance."

"'Tis not your fault. I'll be fine." Leaning on Abigail, Hope clambered to her feet, but her ankle throbbed. She tested it and moaned. "My ankle. I don't think I can walk."

Abigail led her to a small clearing where she eased her down upon a fallen tree trunk. "Wait here. I'll get Nathaniel."

"No, don't bother him. I'll be fine in a moment."

"Don't be silly, I'll return before you know it." And with that, Abigail disappeared into the foliage, casting a reassuring glance over her shoulder. But no sooner had she left than dread surrounded Hope like a dense fog. The warble of birds became an eerie chant. The leaves and branches rustling in the breeze seemed to be reaching for her. Leaning over, she rubbed her ankle, willing herself to remain calm.

The swish of foliage jerked her attention back up in anticipation of seeing Nathaniel. But it wasn't Mr. Mason who entered the clearing.

Chapter 20

Major Paine grinned at Hope just as a ravenous wolf would an injured lamb.

"What do you want, Major?" Hope took a deep breath in an effort to stifle her rising terror.

"Well, well. I went in search of fruit, and it appears I have indeed found a delectable morsel." After a quick glance around, he stepped toward her and raised his brows.

"I asked you what you wanted." Hope heard the tremble in her voice.

"What do I want?" He laughed. "*Now* you wish to know what I want. Earlier today you gave me the impression you cared not a whit for what I wanted."

Placing one hand on a tree trunk and all her weight on her good foot, Hope struggled to rise, all the while keeping an eye upon the major.

He licked his lips. "And yet I have treated you with naught but civility. Certainly more than your situation deserves."

Fury replaced her fear. "And what situation is that?"

Shrugging off his red coat, he tossed it onto the log Hope had vacated and loosened his cravat. "Stifling hot in these tropics. Almost makes one wish we could abandon the need for clothing." His gaze scoured over her, lingering at breast and hip.

"You!" Hope shouted. "'Twas you I saw lurking by the pond."

He stroked the greasy strands of his hair. "I must protest, miss. I never lurk."

Hoped scanned the clearing, seeking an escape, seeking an ally. Her eyes locked on the spot where Abigail had disappeared. "Mr. Mason will be here any moment, sir. Hence, I suggest you state your business and leave."

"Egad, you think that mere carpenter—mere sailor—frightens me?" He flicked one tip of his cravat through the air. "Why, last I saw him, he and that degenerate companion of his were fishing several miles down the shore. Nay, I don't believe he'll arrive anytime soon."

Hope's chest tightened.

Major Paine took another step toward her. She could smell the mildew of his clothes and the staleness of his breath. She tried to step to the side, but a sharp pain stabbed her ankle. Moaning, she leaned back against the tree and met his bold gaze with a defiant one.

"Ah, the little dove's wings have been clipped." He clicked his tongue. "And she cannot fly away."

"I asked you what you wanted." Hope pressed a hand to her roiling stomach. "Or do you enjoy bullying young ladies?"

"Zooks, bullying? Nay, I had quite the opposite in mind." He once again took liberties with his gaze, sending a shiver of disgust through Hope.

"But I fear I am getting ahead of myself." He retreated, clasped his hands behind his back, and took on the air of a gentleman at court. "I came to offer you one more chance to accept my invitation to voyage with us day after next."

"Why do you press the matter?" The man had not shown much interest in her before, save an occasional salacious glance.

"As a man in the service of His Majesty"—he took on a condescending tone—"I represent the nobility of my office. Therefore, I cannot in good conscience allow a lady to stay in the company of men whose reputations are, shall we say, less than refined."

Hope grimaced. Nathaniel's actions had more than proven his reputation, whilst this man's character remained dubious. Major Paine fingered the gold buttons of his waistcoat and waited as though expecting an outpouring of praise for his kindness and honor. She narrowed her eyes. If even a bit of what he said were true, then his concern should also include Abigail. "But what of Miss Sheldon? Is she not worth your protection as well?"

The major flattened his lips and shrugged. "By the manner of her vocation, Miss Sheldon chooses to associate with. . .shall we say. . .questionable sorts."

"She is a missionary, sir, bringing God's Word to those in need. The manner of her vocation, as you call it, exalts her situation high above the rest of us here on this island. And it would seem to me, that fact alone would necessitate your protection."

The lines of his face grew taut. "If she is as exalted as you say, then let her God protect her. She matters not to me." He looked down at the dirt and ground his teeth together. "I will not, *cannot* bear to see a man of Mr. Mason's lowly station enjoy a beauty as yourself."

"Enjoy? How dare you!" Hope drew back her hand to slap his face, but her ankle gave way, and she bent over in pain. "He does not enjoy me at all," she panted, realizing the grim truth of her own words.

"Come now. Let us put pretense aside, madam. I am a worldly man, ergo I understand the way of things." The major took her elbow to assist her, but she jerked from his grasp.

"You understand nothing." Hope hobbled backward.

"This has naught to do with your sense of honor nor your concern for me. 'Tis merely a matter of your wounded pride."

He glanced off as if pondering the question for the first time. "Perhaps." He tugged on his loosened cravat and took a step closer. "But if you're worried about my affections, I'm sure they will come in time." He slid a finger over her cheek and down her neck. Hope slapped his hand away before he could go further. She turned to run, willing herself to endure the pain in her ankle, but he clamped his hand around her arm and swung her around. Wincing, she faced him. Nausea churned in her belly.

Visions of another man, in another place, a time long ago slithered through her mind, awakening terror. A man much like the major. A man who crept into her bedchamber at night. Blood pounded in her ears. Her chest heaved. *Not again, Lord. Not again.*

"Will you come with me or not?" the major fumed.

Hope lengthened her stance and grabbed a lock of her hair. "I will not."

"Foolish girl," he spat, his face reddening. "I will have you one way or another." His gaze crawled to her mouth.

Hope's ankle throbbed. Her heart constricted, and her knees began to buckle. But rather than shrink back in fear, rather than accept her fate as she had done the last time, she narrowed a scathing look upon him. "If you try to kiss me, I warn you, I shall take a bite out of those despicable, slimy lips."

"If you try to kiss her, Major, you'll feel the bite of my sword as well." Nathaniel shoved the last branch aside and burst into the clearing.

Releasing Hope, the major swung around, his hand flying to the hilt of his sword.

Nathaniel stepped toward him and leveled the tip of his

blade at the major's chest. He clenched his jaw, trying to quell the fury storming through every muscle.

"Swounds, calm yourself, man." The major cocked one brow. "The lady and I were merely getting better acquainted."

"I don't believe the lady was enjoying the experience."

The major's hand twitched over his blade, and Nathaniel gave a slight shake of his head.

"I would not consider that, Major. In fact, I suggest you take your leave before my temper gets the best of me and I run you through."

Major Paine stretched out his neck as if trying to untie a knot in his throat. "Very well." A low growl of anger simmered beneath the quiver in his voice. He snatched his coat from the log, his back to Nathaniel.

Relieved, Nathaniel sheathed his blade and dared a glance at Hope. When he'd first caught sight of the major's body hovering over her, terror and fury had charged through him. But aside from the slight quiver of her bottom lip and the moist sheen covering her eyes, she appeared unharmed.

Turning, the major approached Nathaniel, his coat oddly spread over his arm. A bright flash caught Nathaniel's eye, but before he could react, the major swung his blade out from beneath his coat and leveled it at Nathaniel's chest.

Hope gasped and Nathaniel chided himself for not watching the man more carefully.

"You may have her." Flinging his coat over his other arm, the major scraped his sword across Nathaniel's shirt. "What would I want with a mere strumpet anyway?"

Nathaniel would have laughed at the man's pompous display if not for the vulgar name he'd just called Miss Hope. In a swift move, he snatched the major's coat from his arm, flung it around the offending sword, snapped the blade from the major's hand, and hurled it into the air. With a *swoosh*, it whipped through the clearing, flashing where the sunlight caught the steel, before a large clump of foliage swallowed it up.

The major stared after it in disbelief. He opened his mouth to speak, but Nathaniel slammed his fist across his jaw. Head jerking to the left, he stumbled back, arms flailing, and collapsed in the middle of a bush. His dirty boots poked out from the shrubbery, feet twitching.

Pulling out his blade, Nathaniel stormed toward him, parted the leaves with his sword, and pointed it at the villain's chest. "Begone before I finish the job."

Scrambling to his feet, the major rubbed his jaw, his eyes wide with fury and fear. Then turning, he scurried into the undergrowth like a rat caught in the sunlight.

Hope sank back against the tree and stared at Nathaniel. Her golden hair danced across her waist in the light breeze. Her chest rose and fell, and her moist sapphire eyes brimmed with such admiration and desperation, Nathaniel swallowed against the thrill they invoked in him. Sheathing his sword, he approached her, scanned her for injuries and thanked God when he found none.

Tears streamed down her cheeks, and Nathaniel brushed them away with his thumbs, his emotions reeling when she closed her eyes beneath his touch.

"Are you hurt?" he asked.

Hope shook her head. Her eyes opened and searched his as if seeking an invitation. Although he tried to force all desire, concern, and affection from his face, she fell into his embrace anyway. As she molded against him, his body went rigid, unsure, ill at ease with her so close. Then slowly he wrapped his arms around her and pressed her head against his shoulder. She needed him. How could he deny her? Sobs racked her body, and she squeezed him tighter. "Thank you, Nathaniel."

She smelled like sunshine and clean water, and he drew in a deep breath of her, berating himself for not arriving sooner. When Abigail had told him Hope needed his assistance right away, he'd been reluctant to rush to her aid.

The last week of caring for her had taxed his emotions beyond the point of breaking, and he'd hoped to put some distance between them now that she was well. So, after he insisted Abigail remain behind due to the rapid approach of darkness, he'd ambled across the island like a spoiled boy sent on an errand.

"Shhh. You are safe now, Hope."

Her curves pressed against his chest and sent a pleasurable, dangerous shard of heat through him, and he eased her back.

"Ouch," she murmured, and only then did he remember Abigail mentioning her ankle.

Daring to touch her again, he circled an arm around her waist and lowered her to a fallen log. "Forgive me." He knelt beside her.

"'Tis nothing. I told Abigail not to bother you." She sniffed and raised a hand to her nose. "But as it turns out, I'm glad she did."

"May I?" He gestured toward her foot, and when she nodded, he eased the hem of her gown back, wondering all along at his sanity in doing so. Yet the red, puffy skin surrounding her ankle and her groan of pain when he turned it ever so slightly told him all he needed to know.

"My apologies." He lowered her foot to the ground. "I believe 'tis only a sprain, but you should stay off of it for a few days."

A tear slid down her face, and her bottom lip quivered again. He swallowed, searching for the anger, the disdain, he'd once felt for this woman, but the feelings had fled him like traitorous cowards when he needed them most. "The major is a swaggering cur. But we shall be rid of him soon."

Against his better judgment, Nathaniel took her hand in his and held it as he had through the long hours of the night while her fever had raged. He reached up to wipe another tear from her face, but his thumb landed on her lips and he eased it over them, longing to take away her pain.

She closed her eyes and parted her lips beneath his touch. Instinctively, he leaned forward and placed his mouth on hers. A light kiss, meant only to comfort, to erase the memory of Major Paine. But who was he fooling? As expected, it set Nathaniel aflame. He backed away, unable to calm the violent beating of his heart.

Her eyes met his. Innocent, questioning. "What was that for?"

"To comfort you." His voice came out raspy and deep, and he hoped she didn't notice the desire burning within it.

She smiled. "It worked." She brushed her fingers over his stubbled jaw and studied his face. Admiration and a spark of apprehension flickered in her eyes, bringing a tumult of conflicting emotions within Nathaniel.

He brushed his thumb over her moist lips again. When she moaned an encouragement, all control, all resolve flew away, and he claimed her mouth and kissed her deeply, hungrily. Wrapping one arm around her back, he pressed her close. Dizzy with pleasure, hungry with need, he lost himself in her taste, in her touch, in her need for his comfort and protection.

A bird squawked overhead and a gust of wind blew over him, jolting him, and he jerked away from her.

Shock and joy mingled in her sapphire eyes. Her chest rose and fell as heavily as his did. Her sweet breath swirled over him, luring him back into her mesmerizing spell.

Nathaniel tore his gaze from her. "Forgive me."

"Nay, I don't believe I will." She gave him a playful look. "But just to be clear, this time, you kissed me first."

"Aye, I'll admit to that." Nathaniel rubbed the back of his neck, an unavoidable smirk lifting his lips. "I wanted to ease your fears."

"You succeeded."

And he would love nothing more than to continue the treatment. Why did he so easily succumb to her charms? *Lord, where is the strength You promised? And Your promise not to allow me to be tempted beyond what I can resist?* Yet the truth of that verse meant he could have resisted her. He should have resisted her.

Perhaps the real truth was, he didn't want to.

Shame deflated his desire, and he slowly rose.

Her wounded look pierced him. "You want so badly to be angry at me, to hate me."

Nathaniel took a step back. He must distance himself from her—put the temptation out of his sight. "I cannot … I cannot … we must stay away from one another." He turned his back to her.

"'Tis Abigail, isn't it?" Her voice quivered with pain.

"Abigail?" He shook his head but still did not face her. "What has she to do with this?"

A green and yellow bird dove into the clearing, swooped by Nathaniel's head, and landed on a branch, then began twittering as if scolding Nathaniel for his behavior.

He raked a hand through his hair and took up a pace across the sandy soil. "I'm not good for you, and you're not good for me." He could no longer deny his growing affections for Hope, but simply because they existed did not mean they were in God's will. Men were drawn to many things—greed for wealth, liquor, illicit affairs—that in the end caused their destruction. If Nathaniel was to rise above his past, he could not do it with a woman like Hope. He faced her.

"What you mean is, I'm not good enough for you." She lowered her gaze and fingered the lace spilling from her sleeves. "Good enough to kiss, but not good enough to love." Spite rang in her voice, along with despondency.

"That was not my meaning." A pain sliced his heart, and he headed toward her.

She held up a hand. "Keep your distance, Mr. Mason, or you may be tempted to accost me again. Apparently I have that effect on men."

"Accost you? Fire and thunder." Nathaniel halted and

rubbed an old ache burning on his side. He clenched his fists. "You have that effect on men because you freely toss your affections at every man who looks your way."

"How dare you?" Fire shot from her eyes. She tried to move, but winced and shrank back, releasing a sigh of defeat. "Maybe I have done so in the past, but I've not behaved in such a way lately."

"Really, and what of Gavin?"

"What *of* Mr. Keese?"

"Can you not deny you have affection for him? That you constantly flatter him and play the coquette in his presence?"

"I do no such thing!" Hope tugged on a lock of hair and tossed out her chin. "Jealous?"

"Ha!" He snorted, more from the guilt assailing him at the truth of her statement than in defiance of it. Regardless, he must make her see her part in these dangerous dalliances. "'Tis why men take liberties with you." He pointed in the direction Major Paine had gone. Yet even as he said the words, he chided himself for being unfair and softened his tone. "Hope, why do you cast your virtue, your very self— something so precious—to the dogs?"

Her cheeks burned red. She opened her mouth to speak but snapped it shut and raised her seething gaze to his.

Her obstinacy rekindled his fury. "Fire and thunder, woman, I will not forfeit my last ship to rescue you from another wanton affair."

Struggling to rise, she let out a gasp of pain but managed to stand, leaning her weight on one foot. "Never fear, Mr. Mason, I would never allow you to do so again."

She stared at him stone faced, but her expression soon crumpled. Sniffing, she raised a hand to her nose again as grief pooled in her eyes. Despite every effort, Nathaniel's anger fled him once more, and he opened his mouth to apologize. She spoke first.

"How wonderful to be so perfect, so indispensable. You supply our food, build our shelters, preach God's word, and even heal us, all the while looking down your imperious nose at us sinners." She waved a hand through the air. "You are correct, sir. I beg you, do not associate with me further, for I have no doubt the filth of my past, of my very character, will soon tarnish you. And we can't have that. Not while you're building your merchant fleet and making a name for yourself."

Nathaniel grimaced, her words boring deep into his soul. Regardless, they bolstered his decision to keep his distance from her. A decision that should have brought him relief, strength, and resolve, but all he felt was anguish, pain, and regret. He steeled himself to approach her. "I'll carry you back to camp."

"I'd rather crawl." She raised her nose and looked away from him.

"You will do no such thing. I'll not leave you out here to be attacked again."

"Relieve yourself of the burden, Mr. Mason. I shan't expect your rescue in the future."

Back to Mr. Mason, is it? Sorrow tugged at him. He held out his hands. "Nevertheless." Without awaiting further protest, he hoisted her into his arms. She stiffened at his touch but did not struggle, nor reach her arms around his neck, nor even look at him. And the loss he felt threatened to outweigh any prior loss—even that of his ship.

Chapter 21

A distant, sweet chorus beckoned Hope awake. Slowly, she opened her eyes to see the shadows of tiny birds flitting over the sunlit palm branches that formed the roof of her hut. She smiled at the happy way they hopped about, singing their carefree melody. The island boasted a multitude of birds, each one adorned in the brightest shades of green, yellow, red, even purple and blue, that Hope had ever seen—more beautiful than the most elegant gowns on London's aristocratic ladies. These exquisite creatures didn't possess wealth or title, yet they flew about happily as kings and queens of the air, all the while gazing down on the pathetic human race bound to sand and dirt.

The birds' melody heightened and joined in perfect unison as if they were inviting Hope to join them. How she wished she could shed her human chains, her ugliness, and transform into such a lofty creature and fly away, away from her earth bound existence, away from her past, away from the pain of rejection.

A Scripture popped into her mind from a long time ago, something about birds not sowing or reaping or worrying about tomorrow, yet their Father in heaven feeds them and cares for them. Hope sighed, forcing down her longing to be loved—to be cared for in such a way.

True to his promise, Mr. Mason had not spoken a word to her nor graced her with one glance of his handsome brown eyes for three days. In fact, wherever she happened to be, whether sitting on the beach or lolling about the camp, he made every effort to position himself elsewhere.

The stab of his rejection surprised her. Hadn't she always known he deserved a far more chaste and pious lady than she was? Someone like Abigail. Besides, the more Hope tried to prove herself a lady to this virtuous man, the less he seemed to believe it.

No doubt the ease with which she welcomed his kiss did naught to prove her cause.

She rose to her elbows as a bath of heat drenched her at the memory. And what a kiss it was! The gentle way his mouth had explored hers, the yearning she felt in his every movement. The heat that had enveloped her, stealing her ability to think, to even breathe. The kiss was not at all like the one he'd given her on board the merchantman. Merely passion had driven that kiss, but this one … A pleasant shiver ran through her even now. 'Twas as if Nathaniel were kissing *her*—Hope Westcott—not who she appeared to be on the outside. She'd experienced none like it before. And certainly never would again.

A jab of guilt struck her. What of Abigail? Obviously, she harbored affections for Nathaniel. In light of that, Hope should have rejected Nathaniel's advance, should have pushed him away. Could she not resist one man's attentions for the sake of a friend? Hope's heart grew heavy even as the birds' morning ensemble drifted away. The beautiful creatures had no doubt given up on her joining them and flown away in search of a better prospect.

She tested her weight on her ankle and found only a slight ache remained. Running her fingers through her hair, she squared her shoulders and emerged from the hut to a blast of hot salty air and the tiresome smell of fish.

Gavin lay in the sand at the center of camp, his hands pillowing his head. Turning, he gave her a sultry grin and sprang to his feet. "Allow me, milady." He took her elbow to assist her.

Hope smiled at his gallantry. "Thank you, kind sir, but I believe my ankle is much better today. I may even venture out for a walk ... or perhaps a hobble." She warmed to his look of compassion.

"If you would permit me, I'd be honored to escort you." He led her to a chair Nathaniel had fashioned from pinewood and twine and knelt beside her. Taking her hand in his, Gavin brushed his thumb over her skin, and Hope shifted in her seat, uncomfortable with his familiarity. His blue eyes, a shade darker than her own, held a brighter glow than their normal playfulness. Truth be told, after Nathaniel's rejection, Gavin's kindness had begun to break down her resolve to resist his flirtations. His regard dulled the incessant lance in her heart and made the long days on this island pass much quicker. Besides, what did it matter? She'd failed to win Nathaniel's admiration, and since he had already accused her of playing the coquette with Gavin, what harm would it do to prove him right?

Hope sighed and gazed at the calm morning sea, a plate of turquoise glass stretching to the horizon. Her thoughts drifted from Gavin, to Nathaniel, and ended with Lord Falkland. Did the man who once promised to marry her ever think of her? Had he inquired who had purchased her at that heinous auction? A clump of sorrow and remorse lodged in her throat. Perhaps her obsession with Nathaniel was only a symptom of her still-broken heart.

Lifting her hand, Gavin placed a kiss on her bare fingers, drawing Hope's attention back to him.

Bang. Clunk. The sound of wood dropping jolted Hope. Tugging her hand from Gavin's, she peered around him in time to see Nathaniel, wiping his hands—as if he were wiping them of her—and storming from the camp onto the beach, never once looking her way.

"A bit of a grouch this morning, eh?" Gavin watched Nathaniel leave.

Hope let out a ragged breath. "I fear 'tis my presence that dampens his humor."

"But why let him dampen ours?" Gavin grabbed a lock of Hope's hair and fingered it, a mischievous grin on his lips.

A pinprick of unease filtered over Hope. "Where is Abigail?" She scanned the beach then turned to search the jungle.

"She went to get water with Kreggs. And Hanson is gathering fruit on the other side of the island." Gavin lifted one brow in her direction. "We are very much alone."

The taunting glint in his eyes put Hope's fears to rest. "Should I be frightened, Mr. Keese?"

"Do you want to be?"

Her heart skipped, longing to continue this harmless dalliance, but a vision of Major Paine filled her mind, and the smile she intended to give Gavin faded to a frown.

He scratched his thick sideburns. "Forgive me, Hope. I had forgotten about the major."

"You know?"

"Aye, Nathaniel made mention of it."

Hope nodded, wondering why Nathaniel would bring up such a sordid story, especially when the major and his party had been gone now for two days.

She watched Nathaniel walking down shore, his focus intent upon the sand, perhaps hunting for crab.

Gavin released her hair and stood. "The cad. If I had been there—"

"No harm came of it. Nathaniel arrived in time." How could she forget the way he had burst into the clearing—his sword thrust before him, his eyes narrowed like daggers. She'd never seen such fury on his face. And the way he'd dispatched the major so quickly and sent him scurrying off like a frightened rabbit, she would have laughed if she hadn't been so terrified.

And so in awe of Nathaniel.

"You are safe with me." Gavin winked, and Hope longed to reach out and take his hand again, if only to wash away the memory of Nathaniel's touch. But she resisted.

"Thank you, Mr. Keese."

"Gavin, please."

"Gavin." She nodded.

Wiping sand from his breeches, he gestured toward a bucket of fruit. "Something to eat, milady?"

"Cease with the pretensions. I am no lady."

"You are to me." The sincerity in his eyes stunned her. Turning, he plucked a roasted plantain from the pile and handed it to her.

She gave him a puzzled look. Was he flirting with her? Telling her what she longed to hear in order to have his way, like so many men before him? Yet nothing devious appeared in his eyes, just a boyish innocence that belied the worldly man she knew he was. Perhaps he was simply playing a part, a game. Then why did moisture fill her eyes at his kind remark?

She shifted her gaze and thoughts back out to sea and wondered at the fate of Elise and Mrs. Hendrick and the others. Had they made it to Puerto Rico, and if so, had they avoided the Spanish? Even if they did somehow make it to Jamaica, would they bother to send back a ship? If Hope thought God would listen to her prayers, she'd pray for their safety, especially Elise's. But from the sound of her whisperings throughout the long night, Abigail was doing enough praying for all of them. Besides, if God would listen to anyone, He would listen to Abigail. Not Hope.

A blast thundered through the air. Hope jumped, threw a hand to her chest, and rose from her seat. Gavin dashed to her side and together, they peered toward the beach. Nathaniel halted and stared at something offshore.

"Stay here." Grabbing two swords and a pistol, Gavin raced toward Nathaniel. Though she tried, Hope could not remain still. Taking a tentative step on her sore ankle, she limped after him and followed the men's gazes to see a ship, a puff of smoke dissipating in the air above its larboard hull.

A ship!

They were to be rescued at last.

Yet as she approached Nathaniel and Gavin, they did not share her glee.

"Blast it all, my fortune for a telescope." Nathaniel planted his fists on his waist. "Can you make her out, Gavin?"

"Nay, but it appears she raises her colors." Gavin handed Nathaniel his sword, which he grabbed with a nod. "Let us wait and see."

"Do you think they mean us harm?" Hope asked.

Both men swerved to face her. "I told you to stay put." Gavin gave her a scolding look, but Nathaniel barely allowed his eyes to land on her before he uttered a "harrumph" and turned away.

The anchor splashed into the sea and cockboats were lowered. Thoughts of home made her spirits soar. A merchantman perhaps, or a ship sent back by Major Paine. In either case, soon she would be on her way home to her sisters and away from Nathaniel and the disturbing effect he had upon her.

A flag was hoisted upon the mainmast. Beads of sweat formed on Nathaniel's brow as he squinted toward it against the rising sun. His grip on the hilt of his sword tightened.

Gavin groaned. "Well, sink me, of all the luck."

"What is it?" Hope peered at the ship. A black flag flapped in the breeze atop her foremast.

The muscles in Nathaniel's jaw tensed. "Pirates."

Chapter 22

H ope's face paled into bristling fear. "Pirates?" she squeaked. Her gaze flashed back to the ship as her hand went to her throat.

Dread sank like an anchor into Nathaniel's stomach as he once again studied the flag flapping in the light morning breeze … hoping … praying he'd made a mistake. But the white skull and crisscross of swords stark against the black background gave no room for error. Of all the ships to land on this island, why did it have to be a pirate? He eyed Hope again. Her breathing had sped to a rapid pace. As had his own. How was he to protect her and Abigail from these salacious brigands?

Oars splashed into the water, and boats, overflowing with said brigands, surged toward shore, their jeering insults announcing their arrival.

Oh Lord, I need your help. Give their captain some shred of decency toward us.

Gavin shot Nathaniel a wary glance, his jaw flexing. "Should I get Kreggs and Hanson?"

"Nay, 'tis best they remain hidden. They've seen only us so far."

Gavin nodded and planted his bare feet firmly upon the sand. "Any suggestions?"

"Stand our ground." Nathaniel rubbed the rising ache on his side. "And pray."

Gavin snorted, primed and cocked his pistol then shoved it down his breeches.

Hope gripped Nathaniel's arm. Not Gavin's arm, but his. He glanced down at her. "Go back to the hut."

"Please, let me stay with you. I don't want to be alone." Her fingers dug into his skin. "Besides, they know I'm here."

"Get behind me, then." He pried her hand from his arm and eased her back. Though he felt her quiver, she neither whimpered nor swooned like most women would have when facing such murderous villains. "I'll do everything in my power to keep you safe."

"As will I," Gavin added.

Though Nathaniel had no idea how. The bitter taste of fear filled his mouth. He could not stand the thought of Hope or Abigail being hurt, not in this way, not by these men.

Lengthening his stance, he shoved back any evidence of fear, planted the tip of his sword into the sand and awaited his guests. He'd dealt with pirates before. They fed on fear, and he vowed not to give them their meal for the day.

One cockboat struck sand, jolting the boisterous passengers from their seats and sending one man overboard. After the pirates recovered from their laughter, they spilled out of the boat like ants over an anthill and sloshed through the water toward shore. Greed dripped from their twisted lips as they scanned the island searching for anything to satiate their appetites. Their gazes swept over Nathaniel and Gavin and latched on Hope. Trembling, she shrank further behind him.

Gavin gripped the hilt of his sword and frowned at the pirates, some of whom lined up before them, arms across their chests, while a few others wandered over the sand, surveying their new conquest. The men varied in age, girth, and stature, but all wore the same scowl and the same devilish look on their sun-battered faces. Their colorful attire, though mismatched and filthy, bore the elements of nobility in the gold and silver embroidery, the silk lace, and metallic threaded brocade and damask coats—all no doubt stolen. Armed with a cutlass and a brace of pistols across his chest, each man also wore the imperious façade of invincibility. They were masters of the sea, and they well knew it.

Though he could not squelch the fear etching through him, Nathaniel saw behind their masks of insolence. These were lost men, wandering the seas in search not only of treasure, but of purpose, of meaning, of true life. No different from most men's quest, save the method they used.

The second boat hit shore, and more men leapt over her gunwales and splashed through the waves, some remaining in the water, while others lumbered onto the sand.

From their midst, a tall dark man, sporting a blue plumed tricorn and black velvet waistcoat trimmed in silver, marched toward Nathaniel, a jeering grin on his lips.

Doffing his hat, he swept it before him in a bow. The sun glinted off a gold earring in his ear. "Captain Poole of the pirate ship *Enchantress* at yer service." He slapped the tricorn back atop his head. "And ye are?" He asked Nathaniel, but his gaze angled around him to where Hope huddled. His eyebrows rose.

"Mr. Nathaniel Mason, and this is Mr. Gavin Keese."

Gavin slid his fingers over the silver handle of his pistol and inched closer to Nathaniel. Together they formed a wall in front of Hope. With a quick shake of his head, Nathaniel hoped to dissuade his impetuous companion from attempting anything foolish.

"Pleased to make yer acquaintance." Cocking his head, Captain Poole studied them, then he glanced back over his shoulder and lifted his lace-covered hand.

Splashing sounded, and the mob of pirates in the water parted. Major Paine, Mr. and Mrs. Hendrick, and Elise emerged in the grip of four men who dragged them toward their captain. Salt encrusted their filthy clothing, and their faces bore the marks of an arduous journey.

Hope gasped and started to rush forward, but Nathaniel halted her with his arm and forced her back.

"Do these wretched creatures belong to ye?"

Laughter broke out among the pirates.

Nathaniel shifted his stance. His "yes" and Gavin's "no" echoed at the same time above the lapping waves, causing further hilarity among the ribald crew.

"Well, since they told us where to find ye, I'll expect yer the one tellin' the truth." Captain Pooled pointed to Nathaniel then surveyed Gavin. "And ye be the liar." His eyes landed on Gavin's pistol, and he snorted as if it were naught but a stick.

"Unhand me." The major's sullen command drew Nathaniel's attention his way. Stripped down to his white shirt and breeches, his hair hanging in saturated strands about his face, the major looked more like an uprooted kelp than a man wielding the King's authority. Nevertheless, he tossed his chin in the air, as was the habit of all men bred to power, regardless of whether they still possessed it.

Mr. Hendrick fared no better. His sopping red beard clung to his chin like a sea urchin, and both shock and dread swam in his eyes. White faced, his wife and child huddled by his side.

"We found 'em floatin' in the sea, hangin' on for dear life to shreds of wood." Captain Poole chortled, waving a hand in their direction. "We wanted to have some sport with 'em, but since we found ourselves in need of fresh water and fruit, and they swore they knew of a place close by laden with such amenities, we decided not to kill 'em."

"Very kind of you." Nathaniel bowed.

"Aye, we pirates are not without mercy, are we, men?"

Ayes and curses filled the air.

"But since we are here now ...." A malicious look

burned in the captain's dark gaze as he eyed the captives. The pirates shoved the major and Mr. Hendrick to the sand and released Mrs. Hendrick and Elise. The little girl gripped her mother's skirts like a lifeline, her eyes big as portholes, but not a sound escaped her lips. Her mother, however, sobbed, clutching her stomach, and fell into a heap.

Shoving Nathaniel aside, Hope squeezed between him and Gavin and dashed toward Mrs. Hendrick before Nathaniel could stop her. She brushed past the pirates, unaware of the multitude of eyes following her. When she reached Mrs. Hendrick, she knelt and put her arm around her shoulders. Elise fell into Hope's embrace, and she squeezed the girl and planted a kiss on her head. Nathaniel didn't know whether to be amazed at her bravery or appalled at her foolishness.

Captain Poole's eyes lit up. "I see ye have other delicacies on the island as well."

"Some delicacies you are welcome to." Nathaniel forced a commanding tone into his voice. "Others you are not."

The captain belched. "Indeed?" He cocked his head at Nathaniel as if he were studying a specimen under a quizzing glass. He snapped his fingers in the air. "Spread out and search for others," he ordered. As some of his men dispersed, he swaggered up to Nathaniel. "Rather bold for a man with only one sword."

"Two swords and a pistol." Gavin cast a look of challenge his way.

"Ah, I stand corrected. Did ye hear that, men? Two swords and a pistol." The crew chuckled as Captain Poole shoved his face into Gavin's. To his credit, the man did not blink. "Against thirty blades and twice as many pistols, not to mention me guns aboard the ship. Are ye that cocky or just plain stupid?"

Nathaniel clenched his fists and prayed Gavin would hold his tongue, but the young man returned the captain's glare with equal intensity and a spark of playfulness.

"Perhaps a bit of both."

Captain Poole's hard features softened into a grin, and a deep chuckle bellowed from within his gut. "Aye, that be a true word ye spoke. But I'll have to ask ye to hand over yer weapons in any case."

Nathaniel handed his sword hilt first to a pirate who came forward to retrieve it. He prayed Gavin would do the same. Though a groan emanated from his lips, the young second mate followed suit. Relieved the captain seemed to possess a sense of humor and for the moment was disinclined to do them harm, Nathaniel couldn't help but wonder how long it would last.

Hope continued comforting Mrs. Hendrick and Elise. The major struggled to his feet and attempted to brush sand from his breeches, while a jagged wound marred Mr. Hendrick's left cheek as he stared at the proceedings, mouth agape and a look of horror on his face.

"There were others, Captain." Nathaniel said, remembering the other men who'd left with the major. "Four sailors, I believe."

"Aye." Captain Poole stuck his thumbs into his breeches. He nodded toward his ship. "They guard me ship with the rest o' me men."

Nathaniel nodded. When given the choice of turning pirate or dying, most seamen chose the former. But, of course, that was not an option for Nathaniel. He must find another way to convince this man not only to let them live, but to rescue them from this island. "Our ship went down in the storm, and we've been stranded on this island for weeks."

Captain Poole doffed his hat and ran a hand through his coal black hair. "And what d'ye want me to do about it?"

"Since you are merciful pirates, give us safe passage to Kingston."

Captain Poole grinned, revealing an unusually full set of teeth, then kicked sand up with his boot. "And what will ye give me in return?" His gaze locked upon Hope. "We've been out t' sea for quite some time, if ye know what I mean."

"Our undying gratitude, Captain." Nathaniel bowed, hoping to draw the man's gaze off of Hope.

"Strike me down." The captain snickered, but his eyes never left her. "But I was thinkin' of something a tad bit more warm and soft."

Mrs. Hendrick's sobs shot up in volume. Nathaniel ground his foot into the sand, eyeing her protruding belly. Surely these cretins were not cruel enough to harm a woman in her delicate condition.

Captain Poole followed his gaze. "Her? Nay. A bit of a shrew, if ye ask me, but I make it a habit never to steal another man's wife. Was done to me once by a motherless Judas, and I'll not stand for it."

Nathaniel shook his head at the pirate's odd sense of decency.

Without warning, Captain Poole stormed toward Hope and hauled her to her feet. "I'll grant ye safe passage for the woman." He flung an arm around her waist and pressed her against him. Her face paled, and her frenzied gaze met Nathaniel's. The pirate sniffed her hair, recoiled, then fingered it. "Doesn't smell like a lady, but she feels like one."

Blood rushed from Nathaniel's head. His chest tightened. His mind reeled, searching for a way to save her. "You cannot have her."

Captain Poole flinched. "And why not?"

"She's my wife." The thought had barely passed through his mind before it formed on his tongue and left his lips.

Hope's jaw dropped.

"Yer wife, you say?" Captain Poole eyed him suspiciously then examined Hope again.

Major Paine snorted, and for a moment Nathaniel thought he would reveal the ruse. But one stern glance from Nathaniel silenced him, and he turned away.

"Very well. Take yer wife." Poole shoved Hope toward Nathaniel, and she barreled into him.

"I'm beginnin' to hate that code o' mine." Captain Poole spat onto the sand, then crossed arms over his chest. "But now ye have naught to bargain with, sir."

Hoots and hollers blared from behind Nathaniel, where Captain Poole's men broke through the line of trees, Hanson, Kreggs, and Abigail struggling in their grasps. At the sight of Abigail, Captain Poole's eyes once again glinted with delight.

"What have we here?" He sauntered up the beach to meet his men and halted before Abigail. Her chestnut hair flowed in ringlets over her shoulders, and she met the pirate's gaze with brazen confidence. Nathaniel's throat went dry.

"And who might ye be?"

"Abigail Sheldon." She raised her chin toward him as the pirates released her.

Captain Poole eased a finger toward her cheek, but she flinched and backed away, making him cock his head in interest. "And are ye married as well, Miss Sheldon?"

Nathaniel nodded a frenzied yes in her direction, hoping she'd see him over the pirate's shoulder. When she didn't, he faced Gavin, using his eyes to urge the man to claim her. Gavin furrowed his brow then nodded and opened his mouth, but Abigail's voice rang across the beach.

"Nay, I am not married, sir," she replied, her chest heaving. "What is that to you?"

Captain Poole threw back his head as a deep chuckle rose from his belly. Then scanning his crew, he snapped his fingers, and the pirates released Kreggs and Hanson. "Is that all o' them?"

"Aye, Cap'n."

"Very good." He grabbed Abigail's arm and turned to Nathaniel. "This girl will suffice for yer fare."

Nathaniel's heart cramped. He started toward the captain when Hope wove around him and darted to Abigail and Captain Poole, all the while shouting, "Release her at once! She is not for sale."

The captain and his crew froze in mid-stride and gaped at this slip of a woman who dared defy a band of pirates.

Clenching his fists, Nathaniel stormed after her. *Lord, I need your help.*

Hope grabbed Abigail's other arm, attempting to pull her from the pirate's grasp.

"You should control yer wife, sir." The captain huffed.

"Believe me, I have tried." Nathaniel took a stand beside her. "Nevertheless, she is correct. We will not use a human being as barter."

Gavin came up alongside him, his face red with fury.

"Then I'll take her for free." The captain jerked Abigail from Hope's grasp and turned toward the seclusion of the forest.

"Captain, please do not." Hope cornered him and threw herself in his path. "Take me instead."

"No, Hope." Nathaniel barreled after her.

Abigail shook her head, her eyes moistening. "Don't do this."

Captain Poole's lips twisted as his malevolent gaze flickered over Hope. "As I've told ye, I'll not be touchin' another man's wife." Pushing Hope aside, he stormed forward.

"But she is on her way to Kingston to be a missionary." Hope grabbed his arm, stopping him once again. "I am nobody, but she will do great things for God."

"God, you say?" The pirate's face contorted, and his head jerked backward as if someone had punched him. "A missionary?" He dropped Abigail's arm and slowly backed away from her. She fell into Hope's embrace.

Taking the opportunity, Nathaniel threw himself between the ladies and Poole, not caring at the moment by what odd turn of events they had been delivered.

"'Tis a godly woman!" Captain Poole bellowed to his crew crowding around them.

Groans of disappointment, followed by awes of

trepidation, tumbled into the air from the band of men as if their captain had just informed them they were outgunned. Nathaniel shook his head at the madness, but offered a silent prayer of thanks just the same.

Doffing his hat, Poole wiped the sweat from his brow. "No one touches 'er, or the other one neither, or ye'll answer t' me!"

A mixture fear and respect alighted upon the pirate captain's face. "I'll not be riskin' the anger o' the Almighty," he mumbled to himself, his eyes locked upon Abigail. "Well, no matter." He shrugged and faced Nathaniel. "Give us food and water. We shall partake of yer hospitality for a few days and then be on our way. An' if ye don't give us trouble, we may permit ye to live."

Gavin started toward him, his mouth a firm line of protest, but Nathaniel held up a hand to stop him.

The captain huffed out his disgust then directed a probing gaze at Nathaniel. "I see the same anger burns in yer eyes as in yer friend's, yet ye keep it under hatches. The sign of strength." He slapped Nathaniel on the back. "I like ye, Mr. Mason. I may let ye live, after all." And with that, he sauntered toward the camp, his crew ambling after him.

Nathaniel released a heavy sigh. At least the women were safe, though he had no idea how long this pirate's moral code would stand up against his lewd desires. Nor did he know how to convince him to take them to Kingston. With the fruit on the island nearly gone and the fishing uncertain, they would not last much longer. And if he was delayed another week or two, his ship, *The Illusive Hope*, that was to meet him in Kingston, may leave without him. And then he would have no way to get back to Charles Towne.

Hope released Abigail and raised her eyes to Nathaniel, appreciation beaming from their blue depths.

A hideous scream filled the air, jolting him and drawing their attention to the shore.

Nathaniel charged across the sand, Gavin, Hope, and

Abigail on his heels.

Mrs. Hendrick lay folded on the ground, her arms clutching her belly. Mr. Hendrick had his hand on her back and a look of fright on his face, while little Elise sat beside her mother, tears streaming down her face.

Hope and Abigail dropped to Mrs. Hendrick's side and whispered to her. She uttered a loud, sickly moan that sent shivers down Nathaniel's back.

"What is the matter? Is she ill?" Mr. Hendrick asked.

Hope glanced at him and then over to Nathaniel. "Nay, the baby comes."

Chapter 23

Gathering a pile of soft plantain leaves, Hope gently lifted Mrs. Hendrick's head and positioned them beneath her. The poor woman groaned. Her eyelids fluttered as she attempted to open her eyes. Hope turned away, batting tears from her cheeks, avoiding Mrs. Hendrick's inevitable question …

avoiding the answer Hope knew she must give.

On the other side of Mrs. Hendrick, Abigail gathered bloody cloths, a quiet sob escaping her lips. Her eyes met Hope's, and she laid a gentle hand upon her arm.

"There was naught we could do."

"I know." Hope swallowed, not allowing her eyes to wander toward the tiny bundle in the corner of the hut. The tiny bundle who would never have a chance to live, the tiny bundle who would never grow to be a man.

Mrs. Hendrick's agonizing screams continued to blare through Hope's ears, drilling holes in the calm exterior she'd managed to maintain during the ordeal. Each torturous wail had brought Hope back to Portsmouth, sitting in the hallway outside her mother's chamber, trembling in anguish and fright. Only this time, Hope had been forced to watch Mrs.

Hendrick writhe in agony, watch the pain etch lines of misery on her comely face, watch as she expelled the lifeless child from her body.

And Hope saw her mother in each dreadful trial.

The physicians could do no more to ease her mother's pain then Abigail and Hope could do to ease Mrs. Hendrick's.

Forcing back the horrid memory, Hope lifted the sailcloth covering Mrs. Hendrick and peered beneath it. A shudder ran through her. "She's bleeding again."

"I'll go get more bedding and fresh cloths." Abigail stood, her arms full of stained rags. "And some water."

A warm night breeze wafted in through the open flap as Abigail left, bringing with it the smell of smoke and salt. It swept a curl of Mrs. Hendrick's mahogany hair onto her forehead, and Hope brushed it aside, admiring the woman's beauty.

Mrs. Hendrick moaned and grabbed Hope's hand, startling her. Another breeze swept in, sending the two lanterns perched on either side of the hut flickering.

"Boy or girl?" Mrs. Hendrick rasped.

"Boy." A tear slid down Hope's cheek. Wiping it away, she grabbed a cloth and dabbed the perspiration from Mrs. Hendrick's forehead. "You must rest now."

Her breathing grew ragged, and she eased her other hand over her flat belly. "A boy. William, like his father," she whispered as a tear slid from the corner of one eye and trickled into her hair. "I know he didn't survive."

Hope squeezed her hand. "I'm sorry."

"Mr. Hendrick will be so angry." Panic sparked from her eyes.

Hope flinched. "Nay, how could he blame you for what happened?"

"I never do anything right." She struggled to rise.

Hope gently pressed her shoulders down. "That's rubbish, and you know it." Fury raged through Hope. Fury at

Mr. Hendrick's stubborn pride. He should not have taken his wife and child on a raft upon the open sea. If the babe's death was anyone's fault, it was his and his alone.

"Elise." Mrs. Hendrick gripped Hope's arm.

"She is well." Hope patted her hand. "She is with her father. They are both worried about you."

The lines on Mrs. Hendrick's face relaxed. "You've been so kind to me, and I've been naught but. . ." Suddenly she wailed and slumped onto the bed, panting.

Fear shot through Hope. The pains of birth should be over now. "It matters not, Mrs. Hendrick. Just rest. Abigail has gone for more bedding and some tea so you can regain your strength."

"Please call me Eleanor," she managed to squeal out.

Laughter coupled with profane curses rumbled in the distance, reminding Hope they were no longer alone on the island. At least Captain Poole had allowed her and Abigail to attend to Mrs. Hendrick during her lying-in. Not only that, he had provided the cloths and lantern they requested. Perhaps the pirate captain possessed some measure of compassion despite the vile behavior he'd demonstrated when he'd first come ashore.

"He loved me once." Mrs. Hendrick's voice was weak and scratchy as, with glazed eyes, she stared at the roof of the hut, an odd smile on her lips.

"I am sure he loves you still." Hope ran her fingers through the damp hair around Eleanor's face, wondering all the while where her *adoring* husband had gotten himself off to.

"He was so agreeable, so attentive and caring. A real gentleman. All the women adored him. But he had eyes for only me." She winced and pressed a hand to her belly. "He had everything a woman could want: wealth, looks, wit, and charm. I must admit, I was quite captivated."

Eleanor's description brought another man to Hope's mind, a man much like Mr. Hendrick—Lord Falkland.

Oddly, both men had turned out to be anything but attentive and caring. "He is a fine man, I'm sure."

Eleanor laughed. "He is a cad, and you know it." She closed her eyes. "Elise is the only good thing that came from him."

Hope raised a brow at the woman's honesty then peered beneath the sail cloth once again. She glanced over her shoulder, trying to keep the fear from her face. *Where is Abigail?* The bleeding had grown worse.

Mrs. Hendrick's moist eyes burned with sorrow. "Can I tell you something?"

Hope nodded.

"Elise was conceived before we were married." Eleanor searched Hope's face for several moments before releasing a sigh. "I knew you wouldn't judge me. Perhaps that is why I loathed you so much when we first met. I saw myself in you and hated you for it."

Shock held Hope's tongue. She never would have thought this fine lady, this proper, well-bred lady would have behaved with such impropriety, nor especially that she would divulge such an indiscretion to anyone—least of all Hope. That Mrs. Hendrick hated Hope, she had not kept secret, but Hope never could have imagined her true reason.

"He married me, of course." She waved a hand through the air then dropped it as if the effort exhausted her. "But soon after the wedding, he changed. He stopped spending time with me. He rarely paid me a compliment. He spent hours and hours away from home. He drank heavily, and I oft smelled perfume on his clothes. Nothing I did was good enough for him. He criticized the way I managed the household, the way I dressed, my conversation, even the way I laughed." Tears poured from her eyes and dripped onto the leaves beside her head. "And of course I disappointed him with Elise. He wanted a son."

"I'm so sorry, Eleanor." Hope could not imagine the despair she would feel at such rejection. Would Lord

Falkland have done the same thing had they been married? Yet, as thoughts of his recent betrayal burned in her memory, she already knew the answer. Even amidst the torment of the past month, even amidst the despair of the present moment, a bud of relief sprang within Hope. Though she and Eleanor had traveled down the same road, Hope had thus far been spared the same tragic fate. Why? For she certainly did not deserve a reprieve.

"I fear he's never warmed to Elise." Agony cracked Eleanor's voice.

Hope pressed a hand over a tangible pain in her heart—a pain for both Eleanor and Elise, but especially for Elise, for Hope knew what it felt like to grow up without a father's love.

"I gave myself to him wholly, thinking I could win his love." Eleanor struggled to catch her breath. "But in the end all I won was his hate."

"Shhh, now. You must rest." Hope took her hand, shocked by how cold and limp it suddenly felt.

Eleanor shifted her misty eyes to Hope. "I used to be beautiful like you."

"You are still comely, Eleanor." Hope brushed her fingers across Eleanor's cheek. "I was quite envious of you when I first saw you."

She smiled and looked away. "William says I have lost my youthful glow."

"William has gone blind." Hope no longer tried to hide the disdain in her voice.

A breeze blasted over them, sending the lanterns fluttering and shadows crouching across the ceiling of leaves. Abigail entered, her arms full of tattered cloths.

Kneeling beside Eleanor, Abigail lifted the sail cloth and peeked beneath her bloodstained petticoat. A white sheen drained the color from her face as she shared a look with Hope.

Terror curdled in Hope's belly. Once again she was in

Portsmouth, this time beside her mother's bed, holding her mother's hand as she now held Eleanor's.

Eleanor groaned. "I feel so weak." She let out a ragged breath and turned to Abigail. "Thank you, Miss Sheldon. You both have been beyond kind. I wish I hadn't been such a prude and had gotten to know you better." She smiled. "Perhaps we could have been friends."

"I am sure we shall be. There will be plenty of time for that." Abigail cupped her cheek in her hand.

"You know what the worst part is?" Eleanor faced Hope. She swallowed, her eyes foggy and distant. "I still love him."

Tears burned in Hope's eyes, and she squeezed them shut, releasing streams down her cheeks. Oh, how well she understood that kind of love! Just as she understood the heartache of giving it to someone who did not—or perhaps *could not*—return it.

Eleanor coughed and struggled for a breath. She gasped. Hope drew nearer, gripping her hand. "Eleanor!"

Mrs. Hendrick's eyes focused on the leafy roof then went blank. Her chest collapsed, and one final breath escaped her lips.

Abigail dropped her head into her hands and sobbed.

"No!" Hope grabbed Eleanor's shoulders and shook them. "No!" Not again. "Mother. No!" Falling onto Eleanor, Hope embraced her. "Don't leave me."

"Hope." Abigail pulled her from Eleanor and drew her close, wrapping her arms around her. "Shhh, shhh."

Leaning on Abigail's shoulder, Hope threw open the floodgate of years of sorrow and loss and allowed her tears to flow unrestrained—flow for Eleanor, for her baby, for a brother Hope would never know, and for a mother she never had. "It isn't fair. It isn't fair."

Abigail planted a gentle kiss upon her head. "Life isn't fair."

Numb, Hope trudged from the hut, the tiny, cold bundle cradled in her hands. The sultry night air struck her like a wall, thick with sorrow. But she barely felt it. She barely felt anything, save the agony wrenching at her heart. Crushing her toes into the sand, she peered into the darkness. In the distance, flames danced high into the night, circled by a raucous band of pirates, flinging chortles and curses and lewd ballads through the air. Enjoying themselves as if two precious lives had not been snuffed from this earth.

Her gaze moved to five shadowy figures sitting on a log outside the mob of pirates. One pirate, armed with pistols, stood guard over them, yet his attention and his body drifted toward his companions.

Pressing the bundle against her chest, she started toward the men. Above the sea, a full moon flung sparkling diamonds upon liquid ebony. The crash of the waves offered a soothing alternative to the boisterous revelry of the pirates. But she didn't want to be soothed right now. She wanted justice. She wanted revenge.

As she approached the log, Nathaniel's gaze shot to hers, as did Gavin's. The major lay upon the sand, snoring, and Kreggs and Hanson seemed oblivious to anything save the pirate's unrestrained festivities.

She halted before Mr. Hendrick, only briefly glancing at Elise curled up in a ball at his feet.

His drowsy eyes widened and he rose. "'Tis the babe?" He held his arms open to receive the wee bundle.

"I'm sorry, Mr. Hendrick. Your son did not survive." Hope took no care to soften the blow with a sentimental tone. Her only thought was to whisper the ill tidings so as not to disturb Elise.

"What's this? What are you saying? My son?" He took the bundle in one hand and peered beneath the cloth. For a moment his expression registered grief and sorrow and perhaps a bit of remorse, and Hope felt a spark of sympathy for him. But then his eyes flashed dark with anger. He shoved the dead child back into Hope's arms and stormed toward the hut.

Nathaniel shot to his feet as Hope turned and marched after Mr. Hendrick. Though he couldn't make out what she'd said to him, from Mr. Hendrick's reaction, Nathaniel assumed the child had been stillborn. He also deduced from the fury on Hope's face that a barrel of trouble would soon explode.

Grabbing Mr. Hendrick's arm, Hope jerked him around to face her. Her words were muffled, but their effect boomed louder than a broadside.

"Gone! Of all the—gone where?"

Nathaniel reached her side as Gavin circled around Mr. Hendrick, taking a stand behind him.

"The childbirth was too much for her. She is dead." Hope's tone was laced with anger, giving Nathaniel pause.

Mr. Hendrick took a step back, his mouth contorting into an O. Yet his face was devoid of any emotion. "Dead." He glanced at the hut and then at the bundle in Hope's arms.

Nathaniel's throat constricted. *Mrs. Hendrick, dead.* Her ear-piercing screams had trumpeted through the camp all day and half the night, but he assumed they were a result of the normal birthing pains. Hope's expression was drawn. Her shoulders sagged—with exhaustion or sorrow? Perhaps both. What she and Abigail must have endured.

Anger tightened Mr. Hendrick's otherwise placid expression. His jaw twitched. "Stupid woman! She couldn't do even this right without killing herself and my son."

As if in protest to his scornful affront, a massive wave crashed onshore, reaching its foamy fingers toward them.

Gavin shook his head. "Sink me, man, but you are a heartless beast." He voiced the sentiment that rang through Nathaniel's dazed mind.

"What would you know of matters of the heart?" Mr.

Hendrick dismissed him with a wave.

Hope shoved her face into his. "You dare call your wife stupid when it was your choice to take her upon the open seas!"

"The woman insisted on traveling with me." Mr. Hendrick shifted his shoulders. "In fact, she insisted on constantly hovering around me."

"How can you say such a thing?" Nathaniel could not hide the disgust in his voice. "'Tis obvious you did not honor her in life. But fire and thunder, man, at least honor her in death."

Mr. Hendrick lowered his chin as if pondering Nathaniel's words. He kicked the sand with his foot and sighed.

Hope held the bundle closer to her chest and lowered her gaze. "She truly loved you, Mr. Hendrick. Though I cannot imagine why."

The riotous sound of the pirates' merriment faded, and hair bristled on the back of Nathaniel's neck as the sound of their boots sifting through the sand took its place. He had hoped they would have been too far gone in their drink to notice the commotion.

Mr. Hendrick snorted. "You can't imagine why, you say?" The hint of moisture in his eyes dried into a hard sheen. "Many fine ladies set their cap for me—some in possession of quite a fortune, I might add—before I was forced to take Eleanor as wife." He raised his dark brows. "How unfortunate for you that you were not as successful as she with your last beau. Perhaps then, he wouldn't have abandoned you to the auction block."

The smell of unwashed bodies and rum wafted over Nathaniel as shadowy figures circled around them.

Hope's chest heaved. Pursing her lips, she took a step toward Mr. Hendrick. And Nathaniel got the impression she would have struck him on the face if not for the bundle in her arms.

Taking her elbow, he eased her back, hoping to quell her rage and her tongue before she sparked Mr. Hendrick's temper further. The man was grieving, and no matter how heartless he seemed, he deserved to be left alone.

Stifling his own anger, Nathaniel turned toward him. "I realize this must be a shock, but you have no cause to insult Miss Hope. Your wife's death was no one's fault. It was simply her time."

"But it *is* his fault!" Hope pushed her way toward Mr. Hendrick again. But, ignoring her, he directed his rage toward Nathaniel.

"You could have healed her. You healed this strumpet." He nodded toward Hope. "But you wouldn't heal my wife." His face darkened. "And now she is dead!"

The words rang ominous between a lull in the waves, and Nathaniel opened his mouth to explain he couldn't heal anyone without the power of God. But grunts and groans filtered through the mob of pirates, followed by the crunch of sand beneath heavy boots. Captain Poole appeared beside Nathaniel, his hands planted firmly on his waist.

"Mr. Mason, the man has just insulted yer wife beyond what any man should tolerate. And yet ye stand here and do nothing?"

"He's got the heart of a yellow dog, says I," one pirate bellowed.

"Yellow blood runs in 'is veins," another chortled, and the pirates broke into a chorus of insults.

The captain snapped his fingers to silence his men. "Unless, of course"—his voice took on a sinister tone—"she is not yer wife and indeed a trollop, as the man claims." Even in the shadows, Nathaniel could see the lust dripping from the captain's eyes as he gazed at Hope.

Nathaniel ground his teeth together and glared her way. Would this woman's unanchored emotions never cease to cause him trouble?

The apologetic look in her eyes did naught to appease

his rising angst. He lengthened his stance, knowing he could not appear weak in front of these pirates. Their lives—all of their lives—depended on it.

"Mr. Hendrick." He addressed the man in as calm a tone as possible. "You will apologize at once to my wife. And to me."

Mr. Hendrick's eyes flickered between Hope and Captain Poole, igniting a flash of terror in Nathaniel. Would he give them away? Surely the man had enough decency not to offer Hope on a platter to these ruffians. If he would simply apologize and walk away, the whole matter could be put to rest. But instead he snorted. "I will not."

Nathaniel's heart fell to his feet. "Then you shall meet me at dawn."

"It will be my pleasure." Mr. Hendrick fingered his beard and nodded.

The pirates cheered, shoving muskets into the air, one of them firing into the night.

"Since you are the one being challenged, Hendrick, you may choose the weapons," Captain Poole stated as if he often presided over duels.

"I choose pistols," Mr. Hendrick said smugly.

Nathaniel's blood froze. He stood a fair chance with swords, but pistols? He had little experience with them and had never been a good shot.

"Pistols it is!" Captain Poole shouted then turned to survey his crew. "We have ourselves a duel, men."

The pirates cheered. "To the death! To the death!"

Chapter 24

The pirates' riotous celebration of the upcoming duel sent Elise into a frenzy of tears, and Hope spent the next several hours trying to comfort the little girl. Finally she fell asleep, and Hope eased her arms from beneath her and sat to stretch her tired shoulders. At least for the moment, Elise was in a better world—a world where her mother was not dead and her father was not about to duel to the death.

When Abigail and Hope had first broken the sad news to the little girl, shock had kept her silent for quite some time. Then, like a sudden storm at sea, anger raged through her, and she searched the camp, demanding to see her mother. Thankfully, Abigail had already wrapped Eleanor's body in sail cloth, and with the assistance of Kreggs and Hanson, had placed her in the cleft of some rocks down shore, in preparation for burial on the morrow. With the bloody leaves and cloths removed from the hut and fresh ones strewn in their place, it was as if the dear woman had never existed.

Save for the little girl now lying beside Hope who had her mother's blue eyes and the creamy color of her skin.

Hope swallowed against the burning in her throat at the memories of her own mother's passing seven years ago.

Hope had been fifteen, surely more equipped to handle such a tragedy than Elise at only six. Yet the pain of her mother's death remained as fresh as if it had occurred yesterday. Afterward, her father withdrew into his own shell of agony, withdrew from his friends, withdrew from society, and withdrew from his daughters—especially Hope.

She brushed a finger over Elise's soft face, noting even in the shadows how much she favored her mother. Was it Hope's resemblance to her own mother that had caused her father to despise her, or was it, as he so often said, that she constantly disappointed him?

Though she tried to shrug off the sorrow, Hope's heart weighed heavy in her chest.

A hint of red peeked through the leaves forming the walls of the hut. Dawn approached, and with it, the terror of what Hope had caused by her foolish anger. If only she could have kept her mouth shut, Mr. Hendrick would not have insulted her. And Nathaniel would not have to risk his life for her honor. *Honor.* She snorted at the irony and cursed herself for putting him in this position—yet again. No wonder he wished to keep his distance from her.

Rising, she brushed the leaves from her gown and emerged from the hut. A light breeze wafted in from the sea, stirring the coals in the fireplace until they glowed red. Despite the heat, a chill overtook Hope, and she wrapped her arms around her chest. Her eyes ached—from exhaustion, from sorrow, from spending all her energy comforting Elise and all her worrying on Nathaniel's fate.

Where was he now, and what thoughts raced through his mind? Surely he wasn't sleeping. Snores filtered from the men's hut and also from down shore where the pirates had given in to drink and exhaustion and had fallen where they'd stood.

A sliver of yellow floated atop the pink on the horizon, drawing her into dawn's first light. The sound of a male voice drifted to her on the breeze. Turning, she headed toward it, swatting aside tangled foliage as she went. When she emerged onto another part of the beach, the dark shape of a man sitting atop a boulder took form against the pre-dawn glow.

Hesitating, Hope bent her ear toward him, trying to distinguish the voice amidst the roaring surf. It took only seconds for her heart to skip at Nathaniel's deep, resonating tone.

She crept toward him, wondering to whom he spoke and more than curious as to what he said. But as she approached, words like *God* and *Father* spilled from his lips, and she realized he was praying. Ashamed to be eavesdropping, she retreated. He turned in her direction.

"Hope?"

"Yes."

He ran a hand through his hair. "What do you want?" Annoyance rang in his tone.

Swallowing, she approached. His dark eyes scoured over her as if he were trying to see her in the shadows, but giving up, he turned away.

"You were praying," she said.

He nodded. "I thought it wise, since today I may meet my Maker." Humor tainted his voice.

But Hope found nothing humorous about the situation. "I'm afraid I have brought misfortune upon you once again."

Planting one bare foot on the rock, Nathaniel leaned his arm atop it and gazed at the sea. "The man was in shock and grieving. He had no need of your carping wit."

His reprimand stabbed Hope. "That he harbors no affection for his wife or daughter, you cannot deny." She spoke more adamantly as anger flared within her. "But that he shrugged off Eleanor's death so easily was more than I could bear."

"'Tis possible he has other things on his mind." Nathaniel's jaw twitched. He rubbed his eyes as the wind flapped his linen shirt.

"Why do you defend him?"

"I'll grant you he's an ill-tempered mongrel, and perhaps his behavior is deserving of our scorn." He faced her. "But might I suggest that perhaps it isn't wise to allow everything that passes through your mind to slip off your tongue without censoring?"

Hope bunched her fists and looked away, but guilt soon smothered her anger. He was right of course. And once again she'd failed to behave as a lady.

"How is the girl?" Nathaniel's expression softened.

"She cried half the night but sleeps now." The first twitter of birds drew Hope's gaze to the vegetation around them.

"You are good with her," Nathaniel said.

A compliment. Hope's heart skipped, and she gazed up at him. But he'd turned his face back to the sea.

"She is a sweet child, undeserving of this tragedy." Hope shifted her bare feet across the sand. "I also lost my mother in childbirth." Though why she told him that now, she did not know.

Nathaniel shifted on the rock. "I'm sorry." He sighed. "I am sure that made yesterday's task all the more odious."

Hope blinked at his compassion.

"Were you close to her?" he asked.

"Nay. We often fought." Hope tugged a lock of hair.

"'Tis the way with mothers and daughters, I'm told."

"They say we were too much alike—like two grindstones gnashing away at one another." Hope smiled, remembering how often her sisters would tease her with such sayings.

Nathaniel looked at her now, and she caught a whiff of his woodsy scent, a scent she'd come to associate with protection and warmth, a scent she would never tire of. "I am sure your mother only wanted what was best for you."

Hope wanted to believe that was true. Yet more often than not, she wondered if her mother had ever loved her. Or did she see too much of her own follies in Hope to care for her at all? "I wish I could go back and erase all our silly squabbles. I wish I'd spent more time getting to know her."

"We never appreciate someone when they are with us." Nathaniel lowered his foot to the sand and rubbed the stubble on his jaw.

Hope wondered if he thought of his own mother. She didn't know much about her, save she had died when he was young. That they shared the same loss endeared him to her all the more. A memory sparked in her mind—something she'd been dying to ask him.

"You claimed me as your wife," she said with incredulity as she took a bold step toward him. "Why? When I have caused you nothing but trouble." She'd been shocked at the time, overcome with terror and yet, gratefulness.

He snorted. "Surely you don't think me so callous as to feed you to the sharks. Not when it was within my power to save you."

Hope lowered her gaze, her heart shriveling. He'd done for her no more than he would do for any woman. No doubt if Abigail had been there, she would be the one honored with the title. "Nevertheless, I owe you my life once again."

He shifted his shoulders.

Hope inched toward him, longing to memorize every line of his face, every muscle, every inflection … just in case he would be taken from her. "I don't want you to die."

He chuckled. "We are of the same mind."

"I'm sorry for putting you in this position. It was not my intent."

The curve of the sun peered over the horizon, spilling gold and orange ribbons upon the sea. A breeze laden with salt and rain fingered the waves of his hair and flapped his shirt again, revealing his strong chest beneath. He faced her, regarding her intently. Something in his eyes, a depth of feeling, a purity, an honor, made her realize that she no longer yearned just for his admiration and approval. She yearned for his love.

Something she would never have. Not from this man. Gut wrenching, she took a step back. For the first time in her life, her beauty, her charm, and her feminine wiles were not enough to purchase the one man she longed to possess most of all.

He rose and rubbed the back of his neck then let out a deep sigh.

An extreme urge to run into his arms overcame Hope— to feel his strong embrace, to inhale his scent, to remember …. She took a step toward him. Her eyes burned, but she would not let them fill with tears. "Nathaniel, I cannot bear to lose you."

He swallowed, and for a moment the hardness in his eyes softened. For a moment, she thought he might open his arms to receive her. But instead he grunted and wove around her toward the jungle. "Dawn has arrived. I have an appointment to keep."

Nathaniel stood, hands fisted at his sides as Gavin primed and loaded his pistol. The major did the same for Mr. Hendrick, who stood beside him, inspecting his progress. A horde of pirates circled around them, including Captain Poole, who had leapt upon a boulder to survey the proceedings like a prince watching a cricket match. Hope, along with Kreggs and Hanson, stood amongst the pirates to his right. He assumed Abigail was with Elise and thanked God the little girl would not have to witness her father engaged in a duel to the death.

The sun hovered over the horizon, flinging its cruel rays upon them, only accentuating the sweat now dripping down Nathaniel's back. He ran a sleeve over his moist forehead as the pirates' incessant grumbling transformed into wagers and calculations of odds. He tried to drown them out, not wanting to know how much coin hinged on his demise.

The major, looking impotent without his red coat and white baldric, handed the pistol to Mr. Hendrick and sauntered over to Nathaniel. "I fear you have met your match, Mr. Mason." He snickered. "Mr. Hendrick informs me he is an expert marksman. Finally there will be an end to your insolent meddling in the affairs of competent gentlemen." His eyes glided over Hope, and he leaned closer to Nathaniel. "Let me put your fears to rest regarding Miss Hope's safety. I shall be happy to assume the role of *husband* in your stead."

Nathaniel's blood boiled. The intolerable man would never lay a hand on Hope. Not as long as Nathaniel lived. But that was his point, wasn't it? "How did your raft fare upon the seas, Major? Competent craftsmanship of a gentleman?"

The major narrowed his eyes and spun around.

Mr. Hendrick took up a pompous stance, reflecting the cocky assurance of his success. "Ready to die, Mr. Mason?"

"If God wills it, then yes, I am." Nathaniel lifted his shoulders and eyed his opponent. "It is your eternal destiny, however, which concerns me."

Mr. Hendrick snorted and laughed, though his laughter carried a twinge of fear.

"Enough chatter. Let's be on with it," Captain Poole bellowed, and a cacophony of cheers saturated the air.

"Very well." Gavin handed the pistol to Nathaniel with a wink of assurance, bolstering Nathaniel's weakening confidence. "Mr. Hendrick, Mr. Mason, back to back, if you please."

Turning, Nathaniel stared past the horde of pirates onto the green maze of trees lining the beach. He heard Mr. Hendrick shuffle in the sand and felt the heat from his body compress between their backs.

"On the count of six, gentlemen," Gavin continued.

Nathaniel dared one last glance at Hope. Fear bristled in her eyes, along with the same yearning and admiration he'd seen on the beach earlier. The yearning that had nearly broken down his resolve to keep her at a distance. Did she care for him, or was it another coquettish tactic she'd perfected over the years? It mattered not. He tore his eyes from her and focused on the task at hand and the sound of Gavin's thundering shout, "One!"

Nathaniel took a step. He should be angry at Hope for the precarious situation in which he now found himself. Nevertheless, how could he blame her for her outburst? Mr. Hendrick's cold disregard toward his family and his insufferable arrogance were not to be borne.

"Two!"

Nathaniel took another step. The muscles in his fingers twitched over the gun's trigger.

"Three!"

The pirates cheered and thrust their weapons into the air. "Thar be some blood spilt today, says I," one man shouted with glee.

"Put a ball betwixt 'is eyes," another chortled.

"Four!"

The grumbling mob parted as Nathaniel continued. Sweat slid over his palms, and he tightened the grip on the handle of his pistol. Being raised by a reverend had not afforded him the opportunity to master pistols. Swords, yes, for Reverent Halloway enjoyed swordplay as sport. But the man abhorred guns. *Oh why did he have to hate guns, Lord?* Nathaniel clenched his teeth, wondering what a bullet would feel like penetrating his flesh. *Nevertheless, Lord, Your will be done. I only ask that should You take me home, please protect the ladies.*

"Five!" Gavin yelled.

Nathaniel's heart took on a frenzied beat. The cock of a pistol snapped behind him. He gripped his own weapon with both hands.

A white egret flew overhead, squawking a protest.

"Six!" Gavin shouted.

Hope gasped.

"Fire at will!" Gavin and the major roared together.

Nathaniel spun around, pressed his finger over the trigger and aimed at Mr. Hendrick's leg. But before he could fire, the crack of Mr. Hendrick's gun reverberated though the air.

Nathaniel waited for the pain. He glanced down at his shirt, his breeches, but no red spot appeared.

"I shot him. I know I shot him!" Mr. Hendrick's face twisted in unbelief as he pointed his pistol toward Nathaniel. He glanced across the crowd. "You saw me. I shot him!"

The major stared agape at Nathaniel as if he were a ghost. "Egad, the man's luck."

A huge smile spread upon Gavin's lips. "Your shot, Mr. Mason."

"Finish him off!" Captain Poole gave a wave of permission to Nathaniel and then glanced aloft as if he were bored.

"Kill 'im, kill 'im, kill 'im," the pirates chanted.

An expression of terror contorted Mr. Hendrick's features. He tossed his gun to the sand. "I demand we begin again. There's something amiss with my pistol."

"Ye missed him, plain an' simple." Captain Poole hopped down from the rock, and the crowd parted to allow him passage. Planting both boots firmly in the sand, he fisted hands upon his waist and glared at Mr. Hendrick. "Now take yer stand like a man."

Mr. Hendrick's gaze skittered past the captain over the crowd, as if looking for a miraculous escape. His chest heaved. Sweat dripped down his forehead. Turning, he bolted to his left. A snap of Captain Poole's fingers brought the tips of ten swords leveled upon his chest. Sniveling, Mr. Hendrick faced Nathaniel. "I beg you, sir. By all that is decent and holy."

Disgust soured in Nathaniel's belly. This man had wealth, a successful merchant business, a good name—all the things Nathaniel had worked so hard to attain. Yet beyond all the achievements, beyond the respect he received, he possessed not only the heart of a blackguard, but the heart of a coward.

Still Nathaniel could not kill him. *Would* not kill him. He glanced at Captain Poole, who stood urging him with a lift of his brow to complete the task. How to end this without appearing a coward to these pirates?

Nathaniel raised his pistol again, closed one eye, and aimed it upon the trembling Mr. Hendrick.

He pressed the trigger.

Chapter 25

C rack!
A plume of smoke rose from the barrel of
Nathaniel's pistol, and he coughed at the acrid cloud that
blew back in his face.

Mr. Hendrick shrieked, patted his chest for wounds, then
allowed his gaze to follow the direction in which Nathaniel's
pistol was pointed. "You fired into the air." His incredulous
tone was edged with relief.

Nathaniel shrugged and tossed the vile weapon to the
sand. "You're not worth having a man's death on my
conscience."

Grunts and curses flooded over him. Captain Poole
belched and shook his head, glaring at Nathaniel.

But Nathaniel cared not. No one had been killed.
Especially not him. Thank You, Lord. The pirates were not so
pleased. They cursed and spat onto the sand then shot glances
at Nathaniel as if he had deprived them of their only
entertainment for a month.

"What kind o' duel be that? No one be dead!"

"I say we make 'em do it over," another pirate with a
silver ring in one ear and one eye sewn shut shouted toward

Nathaniel.

"Be gone with ye!" Captain Poole waved the crowd aside as he marched into the center. "Nothing more to see here." His men dispersed and ambled away, calling in bets and exchanging coins with clanks and chinks as they went, one of them grumbling, "Perish and plague me, I knew he wouldn't kill 'im."

Major Paine took a wide swath around the pirate captain, casting him a dubious look, and stood beside his still-trembling friend.

Gavin gave Nathaniel a disapproving glance. "Sink me, man. Why didn't you kill him? He would not have hesitated to kill you if he'd possessed a better aim."

"There is no need to take the man's life." Nathaniel rubbed the back of his neck.

Gavin stared at him as if he had just walked on water. "Of course there is. Especially when the man is a blubbering, pompous toad."

Captain Poole chuckled. "A truer word as e'er were spoke."

"The pistol was faulty," Mr. Hendrick whined.

Nathaniel's gaze locked upon Hope, a few yards behind him. Elise stood at her side, clutching her skirts. Even from a distance, he could see the relief and joy beaming from Hope's expression.

Gavin thrust his face toward Mr. Hendrick. "Instead of complaining, sir, you should thank Mr. Mason for his charity. I daresay you would not have received such grace from me."

"Nor from me," Captain Poole added with a grunt. He picked up Mr. Hendrick's pistol from the sand and studied it for a moment. "Ye were beat fair, Hendrick. And as I sees it, ye owe this man yer life."

Mr. Hendrick remained stoic, his jaw firm and eyes hard.

Dismissing him with a wave, Captain Poole took a turn about Nathaniel, examining his back and chest. "Split me sides, but I saw the man's aim. 'Twas dead on. At six paces an' even wit' the unsure accuracy of these metallic beasts, he should o' clipped ye at least." Turning, he glared at the major. "Ye there. Give me some power and shot."

"What is your intent, Captain?" The major eyes flitted across the group.

"None of yer business, ye half-masted cockerel. Now give them to me, or I'll put a shot betwixt yer ears."

The major's sunburned face blanched. He fished in his pocket, pulled out the powder container and a ball, and hurried over to hand them to the pirate.

After loading and priming the pistol, Captain Poole took a few steps away from the group, cast a glance over his shoulder toward where Hope, Elise, and Abigail stood, then cocked and aimed the weapon at a palm tree a few feet down shore. "See them coconuts?" Without awaiting a response, he closed one eye and pulled the trigger. A resounding *crack* whipped the air, and a coconut thudded to the sand. He eyed the weapon, batting away the smoke. "Nothing wrong with this pistol, Hendrick." He stuffed it into his breeches. "Either ye are a horrible shot an' a worse liar, or this man should have a hole in him."

"'Twas God's doing." Abigail's voice shot over them. Captain Poole spun on his heels, his face brightening as he watched the lady approach.

Nathaniel tensed, praying she knew what she was doing. Behind her, Hope and Elise inched closer as well.

"God, ye say?" Captain Poole cocked his head and studied Abigail with interest.

"You have proven, Captain, that the pistol is not faulty," she began, her tone confident and unafraid. "We have Mr. Hendrick's testimony that he is an expert marksman, and why would he lie under these circumstances? And we have Mr. Mason here without a mark on him. What other explanation would you give?"

Captain Poole circled Abigail, fingering the stubble on his chin. A sly grin slithered over his lips. Abigail stood tall, her chestnut hair dancing idly down her back in the breeze. She brushed a few strands from her forehead with the back of her hand and commanded his gaze.

"A wise conclusion, miss," Captain Poole said. "I've forgotten yer name."

"Sheldon. Abigail Sheldon."

"Ah, Miss Sheldon. I should like to discuss this further with ye, if ye don't mind." He proffered his arm as though he would escort her to a ball.

Abigail froze; her jaw quivered. Nathaniel took her arm and eased her away from the pirate.

"Have ye two wives now, Mr. Mason?" Captain Poole snapped. "I wish merely to speak wit' the lady. Ye shall be rid of me soon enough. We set sail on the morrow."

Gavin moved to stand beside Hope in a protective gesture that grated over Nathaniel. Ignoring it, he fixed his gaze upon the captain, both pleased and alarmed at the man's declaration to leave. "So soon?"

"Ye'll miss me, eh?" Captain Poole eyes sparkled with mischief. "Seems ye've picked this island clean of fruit. And we've loaded up all the water we need. There be naught left for us here."

"Will you take us to Kingston, then?" Nathaniel crossed arms over his chest and risked pricking the capricious pirate's ire. But he had no choice. Who knew when another ship would arrive?

The captain inhaled a deep breath as if trying to calm his temper, then nodded toward his ship. "Does that look like a passenger ship to ye, Mr. Mason?" He ground out the words, but then his face softened. "Nay, she be the *Enchantress*— named for me last wife. And upon that beauty, me and me crew have taken three merchantmen, two East Indiamen, one Spanish argosy, a Dutch *fluyt*, and a German barque." He seemed to grow taller with the mention of each conquest then leaned toward Nathaniel and raised one brow. "Now if ye and yer friend here and those two"—he motioned toward

Hanson and Kreggs—"wish to join me crew, then we have somethin' to discuss."

"I can't speak for these others, but I am no pirate, Captain Poole," Nathaniel said without hesitation.

"Too good for the trade, eh?"

"Mr. Mason is a godly man, Captain." Abigail raised her chin a notch. "Pirating would go against everything he believes in."

"Saints' blood." Captain Poole waved his hands through the air, the lace at his cuffs fluttering in the breeze. "This island's crawlin' with godly people. Where have I landed, Christ's Church, London?"

Gavin chuckled and then coughed into his hand beneath Abigail's stern glance.

"What of ye, sir?" Captain Poole directed his gaze at Gavin. "Be there pirate blood in ye?"

"I have yet to discover that, Captain." Gavin winked. "But one never knows."

"I thought so. I can see the fire of the brethren in yer eyes." The captain clapped him on the back, the compliment molding over Gavin like the perfect fit of a garment.

"And ye two." The captain swung about and faced Kreggs and Hanson. Fear skittered across Hanson's face, but Kreggs shifted his stance and furrowed his brow. "We stick with Mr. Mason. He's not led us astray thus far."

Captain Poole turned a curious eye to Nathaniel. "Yer men revere you. Such loyalty be hard to come by." He studied Nathaniel as if searching for the reason then shrugged. "Well, so be it. Ye can all stay on this bloomin' island for all I care."

"We are both able seamen." Nathaniel gestured toward Gavin. "We will work your ship to pay for our passage as long as you don't engage in pillaging along the way."

Captain Poole's menacing laugh bristled the hair on Nathaniel's arms. Instantly, his face turned to stone. "I don't bargain wit' the likes of you." He spat. But when he glanced at Abigail, his face softened. "I tell ye what. Allow me a moment wit' Miss Sheldon, and I'll think on yer offer."

"No." Hope stepped forward. "Leave her be." Abigail sent an appreciative glance toward her friend.

"All I wish is to speak wit' her, an' I'll do it wit' or wit'out yer permission."

Over the pirate's shoulder, Nathaniel saw Abigail nod her consent, though he didn't miss the hesitation in her eyes.

"Very well, Captain," Nathaniel reluctantly agreed.

"There be some sense to ye, after all." Captain Poole proffered his arm again, and this time Abigail took it.

Nathaniel could do naught but clench his fists and say a prayer as he watched them saunter away.

Abigail drew a breath, trying to quell the quiver in her voice and the tremble in her legs. "If you mean to assault me, Captain, I must warn you, I *will* put up a fight."

"Promise?" Captain Poole gave a mischievous chuckle but then patted her hand, still hooked in the crook of his arm. "Ye've naught to fear from me." She caught his gaze from the corner of her eyes—as dark and brooding as any she'd seen. "At least for the time being." His lips curved slightly as he continued to lead her along the shore.

"What would you like to speak to me about, Captain?" His salacious dalliance unnerved her. She wouldn't have agreed to being alone with him—not even to soften him to the idea of taking them to Kingston—save for the fitful yearning she'd seen in his eyes. A questioning, a hopeless pleading that nipped at her heart. And made her believe he had more on his mind than accosting her.

A breeze picked up, bringing with it the scent of the sea and a whiff of rum and sweat from the man walking beside her. His boots crunched over the sand as he swerved away from the waves that crept toward them in arcs of restless foam.

After casting a glance over his shoulder, the captain led her to a boulder beneath a shady palm and gestured for her to sit. Abigail spotted Nathaniel standing at a distance and was thankful for his careful watch. Not that there would be much he could do to stop this pirate from taking whatever he wanted, especially with his savage crew so close at hand.

The rising sun shot its blazing rays upon the island. Abigail ran a hand over her moist neck, thankful for the shade and wondered how the pirate tolerated his velvet coat and breeches. Though seemingly undaunted by the heat, his expression bore evidence of a battle raging within him.

A breeze quivered the fronds of the palm above her until they sounded like the laughter of angels, reminding her that she was never alone. Silently, she thanked the Lord for the good outcome of the duel, for their safety thus far, and for the right words to appease this volatile man beside her.

Captain Poole doffed his plumed hat and tossed it to the sand. His black hair fluttered in the wind over the golden ring in his ear, and she swallowed at the intense look in his dark, flashing eyes. Tall and broad shouldered, he would be handsome if not for the lines of cruelty that often marred his face.

Lowering her gaze beneath his perusal, she waited for him to begin.

He shifted his boots. "Yer a missionary."

Abigail nodded.

"Ye speak of God as if ye know Him." His tone was not accusatory, nor caustic, but carried a curiosity that both shocked and delighted Abigail.

"He *can* be known, Captain. He longs to be known."

He scratched his chin and stared out to sea. Abigail eyed the pistols stuffed in his baldric and breeches, the cutlass that hung at his side, and she knew this man had killed many men in his life. Never before had she been in the presence of such evil, and yet, oddly, she felt no fear.

"I'm wonderin' if ye would enlighten me wit' what ye

know of Him," he said without looking at her.

Abigail blinked. "You want to know about God?"

He cast a glance over his shoulder at Nathaniel then returned his gaze to her. "Aye, as ye heard me say."

A spark of unease shot through Abigail, but she stiffened her jaw. "What do you wish to know?"

He crossed his arms over his chest, his coat flapping in the breeze behind him, and dug his boots in the sand as if preparing himself for a long discourse. "Start at the beginning."

Chapter 26

Hope finally gave in to sobbing. Perhaps it was Eleanor's death, perhaps the terror of the duel, or perhaps it was—one glance toward the beach told her Nathaniel remained at his watch upon Abigail talking with Captain Poole like a fierce sentinel—Nathaniel's obvious affection for Abigail. During the past hour, he had not budged from his post, not even when the blazing heat of the sun scorched the sand, not even after everyone else had abandoned him, not even when it was obvious the pirate had no plans to assault her. From time to time, he would pace ferociously as he was prone to do when he was distraught, but now he stood still, fists planted firmly at his waist.

Hope had longed to join him, but his aversion to her company had kept her standing at a distance for as long as her ankle and the glaring sun allowed. She, too, was most concerned for Abigail's safety, but it truly appeared the captain only wished to speak with her, though regarding what subject Hope could only imagine.

She entered the clearing and sank onto the chair, trying to enjoy the respite from the heat. Wrapping her empty arms around herself, she released a sigh. She missed Elise. Mr.

Hendrick had taken his daughter into his hut with the major, and Hope wondered how she fared. The poor girl obviously feared her father, but he *was* her father, after all. Perhaps now that his wife was gone, Mr. Hendrick would become a better parent. Deep down, Hope doubted it.

Leaning forward, she picked up a shell and examined it, flipping it over and over in her head, admiring the symmetrical ridges—so patterned, so perfect, so unlike real life. Had God intended his children to be this perfect? Did He intend their lives to follow a specified pattern? If so, perhaps one day, they would all end up as beautiful and flawless as this shell.

Gavin bounded into the clearing, his bare chest glistening with sweat. "Kreggs and Hanson are digging the grave." He glanced at Nathaniel out on the beach. "As soon as Abigail is free, we'll bury Mrs. Hendrick."

Hope nodded, even as her gut shriveled. She hated funerals. She hated death.

Scooping a large shell-full of water from the bucket, Gavin poured the liquid over his head. Hope averted her eyes from his muscled chest. Egad, but the man presented a constant barrier in her efforts to become a lady.

"Nathaniel must harbor deep affections for Miss Sheldon, wouldn't you say?" Grabbing his discarded shirt, he dabbed the moisture on his torso then thrust his arms into the garment, and took a seat on a log beside her chair.

Hope shifted against the uncomfortable twinge of jealousy. "Perhaps he is merely concerned for her safety."

"We are *all* concerned, to be sure, but you don't see anyone else standing guard like a marine on watch. Sink me, he's ready to slap the captain's hand should he make a single untoward gesture toward the lady. Nay, seems like the actions of a man quite besotted." He laughed, and his gaiety stung Hope's heart.

Shoving her pain behind a wall of rejection, Hope diverted her attention to the man beside her. His easy smile and flirtatious ways swept over her like salve on a wound. "How would you know the actions of a besotted man?" She smiled.

He took her hand in his and planted a kiss upon it. "Allow me to demonstrate."

And demonstrate he did, through witty conversation, beguiling smiles, amorous looks, saucy jokes, and a constant caress of her hand.

An hour later, when Nathaniel and Abigail entered the camp, Hope released Gavin and leapt to her feet, anxious for news, and only a little embarrassed she'd been caught flirting.

Rising, Gavin placed a possessive hand on her back.

Nathaniel grunted, eyeing them with scorn.

Oblivious to anything untoward, Abigail clasped her hands together, her eyes dancing with joy. "The captain has agreed to provide safe passage to Kingston."

"Indeed?" Hope could hardly believe her ears. From the pirate's fluctuating moods and volatile mannerisms, she'd come to believe their best hope might be that he would simply leave them on the island. "But how?"

"Well, sink me." Gavin eyed Abigail curiously, a slight grin rising on his lips. "What did you offer the man to make him so agreeable?"

"What are you implying?" The sudden flame in Nathaniel's eyes only confirmed Hope's suspicions of his deep affections for Abigail.

Gavin held up his hands. "No disrespect intended. Just wondering."

Nathaniel gave him a glance of warning then crossed his arms over his chest and looked at Abigail with pride.

"I cannot say for sure." Abigail sauntered to the bucket of water and knelt to draw herself a drink. "We spoke about God."

Hope sank back down to her chair, battling a plethora of emotions, shock and jealousy leading the pack.

"God? You spoke of God? With the pirate?" Gavin scratched his whiskers and chuckled.

Hope glanced toward the pirate camp and spotted the captain waving his cutlass in the air and spouting a slur of curses. "Difficult to believe, indeed."

"I can hardly believe it myself." Abigail stood and brought her long hair over her shoulder in a tumble of silken chestnut. Her hazel eyes swept toward Nathaniel. "I will tell you more later, Nathaniel." She smiled, their gazes locking in understanding.

Hope picked up the shell by her feet again, wishing her life would flow along the same perfect pattern. But it wasn't the same shell. This one was chipped and one of the ridges had gone askew. Just like her. Giving a sad smile, she slipped it into her pocket.

"But he wishes to hear more about God," Abigail continued, "so I convinced him to take our party to Kingston with the promise of further discussions."

Gavin shook his head, his expression a mask of confusion. "Do you suppose 'tis a trick, a pretense for his otherwise lecherous intentions?"

Abigail shrugged. "The thought occurred to me as well. But I think not. I saw sincerity in his eyes. He seems to possess a genuine awe for God, along with a fear to harm anyone who knows Him."

"Whatever it takes, I suppose." Gavin snorted. "But I would not have guessed such an interest to be found in our Captain Poole. Not if you'd paid me a chest full of gold."

Nathaniel chuckled. "A miracle of God."

"A miracle, indeed." Abigail said, and they exchanged another intimate glance.

Shaking off the rueful weight that had settled on her shoulders, Hope stood again. "Well, I for one shall be glad to finally get off this island and be on my way home." Her sharp gaze unavoidably landed on Nathaniel, but he didn't once glance her way. Instead he stood with the regal authority of a prince, his hair fluttering in the breeze, his eyes flitting about the camp, toward the hut, Gavin, Abigail, anywhere but on Hope.

"We must prepare," Abigail said. "The captain wishes to set sail at midnight."

"Why not wait until morning?" Hope's nerves tensed as she thought about boarding a pirate ship.

Nathaniel finally met her gaze. Confusion and concern swirled in his dark eyes.

"We sail with the high tide, no doubt," Gavin offered.

Hope lowered her chin. "But we must bury Mrs. Hendrick."

Abigail approached her and took her hand. "And so we shall."

After the dismal funeral, Hope and Abigail convinced Mr. Hendrick to allow them to bring Elise back to their hut. There, they laid down with her, trying to console the devastated child and afford her some peaceful rest before their journey at midnight.

"What an incredible turn of events. I am beyond astonishment." Nathaniel scratched his head and stared out upon the ebony waves.

Abigail chuckled. "I can't imagine what my face must have looked like when he first asked me. I'm surprised I didn't scare him off."

Her eyes sparkled in the moonlight, and Nathaniel thanked God for providing him someone with whom he could discuss spiritual matters. Since he'd left Charles Towne, he'd missed his nightly chats with Reverend Halloway. "And after all you told him, he still wishes to hear more?"

"Yes. Apparently he has a Bible on board, but has been hesitant to even touch it." Abigail stretched her legs out and crossed them at the ankle. "I suspect some miracle happened to him, or perhaps he saw something that convinced him of God's mighty power."

"God *does* work in mysterious ways." Nathaniel rubbed the back of his neck. "For I would have never believed He would send us a pirate who fears Him." He laughed, but then sobered when he saw a shiver run through Abigail.

"I have to admit, I was rather frightened of him at first." She swallowed. "Something in his eyes—a look I have seen once before."

Fear tightened her expression, giving Nathaniel pause. Through all their terrifying circumstances, Abigail had always been the epitome of courage. He longed to inquire what type of look she referred to and where she'd seen it before, but dared not pry. "I have noticed the way he looks at you. He fancies you." Nathaniel rubbed his burning side and stared at the dark horizon, lit up by occasional sparks of lightning.

Abigail sniffed and raised a hand to her nose. When her eyes met his, they glistened with tears.

"What is it? Have I upset you?"

"Nay. I fear the pirate's attentions have resurrected a bad memory, is all." She gave a little smile and brushed the hair from her face.

Nathaniel eased an arm around her shoulders and drew her close. "May I?"

She nodded and leaned her head against him. "Forgive me, Nathaniel. 'Tis been quite a difficult day."

"I am concerned for your safety," he said. "You play a dangerous game with a dangerous man."

"There is no other way. Besides, how could I deny a man's true interest in God?"

"I will do all I can to protect you." Nathaniel squeezed her, knowing she wouldn't misread it as anything other than brotherly comfort.

"And Hope. You will protect Hope?"

He nodded, but he didn't wish to think of Hope right

now. Mainly because he'd done naught but think of her the entire day, wondering what to do about his rising affections for her, wondering if God were not keeping them kindled for a reason.

Hope shot up from her bed of leaves and tossed a hand to her chest, where the wild beat of her heart pounded against her palm. A dream. It was only a dream. She searched her mind for the remembrance of it, but it escaped like a mist before the sun. As her eyes grew accustomed to the pitch-black night, she glanced down and saw Elise curled up beside her, her puffs of deep sleep echoing thought the hut. A dark void loomed on her other side, where Abigail had retired. Where had she gone?

Thud thud thud sounded outside the hut, no doubt the noise that had woken her so suddenly. Her heart squeezed. Some animal? Or worse, a pirate, besotted with rum, seeking a companion. Slowly rising so as not to make a sound, she inched toward the flap and peered behind it.

A dark form sitting by the fire came into view. Gavin. Relief swept away her tension as she eased the cloth aside and emerged from the hut.

He grinned as she approached. "Forgive me, Hope. I didn't mean to wake you."

"What are you doing?" A breeze swirled around her, and she wrapped her arms across her chest.

"I couldn't sleep." He sighed. "I didn't realize I was making noise." He dropped the stick he was holding. The eager look in his eyes gave Hope pause that, once again, she found herself alone with this man who made her feel beautiful and cherished and desired. But was it really love he felt for her? Or just a shadow of the real thing—an imposter drawn by her beauty and not by who she truly was on the inside? For no matter how wonderful his attention felt, Hope knew it would not be enough for her anymore. Not after

Nathaniel.

"Did you see where Abigail went?"

He cocked his head toward the beach. "About an hour ago."

"Alone? With all these pirates on the island?" Hope bit her lip.

"She seems to handle herself well enough with the mongrels." Gavin shrugged, his voice a drone of nonchalance.

"What do you have against her?'

"Abigail? Nothing. I simply have naught in common with the woman. And besides she is married to her God."

Hope sighed. As was Nathaniel. Why couldn't she accept that fact as easily as Gavin had?

Thunder rumbled in the distance as a brisk wind, laden with the scent of rain, ruffled her long hair. Clutching her skirts, she stepped over a log then headed out of the camp. Regardless of Gavin's lack of concern, Hope must ensure Abigail's safety.

"I'll go with you." Gavin gave a frustrated huff and hurried to join her.

Cool sand eased between her toes as the gentle crash of waves washed over her agitation. But it quickly returned when her thoughts drifted to the funeral. A most dreary affair, especially for Miss Elise. The poor child had stood beside her father in abject despondency. Not once did he offer her an ounce of comfort. Her swollen red eyes kept shifting from her mother's wrapped body laid gently in the earth, to Hope, as if somehow Hope could raise her mother from the dead. Hope would have given anything at that moment to possess that kind of power—the kind power of which Nathaniel's God boasted. But where had He been when Eleanor had cried out in pain? When Eleanor had died?

It fell to Nathaniel to speak over Eleanor's grave, sweet words that gave her life and her death meaning and that spoke of a resurrection to glory someday. But Hope had a hard time swallowing any of the placating nonsense, though a part of her longed to believe it more than anything.

"This way." Gavin tugged on her arm as though he knew exactly where Abigail had gone. They made their way through a clustered patch of sea-grape trees and out onto a small bank of sand just in time to see white lightning score the black sky. Shadows emerged on the sand. Two people huddled together—embracing each other. She froze. Gavin halted at her side. Nathaniel's and Abigail's voices drifted to her on the capricious wind.

Spinning around, Hope tromped back through the patch of sea grapes. "Why did you bring me out here?"

"I didn't bring you," Gavin huffed. "You wanted to find Abigail."

"But you didn't tell me Nathaniel was with her."

"How was I to know?" He grabbed her arm, heaving her around. "What ails you? Surely you haven't been blind to their affections for one another?"

Hope swallowed a clump of pain. Of course she'd noticed the attachment between Nathaniel and Abigail. "Forgive me, Gavin. I'm behaving foolishly. My concern was for Abigail, and now that I've found her safe and sound, all is well." She continued on her way, chiding herself for her infantile display.

"You love him." Gavin's words took flight on the brisk wind, taunting her with their truth.

"Don't be absurd." Hope stomped into camp, trying to contain her conflicting passions. One of the signs of a true lady, she had learned, was to control one's emotions. Surely she could do that one small thing. Forcing the anguish from her eyes, she faced Gavin. A frown replaced his roguish grin. She'd hurt him with her callous display.

"Forgive me, Gavin. I've distressed you, and that was not my intention." She stepped toward him. "You've been kind to me."

His smile returned. "I'd like to be so much more." He

brushed the back of his hand over her cheek.

Hope closed her eyes to his gentle touch, but her thoughts drifted to Nathaniel, and then to Falkland. And the pain returned. Why did no one truly love her? Tears spilled from her lashes, and Gavin whisked them away. He eased fingers through her hair, then pulled her toward him. Hope could resist him no longer and fell into his embrace, allowing his strong arms to surround her. Then lifting her chin, he lowered his lips to hers.

Nathaniel walked back to camp in silence, Abigail at his side, as a light rain misted over them. He glanced at the pirate ship drifting nigh thirty yards off shore, and fear stabbed his gut at what lay in store for them all upon it. But Abigail's tale had given him hope that God indeed was with them and would see them through. And then he could bring Miss Hope home to Charles Towne. Thunder cracked with warnings of a storm, and he remembered the tears streaming down her face at the funeral and the tender, loving glances she'd bestowed upon Elise. How could the vixen possess such a caring heart? Yet despite his efforts otherwise, despite his urgent prayers for deliverance, he found himself drawn to her even more. Perhaps Hope could change. Perhaps with God's help she could become a moral, respectable lady. Perhaps God was using Nathaniel's infatuation with her for her good and God's glory.

Happy with the thought, he tramped through the last grove of trees. Against his first inclination to leave Mr. Hendrick and Major Paine on the island, he must wake them for the journey ahead. And of course Gavin—and Hope. But as he approached the camp, the green glimmer of Hope's gown caught his eye. She was awake already. Another step and Gavin's tan breeches came into view. Nathaniel continued onward, peering through the leaves. He halted.

Gavin's arms circled Hope, pressing her against him,

and his lips were on hers.

Swerving around, Nathaniel marched toward the incoming waves. *Infuriating woman!* This morning declaring her affections for him, her ardent concern for his safety, and then tonight allowing another man to take liberties with her. How could he have fallen for her wiles?

"Nathaniel." Abigail followed him. "I'm sorry." She laid a hand on his arm. "I know you care for her."

He dragged a hand through his hair. "Against my every inclination. But no more. Fire and thunder, no more."

Panic shoved its way through Hope's desire, dousing the flame as it went. She pushed away from Gavin. "Forgive me. I cannot."

Gavin flinched. "Why?"

"It is wrong." She swerved around and wiped her lips.

"What could be wrong between two people who care for one another and find comfort in each other's arms?"

"Because we are not betrothed. We are not married. And we do not love each another."

"The first two can be remedied, and the last one"—his feet shuffled over the sandy soil, and she felt his warm breath on her shoulder—"I would not discount so soon."

"I believe you mistake desire for love."

"Are you so sure?"

She swung about. His blue eyes were etched with pain and a spark of expectancy.

"I'm sorry." Hope dashed away from him, stumbled into the hut, and fell into a heap onto the leaves.

Why, oh why, couldn't she behave like a real lady?

Chapter 27

Hope peered inside the tiny ship's cabin that looked more the size of an animal pen in the shifting shadows. "I will not—"

Nathaniel's firm hand over her mouth smothered her protest to a mumble. He removed it as Captain Poole swung about, lantern in hand.

"You will not what, Mrs. Mason?" One dark brow rose on Captain Poole's face as his eyes flashed with amusement.

Mrs. Mason. Good gracious. The sound of it spoken aloud both terrified and elated her. "I will not … be needing anything else." Hope forced a smile. "This is perfect." Clutching her wet skirts, she swished inside the small enclosure, more to hide the look of horror on her face than to inspect her new home—a twelve-by-eight-foot space she was to share with Nathaniel. *As husband and wife.*

"I'm happy yer pleased." The captain's tone tingled with sarcasm.

"Yes, thank you, Captain." Nathaniel had yet to place a foot inside the door. "I'll come assist you in setting sail."

"No need, Mason. 'Tis been awhile since ye've been alone with yer wife, eh?" Captain Poole winked at Nathaniel.

"I'll jest be leavin' ye alone. Oh, and"—his gaze dropped to Hope's dripping gown—"I'll send some fresh clothes fer ye both to wear."

Captain Poole handed Nathaniel the lantern. "So I'd be doffin' yer wet breeches if I was ye." He nudged Nathaniel inside and closed the door with a thud, his laughter fading down the narrow hall.

Thunder roared, sealing Hope's fate. The pitter-patter of rain striking the deck above reminded her of the sound of little feet, and she thought of the orphanage she'd never have. Anything to keep her mind off the man standing just inside the door, apparently too repulsed to be in the same room alone with her. She plopped down on one of two wooden beds attached to the bulkhead and grabbed a lock of her saturated hair.

Nathaniel's deep breathing filled the room, along with the drip-drop of rain spilling from his breeches and shirt. But she didn't want to look at him. Didn't want to see him standing there looking so tall and handsome. Most of all, she didn't want to see the disgust simmering in his eyes.

He'd not spared her one glance all night. Not when they'd gathered to board the cockboat, not during the row out to the ship, not when Hope had crawled onto the deck from the rope ladder, not when myriad eyes swarmed over her and Abigail from the dark figures that spread across the deck. And not even when she shuddered as the realization struck her, she was indeed aboard a pirate ship.

Nathaniel cleared his throat and set the lantern down atop a wooden table. Raking a hand back through his wet hair, he rubbed his side and inched to the furthest corner of the tiny room. "Unfortunately, we must play along with this foolery."

Hope swallowed. "You look as though you'd rather be locked up in the hold with Major Paine." She regretted the words as soon as they left her mouth, but the pain of his rejection was too much to bear along with everything else.

"The fool." Nathaniel spat. "'Twas the only thing I could do to save his life." He looked at her now, but he immediately shifted his gaze away as if the vision sickened him.

"But knocking him unconscious?" Hope couldn't help a giggle as she envisioned the major's staunch refusal to board a pirate vessel. Then of course Captain Poole's obliging response in the form of a pistol leveled at the major's temple. Yet, just when Hope had thought she would be forced to witness a murder, Nathaniel had grabbed a piece of driftwood and slammed it over the major's head.

"The captain would have shot him with no more thought than he gives a belch," Nathaniel offered.

Hope brushed wet hair from her face.

"And no, I wouldn't rather be with the major." His brown eyes locked upon hers and remained there, the golden flecks within them shimmering with a depth of feeling that baffled her.

Shifting in her seat, she glanced down, shaking the vision of him and Abigail together on the beach from her mind. "At least you find my company slightly more favorable than the rat-infested hold."

The ship creaked beneath a wave, and Captain Poole's voice bellowed above deck, issuing orders to weigh anchor and hoist the sails. The pounding of footsteps added to the patter of rain, and Hope pushed back a sudden sorrow at leaving the island. It had been home to her for nearly three weeks, a place made bearable, even pleasurable at times, by the man standing before her now.

"I am sure you would prefer Abigail to be here in my stead." There went her mouth again. Hadn't Nathaniel warned her to test her thoughts before letting them fly from her lips?

"Abigail?" His tone sounded incredulous.

Hope stood, wondering at his reaction. Was he so kindhearted that he attempted to spare her feelings? She sighed. "What does it matter? You're right. We must make the best of this situation." Though as she took in the cramped cabin, the thought of spending three days *and nights* in this space with Nathaniel completely unnerved her. "You sacrificed your freedom to protect me. I thank you for it, and I promise to do my best to make this journey comfortable for you."

Nathaniel gave a derisive snort.

Pound pound pound. Nathaniel released a jagged sigh and opened the door to a spindly pirate with a pointed chin. "Cap'n says to give ye these." He handed him a pile of what looked like a gown, chemise, bodice, and stomacher, in addition to a pair of breeches and a shirt. The pirate sent a leering grin over Hope before he sauntered away.

Closing the door, Nathaniel eyed her. The tight grimace that had taken residence on his face since they entered the cabin relaxed. "This must be quite daunting for you. Being aboard this ship."

"A bit, yes. There are so many pirates. And the looks they give me."

"I will do my best to keep you and Abigail safe."

Hope smiled. Always the honorable gentleman.

"This appears to be for you." His face reddened as he handed the intimate garments to Hope. "Perhaps not clean, but dry nonetheless."

Closing the two steps between them, she took them and bundled them in her arms. The scent of wood and tar and Nathaniel mixed with the musky aroma of rain and swirled around her, sending her senses reeling.

He cleared his throat and tried to weave around her, but they bumped together in the small space. His closeness jarred Hope, and she leapt to the side, trying to escape the overwhelming sensations, just as he dashed in the other direction, tripping on her foot, and slamming headfirst into the bulkhead.

He moaned.

"Are you hurt?"

"Fire and thunder, woman. You will be the death of me yet."

She retreated as his spiteful tone tore through her, gripping the dry garments to her chest, not caring that they got wet. "Perhaps you should call on Abigail to tend your wound."

"Abigail?" He swung around, rubbing his forehead, where a red bump rose upon his skin. "What is all this with Abigail?" He tossed his dry clothing onto one of the beds.

"I saw you two on the beach." There, she'd said it. But the shame of revealing her jealousy stole any satisfaction from the declaration.

His face scrunched, and he shook his head. "You saw us …." He ran a hand through his wet hair. "Blast it all, I saw *you* kissing Gavin."

Hope's breath caught in her throat, and she raised a hand to her lips. "I was not kissing him." She stomped her foot and felt a splinter jab her toe. "He was kissing me." Before the words left her lips, she realized how ludicrous they sounded.

"Of all the … you cannot expect me to …." He took up a pace in the tiny cabin, which only amounted to two steps in either direction. Halting, he glared at her. "You gave me every indication yesterday morning that you felt something for me." He began pacing again, and confusion kept Hope speechless. Why would her feelings matter to him?

"And then you turn around and kiss another man. What am I to believe?"

Tears swam in her eyes. She wanted to give him the explanation he sought. She wanted to tell him she had pushed Gavin away, that his kiss meant nothing to her, that she was trying so hard to be good. She wanted to tell Nathaniel that she loved him. But he wouldn't believe her. He would always think of her as wanton. "Believe what you want. It matters not to me."

He grabbed the door latch.

"Where are you going?"

"Anywhere but here." He opened it and slammed it behind him.

Nathaniel emerged onto the deck to a blast of wind and rain that did naught to cool his humors. Sails rumbled and snapped like thunder above him as the ship veered to starboard. Marching to the railing, he peered through the darkness toward the island, now a black smudge on the horizon.

Lord, rid me of this obsession. I long to do Your will.

A hard slap on the back jarred him from his prayer, and Nathaniel looked up to see Gavin slip beside him. Shaking the rain from his hair, he gave Nathaniel a sly look. "Fight with the wife already?" He gestured toward Nathaniel's forehead. "Looks like she got the best of you."

Nathaniel growled inwardly and gripped the railing, trying to shake the vision of Gavin's arms circling Hope and his lips upon hers. Better to change the subject rather than to succumb to the overwhelming urge to grab the man by his collar and toss him into the sea.

Sudden shame overwhelmed him. *Forgive me, Lord. The woman has clearly driven me mad.* Whatever had happened, it wasn't Gavin's fault. Hope's charms could not be resisted without difficulty—especially for a man devoid of the power of God. Which made Nathaniel's own weakness seem all the more inexcusable.

Hope was an enchantress, just like the name of this pirate ship. An enchantress with blue eyes the color of the sea—eyes a man could dive into and never find his way out again.

"Where is Abigail?" he asked Gavin, attempting to divert his thoughts toward anything but Hope.

Gavin shrugged. "The captain has seen fit to house her in one of the best cabins—even tossed out his first mate to accommodate her."

Rain stung Nathaniel's face as fear for Abigail's safety bristled through him.

"Never fear." Gavin eyed him. "I don't think he means her any harm. Truth be told, he seems quite besotted with her." He chuckled as if the idea were preposterous.

"Why wouldn't he be? She's comely, in possession of a good mind, and is a proper, kindhearted lady."

"Pious and boring, if you ask me."

Nathaniel winced at his friend's poor judgment. He longed to tell Gavin that a pious lady is to be preferred, but he feared it would sound insincere on his lips in light of his infatuation with Hope. "Obviously the pirate finds Abigail interesting enough."

"Baffling, to be sure." Gavin wiped the rain from his face and glanced across the ebony waters. "Ah 'tis good to be out at sea again."

Nathaniel could not agree more. The ship swooped over a roller, spraying them with a salty mist that, joining with the rain, cooled his already wet clothes—and thankfully his temper, along with the heat that always swept over him in Hope's presence. The first eleven years of his life, Nathaniel had spent most of his days cooped up in a room with his mother. He supposed that's why he loved the freedom of the sea so much. "And where are Mr. Hendrick and Elise?"

"Sharing quarters with me." Gavin leaned onto the railing and shot Nathaniel a disparaging look. "And that imbecile, Major Paine, is locked below where he belongs. You should have let Poole kill him."

A cascade of curses swept over them, and Nathaniel glanced over his shoulder at a huddle of pirates on the quarterdeck, playing cards. It had been a long time since he'd been among such vile men. Shaking off their blasphemies, he gazed at Gavin, so young and adventurous, and lifted a silent prayer that his young friend would not follow in their footsteps. "Have you no value for human life?"

"For some, yes. My own, for example." Gavin laughed, and Nathaniel couldn't help but join him.

The rain ceased, leaving behind a refreshing scent in the air. Thunder growled its retreat in the distance, and Nathaniel thanked God the storm had been light. One hurricane was enough to endure. All he wanted now was to meet with his last remaining ship and sail to Charles Towne as soon as possible. He rubbed his forehead, wincing as his fingers grazed the knot where he'd slammed into the bulkhead. Because Hope had tripped him. Yes, the sooner he relieved himself of Miss Hope, the safer he would be. In more ways than one.

A tall man, whom Nathaniel assumed to be the first mate, barked an order to ease off the foresheet and clear the braces, sending the pirates scampering across deck. He had heard pirate ships were havens of disorder and drunken brawling, but the organization he'd seen thus far spoke otherwise.

A group of men emerged from the shadows on Nathaniel's left, Kreggs and Hanson leading them. "We've been telling these men about how you healed Miss Hope," Kreggs said. "They want to hear more."

Elated to discuss the things of God, especially with these pirates, and also to have something to do—anything to do—besides retire below with Hope, Nathaniel's exhaustion fled him. "I didn't heal her. God did. But I'd love nothing more than to honor you with the tale."

"That's my cue to retire." Gavin grinned and disappeared into the darkness, his footsteps fading over the deck. Sorrow overcame Nathaniel at his friend's lack of interest in God, but turning back toward the men, whose wide eyes were trained upon him, he began the story of Miss Hope's healing. Afterward, he shared other stories of miracles he'd witnessed.

At least an hour passed in which the pirates listened with rapt attention to everything Nathaniel said, even periodically asking questions. Amazed at their interest in God and heaven and eternity, Nathaniel spoke with conviction and compassion. And the more he spoke, the more empowered he felt. He knew God was with him, putting the right words in his mouth, and drawing these men to the truth.

But one by one, Hanson, Kreggs, and the pirates excused themselves to go below and get some sleep before dawn, leaving Nathaniel with no reason to avoid his bed any longer. He assumed it was past two in the morning, and he needed at least a few hours of sleep in order to stay alert on the morrow.

Heading down the companionway, he trudged toward his and Hope's quarters, praying she was asleep. Praying she wouldn't hear him enter, that he wouldn't bump into her in the darkness, and that he wouldn't be forced to listen to her soft, deep breaths throughout the night, knowing that if he did, he wouldn't find a second's rest.

Chapter 28

The door clicked shut. Ever so quietly. Not the hollow thud of a ship's cabin door, but the deep clunk of oak—the door of Hope's bedchamber. Lying on her bed, she reached out, her fingers gliding over the silk coverlet she'd not felt since she lived in Portsmouth. Footsteps echoed on the wooden floor. Her breathing halted. Her heart thumped. Her blood rushed, drowning out all other sounds. She opened her eyes, not daring to move, and shifted her gaze across the dark room. Gauzy cream-colored curtains flung wildly at the open window. Lit by moonlight, they danced ghostlike in the breeze. Across the room, eerie shadows danced along with them.

One of the shadows moved.

Hesitant, it stepped toward her bed.

"Faith? Is that you?" Hope whispered and started to sit up. Who else would be in her chamber at this hour?

The dark figure darted toward her. Before she could move, a firm hand slammed over her mouth. Another pushed her down onto the bed. The man clutched a fistful of her hair and yanked her head. Pain shot from her neck down her back. She tried to scream, but only a garbled muffle proceeded from her mouth.

"Not Faith, my dear." The slick voice spilled brandy-drenched breath over her. A voice that made her blood grow cold. A voice that sent shivers of terror over her. The voice of Lord Villemont.

"No! no! Let me go! No, please!"

Nathaniel shot up in bed. His heart slammed in his chest. He scanned the darkness, trying to remember where he was. *The pirate ship.*

Movement beside him. "No! I beg you. Do not!"

Hope. Someone assaulted Hope! In one leap, Nathaniel was at her side, ready to throttle her attacker, but only empty air surrounded her.

"No!" She thrashed and began to sob.

"Hope." Nathaniel gripped her arms and shook her gently. "Hope, wake up."

She struggled against his grip and tossed her head back and forth.

"You're dreaming, Hope. Wake up." Nathaniel grabbed her face with both hands to quiet her.

She jerked, gasped, then placed her hands atop his, feeling his fingers.

"'Tis me. Nathaniel."

She flew into his arms and clutched the back of his shirt as if he were her only lifeline. Engulfing her in his embrace, he pressed her close and felt her heart crashing against his chest.

"Nathaniel." She uttered a breathless appeal.

"Yes, 'tis me. You are safe."

Laying her head on his shoulder, she wept.

"Shhh." He stroked her as sobs racked her body, keeping a firm hold on her, hoping he could make her feel safe from whatever had frightened her so. She cried for several minutes until finally her whimpers softened, and she released a deep, shuddering breath. She fingered the sleeve of his shirt. "I thought I was back there again."

Nathaniel eased a hand down her back, grateful she was fully clothed. "Where?"

"Portsmouth."

Releasing her, he nudged her back and started to rise.

She gripped his arm and held tight.

He gave her a reassuring look. "I'm going to light the lantern."

She loosened her grip and slid her hand down his arm as he left, tightening her fingers around his for a moment before he stepped away.

Swallowing a lump of conflicting emotions, Nathaniel groped through the darkness, finding steel and flint, and finally lit the lantern. Rubbing the back of his neck, he turned to face her. She sat on the bed, her hair a wild cluster of golden curls. Wounded, desperate eyes stared back at him.

His heart shrank in his chest. Something terrible had happened to this woman.

He approached, kneeling beside her, and took her hand in his.

Hope ran her fingers over his calluses. "I'm sorry to have disturbed your sleep. I rarely have nightmares anymore." She looked away and tightened her lips.

"I'm glad I was here." The ship creaked, and the lap of waves against the hull soothed over him. "What happened in Portsmouth?"

She lowered her chin. Her hands trembled. "I cannot tell you."

Nathaniel brushed a lock of hair from her face. She flinched. "Someone hurt you."

Tears spilled down her cheeks, and she squeezed his hand. A shudder ran through her. "My sister's husband."

Nathaniel clenched his free fist, even as the muscles in his face tightened. What had this man done to her to cause such agony? Not sure he wanted to know, he remained quiet nonetheless, allowing her the opportunity to tell him if she needed to.

"He grabbed my hair." She released his hand and seized a handful of her hair as if to demonstrate. Anger and terror screamed from her eyes. "I couldn't move. I couldn't do anything." She dropped her hands to her lap and bowed her head.

Rage tore through Nathaniel, ripping his gut apart. The man had ravished her.

He wanted to punch something ... someone. He wanted to yell. He wanted to pound the bulkhead. Instead, he slid to his knees and took her in his arms.

"I was seventeen." She laid her head on his shoulder again and sobbed.

"I'm so sorry, Hope." Fury set his muscles on edge. How could this man—and a relation at that—hurt such a precious creature? An innocent girl who trusted him? No wonder she harbored anger toward God. No wonder she behaved the way she did. Another emotion shoved its way to the forefront. Shame. Nathaniel had judged Hope, rather severely, without any knowledge of her past.

He buried his face into her hair, breathing in her sweet scent. Her sobs quieted. One final emotion rose to the surface of Nathaniel's heart, drowning out all the others.

Love.

He loved Hope. He could not help himself. And the thought terrified him.

Nudging her back, he ran his thumb over her tears. Her crystal blue eyes met his, brimming with pain, desperation, and something else ... Could it be she returned his affections? Or was the yearning in her eyes just a need for love, a need for attention?

As if reading his confusion, she looked away, and the loss startled him.

"I shouldn't have told you," she said.

"Why not?" He eased her chin forward.

She batted the tears from her cheeks then brushed her hair back as if suddenly worried about her appearance. "I must look a fright."

Cupping her chin, he caressed her moist face. "You're the most beautiful thing I've ever seen." And he meant it. Despite her red-rimmed, bloodshot eyes; her puffy, swollen face; and despite hair that looked like Medusa's, she beamed with a beauty that had naught to do with her appearance.

She laughed, sniffed, and gave him a tiny smile that sent a wave of warmth through him. He didn't know whether to kiss her and declare his love for her or dash from the cabin and throw himself into the sea, risking the swim to land, rather than face the feelings surging through him.

Oh, Lord, please tell me what to do.

When Hope had awoken to find Nathaniel gone, memories of the intimate moments they'd spent in the early morning hours came back to haunt her. As well as the memory of what she had shared with him. Shame kept her below for hours until she could no longer stand the stifling cabin.

Lifting her skirts, she grabbed the rope, climbed up the companionway ladder, and emerged into the brilliant sun reflecting from the open sea around the ship. Planting her bare feet firmly onto the hot deck, she made her way to the railing amidst a wave of whistles and catcalls, as well as a few lewd suggestions that almost made her duck back down below. Instead, she raised her chin and gripped the railing, not daring to glance at the pirates whose eyes she felt boring into her from all directions.

"Good day to ye, Mrs. Mason." Captain Pooled hailed her from the quarterdeck, where he stood regally by the wheel.

She nodded in his direction, ignoring the sardonic gleam in his eyes, then smiled when she saw Abigail making her way toward her from the foredeck, where she had been talking with Gavin. The young sailor winked at Hope before turning to finish tying down a halyard. No doubt Nathaniel was on deck as well, working the ship, but she couldn't face him—not yet.

"Good morning, Hope." Abigail reached her side, a wide smile on her lips as if she were on a pleasure voyage instead of a pirate ship. She held a tiny brown book against her chest.

"Good morning." Hope returned her smile, trying not to picture her in Nathaniel's embrace on the beach. "How have you fared aboard this ship thus far?"

"Other than a few untoward comments, the pirates haven't bothered me." Abigail gestured toward the quarterdeck, and Hope turned to see Captain Poole's brooding eyes leveled upon them. "He protects us for some reason."

"Hmm. 'Tis *you* he protects, and let us pray he does not change his mind." Hope didn't want to alarm her friend, but Abigail's false sense of safety frightened Hope. With her nightmare so fresh in her mind, Hope realized if a lady wasn't safe in her chamber at home, then surely she wasn't safe aboard a pirate ship—no matter the apparent favor of the captain.

"Pray? What a grand idea." Abigail smiled and adjusted the lace binding her sleeves. She'd pinned up her chestnut hair into a loose bun, several curls of which dangled over her collar. She opened her Bible. "Captain Poole wishes to speak to me today about God, and I thought to read him this verse. Would you care to listen to it?"

Although the thought of listening to Scripture unnerved her, Hope nodded in agreement as she gazed over the sea. The sun, now high in the sky, ignited the turquoise waves in silver flames that made the scene so beautiful, it seemed like a dream.

"This is the parable of the sower, where Jesus explains how the farmer scatters the seeds along the ground. The seeds represent God's Word, and the soil represents people. But although they receive God's word, not every type of soil produces a crop. The first seed falls on rocky soil, but troubles and trials fall upon the hearer, and the seed never takes root. Now, here's the type of soil I think most represents Captain Poole." Abigail's voice heightened with excitement as she held down the pages of the Holy book against the wind.

"He also that received seed among the thorns is he that heareth the word; and the care of this world, and the deceitfulness of riches, choke the word, and he becometh unfruitful."

She slammed the book shut and looked at Hope with expectation. "Don't you see? Captain Poole has heard the Word of God, yet the riches of this world have pulled him away."

The words set Hope's mind swirling. She felt a tingling in her toes and shifted her feet across the deck. "Can other things pull someone away?" She gave Abigail a questioning look. "Like other desires ... for love, for affection, for attention?"

"Of course. Riches can be anything someone craves besides God."

A gust of wind, laden with the smell of fish and sunshine, wafted over Hope, and she glanced down to watch foamy waves frolicking against the hull. She had heard the gospel at a young age, but nothing had come of it in her life. She hadn't changed. In fact, she had only gotten worse. Perhaps she would never become like Abigail.

"You will make a good missionary," she said.

"Really?" Abigail smiled. "I wonder."

"You have opened my eyes to many things. My sister Grace is as zealous in her faith as you are." Hope sighed. "Yet she is so judgmental, always pointing out others' faults."

Abigail smiled. "I'm sure she means well."

"I know she loves me. You would like her. She spends much of her time traveling into dangerous places to feed the poor and Indians."

"Very noble, indeed." Abigail nodded her approval.

"Yet, she takes no care for her safety. I fear for her life." Hope thought of the countless times Grace had gone missing for hours, returning muddied and exhausted from some long mission of mercy.

"Pray for her protection." Abigail squeezed her arm, and Hope gazed out to sea, not wanting to inform Abigail that God often ignored her prayers.

The ship bucked over a roller, and Hope gripped the railing as a spray of seawater showered over them. They both laughed and brushed droplets from their gowns.

Hope pointed toward Abigail's gown, a lovely shade of green trimmed in creamy lace. "Very comely."

"Thank you." Abigail nodded. "And yours as well. That shade of blue matches your eyes."

"Truth be told, it feels wonderful to be in fresh clothes devoid of scratching sand and biting fleas." Hope risked a glance at the pirate captain, but he had disappeared from the quarterdeck. She patted her sleeve, where she'd tucked the chipped seashell she'd found on the island. Somehow she couldn't seem to part with it. "I wonder where Captain Poole got these gowns."

"I don't want to know." Abigail shook her head then leaned toward Hope. "How did you manage last night"—a tiny smile lifted one corner of her mouth—"with Nathaniel?"

Hope studied her friend. Shouldn't she be envious of Hope being forced to share lodging with Nathaniel? Yet not a flicker of jealousy marred her comely face. Of course not. Not Abigail.

"We managed well enough." Hope had no intention of sharing the intimacy that her nightmare had caused between them. Especially not with Abigail. But what did it matter? No doubt Nathaniel still found her unworthy. Most likely even more so now that he knew the truth of her past. He might even believe she had encouraged Lord Villemont's assault, as most people had accused her of doing.

He probably wanted nothing more to do with her.

Which was why he had left the cabin so early. Which was also why he hadn't greeted her thus far this morning. "You need not fear, Abigail. There is naught between us."

"Fear? My heavens. I fear only that there *is* naught between you." She chuckled, drawing Hope's confused gaze.

"But you ... but you and Nathaniel." Hope studied her friend. "I saw you on the beach in his embrace."

Abigail's eyebrows rose, and a gleam of understanding flittered across her eyes. "Oh my, you thought—" She laughed. "You thought—oh my, nay, he was only consoling me."

Hope could not help the quick leap of her heart. "Then you don't have affections for him?"

Abigail shook her head. "Not in the manner you mean, nay. I think of him as a brother, and I am sure he feels the same way about me." She laid a hand on Hope's arm. "You poor dear. All this time under such a misconception." She patted her hand. "I assure you, Nathaniel Mason, whether he admits it or not, is quite besotted with you. Although," she added, "I can't say he was all too happy when he spied you kissing Gavin."

Hope huffed and gazed down at the churning water. "That was a mistake."

"I've never seen Nathaniel so distraught."

Shame taunted her again even as Nathaniel's deep voice soothed over her from behind. She glanced over her shoulder, and he came into view, talking with a pirate at the larboard quarter. Wearing a white cotton shirt and clean brown breeches that fit him *way too* perfectly, her body warmed at the sight of him.

She swerved back around. "He could never love me." Hot wind blasted over her, loosening her curls. No matter how hard she tried to pin them up as was proper for a lady, something always came along to tear them down. Just like her efforts to become pure and good. "I cannot behave like a proper lady no matter how hard I try. My flighty emotions get the best of me, and I cannot seem to control them."

Abigail laughed. "There's your difficulty, then."

Hope raised her brows. "What do you mean?"

"You cannot change on your own strength. The power to change comes only from God."

An odd rumble of thunder roared in the distance, and Hope scanned the clear horizon for the source. A crisp line of blue met her gaze. "Why would God help me?"

Abigail laid a hand on Hope's arm. "Because He loves you."

Love me? Hope shook her head. Why would God love her when not even her own father had?

"He will not only change your heart," Abigail said, "but He will also cleanse it from all the filth of your past."

Hope's breath halted in her throat. "As if I were pure?"

"Not *as if,* but He *will* make you pure." Abigail grinned and then raised her face to the sky as if adoring this God of hers.

A gust of chilly air struck them, and Abigail shivered. Her brow furrowed as she glanced across the sea, but all Hope could think about was the girl's last statement. "Pure? How?"

"You have only to repent of your past, and ask God to cleanse you, to change you, and then make Jesus your Lord."

Hope swallowed. "Seems too easy."

"It is a free gift."

The warm rays of the sun dissipated, and Hope looked up to see a massive black cloud swallow it whole.

Abigail huffed. "Looks like we're in for another storm."

Chapter 29

Nathaniel teetered on the topgallant yard, trying to keep his mind on his work and not on the lovely vision of Miss Hope standing below on the deck. But his eyes kept roving her way. And when they did, his palms grew sweaty, his head grew light, and his concentration went flying off with the hot, humid, wind that blasted over him. Why did she have to look so beautiful? With her hair combed and pinned atop her head in a bouquet of glittering gold, and that blue gown flowing in delicate folds about her feet, every man on the ship stared agape at her.

Salacious wretches.

After he had rocked her to sleep, he'd lain back on his bed and tried to quiet his rapid breathing and thumping heart and relax his taut muscles, but when dawn peeked in through the porthole, slumber still had not found him. Rather than staring at Hope sleeping like an angel, he had slipped from the cabin and did the only thing he could think that would quiet the tormenting emotions within him.

He had worked. And he had worked hard.

Now, after hours of the sun beating down on him and sweat streaming off him, he still felt the press of her curves against him and smelled her feminine scent. His muscles ached and exhaustion weighed heavy on his eyelids, but the tumult inside of him had not weakened. In fact, it had only grown stronger.

For all his efforts, he could not shake her sad tale from his mind. Her purity had been stolen when she'd been a mere child. By a trusted relation. And from what Nathaniel knew of her father, she had received no comfort or support from him. 'Tis no wonder she harbored such a low opinion of herself—an opinion that drove her to seek love and acceptance in the arms of whoever offered it.

And Nathaniel had judged her for it.

"Loose topgallants. Clear away the jib!" The command bellowed from below, and Nathaniel worked to loosen the topgallant sail alongside the other men, while his thoughts drifted to his past. Had his mother suffered a similar tragedy in her youth? If so, she had never shared it with him. And he had judged her as well.

Some man of God he was.

Yet the sting of his past, the stain of his mother's profession, would not leave him. Indeed, it only fueled his resentment toward Hope. Regardless of the reason for her actions, Nathaniel would not pursue his feelings for her. For surely, a match between them would only bring them both pain.

"Let go topgallants. Let fall!" The men dropped the topgallant sail, and it began flapping in the wind. Easing across the yard, Nathaniel followed the others down into the shrouds and then climbed onto the ratlines and jumped, thudding to the deck below.

The sail caught the wind with a jaunty snap, and Nathaniel dared a glance toward Hope. With head bowed, she stared at the water, immersed in an intense conversation with Abigail.

Turning, Nathaniel leaned upon the railing, taking in a deep breath of sea air. No matter what he felt, he would not give his heart to a woman who could not help but stomp on it as soon as the next man paid her any attention. He must be strong. He rubbed the sweat from the back of his neck. Surely this was merely a test from God. And one he intended to pass.

"Nathaniel." Gavin's worried tone jarred him as the man clapped him on the back. "You've been working too hard."

"It keeps my mind occupied."

"And off what? Or should I say whom?" Gavin grinned and glanced toward Hope. "I've seen the way you look at her. Although I daresay, she does look rather fetching in that gown."

Nathaniel grimaced and wondered if he should give his friend his blessing to pursue Hope, but a twisting in his gut forestalled the words.

Gavin smirked. "How, pray tell, did you fare playing the part of her husband last night?"

Thunder rumbled, drawing Nathaniel's gaze out to sea where no evidence of a storm revealed itself. "She was asleep when I retired."

"Ah, 'tis the way of those long married, I'm told." Gavin chuckled then grew serious. "If you have no interest in her, I should like to pursue her myself. That is, if you don't mind."

Nathaniel shrugged. "You are free to do as you wish. And so is Miss Hope." His insides twisted into a knot so tight he doubted they would ever come undone.

"Splendid." Facing the main deck, Gavin leaned his elbows back upon the railing. "Sink me, but Captain Poole seems an odd excuse for a pirate."

"Hmm." Nathaniel wished his cheerful friend would depart. He was in no mood for idle chatter at the moment. Not when his insides felt like a grenade about to explode.

"Not only is he quite taken with Miss Sheldon," Gavin continued, "a missionary, no less, but he refused my request to join his crew."

Nathaniel blinked and stared at him. "You wish to become a pirate?"

"Why not?" He crossed one foot over the other and grinned, his eyes alight with mischief. "A life of adventure, freedom, and riches."

"Then I *do* mind if you court Miss Hope." Nathaniel's tone was more caustic than he intended.

Gavin cocked his head and gave him a curious look. "Why?"

"I do not wish to see her associate with pirates."

"Then you do care for her?"

"No more than any other woman." Nathaniel winced beneath his lie but then gazed at his friend, worried for the dangerous path he so casually pursued. "There is more to life than riches, Gavin. And even so, 'tis the way in which these men gain their wealth. Governor Rogers of New Providence has vowed to rid the Caribbean of all pirates who refuse the King's pardon. Do you want to lose your life at the end of a noose? Do you want to be labeled a thief, a brigand?"

"I do not mind dying, if I have truly lived." The sails rumbled overhead as the ship veered to larboard, and Gavin drew in a breath of sea air. "And besides, I care not for the opinions of others."

Nathaniel rubbed his eyes against the pull of exhaustion even as a heavy weight hung upon his heart for his friend. But one thing rang true; Gavin did not concern himself with the judgment of men. A good quality, to be sure, and one that grated over Nathaniel's conscience for his lack of it. Why did he care so much about what society and men of good breeding thought of him? "You have not truly lived, my friend, until you have known God."

Gavin grunted.

The sun's rays disappeared, giving Nathaniel a welcome relief from the heat. But when he glanced up, a dark cloud hovered over the ship.

Gavin followed his gaze. "Another tempest?"

Nathaniel scanned the horizon. Clear and bright. "No, this is something different." Something worse, he feared. He glanced toward Abigail, and her eyes locked upon his in understanding. Hope remained by her side. But what of the others? "Are Mr. Hendrick and his daughter still below?"

"Aye, I believe so." Gavin turned around and faced the sea. "The man wasn't feeling well. When I offered to escort Miss Elise to see Hope or Abigail, he wouldn't allow it."

Nathaniel stepped away from the railing. "I shall see to them. And bring the major some food. I doubt Captain Poole will give a care to provide for the man."

The features of Gavin's face pinched. "I cannot fathom it."

"Fathom what?"

"That you would concern yourself with the major's welfare after all he's done. He would have killed you if he'd had the chance. Yet you saved his life and now bring him food."

"God tells us to love our enemies." Nathaniel headed toward the companionway.

Gavin snorted behind him. "Pure rubbish."

Hope paced across the tiny cabin and smiled when she realized she'd picked the habit up from Nathaniel. Where was he, anyway? Halting, she stood on tiptoe and peered out the oval window. After her discussion with Abigail, thick black clouds had consumed the entire sky, casting a shroud of darkness on sea and ship. Yet, not a drop of rain had fallen. Even Captain Poole proclaimed he'd seen naught like it in all his days. An odd sense of foreboding had driven Hope below deck to the safety of the cabin she shared with Nathaniel, although she was beginning to wonder if he hadn't taken residence elsewhere. She couldn't blame him—not after she'd kept him up half the night with her nightmare.

Abigail had come by, and they had shared a light supper of hard biscuit and plantains, before she'd dashed off to meet with Captain Poole and answer his questions about God. Though Hope had tried, no amount of begging and pleading had convinced Abigail to stay with Hope and away from the man.

Worried for her friend, Hope wiped mist from the window, noting that night had fallen and not a speck of starlight, nor a wisp of moonlight, broke through the thick blanket of clouds. In fact, it seemed the ship floated through a dark void that had swallowed the world whole and was now trying to swallow her.

Dread gripped her heart, and she gazed at the door, longing to go above and find Nathaniel, but not wanting to risk wandering a darkened ship full of pirates. Why was she suddenly so frightened? The lantern flickered, though not a waft of air stirred in the cabin. Flopping onto her bed, she dropped her head into her hands.

Abigail's words would not let her mind rest. *God could make her pure.* Wasn't that what she'd been seeking all this time, to be made pure again? To be a real lady? She had tried so hard to achieve it on her own, but all her attempts had ended in failure.

And now, she may have lost any chance of gaining Nathaniel's admiration. But if God could truly make her pure and help her to behave with propriety, perhaps she could still gain the respect of her community and open an orphanage when she returned to Charles Towne.

Should she dare speak to the Almighty? Fear struck her. Thunder roared outside, shaking the ship and sending a shudder through her. Surely she was not worthy. Surely He would either ignore her, laugh at her, or strike her dead.

I love you, beloved.

Hope wiped the tears from her eyes and glanced over the cabin. She had heard the words as clearly as if someone had spoken them—and yet, she hadn't heard them at all.

You are precious to me.

Precious to God? And then she remembered the fever and how Nathaniel and Abigail told her God had healed her. *God had healed her.* Perhaps He did love her, after all.

Falling to her knees beside the bed, Hope sobbed. "Oh God, help me."

A silent yet imperative voice made Nathaniel wince. He clutched the railing and turned to Abigail, who'd come to see him for counsel before she met with Captain Poole. "Did you say something?"

She shook her head, but her eyes widened, and she gazed across the deck as if she, too, had heard a voice.

Pirates clustered in groups, drinking rum and playing cards. A crowd on the foredeck joined in a ribald ballad. The sails hung limp and lifeless upon the yards. Though black clouds churned above them, not a wisp of a breeze stirred the air nor even ruffled the dark sea.

The ship floated, lifeless, as if it had drifted into a dark cave.

"What did you hear?" Abigail laid her hand on his arm.

"Pray." Nathaniel swallowed. "I heard 'pray,' and then my thoughts swept to Hope."

Abigail nodded. "Then we should." She squeezed his arm and bowed her head, and Nathaniel followed suit. Several minutes passed as they made their appeals to God for Hope and for the safety of the ship. When Nathaniel lifted his gaze to Abigail's, alarm sped through him. "I should go see her."

"Nay." Abigail shook her head, her wide hazel eyes flickering in the light of the lantern hanging from the mast. "Leave her be. She's in God's hands now."

A frigid wall of air enveloped Hope, and she hugged herself and rose, dabbing at her moist cheeks. "Is someone there?" She peered into the shadows beyond the lantern, sensing a presence. Yet the door remained closed, and she had heard no one enter.

Thunder roared through the ship, shaking the hull, and Hope sank to her knees onto the hard deck. "God, if You're there. I'm sorry. I'm so sorry for the things I've done." She lowered her head, ashamed, waiting for the lightning to strike her, but an eerie silence ensued. Only the creak of the ship sounded, accompanied by her own rapid breathing.

A blast of cold air circled her, stealing the breath from her throat. Her heart thumped wildly.

No one loves you. You're not worthy of God's love.

Hideous laughter cackled in her ears, and tears filled her eyes anew, dropping to her gown in blotches.

Clunk. Clank. Crash!

The noise sent Hope bolting to her feet. The lantern had fallen to the deck. Dashing toward it, she snatched it up before the flame caught. But instead, it flickered out and darkness enshrouded her.

Groping her way to the table, she set down the lantern, her breath catching in her throat. The ship had not moved, and no wind strong enough to make the lantern fall had swept through the cabin.

"Who's here?" Terror squeezed her heart. She gripped her throat.

No sound save the tiny creak of the ship.

As she backed away, Hope struck the bedpost and whimpered in pain then crumpled to the deck. "If You're angry with me, God, I don't blame You." She could barely squeeze the words from her constricted throat. "But please, if You find it in Your heart to forgive me, like Abigail says You will"—an invisible hand loomed near her windpipe, threatening to tighten its grip, but she forced her words out in a mad rush—"to forgive me and help me change, to be better, then I beg You, please make me Yours."

Instantly, warmth covered her. A weight fell off her as if

an anchor she'd been holding had been cast into the sea. She began to shake. Tears streamed down her face. A tiny ray of light pierced the darkness of the cabin, and Hope dashed toward the window and peered out. The black clouds drifted away, revealing a myriad of stars sparkling against the night sky. A half-moon splashed its silver light onto the sea in glimmering ribbons.

Hope smiled as she gazed across the glorious scene. God loved her. *He loved her.* When no one else truly had: not her father, or her mother, or even Lord Falkland. The revelation stunned her, sent a rush of joy through her, and she knew in that instant that God had always loved her—even when she had gone astray. A tingling swept through her like a brush scrubbing away the filth, the impurity, the stains of her past. And like a baby dove nestled beneath her father's wings, she felt cherished and safe and clean for the first time in her life.

Chapter 30

T *ap, tap, tap.* Abigail rapped on the door to Captain
Poole's cabin and tried to still the thunderous beat
of her heart. Rustling sounded from within, and she almost
turned and dashed down the narrow hallway. But his "Enter"
blared over her, keeping her from fleeing. Clicking the latch,
she took a deep breath and pushed the door ajar.

"Ah, Miss Sheldon, how good o' ye to come." Captain
Poole rose from his chair, straightened his black velvet
waistcoat, and wove around his desk to greet her.

"Come in. Come in. I won't bite ye." He chuckled and,
taking her by the elbow, led her to a stuffed leather chair.

He closed the door with an ominous *thud,* and Abigail
swallowed, once again wondering about the sanity of
agreeing to meet with this pirate alone in his quarters. She
sensed his gaze upon her and shivered beneath his sensuous
perusal that scoured her as if she were a treasure chest filled
with gold.

As if reading her mind, he smiled. "Ye've naught to fear
from me, miss." But his voracious expression spoke
otherwise.

Tearing her thoughts from their dangerous bent, she set

her Bible on her lap and scanned the cabin, twice as large as
the one she stayed in. A large desk stood guard before the
windows that stretched the width of the stern. Charts, quill
pens, and a quadrant littered the top, as well as a half-full
bottle of rum, a cutlass, and two pistols.

Two high-backed leather chairs flanked the desk, one of
which she occupied. And those, along with the desk and its
chair, made up the only furniture in the room, save the bed
built into the bulwarks on the starboard side. Before the bed,
a cannon—at least an eighteen pounder—stood with its
muzzle pointed toward a closed gun port, reminding Abigail
what type of man she found herself alone with. His gaze
remained fixed upon her. She drew a breath to stifle the
shudder that ran down her back and looked anywhere but
back into those dark, probing eyes.

A glint drew her attention to a row of swords lining the
larboard bulkhead like trophies, glimmering in the lantern
light: a French rapier, a Spanish broadsword, a saber, and an
English long sword. All no doubt seized from the hands of
conquered victims she could only hope were still among the
living.

Despite a sudden chill that overtook her, her palms
began to sweat.

He ambled toward his desk, swerved around, and leaned
back on it, his riotous black hair flinging about his shoulders.
Crossing arms over his chest, he cocked a brow in her
direction as if he enjoyed watching her squirm.

Abigail forced a disapproving glance his way. "I suppose
you've had many women in this cabin, Captain." She hoped
to disarm his superior demeanor, but instead he laughed—
heartily and shamelessly.

"That I have, Miss Sheldon. That I have. Does it distress
ye?"

"Only if I am to be another of your victims." She
straightened her back and pursed her lips.

"Victims? Upon me life, all came willingly and left

happier than when they arrived, if I do say so." He stomped his thick leather boot over the deck, and his lips curved in a taunting grin.

Deciding it best to leave before the pirate assumed she had also come willingly, Abigail stood and made a move toward the door, but Captain Poole dashed toward it, blocking her way. "Me apologies, miss. I meant no disrespect." The gold earring in his ear sparkled in the lantern light as if to affirm the validity of his statement—or perhaps to warn her to take flight while she could.

"What is it you wish, Captain?" She raised her chin.

He searched her eyes as if he could see straight into her soul. She fidgeted but did not lower her gaze. The scent of rum wafted over her, stinging her nose.

"A brave one, ye are. I admire that." He backed away and gestured toward the chair. "If you please."

"I'll stand, thank you." Abigail gripped the Bible closer to her chest.

Captain Poole huffed and gazed out the windows. "'Tis an odd darkness that overcomes us, eh? Thunder, but no lightning. Clouds but no rain or wind."

Abigail nodded and glanced out the stern windows. The same dark shroud she'd seen while up on deck still hovered over the ship.

"I've seen other things—even more odd." He swung around, and this time the arrogant facade had faded. He scratched the dark stubble on his chin as if pondering what to say.

"Odd?" Abigail prompted him to continue.

"Can I tell ye a tale?" He sat back on his desk.

"Of course."

"Nigh about a year ago, me crew and I came across a Spanish merchant ship hauling pearls from Porto Bello. We boarded her with ease." He waved a hand through the air, fluttering the lace at the cuff of his sleeve. "Relieved her of her goods, and set her adrift without benefit o' her sails or rudder." He chuckled as if remembering the jollity of the event, but then his gleeful expression faded to a frown. "We rescued an Englishman imprisoned in her hold. A preacher. Said he was the grandson of the famous pirate, Captain Edmund Merrick." Captain Poole shook his head. "There was something 'bout him."

Abigail brushed hair from her forehead as her heart settled to a normal beat. "What do you mean?"

The captain gripped the edge of his desk. "There was a peace, yet a power about him, that set me nerves to spinnin'." He gazed up at her now. "Much like what I see in yer eyes and Mr. Mason's."

Abigail's heart sped again, but this time from joy.

"We encountered a wicked storm, like none I e'er saw. Fierce winds and angry waves that would have sunk us to the depths for sure, save ...." He released a sigh.

"Save what? Captain?"

"When we thought all was lost, this preacher, Merrick, comes up on deck as calm as if he was walkin' down Bond Street. He speaks to the storm as if it were alive and commands it to cease in the name of his God—this Jesus."

Abigail took a step toward him, excitement twirling within her. "And?"

The captain snapped his fingers. "The storm died off, just like he told it to. The waves settled, the winds died, and the clouds sped away quicker than a trollop from a penniless vagrant." His eyes grew big as he remembered it, and Abigail thought she saw him tremble.

Jumping from the desk, he turned his back on her and stormed to the window. "What do ye make o' that?"

Abigail said a silent prayer for the right words to say. "I think you already know."

He grunted.

"'Tis what we discussed on the island." A renewed strength that could only come from above emboldened her. "God exists. He is the God of the Bible, and He is all powerful, all knowing, and all loving."

As if confirming her words, the dark clouds dissipated, revealing a sky that sparkled like diamonds, and the chill Abigail had felt earlier fled her as well. Raising the Bible to her lips, she placed a kiss upon it. She didn't know what had just occurred, but she knew God had performed a miraculous feat.

"Nathaniel, wake up." A rough hand shook him, and Nathaniel opened one weary eye. Gavin's cheerful face filled his vision.

"What do you want?" Nathaniel asked, groggy with sleep.

"Sink me, 'tis near midday, and you're still asleep on deck."

Nathaniel struggled to sit, every muscle in his back and neck screaming in rebellion. He rubbed his eyes and surveyed the ship, bustling with activity as the pirates scampered across deck tending to their various tasks. Shielding his eyes, he glanced above. White sails, gorged with wind, snapped at every yard.

"Did Hope toss you out of the cabin?" Gavin chuckled.

Nathaniel tried to shake the fog from his mind. "Nay, I was up late and didn't wish to disturb her." Truth be told, he'd waited half the night for Abigail to finish conversing with Captain Poole. Unable to sleep without ensuring her safety, he had loitered outside the captain's cabin for hours. When Abigail had finally emerged on the pirate's arm, Nathaniel had sunk into the shadows and watched as Poole escorted her to her cabin as if they were returning from a concert at Dillon's Inn in Charles Towne.

"Not disturb her?" Gavin cackled. "So you spend a restless night on the hard deck?"

Nathaniel suppressed a laugh, for it would have been a far more restless night's sleep in a cabin with Hope so near.

Besides, the captain had been too occupied last night to notice Nathaniel's absence from his "wife's" bed. So he had curled up under one of the boats on the foredeck, hoping to catch a few hours of sleep before the sun rose. Apparently, those few turned into half the day.

Assisting Nathaniel to his feet, Gavin gazed across the azure sea. "We should arrive in Kingston in two days. It will be good to be in a civilized port again."

"Kingston is anything but civilized, I'm told." Nathaniel stretched.

"As long as it boasts a soft bed, a hearty meal, strong drink, and plenty of women, it could be the middle of Africa for all I care."

Nathaniel chuckled and ran a hand through his unruly hair. "Your definition of civilization leaves much to be desired."

"Speaking of women, where, pray tell, is your wife?"

Nathaniel cringed, but still his heart leapt at the title bestowed upon Hope. Ignoring both reactions, he scanned the deck. "I have no idea."

"Good morning, Nathaniel." Abigail approached with a swish of her green skirts and a beaming smile upon her face.

"Good morning."

"Spent some time with the captain, did you?" Gavin asked, his tone sarcastic.

"That I did. We had a rousing discussion."

"What could you two possibly have in common to discuss?"

Abigail pressed the folds of her gown and gave him a placating smile. "As I have told you, he wished to discuss the things of God."

Gavin snorted then directed a curious gaze toward the captain.

Tall, brawny, and fully armed, by all accounts and appearances, Poole was naught but ruthless pirate. Not a man given to religion.

"I shall leave you to discuss these matters with Nathaniel." Gavin stomped away.

Abigail giggled. "You look a sight, Nathaniel."

He smiled. "I haven't been sleeping well since we boarded this ship."

A flash of blue caught his eye as Hope emerged from the companionway, hand in hand with Elise.

Abigail followed his gaze. "Yes, I see."

He ignored her taunting grin. "What did the captain want?"

She moved to the railing. "He speaks of a miracle he saw aboard his ship. It seems to have both frightened and intrigued him." Shielding her eyes from the sun, she gazed at Nathaniel. "He asked many questions about our Lord, and I answered him the best I could."

"I'm sure you did well." Nathaniel eased beside her, allowing the sun to warm his face. "An odd turn of events. Do you suppose it was the cause of the black clouds yesterday, the oppression we both felt?"

"Perhaps, but Captain Poole thus far wishes only to satisfy his curiosity. Nay, I think something else occurred last night." She glanced at Hope again.

"Miss Hope?" Nathaniel blinked.

"You should speak with her."

"Nay. 'Tis better I keep my distance."

Yet after Abigail went below to rest, Nathaniel could do anything but keep his distance from the enchanting woman. With Gavin engaged in a game of cards and the rest of the crew napping, drinking, or tending the sails, Nathaniel had nothing to do but saunter about the deck. And every time he looked up, he found himself nearer to Hope. Finally, he could hear her conversing with Miss Elise.

Hope embraced the girl, and Elise's little arms wrapped around Hope's neck.

"Then I will go to heaven to be with Mother?"

"Yes, my dear." Hope kissed her cheek, and Nathaniel

nearly leapt at her declaration of belief. "And your mother isn't frightened or sad there. Heaven is a beautiful place with no sorrow and no fear. A place where only love and joy and hope exist."

"Like your name!" Elise smiled.

Hope nodded and brushed the girl's hair from her face. "Only you must love God with all your heart and all your strength for all your days."

Nathaniel shook his head, sure he was hearing things.

"What of Father? He told me there is no heaven." The little girl's lips drew into a pout.

Nathaniel glanced at Mr. Hendrick standing across the deck, staring out onto the sea as if in a daze.

"Your father is sad and angry right now," Hope answered. "We must pray for him."

Shock froze Nathaniel, even as a thrill soared within him. Pray? Could it be true? Could Miss Hope have given her life to God?

"Elise, come here!" Mr. Hendrick bellowed from across the deck.

The little girl turned wide eyes to Hope. "Must I go?"

"He is your father. Be good and love him." Hope rose. "And remember to pray for him. I won't be far away."

Elise started off then ran back to Hope and flung her arms around her. "I wish you could be my new mother."

Nathaniel forced back the moisture that threatened to fill his eyes.

Hope eased a finger over the girl's cheek. "I do, too, precious one." Her voice cracked.

Elise dragged her feet across the deck to where her father received her and drew her close, but not before he fired a disdainful glance Hope's way.

Hope turned to face the sea, and Nathaniel slipped beneath the foredeck ladder, watching her, not wanting her to know he had eavesdropped on her conversation. Was it possible a woman like Hope could change? Yesterday she had not believed in God, or at least in a loving God, and today she spoke of Him as if she knew Him.

For with God, nothing shall be impossible.

Nathaniel's heart swelled. If Hope had given her life to God, perhaps with His strength, she could indeed change—she could indeed become a virtuous lady, moral and good. The kind of lady he longed to share his life with. He must speak to her, find out what happened, confirm what every inch of his heart yearned to be true.

He took a step toward her, but Gavin sped past him and took Hope's elbow. "Miss Hope, would you care for a turn about the deck?"

Startled, she slid her hand through his proffered arm. "Why, thank you, Mr. Keese." Only then did she notice Nathaniel. A sad smile overcame her before she headed off with Gavin, who winked at Nathaniel over his shoulder.

Clenching his fists, Nathaniel resolved to speak with Hope tonight, for he could no longer deny his feelings. He must tell her he loved her.

Chapter 31

F inishing her prayer, Hope opened her eyes to the
most glorious sight—crimson, peach and saffron
ribbons glittered across the horizon as the last traces of the
sun dipped below the dark blue line of the sea. She thanked
God for the beauty of His creation—something she had never
appreciated before. In fact, since she'd given her life to the
Lord, everything seemed more beautiful. Gripping the
railing, she braced herself as the ship rose and plunged over a
swell, feeling truly alive and free for the first time in her life.
And she knew no matter what happened, no matter where life
took her, she had a Father in heaven who loved her, who
found her worthy, and who would never leave her.

Remorse nipped the edges of her joy like the wind that
now clipped her curls, trying to loosen them from her pins.
So many wasted years spent searching for love to fill the void
deep within her—a void she now realized only the love of
God could fill. She shook her head. The stupid choices she'd
made, the pain she had caused. And the loss. Of her
reputation, her purity … of Nathaniel.

She loved him. She would always love him. But her poor
choices had erected a sturdy wall between them that even the

strongest love could not breach. She deserved his rejection and much worse. But the ache of loss remained.

A warm evening breeze swirled around her, teasing her nose with the scent of the sea, with the sweet fragrance of the coming evening, and with life, and she inhaled a deep breath. When she returned to Charles Towne, despite the financial difficulties she would face, despite the impossibility of restoring her reputation with the citizens of the burgeoning port city, she intended to open an orphanage. In her recent conversations with God, He had made His will plain, further bolstering both her confidence and her faith. At last she could offer lost and unwanted children a safe home, where they would be loved and learn about God's love so they wouldn't make the same mistakes she had. So they wouldn't have to suffer for their bad choices.

In addition, she would beg her sister Grace's forgiveness for the way Hope had snubbed all her efforts to tell her about God. Though perhaps she had gone about it the wrong way, Grace's heart had been concerned only with Hope's happiness and eternal destination. She smiled. Perhaps she and Grace could even become close. Something they had never been.

A sail snapped overhead as if sealing her deal with God, and the ship bucked over a wave, anointing her with a refreshing spray. The final traces of light sank beneath the sea, leaving a faint glow on the horizon, but despite the encroaching shadows, the day had not disappeared. The darkness could never hide the sun's bright light for long. Soon, it would rise again, forcing back the gloom as it announced a new day.

Digging beneath the sleeve of her gown, Hope pulled out the chipped shell she had found on the island. Holding it up, she smiled at the way it glistened in the fading sunlight and searched for the chipped section she had seen before. But it was not there. Perfect in form, symmetrical and beautiful, the shell appeared to have been plucked from the ocean, fresh, clean—pristine.

Had she picked up the wrong shell? Confusion twisted through her, followed by a surge of certainty. No she had not. Humbled and awed at the love of God, Hope bowed her head and gave Him thanks.

Wiping tears of joy from her face, she turned around and scanned the ship. Two pirates lit lanterns hanging upon the mainmast and foredeck railing. The rest gathered in huddles, drinking and boasting and playing cards. Better she got below before their revelry got underway and they forgot she was a guest of Captain Poole. She crept down the foredeck ladder and tiptoed across the deck, keeping her eyes straight ahead and not acknowledging the lewd remarks tossed her way. She had not seen Nathaniel since earlier in the day and had no idea where he was. That he avoided her was obvious. That his disdain caused her great pain was something she resolved to endure.

Making her way down into the dimly lit hallway, she saw a thin strip of light shining beneath her cabin door. Had she left a lantern lit? Horrified, she pushed open the door and rushed inside.

Nathaniel stood beside a washbowl, water dripping down his chest glimmering in the lantern light.

Hope averted her eyes. "Forgive me." She turned to leave.

"No, please stay." His voice held a pleading tone that halted her steps.

Leaving the door open, Hope skirted an empty basket on the floor and inched toward her bed, keeping her eyes lowered. It wasn't like she hadn't seen his bare chest oft times on the island, but in this tiny cabin, it seemed inappropriate, and she didn't like the way her heart leapt and her belly quivered.

Grabbing a cloth, he dried his chest and closed the door with an ominous thud.

"You wish to speak to me?" She backed into the hard

bulkhead.

He approached, his shadow absorbing the lantern light. Stopping before her, he released a heavy sigh, showering her with his warm, woodsy breath. Placing a finger beneath her chin, he lifted her gaze to his.

Moist hair, pressed back from his face, eased down his neck and dangled in wet strands across his broad shoulders. Curiosity, concern, and—something she couldn't identify, something she feared to identify—filled his expression, and her head began to spin.

He smiled. Did he notice her discomfort? She tried to look down, but his finger held her head in place.

He brushed his thumb over her cheek, and Hope closed her eyes, relishing in the tender moment. But then he released her and took a step back. She thanked God because her knees had begun to shake and she wasn't sure she could remain standing much longer with Nathaniel so near. Placing her hands behind her, she braced against the bulkhead and dared to open her eyes.

Just in time to see his lips lowering to hers.

Gasping, Hope flattened her back against the wood, but there was no escape. *Lord, help me*, her plea for strength screamed through her mind. She turned her face away. "We shouldn't."

He blinked, and one eyebrow rose in an incredulous arch. "And why shouldn't we?" His tone carried no anger, only curiosity.

Despite the yearning storming through her body, Hope gathered her resolve. "Because we are not courting. Or ever will be courting. You have made that quite plain. And I wish to save my affections for the man I plan to marry." There, she had said it, albeit too fast and perhaps a bit too sharply. But at least she had said the right thing—had done the right thing—and not leapt into his arms and received his kisses like every ounce of her body longed to do.

A grin lifted one corner of his lips. "A new philosophy

of yours?"

"Indeed. One which I intend to live my life by. God has shown me a better way." For it certainly had to be God who was giving her the strength to resist Nathaniel at the moment.

"He has?" Nathaniel laughed. "I am pleased to hear it."

He turned away and tossed the cloth to the table, sending his muscles rippling across his back like swells over a stormy sea. When he faced her again, the respect, the love she had craved to see for so long beamed from his eyes and poured over her like warm sunshine. Hope swallowed and threw a hand to her heart to steady its chaotic beat. "You are pleased?" Her voice squeaked.

He smiled, that mischievous, sultry half grin that set her body aflame. Flustered, she dropped her gaze to the fading wound on his arm and then to the bluish scar marring his left side. She must divert the conversation to a safer topic, away from the possibility she saw in his eyes—the possibility that caused her hopes to soar, the possibility that would leave her devastated once again if she entertained its promise. He had made it clear how he felt about her. Nothing had changed. And she mustn't think otherwise. "What happened to you?"

He followed her gaze to his scar and rubbed it. "I was stabbed."

"Stabbed? Oh my." Hope took a step toward him.

"When I was young." His jaw stiffened. "I was protecting my mother."

Hope nearly stumbled at the pain burning in his eyes. "Your mother. From whom?"

"A man she displeased," he spat then stared out the porthole. Several minutes passed with only the creak of wood and slosh of water to fill the void. Finally, he released a sigh and lowered his gaze to the floor. "She was a harlot."

A harlot? How could such an honorable man have such a wayward mother? The ship creaked over a wave, and Hope gripped the bulkhead.

The muscles in Nathaniel's face twitched, but he refused

to look her way.

"And your father?" she asked.

"I never knew him." He snorted. "My mother thought he was a mason by trade, so she named me Nathaniel Mason." His laughter shook with suppressed fury.

Hope's heart collapsed. "I'm sorry." At least Hope had known her father, though he'd been anything but loving. At least she had a legitimate name, a heritage she could be proud of.

Nathaniel ran a hand through his hair and finally faced her.

She took a step toward him, longing to ease his pain, to smooth the tight lines of sorrow from his face. "What happened to her?"

Leaning back on the table, he gripped the edges and stared at the dirty floorboards. "We lived in Barbados. When I was eight, my mother grew sick. We had no money, no relatives, no help, so I moved her down by the beach on the east side of the island and cared for her." He crossed his arms over his chest. "That's where I learned how to fish and build a hut. Those were good times." He smiled but then grief consumed his momentary joy. "Mother got well again and with the money she made, we traveled to Charles Towne. She had heard the ratio of men to women was four to one. Good odds for someone in her trade." He snickered. "We lived in a room above a tavern. There were plenty of men with enough coin to pay, but some were vicious, even cruel to my mother. They beat her."

"You stayed in the room with her?" Hope's eyes burned with tears as she stepped closer to Nathaniel.

"When I was little, yes. But later I would wander the town for hours while she worked. One night I returned to find a man holding a knife to her neck. When I attacked him, he stabbed me and ran off."

Hope tentatively reached out and eased her fingers over the scar on his side as tears spilled from her eyes. "How horrible."

He took her hand and gently held it. "Odd, it still pains me at times."

Hope nodded, remembering how often he'd rubbed it on the island. "Whenever you feel threatened."

Nathaniel nodded. "You tug your hair for the same reason." He paused and brushed a loose curl from her face. "I hate it that Lord Villemont hurt you."

Hope shifted her gaze away. "'Tis done with." She sighed. "But you never told me what happened to your mother?"

"Mother grew sick again after that. We had no money for a physician." Releasing her hand, he stared off, his eyes a glaze of sorrow. "I couldn't help her this time. I watched her die."

"So much pain for such a young boy." Hope eased beside him. "How did you survive?"

"I wandered the streets for a year before Reverend Holloway found me and took me in." The haggard lines on his face softened. "You know the rest."

Hope leaned against his chest, and he wrapped his arms around her. "I had no idea," she muttered. No wonder he had been repulsed by her licentiousness. No wonder he feared entangling himself with a woman like her. Heat from his skin warmed her cheek, and she could no longer hold back her tears.

"Don't cry for me, Hope. God gave me a good home, and Reverend Holloway loved me as a father." He pressed her against him and leaned his chin atop her head.

"That's precisely why I wish to open an orphanage when I return home." She backed away from him, wiping her tears. "Think of it, Nathaniel. A place for children like you to grow up and receive all the care they need and be taught about God's love and grace."

He flinched in surprise. "Quite a noble venture, and I lo—admire—you greatly for it."

Hope's throat constricted. Though he had not said it, his cutting tone spoke volumes. He had no interest in her plans. Which meant he did not see her in his future. Which meant he did not love her—at least not in the way she loved him. A heavy weight landed on her chest. "Your admiration is all I ever wanted, Nathaniel." She forced a smile. "And much more than I deserve."

"Is it *all* you ever wanted?" He grinned.

She studied him, her heart performing a traitorous leap. "Nay. But it is all I dare to expect. You have made your feelings clear."

Nathaniel shook his head. "I have fought them, to be sure." He caressed her cheek. "But the only thing clear to me now is that I love you, Hope."

Her heart thundered. "You love *me*?"

"Is it so inconceivable?" He chuckled.

Hope searched his eyes, waiting for him to recall his words, deny their veracity, waiting for the jest to play out before she dared to believe it true. A nervous giggle spilled from her lips.

Nathaniel raised a brow. "Am I to be left standing here with no answer but your laughter?"

"No, of course not. I love you, too, Nathaniel." She leapt toward him, inadvertently kicking the empty basket across the deck. Right into Nathaniel's path. He stumbled across the cabin as Hope cringed, praying she hadn't injured him yet again. Thankfully, he regained his balance without bodily harm and faced her. "Still trying to kill me, eh?" He grinned.

"I am a determined lady." She gave him a coy smile, but sobered as she touched the bump on his forehead, where she'd caused him to slam into the bulkhead, then ran her fingers down the scar on his arm, the one from the sword fight with the major. "Truly I don't know what comes over me when you are around."

"I hope whatever it is, it will diminish, for I plan to be around you as much as possible."

She pouted. "Still it would seem I am a constant danger to you."

"That you are." He swung her around, eased her against the bulkhead, and imprisoned her with his arms. "Extremely dangerous."

His gaze wandered to her lips.

"Why do I feel as though I'm the one in danger now?"

He smiled and instantly his lips were on hers, caressing, searching, loving, and the cabin around Hope faded into a dream world—a world where she was safe, secure, and loved.

With Hope's sweet kiss still warm on his lips, Nathaniel leapt upon the deck, lighter and more vigorous than he'd felt in days, despite his lack of sleep. He made his way up to the bow of the ship, hoping the night breeze would cool his heated skin. It took every scrap of strength within him to leave Miss Hope for the night. He had the perfect excuse to stay, after all, with the captain prowling about, but if he stayed with her after declaring his love, he doubted he could keep from holding her close throughout the entire night. And that would not be wise—for either of them.

Gripping the railing, he bowed his head and thanked God for saving Hope, for changing her heart. He also thanked Him that, despite Nathaniel's repeated rejections, she loved him. Not Gavin as Nathaniel had assumed. But him! Something he could no longer deny for he'd seen love burning in her eyes and felt her impassioned response to his kisses.

He shook his head. He had loved Hope from the first moment he'd seen her in Charles Towne, despite the way she snubbed him, despite the salacious rumors about her improper behavior spreading through the city. But now after giving up his prize ship to save her and after all the harrowing events of their journey, as well as his own misgivings about her character, they had finally declared their love for one another. And he vowed to spend the rest of his life giving her all the love she had missed as a child and protecting her from every danger and heartache.

The moon hung high in the sky, smiling down upon him and flinging its sparkling light onto the rolling dark waves. The soothing purl of water as the bow sliced through the sea washed over him, releasing the tension he'd been carrying for weeks. Swerving around, he found a level place near the foremast beside a huge barrel and lay down onto the hard deck. Putting one hand behind his head, he gazed up at the sails fluttering in the moonlight and drifted to sleep.

Hours later, thumping noises jolted him, and he rubbed his eyes and sprang to his feet, ready to defend against some unknown attack. A flash of blue caught his eye, and he glanced to the main deck below where he saw Hope standing near the railing, her blond hair a beacon in the darkness. A dark shadow loomed beside her.

Alarm stiffened Nathaniel. Was someone accosting her? He dashed to the foredeck ladder, intending to pounce upon the villain, when the figure took Hope in a full embrace.

She did not resist.

Slinking into the shadows, Nathaniel rubbed his eyes and peered toward the couple, his heart crumbling in his chest. Perhaps it wasn't Hope after all? Yet after several seconds in which the lovers remained entwined, the woman broke away, stepped into the lantern light, offered the man a tender smile, and descended down the companionway. *Hope.* Nathaniel's legs betrayed him, and he nearly fell to the heaving deck.

The man leaned over the railing, and Nathaniel allowed his anger to surge, overcoming his grief. "Who goes there?" he shouted. Whoever it was, he would pound him to the timbers for touching Hope.

The figure turned into the lantern light. Gavin's sharp eyes met his. "Ah, Nathaniel. There you are. Enduring another sleepless night, I see?"

Shaking the shock from his face, Nathaniel leapt down the foredeck ladder. "Was that Hope I just saw?" He needed to hear it from the man's lips.

Gavin studied him for a moment, then clapped his back and winked. "Aye. We had quite an evening."

"Evening?" Nathaniel fisted his hands.

"You told me I could court her, did you not?" Gavin stretched his arms like a man quite content with life. *Or content from something else.*

Nathaniel attempted to speak, but his tongue had gone numb, along with the rest of him.

"I daresay, the woman moves quick." Gavin chuckled.

Nathaniel moaned.

"Are you ill, my friend? Do you need water?"

"Are you saying that you and Miss Hope, you ...."

Gavin grinned like a cat after a satisfying meal. He glanced across the deck, then leaned toward Nathaniel, "And she was far better than I expected."

Chapter 32

"Hoist the Union Jack if you please, Mr. Drury," Captain Poole bellowed as Hope climbed onto the main deck. A burst of moist wind swirled around her, taunting her with the scent of flowers and musky earth. Making her way to the railing, she shielded her eyes from the sun and peered into the distance where a mound floated upon the horizon like a tortoise shell upon liquid turquoise. *Jamaica.* They had made it.

Swerving about, she surveyed the ship and spotted Nathaniel upon the quarterdeck, speaking to Abigail. No jealous twinge gripped her at the sight of them together, for she finally knew where his true feelings lay. When his eyes met hers, she waved, but instead of returning her smile and dashing to join her, he frowned and turned his back. Her chest tightened. Perhaps he hadn't seen her.

Clutching her skirts and ignoring the pirates' salacious gazes, she started for the quarterdeck ladder when Gavin jumped in front of her, blocking her way.

"You look lovely this morning, Hope." He winked and gave her one of his saucy smiles.

"Thank you, Gavin, but if you please." Hope tried to nudge him aside, but it was like attempting to push an aged tree trunk from its roots. "I need to speak with Nathaniel."

"Indeed?" Gavin scratched his whiskers and gave her a puzzled look. "Can it not wait? Miss Elise is asking for you."

Hope tensed. "She is? Is she well?"

"Yes, quite, but Mr. Hendrick requests your help in dressing her for the trip ashore." His blue eyes would not meet her gaze.

"I doubt it, Gavin." Hope huffed. "Mr. Hendrick's hatred for me is no secret. And he has not required my assistance since we boarded this ship. Why ask for it now?"

Gavin shrugged. "I'm just relaying his message."

Hope studied her friend. "Is this another one of your tricks, Mr. Keese?"

"You wound me, milady." He placed a hand over his heart. "Are we reduced to Mr. Keese again?"

Hope forced back a smile. "You know to what I refer. Last night?" She raised a questioning brow.

He shrugged. "I honestly *did* hear Miss Elise crying and would swear upon my mother's grave, I saw her up here on deck." A spark of mischief flashed across his eyes. "I hope you'll forgive me for waking you so late, but since you have such a good rapport with the girl, I didn't know who else to turn to. She wouldn't come when I called to her. Out of fright, I suspect, and her father was nowhere to be found."

"And yet, she was not on deck after all, but sound asleep in her cabin." Hope glared at him. "With her father, I might add."

"They were not there when I went to wake you." A blast of wind wafted over them and Gavin shook hair from his face then leaned toward her, a pleading frown playing upon his lips. "Do say you'll forgive me."

Hope cast a quick glance toward Nathaniel, still busy with Abigail. If Elise really did need her, Hope wanted to be of assistance. Especially since she'd not seen much of the girl since they'd boarded the ship. "Very well. Lead me to her."

With a smile, he held out his arm and taking it, Hope

followed him below.

Turning his back on Hope, Nathaniel tried to quell the anguish ripping his belly and listen to what Abigail was saying. But though her lips fluttered rapidly, naught but garbled tones met his ears.

"Are you listening to me?" She peered into his eyes.

"Forgive me. I was distracted." Nathaniel ran a hand over the back of his neck where a nagging ache refused to abate. An ache not caused from sleeping on the hard deck, but one that had spread upward from his wounded heart.

Abigail glanced over his shoulder. "Hope waved at you."

Nathaniel stiffened his jaw and shifted his attention to Captain Poole, standing by the helm. A group of pirates crowded around him in deep discussion.

Abigail persisted. "I thought you two had come to an understanding?"

"So did I." Nathaniel released a pained sigh then followed Abigail's gaze. He instantly regretted it as he watched Gavin and Hope descend the companionway, arm in arm. His gut wrenched, and he thought he might lose the hard biscuit he'd forced down that morning. After no sleep. Yet again.

"I'm sorry, Nathaniel." Abigail's brow wrinkled. "She doesn't mean to hurt you."

Nathaniel grimaced and studied the bloodstains marring the deck by his feet and wondered how many battles this ship had seen and how many men had died upon these oak planks. Anything to divert his thoughts from Hope and the questions that had tortured his mind throughout the dark hours of the night. He knew he must speak to her, must give her a chance to explain, but he wasn't ready to hear her answer.

The ship lurched, and he reached out to steady Abigail. "What of you? You must be excited to start your adventure in Kingston."

Yet fear, not excitement flickered in her eyes.

Four pirates swarmed around them, Kreggs and Hanson among them. The other two he recognized as the men he'd spoken to about God a few nights prior.

"Mr. Mason." Kreggs spat to the side and scratched his stained shirt. "Jones and Boone got somethin' ye should hear fer yerself."

Nathaniel turned to the other men, noting an unusual glow in their expressions even beneath the hard crust of sunburn and salt. The stench of unwashed bodies stung his nose, but clear eyes, devoid of red streaks and the usual rum-induced haze, met his.

Jones shifted his feet over the deck and rubbed the scar around his neck. "What ye said the other night about God made sense t' us."

Nathaniel's heart leapt.

Abigail gripped his arm, excitement rippling through her.

Jones crossed arms over his chest. "We gave our lives o'er to yer God. And we is determined t' change our ways an' become good men."

Abigail clasped her hands. "Praise God!"

Nathaniel blinked, allowing the shocking revelation to make its way into his reason. *Gave their lives to God? These pirates?* "All of you?"

"Aye." Kreggs and Hanson nodded. "Us, too."

Nathaniel took Hanson by the shoulders and shook him then clutched the other men in turn. "This is wonderful news!"

Jones's face reddened. Boone's eyes grew wide as he stiffened beneath Nathaniel's touch. Kreggs and Hanson chuckled nervously. They each took a step away from Nathaniel as if he'd gone mad. *Mad indeed. The best kind of mad.* The seeds God had given him that night had landed on good soil, hearts willing to believe and to humbly submit to God. "Fire and thunder, I am most pleased!" He scratched his head and chuckled so loud, it drew the attention of the other pirates hard at work.

"We want t' thank ye for openin' our eyes." Hanson scanned his fellow converts, receiving their affirming nods. "We felt the presence of yer God when we asked Him to show Hisself."

"Not my God. Our God," Nathaniel said then smiled at Abigail, whose eyes sparkled with delight. "Everyone's God. The only God."

"Aye," they said in unison.

An urgency swept through Nathaniel, and he silently prayed for wisdom. "You must read God's Word and speak with Him daily. Promise me you'll do that."

"Aye." Jones glanced at the others. "We will. Those o' us thats can read. An' we'll read to those who can't."

Nathaniel cast a quick look toward Captain Poole standing by the helm. "But what of your pirating?"

"We told Cap'n Poole we be leavin' the ship in Kingston." Boone gripped his baldric with both hands and offered a smile devoid of teeth, but 'twas the most wonderful smile Nathaniel had seen.

As if on cue, the captain barreled toward them, a scowl on his face. Nathaniel braced himself for the rash man's temper, but instead of lashing them with his tongue, he halted in their midst and raised a supercilious brow toward Nathaniel.

"And I'll be thankin' ye to be gettin' off the ship, too, Mr. Mason, before ye convert me whole crew an' I'm left wit' nothin' but a ship full of pious ninnies." His harsh tone belied the twinkle in his eyes. "That won't bode well for pillagin' and plunderin'." He let out a coarse chuckle, and his gaze landed on Abigail and softened.

"I'll be happy to leave your ship, Captain," Nathaniel said. "Unless, of course, you would like to partake of the treasure these men have found?"

"Treasure! D'ye take me for a fool? Nay, I'm seekin' me

own kind of treasure." His hard gaze scoured over the men. "But yer still me pirates until we weigh anchor. So get back to work!" he barked, sending the men scampering off. His dark eyes took in Abigail before he sauntered back to his spot by the foredeck railing.

Beaming, Abigail clutched Nathaniel's arm. "Nathaniel, did I not tell you that you have the gift of evangelism? See the impact you had on these men—hardened sailors and pirates all?"

Truth be told, he'd been exhilarated that night when he'd spoken to the pirates about God. As if his heart and tongue had been on fire.

"Do not deny the calling of God," she added.

Nathaniel shook his head. "You do not know from whence I came."

"But I can see where you are going." Abigail gave him a sideways glance and patted his arm. "Follow your heart, Nathaniel." She released him and turned toward Captain Poole standing at the foredeck railing, staring out upon the fast-approaching island.

A flash of blue drew Nathaniel's eyes to the main deck where Hope had reemerged from the companionway. *Without Gavin.* Nathaniel's elation of moments ago sank back into despair, and he turned around and leapt up into the ratlines before she could spot him. Although he wanted with all his heart to believe otherwise, he could not deny what he'd seen, nor what Gavin had confirmed. Why would his friend lie? The only explanation was that Hope had not changed after all. And although Nathaniel intended to confront her, he could not face her. Not yet. The pain of her betrayal was too raw, too fresh. Had all her talk of God and doing His will been naught but a ruse? A lie? But for what purpose? Nathaniel hoisted himself into the shrouds and made his way to up to the mizzen yard. How quickly she had fallen back into her old ways. And only hours after she had kissed him— and so passionately. He rubbed his lips, trying to rid himself of the memory, but it only increased the heat sweeping through him.

Angered at his reaction, he inched across the yard, battling both the fierce wind blasting over him and the anguish storming within him. A creamy, bubbling wake gushed from the ship's stern, reminding Nathaniel of the joy he'd felt last night with Hope in his arms, but the swirling foam soon faded into the sea. The ship plunged over a roller, and he gripped the mizzen stay to keep his balance, still finding it difficult to believe he was sailing on a pirate ship. The pirate ship, *Enchantress*—appropriately named for the cargo she carried.

For that was exactly what Hope was and always would be—an enchantress.

Abigail eased toward Captain Poole. In between shouting orders to his men, he seemed to settle into a trance—deep in thought and heavy laden with sorrow. Though they had conversed often since their time in his cabin, the captain had not questioned her further on God, and whenever she had broached the subject, he abruptly ended the conversation.

She followed his gaze to the growing mound of land and knew she hadn't much more time with this daring pirate. "Captain Poole, I hope you have given thought to our discussion night before last." Abigail studied him. His stubbled jaw flinched, and he rubbed a rough hand over his chin. Planting his fists upon his waist, he braced himself against a gust of wind that fluttered the blue plume atop his tricorn.

"I have thought on it, aye," he said with finality.

"I am pleased." Abigail laid a hand on his arm. His brooding eyes met hers and she smiled.

The roughened skin of his face softened. "That I have pleased ye warms me down to me soul, miss."

The snap of the Union Jack sounded from above, a disguise of the true nature of the ship. "Do you fear sailing into Kingston?"

"Fear?" He jerked his head back and snorted. "Fear never enters a pirate's head, nor his heart, or he'll be lost forever. Nay, I don't fear it."

"Then what has you so vexed?"

His brows rose and amazement swept across his face. "How can ye know me so well when we have just met?" He huffed. "Kingston, 'tis yer final destination?"

"Yes, I am to join a missionary there. A friend of my father's." Yet even as Abigail spoke the words, dread pinched her chest.

"Man the yards!" the captain shouted, sending pirates leaping into the shrouds. Abigail gripped the railing as the ship bucked over a wave. Before her spread a glistening pool of azure blue. And right in the middle sat the island of Jamaica. Menacing. Waiting to devour her.

"Now I must ask ye, what has *ye* so vexed?" Captain Poole covered her hand on the railing, and although propriety and the dozens of eyes around them demanded she remove hers, his touch brought her more comfort than she cared to admit.

"Is it so obvious?" She sighed. "On Antigua, I found my parents butchered in their bed—murdered by the very people they were there to help."

A twinge of sympathy rose in Captain Poole's eyes, and he squeezed her hand. "'Tis a cruel world, miss."

"Every time I think of it, fear consumes me—fear I will end up with the same fate."

"Humph." Captain Poole doffed his hat, and the wind whipped his dark hair. "Did you not say that this God o' yers loves ye beyond measure and will protect ye?"

"You were listening?"

"To every word that comes forth from that pretty mouth." His dark eyes swept over her lips, before he faced the sea again. "And if ye do meet yer death, d'ye not believe to be goin' to a far better place?"

Abigail nodded, stunned at his words.

"Then what's t' fear?" He plopped his hat back atop his head and shrugged as if that settled the matter.

Guilt and joy battled within Abigail. Guilt for her lack of faith and joy that this wicked man understood everything she had told him about God.

She smiled. "You have put me to shame with your faith, Captain."

"Faith? Perish and plague me. 'Tis yer faith we speak of, not mine. My faith is in me ship, me men, and me skill as a gentleman o' fortune."

"Flighty things to lay your hat upon, to be sure."

He narrowed his eyes and for a moment she thought she had angered him.

"'Tis enough fer me." His black hair fluttered against his coat as he shifted his shoulders.

Abigail stared at the powerful hand still covering hers. "I hope someday you will find it lacking."

"D'ye now?" He grinned, his earring glimmering his mirth. "And if I do, do I have yer permission to seek ye out?"

A rush of warmth sped up Abigail's neck, and she shifted her gaze to the glittering blue waves. He brushed his thumb over her hand. The gesture ignited an unusual sensation in her belly.

"Perhaps I misspoke." He removed his hand from hers and stared out to sea.

"Nay." Abigail took back his hand, her heart convulsing. Against everything she knew to be right, against all her inclinations, she had formed an undeniable attachment to this man—this pirate. "I would be most pleased to see you again."

Captain Poole's handsome lips curved upward, and he placed a kiss upon her hand. "Then I think 'tis fair to warn ye to be on the lookout, miss. For ye'll never know when

Captain Poole may drop anchor in Kingston again."

As the island of Jamaica loomed larger before her, dread loomed in Hope's heart. Nathaniel had been avoiding her all day, just as he had done so many times before, just as if they had not declared their love for one another, just as if they had not embraced so passionately in their cabin below.

After discovering Mr. Hendrick had not summoned her at all and chastising Gavin for his deception, Hope had returned on deck to seek out Nathaniel, only to find him sixty feet above her, clinging to the mizzen royal yard.

But he would have to come down sometime, wouldn't he? She would simply stay put until he did. Then maybe she would discover the cause of his odd behavior. Or perhaps she was just being foolish, for she had done naught to anger him. Then why did a sense of dread clench her heart? Had the man come to his senses and changed his mind about her? She couldn't blame him. Why would he want to associate with a woman whose past indicated a propensity to become just like his mother?

She squared her shoulders into the wind and tried to prepare her heart for his rejection, but for now, she would enjoy the sight of land; the way the white sandy beaches swooped up to meet lush aquamarine mountains rising toward the blue sky, and the circle of emerald trees that now began to take shape as the ship soared over the waves toward them.

"Lay aloft and furl the topsail!" Captain Poole shouted as the wind caught the sails in a keen snap. Soon, they rounded a corner of the island, and a long narrow headland came into view, forming a natural fortress in front of Kingston harbor. Beyond it, ships rocked at anchor in the bay. Was Nathaniel's ship there? She hoped so, for then they could return to Charles Towne as soon as possible. Haphazard buildings dotted the lower hills of the bustling port town while people as small as ants scrambled to and fro. *Civilization.*

The thud of feet upon the deck alerted her, and she spun around to see the top of Nathaniel's head disappearing down the main hatch. Within minutes, he emerged, dragging a rather pale Major Paine to the railing. Squinting in the sun, the major's eyes shot to hers, but a hollow glaze had replaced the impudent spark within them. He drew a deep breath, exhaling it in ragged gasps, and gripped he railing before his thin frame folded over it beneath the next plunge of the ship.

Nathaniel gave him a look of warning and without a glance at Hope, turned to leave.

Before Hope could call to him, Elise barreled into her. "Miss Hope. Miss Hope," she squealed.

Kneeling, Hope took the little girl in her arms and relished the exuberance of her embrace, the swishy sound of her gown, and the sweet smell of her innocence. "Hello, Elise, how have you been?"

"I've missed you, Miss Hope. 'Tis been so dull sitting with Father all day."

Brushing dust from his silk waistcoat as if it weren't a tattered and torn remnant of its former glory, Mr. Hendrick scowled in her direction. His once-handsome face fared no better than his waistcoat, its normal ruddiness faded to a gaunt ashen shade, further marred by the jagged wound across his cheek. No wonder Hope had seen so little of him on the voyage. The seasickness he'd sworn only women succumbed to apparently had dealt him a humbling blow.

Hope smiled at Elise. "No doubt your father needed your care."

The little girl nodded, sending her red curls bobbing. "I took good care of him."

"I'm sure you did." Hope kissed her forehead and stood, pressing the girl protectively to her side.

She glanced across the ship, searching for Nathaniel, but found Abigail instead standing beside Captain Poole, both of them deep in conversation. If Hope didn't know her friend better, she would think the pious woman had become fond of the crusty pirate. Behind them, Gavin hovered with a group of pirates, laughing and partaking of their rum as if he'd been a part of the crew all his life. Hope wanted to be angry at him for his recent deceptions, none of which made any sense to her other than playful antics. But how could she harbor anger toward a man she would most likely never see again after they reached Kingston? In many ways, they were alike; in other ways completely different, especially now that she'd given her life to Christ. But Gavin's interest in her, mischievous as it was, had soothed her pain through difficult times as well as endeared him to her heart. She would miss him.

Hope patted Elise's head as the girl stared toward Jamaica. "We shall soon be on land again. Won't that be nice?"

Elise's blue eyes shone with her unspoken answer.

"Come here, Elise," her father barked, and the little girl's expression faded. With one last glance at Hope, she shuffled to where her father stood by the capstan.

Turning, Hope leaned on the railing and watched the steady rush of water against the hull. The gurgle played a soothing tone in her ears, helping to allay her fears for the young girl. *Oh Lord. Please be with Elise. Don't let her grow up unloved like I was. Protect her. Let her know early on how much You love her.*

"Ease away the sheet. Haul up to leeward!" Captain Poole's commands echoed across the ship, and the thunder of flapping sails being lowered brought Hope's gaze to the marshy headland barricading Kingston Harbor. The noon sun set the bay sparkling like ripples of diamonds as a dozen tall ships drifted majestically among the turquoise waters. Beads of perspiration formed on the back of Hope's neck and began sliding beneath her gown. How she longed for a bath and a fresh change of clothes.

Movement drew her gaze to Nathaniel approaching the foredeck railing. Taking a deep breath, she climbed the ladder, her heart clamping in her chest.

"Good day, Nathaniel." Her palms dampened as she slipped beside him.

He did not so much as glance her way. Dread consumed her.

"Are you ill?"

"Nay, I feel quite well." He crossed arms over his chest. A breeze swirled around him, fluttering his wavy hair across the top of his shirt.

Hope raised a hand to her throat to still her throbbing pulse. "What is the matter?"

"I said I am quite well." The tone of his voice sliced through her heart.

"Nay, I mean …." She took a breath and forced back the burning behind her eyes. "I mean, why are you behaving this way?"

"And what way is that, Miss Hope?" He finally looked at her, and the anger searing in his gaze sent her reeling backward a step.

She looked down. "I thought … I thought we had an understanding." The words choked in her throat. She grabbed a lock of her hair. "In our cabin."

"Indeed, so did I."

"What has changed?"

"You tell me." He stared down at her as if he were a magistrate and she on trial for murder.

"Tell you what? I don't understand."

"Last night?" Nathaniel raised his brow. "I saw you on deck." He looked away as if the sight of her made him ill. "With Gavin. In quite a compromising position, I might add."

Hope recoiled, anger throbbing through her veins. "Oh, you did, did you? And you assumed what? That he and I were engaged in a tryst? That I proclaimed my love for you, kissed you in our cabin, then dashed straightaway into

Gavin's arms?'"

"I didn't need to assume. I was told." Nathaniel gripped the railing and thrust his face into the wind.

Told? The ship lurched, and Hope stared at a belaying pin near the railing, searching her mind for an explanation. A dull ache began to gnaw at her soul. Everything blurred beneath the tears filling her eyes.

"Besides, I saw it with my own eyes, Hope." He glared at her, hard as stone. "Can you deny it?"

How could he think so little of her? How could she convince him otherwise when he had already made up his mind? She swung her hand to slap his face, but he caught it in midair.

She ripped her hand from his grasp.

"Hard to starboard!" The thumping of feet sounded like war drums across the deck.

Nathaniel drew a deep breath but kept his lips stiff as taut ropes. "I wish you the best, Miss Hope, and I shall pray for you."

"I don't want your prayers," she spat as anger crowded out her pain.

"You are a difficult woman."

"And you are a judgmental, merciless clod."

The golden flecks in his eyes simmered. He pushed himself from the railing and tipped his head in her direction. "Then I shall bid you good day." Turning his back to her once again, he stomped away.

Facing the sea, Hope batted away the tears spilling down her cheeks. Her heart plummeted to the dark depths below the ship. What a fool she'd been to entertain the hope of gaining such a noble man's love. Not someone like her.

Never someone like her.

She clung to the railing as the ship rounded the tip of the headland and sailed into the bay.

"Ready the gun!"

The Lord had forgiven her of her past, of all her sins.

Not only that, He had completely forgotten them.

"Ready, fire!" The thunderous boom of a cannon roared across the sky, announcing their arrival, and sending a quiver through Hope.

The Lord had forgotten her past. But Nathaniel never would.

Chapter 33

Nathaniel thrust his oar into the swirling water and pushed with all his strength, sending the jolly boat gliding across the bay. Hanson, Kreggs, Gavin, and two of Captain Poole's pirates rowed along with him, three on each side of the narrow craft. Water gurgled along the hull and splashed cool drops onto his feet and breeches. He jerked hair from his face and tried to avoid looking at Miss Hope, perched like a delicate flower on the bow thwarts, her loose curls glittering like gold, her chin raised, her arms around Miss Elise snuggled in her lap.

Nathaniel's gut churned as he remembered the pain on her face when he had dismissed her affections so ardently, the tears spilling down her cheeks, the life fading from her eyes. It had been almost too much to bear. Almost. For he had nearly taken her in his arms, nearly showered her with kisses of forgiveness. But then he pictured her in Gavin's embrace, receiving Gavin's kisses. And the blood froze in his veins.

Shaking the vision from his mind, he shifted his eyes to Abigail, sitting beside Hope. The young woman's rueful eyes had been locked upon the receding pirate ship ever since they had shoved off from its hull. But one glance told Nathaniel it was not the ship, but her captain that had Abigail so captivated, for Captain Poole stood at the main deck railing, returning her gaze with equal fervor.

One of pirates plunged his oar into the water, sending a spray over the major.

"Be careful, you bumbling fool," Major Paine brayed and swatted at his damp, bedraggled shirt.

"Back to your old self so quickly, Major?" Gavin remarked, drawing a snarl from the man.

Mr. Hendrick moaned and gripped his midsection, his eyes upon the steady shore and what he must consider his only salvation from his riotous stomach.

Gavin and Nathaniel exchanged a knowing smile, both happy to be rid of the portentous merchantman and the obnoxious major.

Nathaniel dipped his oar in the water again as a swift breeze blew over him, bringing with it the smells of the port: stale fish, roasted pork, and horse manure. No matter how unpleasant, the scents brought him comfort, reminding him of Charles Towne. In addition, he spotted his ship, the *Illusive Hope*, floating in the bay, and his excitement soared at the sight of her dark hull and sharp lines. His last remaining ship—named after the woman who had not only stolen his other ship, but his heart as well.

When the jolly boat reached shore and disgorged its passengers, Captain Poole's pirates returned to the ship, while Hanson, Boone, and Jones approached Nathaniel, their gap-toothed smiles reflecting their appreciation.

"We thank ye again, Mr. Mason, fer openin' our eyes to the truth," Hanson said.

"'Twas my pleasure, gentlemen." Nathaniel shook their hands in turn and bade them farewell as they scampered down the dock and onto the main street to their new life. Only Kreggs remained behind.

Leading the rest of their party down the pier to Harbor

Street, Nathaniel halted at the end and glanced across the bustling town. After the earthquake had destroyed Port Royal in '92, the survivors had moved here to begin again. Since then the city had grown into a major trade center. Rows of brick and wood buildings lined the dirt street; drapers, bakers, taverns, blacksmith, warehouses. People scurried across the busy road, weaving among carriages, horses, wagons, and slaves. A bell rang in the distance, the *clip-clop* of horses, the grating of wagon wheels, myriad voices, and the distant music of a fiddle combined in a cacophony of sounds that made Nathaniel long for the peace of their tiny island.

A groan from behind drew him around to see Mr. Hendrick, hand to his stomach, starting in the other direction.

"Elise." He gestured for the little girl to follow him.

She peered at her father from within the folds of Hope's skirts and lifted a pleading gaze to her.

Hope gave the man a worried look. "Where will you take her, Mr. Hendrick?"

"That is none of your concern." He attempted to stand straight and winced. "I have business here in town and a ship awaits us."

Hope knelt by the little girl. "Go with your father now." She brushed the curls from her face. "But always remember God loves you. He loves you very much. And so do I." A tear slid down Hope's cheek, and Nathaniel tore his gaze away, determined to not allow her kind gesture to soften his anger.

The little girl shuffled over to her father, who immediately dashed off, dragging her behind him. Hope rose, wiped her face, and stared after her.

Major Paine cleared his throat. Stripped of every insignia, regalia, and frippery save his white breeches and shirt—neither of which could be called white any longer—and with his brown hair spiraling in all directions like a sea anemone, he looked more like a pirate than a major in His Majesty's Service. "I know we've had our differences, Mr.

Mason, but I hope we can part with civility."

"If I were you, Major," Gavin hissed, "I'd be kissing Nathaniel's bare feet for not only saving your life but for bringing you necessities aboard the pirate ship. 'Twas more than any of us would have done."

"Humph." The major glanced over the town as if anxious to leave.

"Where will you go, Major?" Abigail asked.

"I am to report to the fort to procure passage to England. No doubt they anxiously await my arrival." His gaze sped to the bay. "And first on my list of duties will be to inform them of the presence of a certain pirate."

Hope took a step toward him. "How can you? He saved your life."

Major Paine's gaze took her in from head to toe, causing Nathaniel's blood to boil. "'Tis my duty, miss, and what separates me from men devoid of honor." He waved a hand in Gavin's direction.

Gavin's eyes narrowed. "Then you had better be about it, Major, for I believe the *Enchantress* sets sail." He nodded toward the harbor and grinned.

White sails rose like handkerchiefs waving farewell on the ship's masts as she picked up speed near the mouth of the bay.

"The best to you, Major," Nathaniel said.

With a lift of his nose, the major turned on his heel, stumbled on a rock, cursed, and hastened away.

Abigail bit her lip as she stared at the *Enchantress*. "He will escape, will he not?"

"Never fear." Nathaniel gave her a curious look. "Captain Poole shall be long gone before the major makes his grand entrance into the fort."

Abigail faced him. "I must part ways with you here as well."

Dashing to her side, Hope gripped her hands. "Can't you come with us to Charles Towne? Oh, say that you will."

"Nay, my dear friend." Abigail's eyes glistened. "My place is here." She looked at Nathaniel. "I know it now."

Assurance and conviction shone from Abigail's eyes, and Nathaniel gave her a nod of understanding. "So you are no longer afraid?"

She glanced toward the ship, now almost clearing the headland. "A certain pirate convicted me of my fears and reminded me to keep my eyes on God."

Gavin snorted.

Abigail turned back toward Hope and squeezed her hands. "We shall always be friends."

"Always." Hope sobbed. "You have been my only friend. You spoke the truth to me when I refused to hear it. You sat by my side when I was sick. Your words of God changed my heart."

Abigail cast a quick glance at Nathaniel. "So I have been told. I am most pleased to hear it. Please say you'll visit sometime."

"I shall make every attempt." Hope swallowed down her agony.

Nathaniel shifted his gaze away. Why did the blasted woman always cause his heart to wrench? "Do you need an escort to the reverend's house?" he asked Abigail. "It isn't safe to walk these streets alone."

"I'll be happy t' take her." Kreggs finally spoke. "I wouldn't mind talkin' to a reverend. Mebbe even workin' fer him, if he'll have me."

Nathaniel scratched his head, still amazed at the sailor's transformation. "Very well. Miss Sheldon, would you mind?"

"Of course not." Abigail smiled at Kreggs then turned to Gavin. "Mr. Keese, 'tis been a pleasure."

Gavin took her hand and laid a kiss upon it.

Abigail swept a loving gaze over Hope and Nathaniel as tears filled her eyes. "I shall see you all again." Then turning, she took Kreggs' outstretched arm, and together they made her way down the dusty street.

Gavin shifted his bare feet over the sand, flexing his hands into fists, gazing nervously about the town. Odd. Nathaniel had never seen the man so agitated.

"Are we to go to your ship now?" Hope's shaky voice pricked his guilt. "That is, if you still wish to escort me home." Though she had suffered the loss of a good friend, the loss of Elise, and Nathaniel's rejection, Hope carried herself with a humble strength that only increased his ardor for her.

"I am a man of my word, Miss Hope." He stiffened the lines of his face so as not to express the emotions battling within him and turned to Gavin. "And what are your plans?"

"At the moment, I have none." Gavin's customary joviality returned.

"Then join us." Nathaniel hoped he would, for he could not bear to be alone with Hope. "I am to meet my first mate at the Stuffed Boar."

"A tavern?" Gavin rubbed his hands together. "I do believe I will."

Nathaniel started to offer Hope his arm, but instead he pulled away from her and marched toward the tavern, leaving her in Gavin's company. Each thud of his feet over the hot sand reminded him of the time not too long ago when he'd barreled toward another tavern in another port town, Miss Hope in tow, having sold half his fleet to save her life. At least this time, he hadn't lost a ship on her behalf.

Entering the dim tavern saturated with the stench of rum and sweat, Nathaniel ran a sleeve over his forehead as his bare feet landed in a sticky pool on the floor. Ignoring it, he made his way through the maze of tables, searching the shadows for his first mate and friend, Richard Ackon.

Hope gasped behind him. No doubt she stepped into the same slimy puddle he had. He heard Gavin hastening to her aid, his indulgent ministrations causing Nathaniel's stomach to fold.

A boarding house as well as tavern, the Stuffed Boar was

accustomed to having feminine clientele, yet that did not prevent the lewd calls and whistles sent Hope's way from the men scattered about the room. Nathaniel longed to draw her near to keep her safe, but that was no longer his job. 'Twas Gavin's for the time being, and after him, the next man who took his place. Besides, Nathaniel had heard she frequented these types of places in Charles Towne and no doubt knew how to handle herself.

After determining that Richard was nowhere in sight, Nathaniel chose a table in the back, kicked out a chair, and sat down. The man would show up sooner or later, and Nathaniel could use a drink. Hope lowered to a chair across from him while Gavin went off to get their libations.

An awkward silence ensued as if they'd been plunged underwater, even muting the boisterous conversations of the men around them. A lantern on the table flickered its light over Hope's face, and he dared a glance into those deep blue eyes. Though laden with sorrow, they returned his gaze with the same passion, the same affection, the same yearning he felt inside. He shifted away.

Her gasp brought his gaze back as with wide eyes and open mouth, she stared at someone who had just entered the tavern. A tremble nearly rocked her from her seat, and she raised a hand to her throat and seemed to be having trouble breathing.

Nathaniel laid his hand on her arm. "Hope, what is it?" He followed her gaze to a man of medium build with a plumed hat in one hand and cane hanging on his other arm. The jewels decorating his fingers sparkled in the lantern light from beneath the heavy lace at his cuffs. His satin waistcoat and breeches bespoke either great wealth or ostentatious pride, and he perused the room with haughty disdain as if he owned the place.

Hope panted out a ragged breath. "Lord Falkland."

Chapter 34

Hope stared at the man standing before her, hardly daring to believe her eyes.

When Lord Falkland insisted upon speaking to her in private, she'd turned to seek Nathaniel's consent, hoping secretly he wouldn't give it—that he'd take a protective stance between her and this monster. But although a flicker of apprehension crossed his eyes, he shrugged and dashed off as if he couldn't get away from her fast enough. Gavin, on the other hand, barely looked her way. Instead, he and Falkland exchanged a glance that caused Hope's nerves to tighten even further, before he joined Nathaniel.

Now as the shock of seeing him faded to into a raging fury, she regretted agreeing to speak with him.

Feeling returned to her legs, and Hope slowly rose. With one hand perched on his hip, Falkland slid his fingers over the gold trim of his waistcoat and studied her. His dark hair was pulled back and tied with one of his gaudy bows—this one a bright purple that matched the satin of his waistcoat. He tugged on his white cravat.

"My dear, I must say I expected a more amorous greeting." His stern jaw flexed as green eyes scoured over her, claiming his possession.

Hope cast a quick glance at Nathaniel and Gavin leaning against the far tavern wall, their eyes peeled in her direction. "The last time I saw you, Arthur, you were strolling away from me as I was being auctioned off into slavery. With your *wife* on your arm. What are you doing here?"

"I came for you." He grinned and took a step toward her, holding out his hand.

Hope backed away. "Keep your distance, sir, or my friends will be upon you in a second." Moist heat suffocated her, stinging her nose with the putrid smells of the tavern.

Lord Falkland cast a dismissive glance at Gavin and Nathaniel and chuckled. "Harmless rodents, by all appearances." He pouted. "And when did you begin to call me sir again, my sweet one?"

Hope cringed at the sound of Falkland's pet name for her. "I don't know why you are here, nor do I care. But if you think to make amends for what you did, you are sorely mistaken." Belying her outward composure, she grabbed a loose curl at her neck and tugged upon it. *Lord, help me. Why are You doing this to me?* Not long ago she had hoped with all her heart that she would see this man again, hear his words of love. Now that he stood before her, she couldn't be sure of anything.

His eyes narrowed and he cocked his head. "You have changed. You are stronger. More defiant." He raised one brow and leaned toward her. "I find it quite alluring."

Hope's stomach knotted. "Did you expect me to run into your arms?"

"You are so beautiful." He brushed a knuckle against her cheek, but she jerked out of his reach. He frowned. "Will you at least hear my explanation?"

"Pray, get on with it."

"I did not abandon you to the fate you assume." He laid his cane atop the table with a clank and straightened the cuffs of his sleeves. "Do you remember Mr. Garrison?"

A vision of the stocky, puffy-faced man at the auction block came into Hope's mind, renewing her revulsion. "The merchant who nearly purchased me? How did you know …."

Arthur smiled.

Hope blinked. "He was in your employ?"

"I paid him quite handsomely to purchase you. All money lost, of course." He sighed and patted his money pouch like an old friend.

The jangle of coins grated over Hope. Her mind reeled, and she gulped for a breath of fresh air, not the stagnant muck that infiltrated the tavern. "For what purpose?"

"To keep you safe, of course. Captain Grainer had his heart set on selling you. Though I tried desperately to dissuade him." He shrugged. "My only other option was to purchase you myself. And my plan would have worked, too, if that poor excuse for a hero"—he pointed toward Nathaniel—"hadn't swept in to the rescue."

Hope's anger cooled. So Arthur hadn't abandoned her, after all.

He gave her one of his charming smiles, and Hope waited for her heart to leap as it always did at the sight. But then a vision of Lady Falkland—Arthur's *wife*—lifting her pert little nose in the air broke the spell. "And what, pray tell, would you have done if your plan had worked?"

"Sent you home safely on one of my ships, of course." His brow furrowed in concern. "Do you think I would ever do anything to harm you? I love you, sweet one. I always have."

Hope's knees turned to pudding, and she sank into her chair. *He loves me still.* "What of your wife?"

Lord Falkland stooped before her and reached for her hands, but she snatched them away. "I meant to tell you about her, I truly did." He sighed and looked down. "But there was never a proper time."

"A proper time?" Hope shouted, drawing the gaze of Falkland's two men sitting at the next table. "You promised to marry me," she whispered, seething.

"And I still intend to, sweet one. All in good time." He placed a hand on her leg, and Hope shot to her feet, knocking her chair over behind her. Not long ago, his touch would have sent waves of heated pleasure through her, but now his hands felt as cold as ice.

A look of genuine pain sparked in his eyes. "My wife is quite ill. The doctors do not expect her to live much longer."

"She looked quite well to me," Hope snapped.

"'Tis an insidious disease that does not manifest itself in obvious ways." He sent her a look of appeal. "I cannot tell you how taxing it has been."

Hope rubbed her brow, unsure whether to believe a word this man said. "Taxing? How taxing can it be when your wife lies near death and you are bedding another woman?"

"Can I help that I fell madly in love with you?" He stepped toward her again. "It was not my intention. I would have left her if not for the disease."

Hope eyed him, searching her heart for any scrap of affection, any spark of tenderness remaining for this man, but all she felt was confusion and doubt.

"So you see," he continued, "I have been ardently searching for you for months, until I discovered Mr. Mason had a ship berthed in Kingston, and came straightaway."

"You have wasted your time, Arthur. You already have a wife."

"Nothing has changed between us, my sweet. Nothing. We are still betrothed. I still intend to marry you." He inched toward her, sweeping his gaze over her hair, her face and down to her lips. "I have a ship. I can take you back to Charles Towne post haste, and we can carry on as if none of this nightmare had ever occurred." He waved a hand through the air as if to dismiss the agony she had suffered the past few months.

He still loved her. He still wanted to marry her. Isn't that what she had longed for? Isn't that what she had endlessly cried for after he'd abandoned her? She glanced at Nathaniel. His rejection proved no honorable man would ever want her. If she didn't accept Arthur's proposal, she would most likely spend the rest of her days alone and unloved.

Never alone and always loved. The soft voice filtered through Hope, soothing her and lifting her spirits.

Falkland's scent of lavender crept over her, but instead of setting her senses aflame as it used to, nausea brewed within her belly. How could she ever go back to this man? Not only was he married, but his love paled in comparison to the love of God. Hope gazed into his green eyes that suddenly reminded her of a lizard's. And she knew. She knew she no longer loved him, no longer needed him. In fact, she suddenly wondered why she ever had.

Thank You, Lord.

Clasping her hands before her, she raised her chin. "But this nightmare *did* occur, your lordship, and you are right, I have changed. I find I no longer have a shred of affection for you. In fact"—she could feel Nathaniel's piercing eyes upon her from across the gloomy room—"my affections lay with God. And with another."

"God, bah." Lord Falkland glared at Nathaniel. "I see." He faced her. "But what would I have expected from a woman who so freely offers her wares to any man with interest."

"How dare you!" Hope slapped his face.

He rubbed his jaw, a devious grin slithering over his lips. "I have learned much about Mr. Nathaniel Mason over this past month. I would hate to see the young merchantman's business ruined before it has begun."

Fear spiked through Hope, and she stepped back. Her bare foot landed in something almost as cool and slimy as the man before her. "What are you saying?"

"Shall I spell it out for you, my sweet one? Either you come with me willingly and remain my mistress, or I will ruin your lover. Mark my words, I will ruin his business, I will ruin his reputation, and Mr. Nathaniel Mason will end up a beggar on the streets."

Nathaniel took up another pace across the sticky floor. He crossed arms over his chest, scratched the back of his neck, then crossed his arms again. Why did Hope give that pig an audience after what he had done to her? And what was that odd look on her face when she first saw Falkland. Shock … anger … love? The chaotic spin of his own emotions made it impossible to tell.

Hope had committed her life to Jesus, yet since that time she had betrayed Nathaniel's trust, thrown herself at Gavin, and now appeared to be falling back into the trap of the charlatan who had started all this madness. And after Nathaniel had rescued her from near slavery, had given up his ship, had endured over a month of starvation, discomfort, and danger. He didn't know whether to be angry at his losses, at her betrayal, or be sorry for her quick slip away from the Lord back into her old ways.

Regardless of the pain she'd caused him, Nathaniel longed for her to remain true to her faith. *Oh, Lord, please help her do the right thing.*

Gavin's whistling began to chafe over Nathaniel. The man had not said a word nor even looked at Nathaniel since they had crossed the tavern. Instead he spent his time kicking a piece of stale bread across the floor.

Movement drew Nathaniel's gaze to Lord Falkland advancing toward Hope. She backed away, and it took all of Nathaniel's resolve to stop himself from charging toward them and pummeling the man to the floor. He couldn't make out Hope's expression or hear her words, but two things were sure. Lord Falkland made a heartfelt appeal, perhaps even begging for her forgiveness. And Hope was listening. Though she seemed to resist at first, now her shoulders slumped and she sank back into her chair.

Falkland snapped his fingers, and his two men leapt to their feet and flanked Hope. Nathaniel started toward them, wondering how he and Gavin were going to take on three armed men. Turning, he gestured for Gavin to follow, but the man's attention remained riveted on the floor. "Gavin. Come on." But still his friend ignored him. Growling, Nathaniel charged forward toward an advancing Lord Falkland.

"Calm yourself, Mr. Mason. Your lady is unharmed. Or should I say, *my* lady." The pompous fop halted and tapped his cane on the wooden floor, the sound as hollow as Nathaniel's heart. Behind Falkland, Hope bowed her head.

"What's the meaning of this?" Nathaniel asked.

"I'll make it simple for you, Mason, since you are a simple man." Falkland gave him a malicious grin. "Miss Hope and I have reconciled our differences, and she has agreed to set sail with me this evening for Charles Towne."

Nathaniel's throat went dry. His heart seemed to collapse in on itself. It couldn't be true. Not after all they'd been through. Not after her encounter with God. "Hope?" He peered around Falkland. He must hear it from her lips. "Is this true?"

Hope lifted her head then quickly looked down again. Her eyes pooled with tears. For him? For Falkland? For her shame? Fire and thunder, he was weary of trying to figure her out.

Falkland cleared his throat.

"'Tis true," she muttered.

He brushed dust from his satin coat. "But I do wish to thank you, Mason, for keeping her safe thus far." He turned toward Gavin. "And I believe I owe you five pounds, Mr. Keese."

Gavin shuffled forward as confusion rattled through Nathaniel.

Plucking out his money pouch, Falkland counted the amount into Gavin's outstretched hand.

"Gavin?" Nathaniel's voice came out like sludge from

the bilge.

"I'm sorry, Nathaniel." Gavin pocketed the coins, their clank piercing Nathaniel like arrows.

Hope gasped.

Falkland's brows shot up. "Oh of course—you didn't know. Mr. Keese is the first mate aboard my ship. After you purchased Miss Hope, I offered him five pounds to follow her, both to ensure her safety and keep her from, shall we say, any untoward liaisons. As she is prone to do." He shot a quick glance at Hope then leaned toward Nathaniel with a grin. "I know how enchanting she can be, and I wouldn't want her sullied before she was returned to me."

Hope's shoulders fell beneath Falkland's insinuations.

The fangs of yet another betrayal sank deep into Nathaniel's gut. "You work for him?"

Gavin gave a half smile. "You know me, Nathaniel. I love an adventure, especially one that pays. How could I resist?" He lowered his gaze, but not before Nathaniel saw a spark of remorse.

"Enough of this triviality." Falkland tapped his cane as if that put an end to things. "I shall bid you adieu, Mr. Mason." He nodded toward Nathaniel then faced Gavin. "Are you coming?"

Then in a flourish of satin and lace, Falkland swerved about, grabbed Hope's arm, and escorted her from the tavern, his men and Gavin following on their heels.

Chapter 35

The rising sun cast glittering shafts of gold and white onto the sleepy waves of Kingston Bay, caressing them to life around Nathaniel's ship. He wished it were so easy to breathe life back into his own body. For he felt as dead as if a cannonball had blasted through his chest, and all that remained was to toss his carcass into a watery grave.

Ships of all shapes and sizes rocked in the bay. Beyond their bare masts, the mountains of Jamaica rose in a glistening mound of bluish-green that normally inspired awe within Nathaniel at the beauty of God's creation. But today he found no pleasure in the sight.

Activity in the port drew his gaze to the slaves and dock workers scrambling across Harbor Street, crates and barrels hoisted on their heads and shoulders as the rising heat of the day shoved aside the shroud of slumber—that sweet repose of the night that had eluded Nathaniel, yet again.

Lord, what is wrong with me? He should be happy to be rid of Hope. She had brought him naught but hardship and heartache. Now, he had been spared not only the trouble of escorting her to Charles Towne, but also the vexation of her company. Then why did the vision of her walking out of the tavern—and out of his life—yesterday make his heart feel as though it had been ripped from his chest?

He paced across the deck, his boots thumping over the wooden planks. At least he had connected with his first mate and was once again aboard his ship, the *Illusive Hope*. He gave a sorrowful chuckle. He had named the ship after Miss Hope, a condition he intended to rectify as soon as he returned to Charles Towne. For once again she proved to be as elusive as ever, not only to him, but to God as well. Perhaps she'd had no real encounter with the Almighty after all. Perhaps it had all been an act to win Nathaniel's affections. Then why had she run into Gavin's arms after she had what she wanted? Nathaniel would never understand women. Especially those like Hope—those like his mother.

He sank into the chair behind his desk. *Lord, take this pain from me. I fear I cannot bear it.*

Drawing a deep breath, he allowed the familiar smells of his ship, tar, wood, and oakum to ease through him. He glanced over his desk: Charts, books, a quill pen, his hourglass, logbook, and quadrant spread haphazardly across it. He let out a final sigh, expelling his sorrow, and stood. He had one ship left, and one being built in the dockyard at Charles Towne. He had pocketed some coin from the cargo his first mate had sold in Kingston. Now he would put Miss Hope and the past few months out of his mind and continue with his plans to build a merchant fleet, a fortune, and a name.

I want you to preach. I want you to lead others to Me. The gentle words pierced his heart.

Nathaniel bowed his head. *I cannot, Lord.*

True, Nathaniel's preaching may have influenced a few pirates. But not the most important person. *I failed You. She is back with the enemy. Do not ask this of me.*

A knock on the door jolted Nathaniel from his prayer. "Enter."

Mr. Simmons, his steward, appeared in the doorway, his

face a twist of confusion. "A note for you, sir." He approached and held out a piece of paper. "And a child arrived with it."

"A child?" Nathaniel grabbed the note and tore through the wax seal.

Mr. Mason,
I deeply regret the course of my present actions, but I find I have no other choice. As you must imagine, I am a man of enormous responsibilities and cannot possibly care properly for a child. I am rarely home and would be constantly afflicted by guilt should I assign Elise to the care of a governess who would possess no real affection for the girl. Hence, I am handing her over to Miss Hope. Having seen the attachment formed between Miss Hope and Elise, and Miss Hope's reluctance to bid farewell to my daughter, I believe this is the right course of action. I trust Miss Hope will be pleased with the arrangements and both she and Elise will be better off for it. It is the kindness of my heart which prompts me to this action.
Truth be told, I am unsure whether I am even the girl's father.
Your humble servant,
Mr. William Hendrick.

Humble indeed. Nathaniel dropped the letter, allowing it to flutter to his desk, and stormed from the room, shoving past Simmons. "Is he still here?"

"Who, Cap'n?" Simmons's footsteps pounded after him.

"The man who left this note."

"Nay. He handed me the letter and the girl and shoved off before I could speak a word."

Nathaniel leapt onto the deck, spotted Elise trembling beside Haines, one of his sailors, then dashed to the railing and scanned the bay. A small boat manned by two rowers made its way toward the dock. A third man sat in the midst of her, but even at a distance, Nathaniel could tell it was not Mr. Hendrick.

Simmons approached. "He did say to tell ye Mr. Hendrick had already left the island. Last night, he said."

"Fire and thunder!" Nathaniel swerved about. Elise's wide blue eyes stared up at him, her tiny face contorted in fright. "Where is your wife, Mr. Simmons?"

"In the galley, Cap'n."

"Please ask her to come on deck." Nathaniel raked a hand through his hair and knelt beside Elise. He dismissed Haines and took a deep breath, trying to calm his fury. "You remember me, Miss Elise?"

She nodded, sending her red curls shimmering like rubies in the rising sun. Her bottom lip quivered. Nathaniel clenched his fists. What sort of man abandoned his daughter? And in the pretense of being kind—of doing the right thing.

"Where is Miss Hope?" she squeaked.

He took her hand in his. "She is not here."

Her blue eyes swam with tears that soon streamed down her cheeks. Nathaniel knew how she felt. Pushing aside his anguish, he forced a smile.

"But I am here. And I'm going to take good care of you."

"Where is my father?" Elise whimpered, the quiver in her lip radiating throughout her body.

"Your father had to go on a trip. But you'll be safe here with me."

"Father always goes away." Her face took on a haunted look.

Nathaniel gripped her shoulders, not knowing what to say to bring her comfort.

Mrs. Simmons emerged from below deck, a portly woman in her forties. She huffed from the exertion of climbing the companionway stairs, but when her eyes landed on Miss Elise, she rushed to her side. "What 'ave we 'ere?" She stooped and gave Elise such a huge smile that the fear from only a moment ago faded from the little girl's face.

"Mrs. Simmons. It seems we have a special guest on board," Nathaniel said. "Would you be so kind as to escort her to your chambers and look after her? Make her as comfortable as a princess."

Elise's eyes swept to his, sparkling even amidst the tears.

"I would at that." Mrs. Simmons opened her arms, and without hesitation Elise flew into them. "Oh you poor dear. Nothin' to be afraid of." She patted her back and looked up at Nathaniel. "What o' me duties, Cap'n?"

"I'll have Mills take over the galley."

Grumbles flung his way from all around, no doubt due to Mills's lack of culinary skills.

"A boat approaches, Cap'n." A shout from the foredeck brought Nathaniel's attention to the harbor, where a small craft, manned by one person, made its way toward them. Now what? He faced Mrs. Simmons and Elise.

"Thank you, Mrs. Simmons."

Elise's arms clung to her neck like barnacles to a ship's keel, but she managed to rise and head toward the ladder. "Come now, little one."

Nathaniel raked a hand through his hair. What in heaven's name was he going to do with a little girl? "Mr. Ackon, spyglass, if you please."

His first mate leapt down the foredeck ladder and thrust the scope into Nathaniel's hand. Raising it, he surveyed the approaching craft. Gavin Keese came into view. Fury knotted his back. "Man the swivel!"

Ackon looked dazed. "Cap'n?"

"You heard me. The swivel gun." Nathaniel lowered the glass and slapped it across his palm.

"Are we to shoot an unarmed man?" His first mate's voice heightened.

Nathaniel would like nothing better. "You are mistaken, Ackon. This man comes with all guns loaded. Trouble is, he hides his weapons well." Nathaniel had been so distraught over Hope, he hadn't taken time to ponder Gavin's betrayal. All this time, the man had been naught but one of Falkland's minions. Memories surged into rage as he remembered all the times Gavin had indeed come between Hope and Nathaniel. And all the while, pretending to be Nathaniel's friend.

"Gregson, Matten, load the swivel," Ackon bellowed.

"Aye, sir." Two men scrambled to the gun mounted amidships on the railing and began loading it as Gavin continued to row toward them.

"Ready, Cap'n," Matten announced.

"Fire on my command." Nathaniel squeezed his eyes shut for a moment. "But do not hit him."

"Do *not* hit him, Cap'n?" Gregson scratched his head, and a wave of disappointment soured his features.

"That's what I said." Nathaniel glanced back at Gavin, assessing his position. "Fire!"

The men lit the fuse, and the swivel exploded in a thunderous boom. The ball splashed inches from Gavin's boat, dousing him with a spray of seawater. An obscenity drifted to them on the wind, but he continued rowing, albeit more energetically than before.

Nathaniel batted away the acrid smoke. "Load another shot," he ordered, and the men worked furiously to remove the breech, swab the barrel, and load another round, but before too long, Gavin had brought his craft within earshot of the ship and too close to be fired upon.

"Sink me, Nathaniel, what are you trying to do?" Gavin's indignant voice rose from the small boat. "Sink me?"

Nathaniel leaned over the railing. "Precisely," he shouted. "Now take your leave, or I *will* sink you, Mr. Keese."

"I must speak to you." Gavin sent up a look of humble appeal.

"I've heard all I care to hear from you. Now be gone with you."

The boat thudded against the hull. "Permission to board,

Captain?"

"Nay." Nathaniel turned toward Ackon, who stared at him as if he'd gone mad. "Shoot him if he tries to board," he said loud enough for Gavin to hear.

"Egad, man, I have information you must know."

Nathaniel rubbed his left side and paced before the bulwark. Perhaps he should hear the man out. Perhaps he had news of Hope. Perhaps she was hurt. He leaned over the side, battling the rage churning inside of him at the sight of the charlatan whom he had once called friend. A twinge of guilt pricked his soul. He was supposed to love his enemies, not hate them.

"Come up." He shouted then stood back as Gavin climbed the ropes and leapt with ease over the railing, the usual cavalier smirk missing from his boyish face. Freshly shaven and clad in a white shirt and dark breeches, leather boots, and a black cravat, he no longer looked the part of the madcap he so often played.

Nathaniel planted his fists on his waist. "Out with it."

"In private." Gavin raised his brows and glanced around at Nathaniel's crew, who closed in on the newcomer, no doubt expecting an altercation.

Nathaniel gestured to the foredeck and then followed Gavin up the ladder to the bow, dismissing the few sailors who loitered about.

Eyeing his one-time friend, Nathaniel tried to quell the fury gripping every muscle, the urge to beat him to dust. But he would hear him out first.

Gavin shifted his boots over the deck then met Nathaniel's gaze. "Nice ship. You built it?"

Nathaniel nodded.

"Nathaniel. I deceived you. I don't blame you for trying to blast me out of the water." He chuckled, but the smile slipped from his face beneath Nathaniel's glare.

"I trusted you. I called you my friend."

Gavin swallowed. "I didn't know you. I didn't know

Hope when I agreed to do the deed." He shrugged. "It sounded like an amusing diversion. I meant you no harm."

"What is it you want, Gavin? I'm a busy man."

"I gave Falkland his money back. I'm no longer his first mate."

"Why?"

"It wasn't right. What I did." Gavin ran a hand over the back of his neck and gazed out upon the bay. "You changed me."

Nathaniel narrowed his eyes. What was the man up to now? Was this another trick of Falkland's?

"You are so honorable, so good—even to those who do you harm." Gavin huffed as if he found the qualities frustrating. "You always do the right thing."

"Not always." Nathaniel thought of his obsession with Hope. Pursuing her had never been right.

Seagulls flapped overhead, squawking.

"Despite every effort to the contrary, I found my respect growing for you daily." Gavin jerked his hair behind him and leveled a sincere gaze upon Nathaniel. "My friendship was real."

"Friends don't lie to each other." Nathaniel looked away. The sound of water purling against the hull did naught to ease the acid fermenting in his stomach.

"I know." Gavin gripped a halyard and shook his head. "Then the miracle of Hope's healing. All this talk of God, and Captain Poole." His laughter came out a bitter chord. "I always wanted to be a pirate. And then this notorious pirate advises me against it. Not only that, he pours his affections upon Abigail. Sink me, a woman of God?" Gavin snorted. "I could not fathom it. You represent everything I loathed: rules, integrity, honor, religion, piety. Everything I avoided my whole life. But I found I admired them. Egad, I *actually* admired them."

Nathaniel studied the man, searching for a hint of deception, wondering what purpose this confession—even if it were sincere—would serve.

"I now know these qualities make a man strong, make him good. They give him a higher purpose than serving himself. After Falkland gave me the money and I went back to his ship, I realized I no longer want to live without them."

Nathaniel gazed at the sky, half expecting lightning to strike the man for such blatant lies.

Gavin scratched the whiskers lining his jaw. "I don't expect you to believe me. But after I came to know you … and Miss Hope, I—"

"You did your job well coming between us." Nathaniel interrupted, weary of the man's suspicious explanation. "Of course, Miss Hope lavishes her affections so freely, the task could not have been too difficult. Nor unpleasant."

"That is another matter I have come to clear up. I lied to you regarding Miss Hope."

"What is one lie among so many?"

"Nay, you misunderstand. She never gave herself to me."

"What are you saying?" Nathaniel's eyes snapped to his. Despite his suspicion of everything Gavin said, a spark of hope lit within him.

"I lured her on deck under the pretense Miss Elise was in need of her. I knew you would see us."

"So you didn't?" Nathaniel clutched his arm. "She didn't?"

"Nay." Gavin shook his head and grinned. "Not that I didn't try. Truth be told, despite my pretending, despite my promise to Falkland, I became quite enamored with her. But when I declared my love and tried to seduce her, she spurned me. Gave me some balderdash about loving you and never giving herself to a man who wasn't her husband."

Releasing Gavin, Nathaniel gripped the railing and glanced over the bay, his vision blurring. "So you never?"

"Sink me, are you daft? That is what I'm trying to tell you. Her affections have always been for you and you alone."

Hope hadn't betrayed him. Agony wrenched his gut. He'd treated her so horribly, rejected her so cruelly. His throat burned, and he clamped his fingers on the wood until they ached. "What does it matter? She chose Falkland."

"Is that what you think?" Gavin chuckled. "Then you're not only daft but mad as well." He gave Nathaniel an accusatory look. "I don't know what spell Falkland may have cast on Hope, but from the way she was behaving on his ship, I don't think she was at all pleased to be there."

Nathaniel's mind spun. "What are you talking about?"

"Miserable, heartsick, more like a prisoner than a lover."

Miserable? But why? When she'd willingly gone with him.

"Did you hear me?" Gavin asked.

"Aye, and I cannot believe it."

"You are quite a pair." Gavin snorted. "Neither of you believes the other one loves you when 'tis plain as a white sail against a dark sky to the rest of us."

"Which one is Falkland's ship?" Nathaniel stormed across the deck.

"He set sail last night."

"For where?"

"Charles Towne."

"Lay aloft, yardman. Lay out and loose the sails!" Nathaniel barked to his crew. "I must speak to her," he shot over his shoulder toward Gavin.

Gavin's boot steps pounded behind him. "His ship is well armed. Twelve guns, not counting his swivels. You have only two." He caught Nathaniel's shoulder. "I doubt Falkland will grant you an audience with her. He will fight you. And you will lose."

"I cannot let her go without knowing her reason." He scanned the bay. "Where can I get a well-armed ship?"

"Why not the *Enchantress*?" Gavin grinned.

"Captain Poole sailed yesterday. I watched him leave."

"Aye, but I have it on good authority, he's anchored

around the bend in a hidden cove." Gavin lifted a brow.

Even if they found Poole, Nathaniel wondered if he'd be able to convince the self-serving pirate to help him find Hope. But what choice did he have?

"Then let's pay him a visit, shall we?"

Chapter 36

"Ah, and to what do I owe the pleasure of yer company this fine evening." Captain Poole failed to rise from his seat behind a desk that looked more like driftwood than a piece of furniture. Leaning back in his chair, he crossed his booted feet atop the wooden slab that was home to sundry charts and maps, a set of brass flintlock pistols, a near empty bottle of rum, two flickering candles, and oddly, a fiddle.

The pirate who had escorted Gavin and Nathaniel below waved them inside, showering them with the rancid odor of his unwashed body.

"Miss me so soon, Mason?" Captain Poole took a bite out of an apple.

"We have a business proposition, Captain." Nathaniel glanced over the cabin, a room he'd not been permitted to enter on his last voyage aboard *The Enchantress*.

Captain Poole grunted. "Well, I hope 'tis a better proposition than the last one. What did I get for me trouble escortin' ye to Kingston? Naught but one of His Majesty's ships sharp on me tail."

"Major Paine," Gavin uttered beneath his breath and

plopped into a chair.

"Yet I see you have managed to evade them," Nathaniel said.

"Would ye expect any less?" The pirate grinned. "I'm Captain Poole, after all." He took another bite of his apple and tossed it across the room. It landed in a barrel with a precision that defied the rum-induced glaze across his eyes. "But how did *ye* find me?"

Nathaniel crossed arms over his chest and replied in a waggish tone, "I'm Captain Mason, after all."

A faint smirk took residence on the captain's lips, followed by a deep chuckle. Slamming his boots down onto the deck, he stood, grabbed the bottle of rum, and took a swig.

"Well, out with it. What be yer business?"

"I need your ship."

A shower of rum sprayed from the captain's lips, and Nathaniel jumped back to avoid getting wet.

"And how d'ye propose to take it from me?" A sharp challenge skipped across Poole's dark eyes.

"I don't propose to take it at all, Captain." Nathaniel rubbed his chin, praying the rum would put the captain in a fair mood instead of a more belligerent one, as it did most men. "I am no pirate. I simply wish to borrow it, along with you and your crew."

"Borrow, ye say." Captain Poole cocked his head. "And what be yer purpose?"

"To rescue Miss Hope."

"Miss Hope?" Captain Poole circled the desk. "The fair mistress with the hair of gold? Yer *wife*?"

Nathaniel swallowed. Amidst all the stress, he'd forgotten their ruse. "I must beg your forgiveness. She is not my wife."

"A truer word ne'er been spoke." Captain Poole chortled. "D'ye take me fer a fool, Mason? I knew it all along." He fingered the pistol on his desk, and Nathaniel wondered if he intended to shoot him for his deception. But then his gaze drifted to the thick darkness outside the stern window and for a moment, he seemed to get lost in it. "And why does yer fair lass need rescuin'?"

"She may have been taken against her will." The sound of the words ignited an urgency within Nathaniel.

"By Lord Falkland," Gavin said. "They are headed for Charles Towne."

"A lord, eh?" Captain Poole spit to the side, his dark eyes shifting between them. "But ye've got a ship, don't ye, Mason?"

Gavin stood. "Lord Falkland's ship is heavily armed."

"Heavily armed, ye say." The pirate scratched the stubble on his chin. "Which means he's got somethin' worth stealin' aboard."

"That he does," Gavin said. "A belly full of goods he intends to sell at Charles Towne."

At the mention of the wealth, Poole's face lit up.

Nathaniel shifted his stance. "However, if you agree to our plan, you cannot plunder his ship."

Captain Poole jerked back as if Nathaniel had hit him. "Of course I can. I've done it many a time before."

"I have no doubt." Nathaniel sighed. "What I meant to say is that I cannot allow you to steal anything nor to take the ship as prize." Though Nathaniel would do almost anything to speak with Hope, he would not break God's law.

"Cannot allow?" Captain Poole's brow furrowed into a jumble of lines as if no one ever dared tell him such a thing. "Are ye tired of yer life? If ye dare hire a pirate, ye cannot expect him *not* to pirate."

Nathaniel glanced at Gavin, who shrugged his agreement with Poole. Untying the pouch at his side, Nathaniel tossed it to the captain, who caught it in midair. "Here is your pay for the deed, Captain. But I cannot in good conscience be a part of thievery."

"Ah, there's yer problem." Captain Poole gave a

mischievous grin. "Ye must rid yerself of that good conscience."

"By God's grace, that will never happen."

"Hmmph." The captain eyed Nathaniel with disdain then opened the pouch and poured the coins onto his desk. Clinks and clanks echoed through the cabin as the glittering pile grew into a gold and silver mound. "So allow me to get a clear understandin'." Tossing the empty pouch down, Poole clasped his hands behind his back, the silver trim on his coat glimmering in the candlelight. "Ye want me to attack this Lord Falkland's ship, but I can't sink 'er, can't pillage 'er, can't steal 'er, and all I'll be gettin' is this measly bag of coin?"

"That is the way of it, yes, Captain." Nathaniel tried to keep his voice calm and his tone commanding, all the while praying for God's grace to change this pirate's heart.

Grabbing the rum bottle, Captain Poole took another gulp and wiped his mouth on his sleeve. "I've got to hand it to ye, Mason, ye've got pluck." He chuckled. "The pluck o' a pirate, to be sure."

"The money is all I have, Captain. But it's yours if you'll help me."

"Not all ye have." His dark eyes glinted greed.

Nathaniel shook his head. Had the rum gone to the man's head? What else could he mean?

Captain Poole's brows lifted. "I believe ye own a ship?"

Hope paced across the captain's cabin, wringing her hands. Soon Falkland would join her, as he always did this time of the evening. So far he'd been a gentleman, but behind his docile facade, impatience simmered in his eyes. He was not a man accustomed to rejection, and she'd seen him unleash his cruel temper many a time on those who dared to cross him.

Three miserable days had passed. And although she'd

been treated like nobility, given the run of the ship, and fed like a queen, Hope much preferred to be locked in the hold than to face Lord Falkland's constant advances. Her thoughts drifted to Nathaniel, as they always did, and she wondered how he fared. Was he on his way back to Charles Towne? Did he think of her, and if he did, were his thoughts consumed with his poor opinion of her character? But how could she blame him? He believed she'd betrayed him with Gavin, and now he must believe she had rushed back to her old ways. No doubt he was glad to be rid of her.

Shoving memories of Nathaniel aside, Hope approached the bulkhead and swerved to cross the cabin again, tripping on the plush Turkish carpet at its center. Lord Falkland liked to surround himself with beauty, even in his ship's cabin: from the intricately carved mahogany desk, to the velvet upholstered Queen Anne chairs, to the twinkling brass lanterns and the tapestries depicting scenes from the English countryside that decorated the walls, to the imposing oak bed in the corner, complete with silk coverlet. Hope shivered at the sight of it. Perhaps she was just another one of his trophies—another thing of beauty to add to his collection.

And like all his precious possessions, he enjoyed putting her on display, all the while keeping her close and guarded.

But Hope didn't need Lord Falkland any longer. She didn't need his wealth. She didn't need his title, and she certainly didn't need his attentions to make her feel valued and loved. That empty yearning within her had been filled to the full by the love of God.

The ship creaked as it rose over a swell, and Hope braced her feet on the deck and glanced out the stern windows. The sun dipped below the horizon, absconding with the light of day and pulling a dark blanket over the sky. She rubbed her arms against a sudden quiver. Everything seemed worse at night, more threatening, more frightening. As if God took all that was good in the world and retired with it to His chamber for the evening.

I am here, beloved.

Hope's eyes burned at the soft inner voice, and she glanced over the cabin. "Thank You, Father. For I fear I will need Your strength tonight." She doubted she could put off Lord Falkland one more night. What would he do when she rejected him again? Would he force himself on her? Would he lock her below? Cast her into the sea? Or perhaps sail to St. Kitts and complete the task of selling her to one of the island's grotesque planters.

But this time who would be there to rescue her?

She tugged a lock of hair and hurried her pace as fear stole her breath. *Oh, God, please help me.*

The thick oak door creaked open, and in swaggered Lord Falkland as if he were entering a levee with the king. "Ah, my sweet one." He smiled, but beneath the smile, frustration stewed. He shut the door with an ominous thud. After laying his cane atop his desk, he doffed his tricorn and shrugged out of his coat, draping it over a chair. Then, straightening the lace at his cuffs, he approached her. Hope swallowed.

"You look lovely tonight." He perused her, his eyes burning with desire.

"You provided the gown, Arthur." Hope swished away before he saw the fear in her eyes. "Your wife's perhaps?" She faced him, willing to do anything to deter him, even anger him if necessary.

"Nay, love. My wife could never"—his licentious gaze swept over her again—"shall we say, fill a gown quite like you do."

Hope's stomach sickened under his salacious perusal. Why had she ever been attracted to this man?

He laid a finger on his chin and approached her. "But come, come, are you to be cross with me forever?"

She stepped back. "You have a wife, Arthur. It is no little thing."

"Hmm." He loosened his cravat and tugged it from his neck. "But it is of no importance, sweet one. Or she is, I should say."

Hope groaned in disgust. "How can you be so cruel?"

"There's naught I can do about her ailment." He shrugged. "And 'twas not a marriage based on love." He slid his fingers over his cravat and snapped it tight between his hands as if he intended to choke her with it. "But do not speak of her. It puts me in such ill humor." He yanked her close and kissed her cheek. "I have missed you, Hope," he whispered into her ear.

The nauseating stench of lavender and tobacco swirled around her, and she tore from his grasp and walked away. *Lord, what do I do?* She had to stay with Falkland, or he would ruin Nathaniel. Yet even if the thought did not repulse her, she could not give herself to him and be true to God.

His boots thudded over the deck, and Hope spun around to see him opening his desk drawer. He pulled out a bottle of port and poured himself a glass. Taking a sip, he glared her way.

"Why did you marry her?" Hope thrust her nose into the air in a pretense of composure.

"For her wealth, what else?" His eyes glinted in the lantern light. "Not that it impressed the grand Earl of Wrexham." Arthur gulped down the rest of his port and poured himself another. He skirted the desk, bottle in hand.

"Who is the Earl of Wrexham?"

"My father." He took a sip and sank into one of the Queen Anne chairs.

By the sullen look on his face, Hope surmised this new subject would cause him to become either extremely morose or extremely angry. Either emotion might save her for one more night. "Did he not approve of the match?"

"Approve? Humph." Arthur grunted. "I doubt the man knows the meaning of the word, save when it came to my brother, Gifford."

"I didn't know you had a brother." Clutching her skirts, Hope moved to the chair farthest from Arthur and sat down.

"The grand Viscount of Buckley." He lifted his glass into the air in a feigned toast.

"Your older brother?" For only the eldest son assumed a title, and Arthur called himself Lord. No matter. If Hope could keep him talking—and drinking—perhaps he would eventually pass out.

"Older, and apparently, much wiser." Arthur downed his glass and poured another. "Much better at every task he undertook, if you ask my father." He slouched into the chair, appearing more like a little boy than a man.

"Was it my fault I was always sick as a child?" He tone grew caustic and threaded with pain. "How could I keep up with strong, robust Gifford—a head taller and a pound wiser? Whatever I did, it was never good enough." He stared off into the room, a dull haze covering his eyes, and snickered. "*I was never good enough.*"

Hope eyed the man she'd once loved and suddenly felt sorry for him. Falling short of a father's approval was something with which she was quite familiar. "I'm sorry."

"I don't want your pity!" He sprang to his feet and thrust the half-empty bottle toward her.

Hope shrank back, her heart thumping wildly.

He slammed the bottle onto the desk and snapped his remaining drink to the back of his throat. "I need no one's pity. For I have made a success of myself without anyone's help. I possess more wealth and land than my brother ever will. That is why I give myself the title due to my brother by birth." Setting down the glass, he turned and leaned back on the desk. "For he that is least among you all, the same shall be great."

She cringed at his distortion of the Scriptures.

Rising, he stumbled toward Hope, tearing at the buttons on his shirt. "Enough of this talk. You are mine, and I will have you. It will be just as sweet as before."

Hope slowly stood and sucked in her breath. Her fingers went numb. Retreating, she held her hand up. "It can never be that way again, Arthur."

"What do you mean? Of course it can." Pulling his shirt over his head, he laid it on the chair, then clutched her arms. Pain spiked into her shoulders. "I know you love me. Tell me you love me." He shook her. The smell of alcohol stung her nose.

"I *did* love you, Arthur. But I cannot give you that kind of love anymore." She gazed into his eyes, rife with anger, confusion, and pain. He could still harm Nathaniel. He *would* still harm Nathaniel. "I cannot be yours until we are married." She blurted out her agreement to marry him though it made her heart crumble to pieces. But it was the only way to keep Nathaniel safe.

"Balderdash." He shoved her down on the bed. "You had no compunction giving yourself to me before."

Hope's skin grew clammy. Her hands trembled. Surely he wouldn't force himself upon her. "You don't love me, Arthur. Don't you see? I'm simply a prize in your battle for supremacy over your brother. A trophy to display before your father."

He studied her. "You *have* changed."

"Yes, I have." She was no longer the desperate, wanton girl who tossed her affections like garbage to ravenous dogs. She was a precious child of the King. Cleansed, purified, made holy. A burst of joy flooded her, despite her dire circumstances. For no one could take that away from her. Not even Lord Falkland.

She gave him a determined look. "I have changed for the better."

"I shall be the judge of that." He snorted and slid fingers over her cheek.

Taking his hand, she pressed it between hers. "Arthur, I have found God. Or should I say, He found me. He exists. He loves me. He loves you. There is a better way to live." *Oh, Lord, please help him to see.*

He snatched back his hand as if she'd stabbed it, face

contorting like mass of tangled rope. "Scads, I knew I shouldn't have allowed you to spend time with Mr. Mason. A reverend's son, isn't he? He has poisoned you with that pious rubbish."

"It's not poison. It's truth and life."

Falkland took a step back, disgust simmering in his gaze. "You gave yourself to that carpenter, Mason. He's sullied you." He wrinkled his nose.

"I did no such thing!" Hope's voice emerged in strangled tones, boiling with temper. She grew tired of being accused of things she had not done.

"And Mr. Keese, too, I am sure. That's what all this talk of God is about—a diversion, an excuse." He narrowed his eyes. "You forget, my sweet one, I know you too well. You, religious? Absurd!" Turning, he stumbled across the carpet and grabbed the back of a chair.

"I assure you, I did not—"

"Mr. Keese gave me my money back." Retrieving his shirt, Arthur swerved around, struggling to toss it over his head. "No doubt he'd already been well paid for his services." He gave a huff of disdain.

"How dare you!" Hope leapt to her feet, resisting the urge to charge him and slap away his insult.

He clicked his tongue. "I'll hear no more talk of God. *Or* of marriage. You've ruined my mood for tonight. But mark my words, you will be mine tomorrow. And if you resist, I promise you, I *will* ruin your precious Mr. Mason."

Hope dropped back onto the bed, her heart plummeting.

"You haven't changed." Arthur grabbed his cane and the bottle of port and marched toward the door. Opening it, he gave her a scorching look. "God or no God, you're a trollop, and you'll always be a trollop." Then storming out, he slammed the door, the loud *bam* shaking the foundations of Hope's newfound faith.

Chapter 37

B *oom!* The blast jarred Hope awake. Rubbing her eyes, she glanced across the room, the details of Falkland's cabin forming in her hazy vision. The pounding of boots sounded above, adding to the wild thumping of her heart. Thunder? Were they in the midst of a storm? The rays of sunshine filtering in through the stern windows defied her assumption, but she flung off the coverlet and dashed toward them anyway. The rising sun cast golden sparkles over the sea while white, puffy clouds dotted an otherwise clear azure sky.

Boot steps pounded louder, and Falkland's nasal shouts echoed across the ship. Though Hope couldn't make out what he said, she could tell from the urgency in his tone, something frightening was upon them. She scanned the horizon, just catching the stern of a ship passing beyond the window on the right.

A ship!

Without concern whether it be friend or foe, Hope donned her gown, slipped on her shoes, and dashed into the dark hallway. Weaving around sailors rushing past her, she grabbed one by the arm. "What is happening?"

"Pirates." His eyes bulged, his face twisting in fear. Yanking from her grasp, he darted away.

Hope's breath quickened as a chill coiled up her back. Pirates. *Lord, Your salvation does indeed come in odd forms.* Bumbling through the crowded companionway, she leapt up the ladder and emerged onto deck. A mad scene of fury and frenzy met her gaze as men dashed to and fro, some arming themselves, some climbing the ratlines, others tugging upon ropes and halyards. The acrid scent of gunpowder, sweat, and fear assailed her.

"Run out the guns. Man the swivels!" Falkland's shrill voice, rippling with terror, crashed over her as he marched across the deck, staring at something off their larboard side.

Hope slunk into the shadows of the quarterdeck and glanced aloft. Her heart stopped. She tossed a hand to her throat.

The *Enchantress.*

She'd know that ship anywhere: her creamy sails bursting with wind, foam bubbling against her hull, and the black flag of Captain Poole flapping from the mainmast. Squinting, she tried to make out the men who stood atop her foredeck, but only Captain Poole came into focus, his black velvet coat clapping in the wind, his dark hair flailing about his face in abandon. Had he come for her? But she'd made no connection with the capricious pirate. Perhaps this was simply a routine raid, an event of happenstance, and she another of his unfortunate victims. Regardless, she would take salvation in whatever form it came.

Oh, Lord, make his attack swift and sure and allow no deaths this day.

"Hope, go below!" She turned to see Falkland's eyes glinting with anger and his face mottled red. "I cannot be bothered with you now." But before she could respond, he spun around and bellowed further orders to his crew.

"She's coming around again, Captain," a sailor cried from the crosstrees.

"Blast!" Falkland loosed a string of curses that stung Hope's ears. She prayed he would take no more note of her, for she had no intention of leaving. Whether she lived or died was in God's hands, and if her future held naught but the company of Falkland, then she preferred the latter.

The *Enchantress* veered to larboard, showing them their rudder, and opened fire with their stern chasers. The air quivered with the roar of guns. Hope ducked beneath the pelting shots. Profanities marred the silence that followed, and she rose and gazed upward to see the slivered remains of the *Victory*'s main and mizzen topsails.

Cursing, Falkland stormed across the deck, pounding his cane against the hard oak as he went, his chest heaving beneath his satin waistcoat. "Fire on my command," he barked, his voice a dissonance of fear and rage. His white shirt dangled atop his breeches while strands of tawny hair had loosened from his tie and tumbled over his face and shoulders. Hope had never seen him so out of sorts.

The *Enchantress* swung fully about and shouldered the sea high and wide as she brought her starboard guns to bear.

"Fire!" he shouted, and Hope plugged her ears as thunderous booms exploded one after the other, trembling the ship and sending her heart into her chest. Black plumes shot into the air. Coughing, eyes stinging, she batted the smoke away and squinted toward the *Enchantress*, slowing on its tack and sailing by them with no apparent damage.

"Did we hit her?" Falkland leapt onto the bulwarks, his voice spiked with urgency.

"Nay, Captain." A tall man beside Falkland spat with disgust. "Not a scratch. She's out of our range."

Falkland swore, gripped the hilt of his sword then faced the foredeck. "Back astern and bring our other broadside to bear, Mr. Deems. Load the starboard guns!" he bellowed then lowered his hardened gaze to the deck. "We'll come in closer," he said to no one in particular. "Closer, yes. Then I'll blast her from the sea."

But before the crew could respond, an ominous boom split the air. Hope snapped her gaze to the *Enchantress.* A spike of gray smoke darted from the hull.

"Hit the deck!" Falkland commanded as a metallic *zing* and *zip* rang through the air above them. An earsplitting *crunch* thundered. A shudder ran through the ship. Eerie silence ensued. Hope opened her eyes to see the crew slowing rising to their feet.

Crack! Snap! The sound of splitting wood grated over her ears, followed by the shouts and screams of the men. "The mainmast! Clear away!"

Falkland stumbled backward, falling to the deck, his eyes as wide as doubloons. Hope pressed against the bulkhead and winced. The giant mast toppled, showering a web of lines, spars, and billowing sails upon the men. The ship staggered beneath the blow, and Hope clung to the quarterdeck to keep from falling.

Cheers and hollers blared from the *Enchantress.*

Biting her lip, Hope peered through the tangled mass of ropes and spars, praying no one had been injured. But no screams of pain emanated from the sailors who made their way from beneath the wreckage.

"What do we do, Captain?" one of them asked Falkland, who stared benumbed at the shattered mast as if he could resurrect it by sheer will. His gaze swept to the *Enchantress,* her decks littered with pirates thrusting weapons and curses into the air.

"Captain?"

"Set the white flag aloft," he finally said, his voice heavy with defeat. His eyes shifted to Hope's, and she thought he would order her below again, but his gaze breezed past her as if she didn't exist.

The *Enchantress* swept around again, lowered sails, and came even on the *Victory*'s keel.

Hope's throat grew dry. Her chest heaved. Without Nathaniel, without Abigail, who would restrain the licentious urges of Captain Poole? Had she been delivered from one monster's hands into another's?

The pirates, many of whom she recognized, lined the railing of the *Enchantress*, their grins dripping with wicked intent, their weapons glinting in the sunlight, and their mouths spewing insults.

"Out, grappling hooks! Prepare to board." Captain Poole howled, though Hope could not yet see him through the crowd.

Falkland brushed the dirt from his waistcoat, tucked in his shirt, and ran hands through his hair, then took a stance upon the deck as if he were greeting royalty. Some of his crew amassed behind him; others draped themselves over the quarterdeck railing, their sweaty faces streaked with black lines of defeat and fear. Being overtaken by a pirate was a death sentence. If the sailors weren't killed, they would be marooned at sea or on an island. Often their only choice was to join the pirate crew. Hope's heart went out to them despite her fear for her own safety.

Grapnels clanked into the deck. The snap of splintered wood filled the air. Poole's pirates tugged on the ropes, and the two ships thumped together, sending a tremble through the timbers. Captain Poole leapt to the bulwarks, cutlass in hand, a brace of pistols slung over his chest. "Board 'em, ye swabs!"

He leapt onto the *Victory*, his boots sounding an ominous thud on the deck.

Hope's gaze shifted to the pirates behind him, and she threw a hand to her mouth and shrieked.

Chapter 38

Nathaniel scanned Falkland's ship for any sign of Hope. A flash of crimson silk caught his eye. There. She stood by the quarterdeck, trembling, wide-eyed, but from all appearances, unharmed. Her gaze met his, and he offered her a reassuring grin, but her face blanched and she jerked backward as if she saw a ghost.

Gavin appeared beside him, the thrill of excitement beaming on his boyish face. Nodding his way, Nathaniel thrust out his blade and charged onto the *Victory*. A horde of pirates followed in his wake, brandishing swords that were quickly leveled upon Falkland and his crew.

Falkland swallowed but did not move. His sailors stumbled backward, their faces twisting in fear.

Captain Poole sauntered toward the defiant captain, the tip of his sword steady upon his chest. "I'll ask ye to lay down yer arms, Captain, if ye please."

Fury stormed across Falkland's face. His lip curled and for a moment it seemed he would not comply. "Do as he says," he shot over his shoulder but made no move to deliver his own blade. His crew tossed their swords, knives, and pistols to the deck in a series of clanks and clunks, and a snap from Poole's fingers sent four of his men to gather the weapons.

Lifting his nose in disdain, Falkland addressed Gavin. "Traitor! I suppose you led them to me. I should have known I couldn't trust you."

"Kindred spirits, you and I, Falkland." Gavin gave a mock bow.

Snorting, Falkland faced the pirate captain. "Be about your business, pirate, and then leave us be."

"Me business?" Captain Poole chortled. "Well, I'm glad ye asked." He pointed his cutlass toward Hope. "We require an audience with the fair lady."

"An audience?" Falkland laughed. "What business could you possibly have with her?"

"'Tis Mr. Mason who has the business, ye snivelin' toad." Poole gestured toward Nathaniel. "Not that it be any of yers. An' he'll speak to the lady in private, if ye don't mind."

Silence invaded the ship. Falkland's face crinkled into a tangle that resembled the mass of cordage littering his deck. "Did I hear you correctly?"

"Aye, I believe ye did, unless yer hearing's gone by the board along wit' yer mast."

Hope crept out from her spot by the quarterdeck, nudging pirates aside as she went. Her gaze locked upon Nathaniel, and he tried to offer her a reassuring look, but it did naught to penetrate the look of dismay on her face.

Falkland shifted his stance. "Do you mean to tell me that you destroyed my mainmast and disabled my ship for a mere parley with the likes of her?" he spat. "Why did you not signal me and send a boat?"

"Where'd be the fun in that?" Poole grinned.

Falkland moaned. "What else do you want while you're here?"

The captain's jaw twitched. He scanned the ship as if accessing its value. "Nothing." He seemed to force the words out with difficulty. "For now."

A collective sigh of relief emerged from Falkland's crew.

"Get on wit' it, Mr. Mason." Poole nodded toward Hope.

Sheathing his sword, Nathaniel took Hope's arm and led the dazed girl up the quarterdeck ladder to the stern of the ship. She stumbled along beside him but said not a word until they reached the far railing, well out of hearing of the crew and pirates.

She faced him, a glaze of disbelief covering her eyes. "What are you doing here?"

"Precisely what I came to ask you."

"I don't understand. Why did Poole attack Falkland?"

"Answer *my* question first."

Hope swallowed and gripped the railing, swerving her face away from him. "Falkland still loves me. He asked me to go with him." Her tone screeched as if saying the words pained her.

"Love? Is that what he says?" Nathaniel clenched his jaw. "I would have thought you could recognize *real* love by now." A wave lifted the ship, and he laid a hand upon the small of her back to steady her.

Her knuckles whitened on the railing, and she looked down at the foamy crash of the sea against the hull.

"Tell me you love him." Nathaniel grabbed her shoulders and turned her to face him. "Look me in the eye and tell me you still love him."

Hope released a fearful sigh, not meeting his gaze. "Nathaniel, I beg you, please leave. Make your apologies to Arthur, take Poole, and go. For your own good."

"Leaving you with Falkland would not be for my good."

A flash of confusion twisted her face. "Trust me, it will."

He lifted her chin, forcing her to look at him. "Do you love him?"

She squeezed her eyes shut, the lines of her face etched with sorrow.

Nathaniel released her and stared across the restless sea,

as unsettled and ambiguous as the lady before him. "You cannot admit that you love him, yet here you are, playing his mistress once again. After you gave your live to God? What ails you, woman?"

Taking a step back, Hope hugged herself. "Falkland is powerful. You must get as far away from us as you can."

Nathaniel gazed into her moist eyes, searching for an explanation. Love and sorrow pooled there, along with a smoldering determination.

And then he understood.

The revelation crushed him to the core. "He threatened to hurt me, didn't he?"

A tear spilled down her cheek. She looked away.

Nathaniel took her hand in his. "Didn't he?"

"He can ruin you, Nathaniel. Everything you've worked for. I can't let him do it."

He kissed her hand. She had sacrificed everything to save him, even after he'd believed the worst of her. Shame weighed upon him. He had not believed she had changed. When in truth, it was he who hadn't changed. He was still the judgmental, merciless, cad she'd claimed he was.

He drew her close, and her initial resistance melted as she folded into him.

"I owe you an apology," he whispered in her ear.

Hope stepped back. "Whatever for?"

"For not believing you." He bowed his head. "I thought you and Gavin ...."

"How can I blame you?" Hope lowered her gaze, a pink flush rising up her neck. "My reputation has not been ... well, it has not been one to foster much faith in my conduct."

"I should have believed you."

"It doesn't matter now." She withdrew and wiped the moisture from her face. "I will not see your life destroyed. Not because of me. I could not bear it." Reaching up, she brushed fingers over his jaw. "Promise me you will leave and never try to find me again."

Nathaniel shook his head. "I cannot. Don't you see? I don't care if he ruins me. The most profitable merchant business in the world will mean nothing without you."

Renewed tears filled her eyes as they flitted between his as if not believing his words. "Truly?"

He nodded.

A half-sob, half-cry of joy burst from her lips, and she hurled herself into his arms.

Minutes later, Nathaniel led Hope down to the main deck where the pirates lumbered about, grumbling from boredom, and the sailors stood stiffly behind Falkland awaiting their fate. Captain Poole perched on a crate, conversing with Gavin. Nathaniel approached Falkland. "Miss Hope agreed to accompany you under false pretenses, sir. She will be coming with me now."

Lord Falkland's upper lip twitched, and he turned a cold eye onto Hope. "Is that so? You choose this carpenter, this nobody, over me?" His face darkened.

"Arthur." Hope stepped toward him. "I am changed now. God has changed me, and I realize my feelings for you were not love at all. Neither are yours for me."

Nathaniel grimaced at her close proximity to the beast, while at the same time admiring her tender, forgiving heart toward a man who had caused her so much pain.

The agony on Falkland's face flashed to rage, and in one quick motion, he grabbed Hope, drew his sword, and pressed the edge of his blade against her throat.

Nathaniel's heart turned to stone. Gavin charged toward them, but Nathaniel held up a hand, halting him.

"All this talk of love. Quite touching." Falkland snorted, pain threading his voice. "But I am not ready to give her up, Mason. Ergo, you will take this pirate and his crew of thieving vagabonds and leave."

"Gentlemen of fortune, if ye please." Poole approached, waving a jeweled hand through the air in unruffled disinterest. But the hard glint in his eyes told a different story.

Falkland snorted. "Begone with you. All of you! I'll see Hope dead before I let her go with the likes of you."

Hope struggled in the man's grasp, wincing beneath the steel biting her neck.

Nathaniel stiffened. The fiend would do it, too. Blood rushed through every muscle, sending his fury into a boil. Sweat trickled down his back. He squeezed his fingers around the hilt of his sword, waiting for one perfect moment when Falkland's concentration would falter. The sounds of the ships thundered like warning knells in his ears: the rustle of waves over their hulls, the flap of sails, hanging impotent on their yards, the threats and flourishes of pirates and sailors.

Falkland's blade gleamed in the sun, and Nathaniel squinted against the glare. Above it, Hope's eyes sparked with fear, yet she shook her head ever so slightly as if to dissuade him from making a move. A thin line of blood appeared on her pristine neck, and Nathaniel ground his teeth together until they ached. He had not come this far to lose her now.

The sun rained hot arrows down upon them, and Falkland shifted his stance on the rolling deck.

Nathaniel curved his lips in his most unnerving grin. Producing the desired result as a cloud of uncertainty crossed Falkland's eyes. He loosened his grip on the sword. Just for a moment.

But it was all Nathaniel needed. He charged Falkland, sending him careening backward, Hope still in his grip. Before Falkland could regain himself, Nathaniel grabbed Hope by the waist and tore her from his grasp, shoving her aside. Gavin caught her before she fell to the deck.

Falkland recovered his stance and looked about wildly. He raised his sword. His brow grew dark as his eyes smoldered with fury. "Then I shall kill you. No matter."

"You may try if you wish." Nathaniel lifted his sword.

Falkland's crew moaned, but a wave of excited laughter and yelps emanated from the pirates. "A duel! A duel!" They began to chant.

Captain Poole sauntered forward. "A duel, indeed. Seems only fair t' me." He grinned, planting his fists at his waist. "An' the winner gets the girl."

Cheers erupted from the pirates.

Nathaniel cast him a look of protest. A duel had not been part of their bargain, but it was obvious from the gleam of anticipation in Poole's eyes and the prevailing furor of his men, it was not to be escaped.

"No! Falkland will kill him!" Hope's scream drew Nathaniel's gaze to her as she struggled in Gavin's grasp.

"I am overcome by your confidence." He smiled, trying to allay her fears, but she shook her head as if she were privy to a secret.

A sinister grin fell upon Falkland's lips. He pointed his sword at Nathaniel and raised a haughty brow. "I accept," he snapped.

He leapt toward Nathaniel.

Nathaniel met his blade with a ringing *clank*, amazed to find strength behind the fluff and pomp with which Falkland arrayed himself. Falkland swooped at him from the left. Nathaniel sidestepped his attack and spun to the right, striking a blow to Falkland's side.

Shock tightened the man's features. He rubbed his torn waistcoat and withdrew fingers painted red with blood. In a flurry of rage, he charged Nathaniel, slashing his blade back and forth, the glint of sun on steel nearly blinding Nathaniel.

Meeting each forceful blow, Nathaniel retreated into the mob. The crowd shrank away from the dueling pair, some spitting encouragements, some spitting insults. Forcing Nathaniel against the starboard railing, Falkland pulled back. A smug look settled on his face like a royal robe on a king, the kind of look that spoke of a sudden awareness of his advantage in the match—and of his impending victory.

Wiping sweat from his eyes, Nathaniel caught his breath. He could not lose. He would not lose. He swooped down upon Falkland. Their blades crossed, echoing an ominous *clang* over the ship. Falkland stepped to the side, grinned, and twirled his sword in the air as if he were engaged in an afternoon contest.

Rage clamped every muscle, urging Nathaniel forward. God forgive him, he wanted to kill Falkland. He wanted to kill him for using Hope. He wanted to kill him for hurting her. But right now, he wanted to kill him for being such an insolent dog. They circled each other. *Lord, forgive me. Give me the strength to win this battle and the courage to do this man no harm.*

Yet even as he breathed the words, Nathaniel feared he should have prayed for his own life. Falkland's attacks came swift and skilled, and it took all of Nathaniel's concentration to ward them off.

Then, as if Lord Falkland grew tired of the match, he turned on Nathaniel, his red face streaked with sweat and fury. With a fierce swipe, he sliced Nathaniel's breeches.

Pain etched up his leg.

Hope shrieked.

Nathaniel backed away, panting, gulping in the oppressive air.

"Had enough?" Falkland leaned on the hilt of his sword and cocked his head.

Nathaniel longed to slash that supercilious smirk from his lips.

"Surely the trollop isn't worth dying for?" Falkland eyed his fingernails.

"Perhaps you should ask yourself that, your lordship." Raising his blade, Nathaniel charged the man. Off guard, Lord Falkland still met his blow, their blades ringing over the ship. Their hilts locked and Nathaniel shoved him backward. The arrogance slipped from Falkland's face.

Snapping their swords apart, Nathaniel plunged the tip of

his blade into Falkland's boot. The man uttered an indignant shriek and glanced down. Taking quick advantage of the distraction, Nathaniel slammed the hilt end of his sword onto Falkland hand, sending the man's blade clanking to the deck.

Lord Falkland clutched his hand, his face a mottled mixture of shock and agony. His breathing became ragged as the reality crashed over him; he'd been bested—by Nathaniel, a commoner. Squaring his shoulders, he assumed a thin mask of superiority.

"You can have the wench. She's only good for one thing, anyway."

Nathaniel slammed his fist across Falkland's jaw, sending him reeling backward. Lud, but that felt good! "She is a lady. And daughter of the King. You'll pay her the respect she's due."

Falkland slumped to the deck and moaned. "Daughter of the king, indeed." He sneered. "What king is that?"

"The King of Kings." Nathaniel's gaze swept to Hope. She clutched her skirts and dashed toward him. Dropping his sword, he took her in his embrace, breathing in her fresh scent. She lifted her eyes to his, tears streaming down her cheeks, and he brushed them away and lowered his lips to hers.

Chapter 39

H ope stood at the bow of the *Enchantress* and leaned back on the foremast. A gust of wind, sweetened by the Caribbean, eased over her as the ship rose and plunged over a turquoise swell. A spray of salty mist refreshed her face and neck, and she smiled and shifted her gaze to the setting sun in the west—a bouquet of purple, crimson, and saffron.

She was finally going home.

Captain Poole had begrudgingly agreed to drop her and Nathaniel, Mr. and Mrs. Simmons, and Miss Elise as close to Charles Towne as "his good sense would allow him to come within range of the filthy, pirate-hanging town."

Elise.

Warmth spread through Hope as she remembered the little girl leaping into her arms when she had first boarded the *Enchantress* from Falkland's ship. Overcome with joy, Hope had been reluctant to release the sweet child, fearing she was only a dream conjured up by Hope's continual prayers for her safety. But the trembles coursing through Elise were real enough—no doubt due to the gun battle and being aboard a pirate ship—and after comforting her for hours, Hope had finally eased the little girl to sleep nestled in her berth.

Hope closed her eyes, relishing in the final warm kiss of the sun. *Thank You, Lord. Thank You for Elise, and thank You for sending Nathaniel to rescue me. Thank You for his love, a love I no more deserve than I do Yours.*

Unable to find Nathaniel, Hope had ascended the foredeck to pray and watch the sun set. Perhaps he would find her here. She hoped so, for she had many unanswered questions. What had changed his mind about her? And what was the strange ship that followed them off their larboard quarter?

A warm, strong hand touched her shoulder. Flinching, she opened her eyes to see his handsome face smiling down at her, a hungry gaze that took her in like a man long deprived of sustenance. He ran his palm over her cheek.

"Oh, Nathaniel, how can I ever thank you for saving me?" Hope's throat burned, and she swallowed, afraid to embrace the love beaming from his eyes. She dropped her gaze to the bloodstained slash in Nathaniel's breeches. "Once more, I have caused you harm."

Nathaniel stretched out his leg. "Falkland wields quite a skilled sword."

"An expert swordsmen. Or so he claims." She shook her head, then giggled. "The look on his face as we sailed away, leaving him foundering in the water."

Nathaniel chuckled. "Indeed. Especially after Captain Poole threatened to come back and finish the job." He gazed across the darkening sea. "Have no fear. Falkland will survive. He'll make it to Charles Towne." He grinned. "Albeit a bit later than planned."

The ship bucked, and Hope gripped Nathaniel's arm. "His welfare is of no concern to me. I hope I never see him again." She took in a deep breath of salt-laden air, amazed at the truth of the words she'd just spoken.

Nathaniel cupped her chin and ran his thumb over her cheek. A warm tingle swirled within her, and she took a step back. He affected her like no man ever had. It frightened her, for she no longer wished to give in to every impulse storming through her.

She clutched her hands together and squinted toward the sun still sinking beneath the sea, fluttering feathers of gold and crimson over the choppy waves. A breeze tore a curl from her pins, but she no longer associated it with her inability to be pure. Nay, God would give her the all strength she needed in that endeavor. "Falkland can still harm you."

"How? I've nothing left for him to destroy."

She faced him. "You still own a ship."

Nathaniel's gaze slipped to the two-masted vessel behind them. A sense of longing tugged at his features.

"Is that your ship? The one that sails behind us?"

"Not anymore."

Dread clutched her heart.

"I gave it to Captain Poole." He waved the ship away as if it were but a trifle.

The words sank like anchors in her belly. "Why?" But she already knew the answer.

"Do you think he aided in your rescue out of the goodness of his heart?" Nathaniel chuckled and ran a hand through his hair.

"What of your crew?"

"Most of them stayed in Kingston to find work on other ships. Some joined the pirates."

Hope shrank back. "You gave up your last ship to rescue me when you didn't even know for certain whether I went with Falkland willingly?"

He shrugged and gave her a playful grin. "It worked out well."

Hope shook her head. "You've lost everything because of me. And"—she glanced at the wounds on his leg and arm and the bruise on his forehead—"I've nearly killed you—several times."

Her foolish actions had caused the man she loved unthinkable pain and loss. Turning her back to him, she stormed to the railing.

His boot steps thudded behind her. Strong hands grabbed her waist and pulled her back against him. His arms wrapped around her as his hot breath swept down her neck. "Worth every timber, plank, sail, and wound."

Elation and fear tangled in her throat. Placing her hands atop his, Hope lowered her gaze to the restless sea below, allowing his loving words to soothe her doubts. As hard as it was to believe, Nathaniel must truly love her. Yet she couldn't help but entertain one remaining fear. Why would he attach himself to a woman with her sordid past?

Remember ye not the former things, neither consider the things of old. Behold, I will do a new thing; now it shall spring forth. The words Hope had read in Isaiah that afternoon eased over her. She lifted her face to the sun.

Nathaniel turned her around to face him. Specks of gold gleamed within his dark eyes. "I love you, Hope. Why do you not believe me?"

She swallowed, breathing in the scent of wood that always clung to him. "Nobody has ever loved me before. Not truly loved me."

He brushed a curl from her cheek. "Then allow me the privilege of being the first." His lips met hers.

Hope folded into his embrace, submitting to his kiss, and finally permitting herself to believe this honorable man loved her. He pressed her close, caressing her hair and exploring her mouth with gentleness that soon rose to a hunger that matched her own. Heat exploded within her like a thousand cannons set ablaze. The ship, the sea, the sky melted away. Her knees weakened.

Withdrawing, he hovered close to her face. His warm, musky breath tingled over her skin. And for the first time, Hope longed to give herself to a man completely, wholly, for no other reason than pure love.

But no.

Breathless, she spun away, searching for her traitorous

wits amidst the passion that had set her insides aflame. "What will you do now? You have no ships left." She waved a hand over her face and neck, directing the breeze to cool her torrid skin and remove the flush before she faced him again.

Nathaniel drew a deep breath and rubbed a hand over the back of his neck. The woman caused every sinew, every fiber, every particle within him to explode. And then she tore away from him, leaving him in a cold sweat. He gripped the railing, dragging his fingers over the rough wood. A splinter tore his flesh. Good. The pain would jar him from her spell.

"Perhaps God is trying to tell me something," he finally said, cursing himself for the passion still thick in his voice. He cleared his throat. "Perhaps I should heed his call on my life to preach."

"Preach?" Hope twirled around.

"I seem to have a talent for it." Nathaniel shrugged, concerned by the anxious look on her face. Perchance she did not approve. Perchance she did not wish to marry a poor preacher. His stomach tightened. Regardless, he must follow the call of God on his life. The loss of his last ship had not left the gaping hole within him he'd assumed it would. Instead, when he'd made up his mind to become a preacher, a peace like he'd never known had fallen on him. "I suppose I've been running from God for quite some time, hoping to make a name for myself through status and wealth, trying to remove the stain of my past."

"Only God can truly cleanse you." She gave him a sweet smile, her blue eyes beaming with an innocence that had not been there before.

"You learn quickly." He returned her smile. A gust of wind blasted over him, cooling his skin. He tossed the hair from his face as the sails snapped overhead. "But I've also learned that status and reputation do not make a man. Look at

Hendrick, Paine, Falkland."

"You need say nothing more. Hendrick." Hope blew out a sigh. "I cannot fathom a man who abandons his own daughter."

"You read his note. Perhaps he truly believes she is not his child."

"No matter. He is the only father she has known. Poor Elise." The ship bucked and Nathaniel reached out to steady Hope, keeping his hand upon her arm.

"But it is an answer to prayer." She gazed up at him. "I shall raise her as my own daughter, give her all the love she needs and teach her about the everlasting love of God."

Nathaniel forced a smile. What did he know about raising children? His only parent had been a prostitute. *Lord, if Hope is to be a part of my future, I will need Your help with this.*

If she was to be a part of his future.

"You will make a good mother."

"With God's help, I hope so." She glanced toward the sun. The frown of its arc now cresting the horizon mirrored the one on her lips.

Nathaniel drew her close, longing for her smile to return. "What troubles you?"

"Elise needs a father, too." Her blue eyes searched his. Anticipation sparked in their depths.

Nathaniel looked away, unsure of the intent of her statement, unsure whether Hope would choose to live without the luxuries to which she'd grown accustomed.

When he looked at her once more, the gleam in her eyes had faded to disappointment, and she lowered her face.

Lifting her chin, Nathaniel brushed his lips against hers. "I love you, Hope," he whispered.

"I love you, too, Nathaniel." Her words melted over him. "With all my heart."

He pulled back and studied her. "I have nothing to offer you."

"You offer me more than anyone else ever has."

Heart thumping against his chest, he took her hands in his. "Then will you marry this poor preacher?"

Hope leapt into his arms, giggling, and showered him with kisses. "I thought you'd never ask."

Embracing her, Nathaniel stumbled backward as the ship lurched over a wave. Unable to keep his balance—or his concentration—as Hope continued planting kisses on his face and snuggling her body next to his, Nathaniel bumbled and slammed into the railing. The ship canted again, and quickly releasing Hope, he clutched the railing just before he would have toppled over the side and plunged into the sea.

Hope braced her feet on the deck and threw a hand to her mouth, her eyes wide.

He raised a playful brow her way. "Perhaps we should marry as soon as possible before you do, indeed, manage to kill me." He chuckled, and she fell into his arms, her laughter joining with his.

Epilogue

"A sail! A sail!" A man on the yards above Hope roared across the ship. She looked up from her spot sitting on a barrel beside Elise, reading her a copy of the *Tales of Mother Goose* that Mrs. Simmons had procured.

Captain Poole leapt upon the foredeck, grabbed the glass from Hawkins, and raised it to his eye.

Across the deck, Nathaniel instructed a group of pirates on the use of the quadrant. Glancing at her, he gave her a reassuring nod and gripped the hilt of the sword he now wore constantly aboard the pirate vessel.

Gavin slid down the backstay and landed with a thud beside her. He tickled Elise beneath her chin, sending her into a flurry of giggles, and then winked at Hope. He'd taken the news of her and Nathaniel's engagement with more joy than Hope would have expected. Either he had never harbored any affection for her, or he hid his feelings well beneath his usual facade of charm. Regardless, he seemed somehow different these past few days.

He sauntered over and stood beside Nathaniel, who clapped him on the back. The two had recently formed a close bond. One which Hope prayed would drive Gavin to his knees before God.

A band of pirates gathered on the main deck, waiting their captain's assessment of the intruder.

Within a day's journey of Charles Towne, Hope could hardly contain her excitement at seeing her sisters again. She'd been praying for Faith, whom she'd last seen in the Watch Tower Dungeon awaiting trial for piracy. Even now, Hope found it difficult to believe she'd been so self-centered as to leave her sister in such a predicament with her fate unknown. But thanks be to God, Hope was a different person now.

Putting the book aside, she shielded her eyes and peered in the direction of the men's gazes. They'd not come across another vessel in two days, and she'd been praying for a safe and uneventful passage home. Hope didn't know if she could endure any further excitement.

Lord, let this be a friend and not a foe.

"Scupper, sink, and burn me," Captain Poole exclaimed. "'Tis the *Red Siren*."

"The *Red Siren*." Hope snatched the glass from Poole's hand, and a foul curse spewed from his mouth.

Ignoring him, she held the telescope to her eye and twisted the ship into focus. The words *Red Siren* stood in bold red across the ship's bow. Excitement soared through her. "'Tis my sister."

"Yer sister?" Poole swung a startled gaze her way. "But the *Red Siren* be a pirate vessel."

"Her sister *is* a pirate." Nathaniel eased beside her, slipping a protective arm around her waist. "Or at least she was."

"Your sister be the notorious Red Siren?" Poole's eyes lit up, and he slapped his knee. "Well, upon me life."

Gavin gripped the railing and stared at the fast-approaching ship. "Why, pray tell, would you withhold such an intriguing fact? Quite astonishing!" He pushed from the railing, his blue eyes alight with interest. "Will she fire upon us?"

Poole spit to the side and thrust his hands upon his waist. "I'll introduce her to the sharks, if she does." He gave a sideways glance at Hope. "Beggin' yer pardon, miss, sister or no, no one fires upon Captain Poole without a sharp reply."

"I would expect nothing less, Captain." Hope forced a smile that belied her churning insides. "But I assure you, if it is my sister, and she spots me on your ship, she'll not fire upon us." Bracing her shoes against the heaving deck, Hope raised the spyglass once again, scanning the oncoming vessel, squinting into focus the people on board. What if it wasn't Faith? She could have sold her ship, or it could have been stolen. Perhaps she had been sentenced to the gallows, after all. A sick brew welled in her stomach. *Oh, Lord, don't let it be so.*

A shock of red hair swept across her vision, and Hope swung it back and twisted the handle.

"'Tis my sister, indeed!" Hope leapt for joy.

"Are you sure?" Nathaniel asked.

"Yes, and there's a man beside her." Hope hesitated, peering through the glass. "Captain Waite. 'Tis Captain Waite, I'm sure of it. Ah, this is good fortune indeed."

"Who the blazes is Captain Waite?" Captain Poole tore the glass from her eye and pressed it against his own.

"A lieutenant in His Majesty's Royal Navy." Too late, Hope realized the implications of her words.

Poole lowered the glass. "Be ye out of yer head?" He swore then stomped to the foredeck railing and stared at the mob of pirates clustered on the main deck. "Load the guns! Clear the deck! Run up our colors."

As the men scrambled to do their captain's bidding, Hope dashed to Poole's side, daring to touch the raging pirate's sleeve. "Nay, Captain. He is not in uniform. And he does not sail under British colors. I assure you he will not fire upon us." At least Hope prayed he would not.

Captain Poole's narrowed eyes sent a chill through her as he shifted his gaze between her and the ship.

Nathaniel approached, nudging Hope behind him. "They've no doubt seen us by now, Captain, and their gun ports are still closed. Lend us a boat and send us to their ship. If their intent is anything but friendly, you have my word, we will convince them otherwise. In either case, you shall be relieved of our company, as I am confident Miss Westcott and Captain Waite will be happy to escort us into Charles Towne harbor."

"I'll join you," Gavin shot over his shoulder from the railing.

"I thought you were turning pirate?" Nathaniel faced him, a faint smirk on his lips. "Or have I managed to persuade you otherwise?"

"Perhaps." Gavin gave one of his boyish grins. He scratched his sideburns and gazed at the *Red Siren*. "But truth be told, I can't pass up the opportunity to meet a lady pirate."

"Belay me orders," Poole shouted below, then grunted and crossed arms over his chest. "So be it. But if she fires upon me, I'll hold to no bargain."

Nathaniel extended his hand. The pirate gripped it. "'Tis been quite an experience, Captain. I shall not forget you."

Captain Poole snapped his hand back and shifted uncomfortably. "Be gone wit' ye now before I change me mind."

"Where will you go now, Captain?" Hope asked, realizing she'd grown oddly fond of the beastly pirate.

He scratched his chin, the twinkle in his eyes matching the glitter of the ring piercing his ear. "I hear there be a pretty young missionary back in Kingston. I have it in me mind to pay her a visit."

Hope's heart lodged in her throat as she allowed

Nathaniel to assist her over the railing of the *Red Siren.* Before she placed both feet on the deck, a flash of red filled her vision, and Faith barreled into her, wrapped her arms around her, and squeezed the breath from Hope's lungs.

"Hope, Hope ... I cannot believe it is you!" She held her out for a moment and inspected her from head to toe then pressed her close again, her voice a cacophony of sobs and laughter. "Where have you been? We've been searching for you!" Her joy snapped to anger in seconds—as only Faith could do—and she released Hope and took a step back, placing her hands on her hips. Curls of flaming red fluttered around her face in the ocean breeze—a face that now grew tight with anger. Her white cotton shirt flapped beneath a leather baldric. Brown breeches were stuffed into dark boots that tapped an ominous chant over the wooden deck.

Hope couldn't help but smile. "I'm glad to see you, too, even if you do look like a pirate." She swiped a tear slipping from her eye and placed a hand on her sister's arm. "Never fear. I am well."

Faith's gaze shot to Nathaniel, who assisted Mr. and Mrs. Simmons and Elise on board, then swung to Gavin as he swept over the bulwarks after them, plopping to the deck with a smile, before she cocked a curious brow at Hope, awaiting an explanation.

Mr. Waite's imposing figure stomped past them and gripped Nathaniel's shoulders. "Nathaniel. How did you ... what on earth are you doing here?"

Hope smiled. "You remember Mr. Nathaniel Mason, Faith, do you not?"

Nathaniel nodded at Faith. "Miss Westcott. We have much to tell you."

Faith slid her arm through Hope's. "As in, what you're doing with my sister? And who these people are?" She gestured toward Mr. and Mrs. Simmons, Elise, and Gavin. "And isn't that a pirate ship? Captain Poole's, I believe?"

Hope glanced at the *Enchantress,* where Poole's pirates

scrambled to unfurl sail as soon as the cockboat returned. "Yes. But how did you know?"

"I've heard of him." A wind thick with moisture swirled around them and seemed to wash away the anger from Faith's face.

Elise inched her way to Hope, grabbed onto her skirt, and hid herself among the folds.

Faith knelt and smiled at her. "And who might this be?"

The little girl curtsied. "My name is Elise, and Hope is my new mother."

"Indeed?" Faith took her hand. "Pleased to meet you, Miss Elise." Then rising, Faith tossed her hair over her shoulder. "You *do* have much to tell me."

"And I will in good time." Hope clutched her sister's arm. "Did you receive the pardon from the governor? I was so frightened for you."

"I did." She glanced at Mr. Waite conversing with Nathaniel.

Gavin approached and gave a gentlemanly bow. "I am honored to finally meet the notorious Red Siren." His blue eyes took her in with interest.

Clearing his throat, Mr. Waite slipped beside Faith, laid a hand on her back, and glared at the young upstart.

Hope giggled. "Faith, Mr. Waite, may I present Mr. Gavin Keese. Mr. Keese, my sister, Miss Westcott, and Captain Dajon Waite."

Faith smiled. "Mr. Keese, my pleasure, but my sister errs. I am no longer Miss Westcott. I am Mrs. Waite." She smiled at Dajon.

"Married?" Hope flew into her sister's arms, laughter bubbling from her lips. "Oh, I knew it. I knew it! I'm so happy for you." Withdrawing from Faith, Hope took Mr. Waite's hands in hers. "For you both!"

"Thank you, Miss Hope." Mr. Waite gazed at his wife, his eyes warming with love—a love Hope had never dreamed she'd experience. Not until Nathaniel.

"God has abundantly blessed us," he said.

"God has blessed us as well." Hope slipped her hand into Nathaniel's.

"Did I hear you say God?" Faith gave her a questioning look.

"You did."

"And does this blessing include Mr. Mason?" Mr. Waite asked.

Hope gazed up at Nathaniel and nodded. Warmth flooded her at the consuming look in his eyes.

"I am truly happy." Faith hugged her. "I cannot wait to hear all that has happened." The *Red Siren* careened over a wave, spraying them with salty mist. The joyful exuberance slipped from Faith's face. "But there is a matter of grave importance we must attend to first."

Hope's heart shrank.

Faith's jaw tensed. "It is the reason we have set sail."

"What is it?" Hope clung to Nathaniel.

"'Tis our sister, Grace." Faith swallowed and glanced at Mr. Waite. Her face twisted in fear. "She's been kidnapped."

Look for ***The Raven Saint***
Charles Towne Belles, Book 3 coming Fall 2015

About the Author

BEST-SELLING AUTHOR, MARYLU TYNDALL dreamt of pirates and sea-faring adventures during her childhood days on Florida's Coast. With more than fifteen books published, she makes no excuses for the deep spiritual themes embedded within her romantic adventures. Her hope is that readers will not only be entertained but will be brought closer to the Creator who loves them beyond measure. In a culture that accepts the occult, wizards, zombies, and vampires without batting an eye, MaryLu hopes to show the awesome present and powerful acts of God in a dying world. A Christy award nominee, MaryLu makes her home with her husband, six children, two grandchildren, and several stray cats on the California coast.

If you enjoyed this book, one of the nicest ways to say "thank you" to an author and help them be able to continue writing is to leave a favorable review on Amazon, Barnes and Noble, IBooks, ITunes, Kobo (And elsewhere, too!) I would appreciate it if you would take a moment to do so. Thanks so much!

Comments? Questions? I love hearing from my readers, so feel free to contact me via my website: http://www.marylutyndall.com

Or email me at: marylu_tyndall@yahoo.com

Follow me on:

FACEBOOK:
https://www.facebook.com/marylu.tyndall.author

TWITTER:
https://twitter.com/MaryLuTyndall

BLOG:
http://crossandcutlass.blogspot.com/

PINTEREST:
http://www.pinterest.com/mltyndall/

To hear news about special prices and new releases that **only my subscribers receive**, sign up for my newsletter on my website or blog! http://www.marylutyndall.com